# SURVIVE

## SAL MASON

ISBN: 978-1-9164743-0-7
2nd edition
Rapid River Publishing

Book cover design by render/compose
Edited by Ayers Edits
The text type was set in Adobe Garamond Pro

For more information or to sign up to my newsletter, visit
www.salmasonauthor.com

Trigger Warning: This story includes relevant social topics such as
self-harm, as well as references to rape/abuse which could be upsetting to
sensitive readers.

*To my kids for all the burned pizzas, missed laundry, and extra chores they had to do. Without them, I would have long given up.*

# Prologue

They appear behind me out of nowhere. Four big guys, towering over me by at least a foot. The one with the cocky smirk must be the ringleader. His eyes have a predatory look that sends a shudder down my spine—it's a malicious glow that blends in with the surreal light of the setting sun. A sudden stench of alcohol and sweat sickens my stomach. I don't have to look around to know there is no place to hide. They have strategically positioned themselves throughout the alley with two of them blocking the only exit.

"Hey there." The ringleader's grin is wide, exposing a couple of golden teeth in the front. His eyes undress me as they roam over my body, coming to rest on my cleavage.

"I'm—" I clear my throat. "I'm waiting for my boyfriend." Despite my best effort, a slight tremble sneaks into my voice. "He's a cop."

A cruel laugh escapes the leader's throat. "He ain't coming, baby. Your boyfriend likes to bet on the horses and owes us quite a lot of money." He shifts his weight, exposing a bulge in his stained jeans. "He and I came to new repayment terms, and fortunately for me, you have to pay up."

I squint at him, not wanting to believe that Paul would do that to me. In response, the ringleader pulls out the picture my boyfriend carries in a secret compartment in his wallet.

"He called you, didn't he, and asked you to meet him here? Sorry, baby, but he set you up." The smirk is like a punch to my stomach. "But don't be sad. You'll have a great time with us."

The truth is slowly sinking in. My mind screamed caution when Paul had wanted to meet me here—in one of the most rundown parts of the city—but he had been working undercover and said it was the only way for us to spend a few stolen moments together. Like a fool, I believed him. Just shows I should trust my intuition more.

My fists ball tightly and my body tenses—if they thought I would be easy prey, they will be in for a surprise. My father is a special-forces operator and has trained me in self-defense and survival since I was a little girl.

When one of the younger guys tries to grab my wrist, my knee connects with his groin. He howls in pain and the few seconds of commotion are all I need to seize the opportunity. Lunging forward, my shoulder rams into the side of the guy blocking my way. He is so stunned by my attack that he doubles over, gasping for air.

I glance at the road a few yards ahead. If I make it, there are at least places to run and hide. The muscles in my legs flex as I dash through the alleyway, trampling footsteps follow.

"Fuck." Heavy panting is right behind me.

These guys are so out of shape. Probably all drug users or at least smokers, not able to keep up with a fitness maniac like myself, who runs five miles every morning before class. They will hopefully give up by the time I turn the corner.

In the end, my long hair proves to be my downfall. When one of them gets ahold of a fistful, my head jerks backward. The sudden pull almost takes me off my feet. I scream as I try to tear loose, my scalp on fire. As two arms enclose my upper body, I kick randomly, clawing my fingernails into the skin of my assailant. He shouts a curse, but his embrace is like a steel belt I can't break no matter how hard I try. Sweat trickles down my forehead and my back as he cuts off my air supply. My stomach is so tight I'm about to throw up.

One of his buddies comes to his aid and catches my legs midair. Pain forces me to still as he starts to twist my ankles.

"Behave or I swear I'll break every bone in your body." The leader's hissed words make my skin crawl.

I consider my options, but for now, I'm immobilized and need to preserve my strength. Without objection, I allow the guy holding my legs to set my feet back on the ground. He and his friend secure my arms and shoulders in an iron grip.

The leader studies me before stepping closer. When I struggle against my captors, he warningly narrows his eyes. "Hold her."

The grip becomes tighter and a sharp pain stabs at my shoulders when my arms are pulled backward. One wrong move and my joints will pop out of their sockets.

He opens the button of my jeans and lowers the zipper before his hand finds its way into my panties. A sudden rage bubbles up inside me and I spit right into his smirking face.

He chuckles. "You're a feisty one, aren't you?" The lust burns in his eyes as he wipes my spit off his face with his sleeve. "I like girls who can stand their ground—it makes fucking them so much more challenging." His hand cups the back of my head and he pulls me closer, his alcohol stained breath tickling my neck. "But make no mistake, my dick will end up inside you tonight. Play nice and you might even enjoy it."

They drag me away, shoving me in the trunk of a car with a loud cheer. Needless to say, no one comes to my rescue—it's not the part of town where people get involved. I am their play toy for the night. The man who I thought loves me has sold me out to the wolves.

~~~~

The sun already peeks over the horizon when they drop me back at the entrance of the alley. It rained overnight and the pavement is wet, the water puddles mixing with my blood as I crawl along the street. My whole body screams in agony and tears roll down my cheeks. I cry for someone to help me until I'm so hoarse that my voice cracks with every new breath.

Again, no one comes to my rescue. I am all alone—beaten, raped, and utterly broken.

# Chapter 1

"Paper or plastic?" With my best fake smile, I gaze at the old lady in front of me, my fingers drumming on the small ledge next to the cash register when she doesn't respond. My eyes wander to the line of customers behind her and I sigh—so much for the extra bathroom break I so desperately need.

"What did you say, dear?" She fiddles with the small plastic hearing aid behind her ear.

"Do you want paper or plastic?" I ask a few octaves higher, hoping my words get through this time.

"Oh, paper, dear." Her lips split into a toothless grin. "Plastic is bad for the environment."

This time, my smile is genuine—someone her age who is concerned about the pollution future generations will have to endure totally rocks. My attention turns to Ricky, our bagging clerk, and I give him the thumbs-up, our sign for paper bags. He nods, but I'm not sure if he understands or just bounces to the music blasting through his earplugs.

He grabs a paper bag and I start to scan the first item. One by one, the groceries move forward on the belt, a low metallic beep indicating I'm doing it correctly. The lady is a health nut, buying mostly salads, fruits and vegetables, and lean chicken breast. The only sin is a small box of chocolates.

"That will be forty-two sixty-five," I say when I'm done.

"Can I get a lottery ticket, please?"

I point to the customer service desk. "Sorry, we don't sell them at the register anymore. You have to go over there."

It takes her forever to count out the money, the line growing with every penny she places on the small space in front of me. I peek into her wallet and see an extra ten dollars, but she insists on giving me the exact change. After that, she is on her way.

I turn to the next customer with my fake smile, but the voice of Mr. Hill, the store manager, stops me before I can get started.

"Aeree, a word, please."

Usually, he is friendly enough, but this time, he looks like he just choked down a glass of lemon juice. His lips are pressed together in a thin line as he regards me with a sullen expression.

My eyes dart from his face to the long line of customers and back to him. "Now?"

"Yes." He signals for Tammy from the customer service desk to come over.

"Finish here," he hisses before shooting me a nasty glare.

Somehow, I can't shake the feeling I'm in trouble, though I can't figure out what I could have possibly done wrong. I'm always polite, on time, and never have any cash shortage in the register. This is an entry-level job at the supermarket and hard to screw up.

He ushers me into his office and, to my surprise, closes the door behind us. The hairs on my neck rise in alarm—I'm not comfortable being around men on my own, especially those I don't know well. My body tenses when he gives me a curt smile that doesn't hit his eyes and points at the chair in front of his desk.

"Sit down."

I oblige with hesitation, lowering myself on the front edge of the chair with my feet firmly planted on the ground. I measure the distance to the door—five, maybe six steps—too far to make a safe escape. If he tries anything, he will taste blood.

"Well, Aeree, it has been brought to the shop's attention that you lied on your employment application."

This earns him a frown. "Excuse me, what are you implying, sir?" Playing ignorant might be my only chance to salvage my job. Not that it's a great job, but with my rocky past, my options are severely limited.

"We received information that you have a criminal record you did not disclose."

Busted. I force a sweet smile. "Well, don't they always say people deserve a second chance? I'm an outstanding employee—that should count for something."

"You still lied. Store policy is clear that, in an instance like this, I have to let you go."

"Don't you at least want to hear my side of the story?" The desperation in my voice makes me cringe. I swear to myself that I will not resort to begging like the last time—screw him and his job.

"It's a little late for that. If you raised this in the interview, I would've been more than willing to listen, but not now." His face is stern; he reminds me of the judge who sentenced me four years ago when all that shit happened.

"Okay." I hate how timid I sound.

"You have fifteen minutes to clean out your locker. Your last paycheck will be available on Friday." He makes a sour face and scribbles something on a piece of paper before waving his arm, apparently his way of dismissal. "I'm sorry it has come to this. You can go now."

"Fine, your loss." I jump to my feet and storm out, my heart screaming about another injustice. There's no way the prick would have hired me if I had been truthful. People with felony convictions don't make good employees, no matter what they say. It's a fact of life I have learned the hard way. My chances of ever finding a decent job are nil.

I purposely bang the door of the locker against the wall a few times to blow off steam, but it doesn't help, even when I kick against it and leave a good dent. The result is only a sore toe. Cussing under my breath, I stuff my phone and lunch box into my backpack, glancing around the staff room one more time. The job sucked anyway. I don't need this. My husband earns enough money and will take care of me for the rest of my pitiful existence. Screw these people and their judgmental attitudes.

Chin held high, I march out of the shop without bothering to say goodbye to anyone. Mitch can pick up my paycheck or they can mail it—I don't intend to ever set foot into this hellhole again. I swallow down the lump in my throat as the automatic doors slide open. Only the cold, harsh world waits on the other side.

As I walk to my car, a tingling sensation spreads along my scalp. I gaze around. It almost feels as if someone is watching me. The parking lot is empty except for a woman and her kid who mind their own business. I squint at the windows of the supermarket; no set of eyes gawks back. An empty soda can rattles and holds my attention as the wind carries it over the smooth asphalt, which glimmers from the heat of the midday sun.

I tear my gaze off the can and continue my way to the car. The feeling of eyes burning into my skull persists. By the time I slide into the small convertible that Mitch got me for Christmas, my body screams from the tension, and I'm covered in cold sweat.

I try to ignore the prickling feeling in my scalp when I start the car and pull out of the parking lot. The heat is probably driving me crazy—nothing a cold drink can't fix. On my way home, I stop at another supermarket and pick up a few cans of zero cola and a six-pack of beer for Mitch. Slurping the ice-cold drink, the liquid runs down my throat with a tingle, taking off the edge. The prickling is still in my scalp, but I'm probably just getting paranoid. There is no one watching me—my life is way too boring for that.

~~~~

By the time Mitch comes home from work, I'm hiding under the covers after devouring a big bucket of ice cream. Usually, I frown on too much sugar and constantly watch my calorie intake, but what is sulking without a good brain freeze? I allowed myself a good cry and feel halfway better, though the sting that I have lost yet another crappy job hurts more than I want to admit.

In a forgotten lifetime, I was a straight-A student at Columbia with a brilliant accounting career ahead of me until my criminal conviction took my future away. Admittedly, it could have been worse—I could have ended up behind bars for the rest of my life if my dad hadn't taken the fall.

When Mitch pulls the blanket away, I squint at him against the bright light from the afternoon sun, peeking through the gaps in the curtains. "Go away."

He ignores my protests and lowers himself next to me on the bed. "What's the matter, babe? You look like you've been crying."

My nose wrinkles to keep the tears locked away. "I got fired again."

"Oh, I'm sorry." He strokes my back. "What happened?"

I hug my legs, propping my chin up on my knees to focus on his face. "They found out about the conviction."

"That's too bad."

I expect a flinch or some other reaction, but he keeps a straight face while he searches my own with his hazel eyes. When the sunlight reflects in them, they sparkle like golden nuggets, but in the confinement of the house, specs of green stand out.

"I did suggest you should be truthful this time," he says, and I deflate like a balloon by the slight annoyance in his voice. "Employers like it if you admit to your mistakes *before* they discover them on their own."

"I know." My smile is guilt stricken to show that I'm sorry for not listening to him. "I just didn't think they'd hire me if I told them I was convicted of assault. Who would want someone like that around customers?"

"I suppose. How did they even find out?"

Good question. "The manager called the cops the other day when a couple of kids got caught stealing. One of the officers looked really familiar—I think he used to work in Paul's unit and recognized me. I'm sure he squealed on me."

"Well, what's done is done." Mitch bends forward and brushes a kiss on my forehead. "Why don't you get up and I'll take you out for dinner? I have a surprise that might cheer you up."

A tingling sensation spreads in my stomach—he always has the most amazing ideas. "What kind of surprise?"

"Get up, and I'll tell you on the way to the restaurant."

Jumping out of bed, my mind already scrambles what to wear. "Where're we going?"

"I made a reservation at Buddakan for eight o'clock."

I squeal. "We're going into the city?" He knows how much I love Manhattan, though we usually never go downtown during the week. "Don't you have to work tomorrow?"

"I do, but I thought a special occasion calls for special plans." When he notices my puzzled expression, his lips twist at the same time as his eyebrows rise. "Don't tell me you forgot?"

I don't have the slightest idea what he's getting at, but from the boyish sparkle in his eyes, it's not only big, but something I should definitely know. I scan the room for a clue, stopping on the calendar. The date is circled with a big heart.

My hand slaps my forehead. "Oh, Mitch, I'm so sorry." How in the world could I have missed that today is our anniversary? The two years have gone by so quickly that our wedding seems like it was yesterday.

My cheeks sting when he pulls me into his arms, laughing. "Aren't guys usually the ones who forget?" He plants a kiss on my lips when I stay silent, my whole face burning up. "Don't worry, babe, you can apologize later." Wiggling his eyebrows, he playfully slaps my behind. "In bed. I'll make you work for my forgiveness."

My smile is automatic in the hopes of camouflaging my apprehension. Though the promise of snuggling and falling asleep in his tight embrace is enticing, the thought of sex fills me with dread. Too many painful memories, which always end with nightmares. Only my need to keep him happy lets me endure the ordeal at all.

I rest my head against his broad chest. "You know, you're the best husband in the world." His tie tickles my cheek and I take in his aftershave, thanking my lucky stars to have him in my life. "I *really* am sorry."

"Enough." He catches my chin and forces me to look at him. "I love you and want to have a wonderful evening with my wife. No more sulking, apologies, or other such nonsense. Okay?"

I nod, swallowing down another apology. His strong, even heartbeat is comforting and, just like so many times before, sucks any remaining sadness right out of me. "Give me fifteen minutes and we can go."

"Can I watch while you get ready?" His lips curl in a mischievous grin.

"Of course." I pull the clips out of my hair, which have held back my long fringe, and attack it with a brush. The soft bristles run through my raven hair like silk. To finish it all off, I use the curling iron to give some of my tendrils a slight bounce. Buddakan is one of the best Asian restaurants in New York and I plan to wear my new cobalt blue cocktail dress, which highlights my curves. Since I already forgot our special day, I can at least look my very best for Mitch.

A giggle outside distracts me and I peek around the curtains. A young woman a few years older than me sits on the swing set next door. She is having a blast while a guy who looks like he just escaped from a high security prison pushes her up in the air. A second guy sits with his back against the fence in the grass, bouncing a small baby on his lap. Another child is sleeping in a car seat next to him, oblivious to the ruckus the woman on the swing is causing.

"I think those are the new neighbors," I remark. The real estate agent who had sold us our house stopped by about a week ago to tell us they had finally found a buyer for the old fixer-upper, which had been on the market for years.

Mitch steps next to me. "I met them on my way in. They seem pretty nice. Her name is Kelsey and the one sitting down is her husband. They've got twins."

"What about the big dude?" I can't help the shudder running down my spine. "He looks like a drug dealer."

Mitch chuckles. "Looks can be deceiving, my dear. Kelsey said she and that guy both work in law enforcement."

I grunt—having a cop live next door is the last thing I need. "Well, I'll make sure I stay as far as possible away from them."

Mitch's arm slides around my waist, his lips brushing against my temple. "Don't worry, babe. When I make partner at the law firm in a few years, we'll move anyways."

I finally tear my eyes off the scene next door. Feeling self-conscious about my stomach with Mitch's arm wrapped around my middle, I grab the dress from the closet and head for the bathroom. My hands shake slightly when I apply my lipstick, trying to get the image of the big guy out of my mind. He reminds me so much of the ringleader who raped me. I battle to keep my tears under control. What happened back then is a thing of the past—though the ripples of the aftermath will probably haunt me for the rest of my life.

# Chapter 2

As soon as I lean back in the soft leather seat of the SUV and the engine starts, I gaze at my husband with bubbling excitement. "And? What's the surprise?"

He laughs while he pulls out of the driveway, waving to the new neighbors as we pass by. The woman, Kelsey, waves back, her cheeks flushed from the heat. Happiness practically oozes out of every pore, and I wonder how someone's existence can be so perfect. She's probably gotten everything handed to her for her entire life.

For a moment, envy shows her ugly face until I remind myself that things haven't turned out as badly for me as they could have. My husband is pretty awesome, we have plenty of money, and for the rest—well, things will work out eventually. My father always taught me to view a glass as half full, a notion that has pushed me forward through some pretty dark hours.

My attention returns to Mitch, but he continues to ignore my question. A small smile plays on his lips. He loves to be mysterious and suspenseful and will probably torture me until dessert before spilling the beans about his big secret. I play along, soaking in his handsome face. His chiseled chin is clean-shaven as expected in his profession—he only allows the stubble I like so much to grow on long weekends and during vacations.

My mind drifts off to the first time I laid eyes on him. I had just been arrested for attempted murder and was being held at Rikers Island. The public defender they assigned me totally sucked and my mood was accordingly sullen. I was looking to spend the next fifteen years behind bars.

When the guards told me a lawyer wanted to see me, I fully expected that bitch, Rose Hamlin, but instead, two men were waiting for me. Each of their suits must have cost more than my dorm room at Columbia. The older guy, especially, had a look to him that screamed old money.

He extended his hand for a firm handshake. "Aeree, my name is Jonathan Buren of Buren, Buren, and Larson. This is my junior associate Mitch Cahill."

When Mitch's and my hand met, a surge of electricity shot up my arm. For a second, we just stared at each other before he cleared his throat and pointed at the metal chair across from him.

Jonathan's smile was thin as he took the lead. "Aeree, since you are represented by another attorney, it is totally your choice to talk to us. We can only stay if you explicitly ask us to."

I frowned, unsure what he was getting at. "Sure, no problem."

The smile turned more amicable. "Good. Your case caught my firm's attention and we might consider representation."

The frown on my forehead deepened. "I don't have any money."

"We wouldn't charge you." Jonathan leaned forward and propped his head on his palms. "The New York Bar Association requires every attorney to perform pro bono work, so we always look for high-profile cases to represent for free. Your case qualifies."

"Really?" I glanced at Mitch for confirmation. He was playing with a pen, his eyes glued to a notepad in front of him. "And why does my case exactly qualify?"

Jonathan opened a file, his face turning all business. "Well, you were charged with attempted murder for"—he hesitated—"for castrating your ex-boyfriend. Under normal circumstances, this would constitute aggravated assault, but since he's an NYPD detective, they're trying to throw the book at you. We consider this alone a grave injustice, especially since there were mitigating circumstances."

I turned my head and realized that Mitch was staring at me. His lips twitched and I could swear he thought it was funny.

"Well, yeah, I guess you could call it that." I leaned back and folded my arms in front of my chest. There was something about Jonathan I didn't trust, but for the moment, he seemed the only one who could help me.

"Why don't you tell us what happened?" he asked with a benevolent tone.

A lump the size of Texas formed in my throat. This was always the hardest part. "I was gang-raped. Paul, my ex, was the one who sold me out, so I figured he deserved to share a little of my pain."

"And your father took care of the rest?" Mitch asked.

He was silenced with one dark look from Jonathan.

I was not sure whether I was expected to answer but decided to be cooperative since my dad's charges were a matter of public record. "He pled guilty to quadruple murder and got twenty-five years."

Jonathan's eyebrows rose. "Why didn't he take it to trial?"

"I don't know." My gaze dropped when Mitch kept staring at me with those intense eyes.

The truth was that after my assault, my father's team had decided to pay those guys a visit. Four dead bodies were the result. Up to this day, we don't know why the cops zoomed in on them. As trained operators, they would have never left fingerprints or any other evidence behind that could tie them to the scene of the crime, but when the investigators kept digging, my father wanted the truth buried. A plea bargain was the only way to protect the others, so my dad alone took the fall.

His second-in-command thought it had been a setup, but he had never found any proof that someone from the unit had double-crossed them. My father had dismissed his theories as paranoia. No one in his team would betray him—snitching would be an automatic exit pass. He had called the police investigation a string of bad luck. It was probably what had happened.

Jonathan cleared his throat. "Well, we can't make any promises, but we'd try our best to have your charges reduced and work out a good plea bargain if you'll allow us to represent you."

I slowly nodded. "Do you think I could win in front of a jury?"

"Probably not," he admitted, and I appreciated his candor. "Your fingerprints were all over the knife, and Paul Turner is a highly decorated police officer who'll come across as very believable. Are you saying you didn't do it?"

"No, I did it." I tried to sound remorseful but failed miserably. Payback had been an exhilarating feeling.

"I cannot properly advise you until I know all the facts and review the evidence against you. There's always a chance the cops screwed up and you walk, but truthfully, this is not very likely in this case." He placed a sheet of paper in front of me. "Sign here if you wish my firm to represent you."

There was not a single doubt that Jonathan and his people would be better than my current lawyer, so my signature was just a formality. With his help, things might even work out in the end.

"I'll be the official attorney of record, but Mitch will be your main point of contact." Jonathan tucked the paper in between the covers of the folder. "We will request a substitution of attorney and get the files from the prosecutor's office." He stood and offered me his business card. "In the meantime, do not talk to anyone about your case, especially not other inmates. We'll be in touch."

Mitch winked boyishly at me as he left, and for the first time since my rape, I didn't mind his flirtation. There was something about him that put me at ease. Besides, he was probably just trying to be friendly or felt sorry for me. In any event, he was my lawyer and there was no way there could ever be anything else between us. Little did I know that as soon as I was released from prison less than two years later, we would be married by none other than Jonathan Buren, who had just been appointed to the federal bench.

"We're here, honey."

Mitch's words tear me back to the present and I blink at the restaurant's valet, who had opened the passenger door for me. I slide out of the SUV and wait for my husband to turn his keys over and offer me his arm.

"Hungry?" he asks when my hand comes to rest on his lower arm. My thumb runs over his flexed muscles. He took off his suit jacket and rolled up his sleeves, his bronze freckled skin in sharp contrast to my pasty color. We both love the outdoors, but while I protect myself from the dangerous rays at all cost, he enjoys the warmth and comfort of sunshine.

Buddakan is already packed with a long line of customers waiting at the hostess station. The hostess is a young girl, who is desperately trying to get everyone seated as fast as she can.

Mitch disregards the rest of the patrons and pushes his way to the front. A few angry mumbles follow his path. He seems oblivious to the annoyed glares tossed his way.

"I reserved a table for eight o'clock." He gives the hostess one of his beaming smiles. I peek around him at the other guests, using his impressive frame as my shield.

"We all reserved," mutters a young man next to him dryly and Mitch arches his eyebrow. With his slicked-back hair and the half-unbuttoned shirt, the guy looks like one of those typical rich kids who live off their trust-fund money. Mitch hates those types of people since they always seem to look down on the less privileged.

Mitch's mouth opens, probably to tell him what he thinks of him, when a waiter rushes toward us. "Mr. Cahill, welcome. I have your table ready for you."

"Thank you, Dimitri." Mitch's face is full of triumph when he shoots a nasty glance at the young man who dared to speak up. Buren, Buren, and Larson, Mitch's employers, must frequent the restaurant or we wouldn't get this type of preferential treatment. It shouldn't be surprising—they are one of the biggest law firms in Manhattan, with a lot of money behind them, even if their reputation is questionable. Usually, eyebrows rise when people find out that the firm's top client is the mob.

The usual stares follow us as the waiter leads us to our table at the end of a long row. He pulls out the chair for me while Mitch claims a seat on the bench. When I accept the offered menu, I raise my chin to show everyone that I'm not just a trophy wife Mitch bought in a catalog. Even in New York City, Asian-White couples are still a reason for whispers. There are plenty of women in Asia who are trying to enter the US through a marriage of convenience, but those prejudices are something I've come to accept during the course of our relationship.

"You look gorgeous tonight," Mitch says and pulls my palm to his lips. "I'm so lucky to have you as my wife."

My cheeks sting a little under his burning gaze and I pretend to get lost in the menu. "Don't you think I'm too fat?"

He sighs with a hint of disapproval. "No. You're perfect."

I swallow a doubt, not wanting to spoil the mood. As my husband, he is supposed to tell me these things, even if they are untrue.

"Get anything you want." He squeezes my hand. "I won't tell you your surprise until all the food is gone and we at least share a dessert."

I pout, but a small chuckle is his only response. He insists on an appetizer and a main dish, and I go for King Crab and Lobster Shu before devouring the Kung Pao Monkfish. The food is divine, as always, and I enjoy every bite, already knowing how the evening is going to end. For dessert, we order the Crying Chocolate, a malted chocolate ganache with Vietnamese coffee cream.

When I'm stuffed to the brim, I give him my best puppy dog eyes. "Now, please, tell me—what's the surprise?"

He fiddles with his napkin, obviously enjoying keeping me in suspense. "Well . . ."

My fingers drum on the table in anticipation. "Mitch, please."

"Okay." His whole face has transformed into the widest grin when he pushes an envelope in my direction.

I tear it open with trembling hands. Inside is a voucher for a weekend getaway to the Green Mountains over the upcoming Fourth of July holiday.

"We're going away?" I squeal, not bothering to keep my voice down.

"We'll leave on Friday afternoon and I took a couple of extra days off. It's nothing fancy but includes whitewater rafting and a bungee jump. I know you always wanted to try that."

"Oh, Mitch." I excitedly clap my hands. "We haven't been on vacation in ages." It's just what I need—some time away from the city to get my head cleared. Maybe I can even figure out what I want to do next with my nonexistent career.

"So do you like my surprise?" he asks with a fond smile.

"I love it." I lean over the table for a kiss. "Thank you. It's great." When I sit back down, the food weighs heavily in my stomach. "Would you excuse me? I have to use the bathroom."

"Sure. Do you want anything else or should I get the check?"

"I'm ready to go." I wiggle my eyebrows. "Time to enjoy the rest of the evening at home."

His eyes scorch me while I walk toward the bathrooms. I shake my hips gently for good measure, yet my mind is already on what is ahead. For the second time today, I will have to purge myself from my sinful feast—first the ice cream at home while I was sulking in bed, waiting for Mitch to make me feel better, and now this lavish meal.

I close the stall behind me and slide out of my heels before going down on my knees. I stare inside the toilet. Sucking in a deep breath, I stick my index finger all the way down my throat. The gag reflex is almost instantaneous, but I don't remove my hand until I taste vomit in my mouth. Over and over, my stomach heaves and half-digested food spills into the toilet until the entire meal is regurgitated.

I flush and lean against the stall wall to catch my breath, my throat burning. It takes only a few minutes before the cramping in my stomach subsides and I manage to calm my trembling body. With a grunt, I heave myself up, pee before flushing again, and slip back into my shoes.

Without glancing at any of the other women in the bathroom, I approach the sinks and wash my hands while observing myself in the mirror. A few tears, forced from my eyes while I barfed, smudged my mascara. I carefully dab the streaks away with a tissue before applying a new coat. A little bit of powder covers the blotches on my cheeks.

My tongue runs over my teeth to get rid of any food residue. Without a word, the girl next to me offers me a mint. Though I have my own mints in my purse, I graciously take it to show my solidarity. This is New York City and bulimia is a common occurrence most women don't even think twice about. We all compete with the fashion models and young actresses who arrive daily, on the lookout for a boyfriend or husband who can afford places like Buddakan. Only the thinnest of us survive, and with my twenty-three years, I have to seriously watch my weight. Exercise alone won't cut it anymore.

I stroll out of the bathroom and meet Mitch at the table as he signs the credit card slip. Two hundred and fifty dollars—and half of it just went literally down the toilet. Even though I'm convinced he knows what I'm up to when I excuse myself after every big meal, he never talks about it, which shows he secretly approves. He loves having a thin wife just like everyone else.

Two hours later, I cuddle next to him in bed, totally exhausted and dizzy after a couple of rounds of sex. As usual, the actual intercourse was pure agony, but I have mastered the art of faking my high for many years. Mitch wraps his arms around me, pulling me closer. A few tears roll down my cheeks, which I manage to hide. He only knows the strong me. I will never allow him to see the girl who was broken—and who has never been completely fixed.

# Chapter 3

On the first Friday of every month, I drive the two and a half hours from Staten Island to the Shawangunk Correctional Facility just north of Wallkill to visit my father. This month is no exception, even though I will have to end the visit a little early to be home in time for our weekend getaway.

Morning traffic is just easing up. I floor the pedal when I get onto the highway, hoping the cops are busy with criminals committing more serious offenses than breaking the speed limit. If not, Mitch will probably have a fit since it'll be the third ticket this year. His bad—he shouldn't have bought me a red car that sticks out like a sore thumb.

The weather couldn't be better. It's still fresh from the night, but the cloudless sky promises another day with record temperatures. The forecast predicted nonstop sun over the holiday weekend, even though the climate in the mountains will be cool enough for us not to sweat like pigs. The whole week, I have been beyond excited and can't wait to leave the city and its problems behind to spend a few special days with my husband.

The ride gets boring after a while and just as so many times before, my mind drifts to that fateful night that landed my dad behind bars. My thirst for revenge had consumed me and I didn't try to stop him even once. To the contrary. Now, he would be spending a long stretch of his life in prison, and I would be driving up to see him. Though he has never blamed me, the guilt that I'm at least partially responsible has left a constant stale taste in my mouth whenever I think about that night.

Just before I get to the prison, I pull into the parking lot of a diner for coffee. I smile when my eyes fall on the familiar truck—Eltas got my text message and is able to meet me after all. He was my dad's second-in-command and now runs his old unit. Having breakfast has become a little ritual whenever I visit my dad and Eltas happens to be in town.

The smile is wiped off my face when my scalp prickles like the other day in the grocery store parking lot. I glance around. My parking space is fully hidden under an arched tree branch, and other than a bird chirping, there's not a sound. I need to get a grip on this paranoia. The world isn't out to get me just because someone caused me to lose a crappy job.

As soon as I enter the diner, Eltas's big grin puts my mind at ease. He gesticulates wildly to join him at the table. To my surprise, he is not alone. The young guy who occupies the chair next to him jumps up as I approach. His body goes rigid until he stands straight as a stick, his hands automatically smoothing his shirt before running his fingers over his almost bald head. I have to admit that he is kind of cute. Just a few shades lighter than Eltas, his skin has that deep glow that black people get when they spend a lot of time in the sun. His age is hard to tell—I would guess him to be in his early twenties.

Eltas has also risen, and he and I embrace. I take in a whiff of his aftershave. His smile is just as pearly as I remember—he has always been a charmer. My father called him the greatest manwhore of the unit with a girl in every city. Yet he was the one who could get things done if they ever got in a bind.

My attention shifts back to the young guy, who is gazing at me with a goofy grin. "And who's this?"

"Our latest addition, Staff Sergeant River Cunningham." Eltas slaps him on the back. "Son, say hello to Aeree Cahill, Sergeant Major Phan's daughter."

"Good morning, ma'am." The goofy smile has disappeared and River stares straight ahead at the picture of some country singer with a guitar like it's the most interesting thing in the world. His posture is again all military—I could punch him in the stomach and he wouldn't flinch.

"Hello, Staff Sergeant." I smile but his attention is still focused on the picture. He won't divert his gaze unless Eltas gives him the go-ahead. That's how it works with new recruits—it's a grinding routine until they can call themselves a full member of the team. My father claimed it toughened them up.

"Hope you don't mind that I brought him along, but I had wanted to introduce him to your dad."

"No, not at all. I know how much my dad loves rookie introduction, and I appreciate you're still keeping him in the loop."

Eltas smiles. "Your father will always be one of us."

"That really means a lot." I return the smile before my gaze focuses on River. "What's his specialty?"

"Sniper and explosives. Kid's a natural. Your dad was very impressed."

River's lips twitch slightly; otherwise, he doesn't acknowledge the praise. Over the years, I have met many rookies, and he seems like he'll be a perfect fit with the right amount of modesty under a tough shell.

"So you already saw my dad?"

"Yes, we caught the first visitor group before it gets too busy. He's doing okay."

My smile is crooked—I suppose it's a matter of perspective. Personally, I can't see anyone doing okay in prison, but it's a hard concept to grasp for a bystander who has never gone through the experience. Being locked up in a cage, having to ask permission for even the most basic things, and being degraded by guards and other prisoners alike on a daily basis leaves scars from which it is hard to recover. Even now, a shudder runs down my spine whenever I think of the days I spent as an inmate.

"Why don't we sit down?" Eltas says and I realize that both men have been staring at me with an awkward expression during my trip down memory lane.

I plop into the chair and Eltas pushes the menu in my direction. "Breakfast?"

"Just coffee for me."

"You should eat something."

"I already ate at home." I smile at the waitress when she fills up our cups to escape Eltas's critical eyes. Lying to him has always been hard for me.

"I think you lost weight again. You're practically just skin and bones."

"Trust me, I'm eating enough." I stir creamer into my coffee, forgoing the sugar, even though I hate the bitter taste of unsweetened coffee. "So, what else is new?"

He doesn't go for my diversion tactic. "You used to be a foodie when you still had your catering business. You tried out every dish and loved to experiment."

"Yeah, well, that was a long time ago." I twitch in my seat when his eyes keep drilling into me. "I'm exercising a lot lately since there's not much else to do. Maybe that's why I lost a few pounds."

Eltas's gaze shifts to River. "You know, coming home used to be a special treat because there was always a meal waiting for us. Aeree managed to feed the whole unit. Best cook in the country."

"You're totally exaggerating." I blush when I meet River's warm smile. To my surprise, there is a softness in his features, which is unusual for a special-forces operator. If I didn't know better, I could bet he had never killed before.

"I would've loved trying out your cooking," he says.

His voice is deep with a hint of velvet. It raises the goosebumps on my arms. Something in his gaze is captivating—there's an openness that screams "trust me." Before Paul's betrayal, guys like him had been my weak spot.

"Well, enough of that. How is the husband?" Eltas asks.

I clear my throat, still dazed from River's intense gaze. "Mitch is doing very well, thanks. We're actually planning a camping trip this weekend into the Green Mountains."

"That sounds awesome." Eltas's phone rings and he checks the display. "If you'll excuse me. I have to take this."

A sudden awkwardness falls over the table after his departure. I feel obliged to say something when River stays quiet. "Any special plans yourself for the holidays?"

"Not really." He grimaces. "Plus this might be *the* call."

"The call"—my childhood nightmare. Every time the phone rang, my father was off to save the world. Broken promises, tears, and worry were associated with it, something my mother couldn't handle. Her solution was to stick a pistol in her mouth, leaving me to fend for myself when I was only fifteen.

Eltas returns to the table and drops a twenty-dollar bill next to his cup. "Hate to do this to you, kiddo, but you know how it is. The staff sergeant and I gotta run."

"Well, you take care of yourself." I embrace Eltas quickly before smiling at River. "It was nice meeting you, Staff Sergeant."

"Same here, ma'am."

"And you both stay safe."

I watch them leave, wondering if River will turn around once more and smile. He doesn't. That puts a damper on my good mood, though I have no clue why this even bothers me.

~~~~

It is almost four by the time I'm back home and my mood has turned for the worst. The whole way home, I had to squint against the glaring sun after forgetting my shades in Mitch's car. Sweat pours out of me by the bucket and I'm starving, a crumbly granola bar my only food source all day. To top it all off, I had to cut my visit with my dad even shorter since the stupid guards had made me wait for almost two hours before I was allowed to see him. He was miffed, though he claimed he understood.

Rummaging through the garage to find the second flashlight, I curse the incompetence of the New York prison staff. They are, without exception, arrogant pricks who treat visitors like common criminals, and they have zero compassion for inmates' families and their obligations. Today's asshole even insisted that a female officer pat me down, like I would be stupid enough to bring in contraband. I hate when strangers touch me—even women—having had my fair share of bad experiences when I was incarcerated for thirteen months on my assault charge.

"Excuse me, could I borrow a screwdriver?"

With a startle, I catapult upward, my head colliding with the bottom board of the shelf.

"Ouch." I rub the sore spot, my eyes cutting to the guy standing at my garage door. "Gee, can't you knock? You scared the shit out of me."

"Sorry." He grins at me goofily before I recognize him as the new next-door neighbor.

"It's fine. What type of screwdriver do you need?"

"Phillips." He peeks over my shoulder when I open Mitch's tool box. "It's that one." With an oil-stained finger, he points at a medium-sized screwdriver with a red handle.

If he wasn't the next-door neighbor, I would probably ram it through his eye. He is standing way too close for my liking.

"Here we go." I force a painful smile on my lips. Fortunately, he backs away after I hand him the tool.

"Thanks." That goofy grin stays on his face, reminding me of a creepy clown.

"Anything else?"

"No." He continues to smile as he shuffles his feet.

What an awkward situation.

"I'm Finn by the way." He wipes his palms on his overalls before extending his hand.

My eyes go wide at the sight of his oily, rough hand full of calluses, and I seriously consider ignoring the gesture. When I finally come around, he looks surprised.

"It's nice to meet you, Finn." I shake his hand firmly to show him that I'm not some weakling he can grope. "I'm Aeree."

Silence follows the introduction.

"Well, I better run." His chin points toward his house. "My kids could wake up from their nap any minute."

My eyebrows arch. "Isn't your wife at home?" The babies looked so small when I saw them earlier in the week that I figured she was still on maternity leave. But then, what do I know? My expertise on the baby front is severely limited.

"Nope, she's at work. During the day, it's usually just me."

"Well." I check my watch. "I don't mean to be rude, but my husband and I are going out of town and I still have tons to do."

"Oh, sorry."

His look is more than contrite and I almost feel I should be the one apologizing.

"It's okay." For the first time, my smile is genuine. "I hope I'll get to meet your wife soon. Maybe we could have you over for dinner sometime." The last words take some effort to roll off my lips, but I know that Mitch would be proud. He values relationships with our neighbors, always reminding me that you never know when you need them.

He nods. "That'd be great." He raises his hand for a small wave. "Bye then. Enjoy your weekend."

With that, he retreats, and I can't shake the feeling that this whole experience was just as painful for him as it was for me. Meeting new people has always been difficult, despite the fact that we moved around a lot with the military. It takes me forever to warm up to anyone.

With a sigh, I return to my search and finally locate the flashlight in the box with the fishing gear. Now all I need are my sunglasses from Mitch's car and to pick up mosquito repellent on our way to the airport.

On cue, Mitch pulls into the driveway. Beaming, he jumps out of the car, his arms wrapping firmly around my waist as he spins me around. "How is my beautiful wife today?" He plants a boisterous kiss on my lips. "Are you all packed?"

The liveliness oozing from him sucks the bad mood right out of me. "I just need to change."

His fingernails run down my spine, giving me chills. "Hurry up."

When his lips seal mine, I moan while his tongue gently explores my mouth. It's one of those rare moments I fully indulge in our intimacy. The kiss doesn't last long enough.

Whistling to myself, I bounce up the steps, peeling out of my sweaty clothes as soon as the bedroom door closes behind me. A few minutes under almost-freezing water cools me off, and I quickly pat myself dry. My travel outfit—knee-length pants and an airy T-shirt cut deep in the back—are already neatly spread out on the bed. By the time I'm on the way downstairs, I feel like a new woman.

I halt in my tracks at the sound of Mitch's angry voice drifting out from his study. "No, this is totally unacceptable. It took three years and I'm fucking tired. Get it done, will you? No more excuses."

There's a brief silence.

"Yeah, whatever. Just make sure you'll keep your end of the bargain. Talk later."

I jump back when he tears the study door open. "Aeree." A frown cuts across his forehead. "I didn't hear you come downstairs."

"You were screaming." Curiosity bubbles like a seething volcano. "Is everything all right?"

Usually, he never lets down his guard. He told me his mom used to joke that you could piss on his head and he would still keep his cool.

"Yeah." He sucks in a deep breath. "There're problems with a case that goes to trial in a few weeks. Someone majorly screwed up, but I think I was able to fix it." His lips brush against my cheek. "Sorry I got upset."

"Don't worry." I chuckle. "I guess you still have a little way to go before turning into that superhuman with magical wings, even if you already got the perfect teeth and model hair."

He laughs until his eyes glisten with tears. "God, I love you, honey." He rewards me with another peck on the cheek. "Let's go. The wilderness is calling."

I grab the small backpack from the hanger and scan the hallway one more time. A big lump sits in the pit of my stomach, releasing this itchy sensation that I often get when something bad is about to happen. My father has always called it my sixth sense.

"See you in a few days," I mumble to the coat rack to drown out the feelings. When I lock the door behind me, my mind is already far away in the Green Mountains. Ignoring my premonitions has always been my biggest flaw.

# Chapter 4

As a child, going camping with my dad had always been the highlight of my summer. We pitched a tent in the middle of nowhere, caught a fish to fill our stomachs, and explored the forest. I learned a great deal during those trips but being able to spend some alone time with my dad was undoubtedly the best. Leaving the phone at home made up for the lack of running water and a real toilet.

Mitch's idea of a camping trip is very different. Having been raised in a poor part of Queens and fighting hard to put the Juris Doctor behind his name, he is frugal most of the time, but when he decides to spend some money, he goes all out. The camping site is more like a five-star wilderness lodge with six impressive log cabins nestled at the shores of a small lake and surrounded by mountains.

The cabin lacks no amenity, and I'm stunned to find not only a sixty-five-inch television next to the open fireplace but also Wi-Fi access and a Jacuzzi. When I try to light a fire to give the whole place a little bit of a rustic ambiance, I realize the fireplace is gas with artificial logs that try their best to look like the real thing. Nothing to break a nail or get my hands dirty.

Mitch beams. "Do you like it?"

I smile, trying my hardest to hide my disappointment. "It's great."

He quirks an eyebrow with his "you can't fool me" look.

"I guess I'm just surprised. I expected it's be a little bit more basic." My eyes fall onto the Wi-Fi box before lingering on his laptop bag.

"I'm not going to work." Pulling me into his arms, his nose nuzzles into my hair. "I swear, you'll have my undivided attention."

We both know it's a lie. There will be emails, then quickly checking the database. Before I know it, he will be on the phone with one of the partners, discussing some problem with a case that just cannot wait. That's how we spend the few weekends he is at home, though most of the time, he travels to other parts of the state to meet with important clients. Just as it was with my dad, it's a huge mystery to me why spouses always have to compete with a job. Is it really too much to ask to leave work at the office for at least a few days a week?

The cabin has a separate bedroom with access to the master bathroom. Mitch hauls our overnight bags inside and I start to unpack. Judging from the size of the closets, the lodge management expects us to move in here—the shelves could probably hold all my possessions. Our bags' contents don't even fill one compartment. Hopefully, the other guests won't show up for dinner in a tux and an evening gown.

The room is otherwise cozy. Rich, dark wood paneling covers the walls, which looks like mahogany with hand-carved inlays. The golden and burgundy throws on the king-size bed match the thick, soft carpet. There is also a fireplace across from the bed, but luckily, no television.

When I get back into the living room, Mitch is already on the computer.

"Hey—just checking the weather," he says when he notices my reproachful frown. "I called over to reception and dinner is at seven. Are you hungry?"

"Starving." The bag of peanuts on the plane was tiny, and my body demands fuel. The heat has drained me of my last reserves, and a slight headache crawls up the back of my head.

"Let's test the Jacuzzi," he suggests with a brow wiggle.

The last thing on my mind is sex. "I was going to take a nap. The heat is killing me."

"Oh, okay." His thumb runs over the mouse sensor. "I'm just gonna quickly check my emails then."

I hide an eyeroll—of course he is taking my need to relax for a minute as an excuse to work. It's always the same. "Sure, go ahead." I peck him on his cheek, not really in a mood for an argument. Hopefully, a quick snooze will make me feel better and after dinner I won't even mind getting lost in the Jacuzzi for the rest of the night.

~~~~

To my delight, the dining room is not as fancy as the cabins but reminds me a little of the mess hall at summer camp. A huge table that holds fourteen chairs takes up half the room, and a buffet, from which an amazing scent emits, takes the other half. My mouth waters as soon as I step over the threshold. Mitch's lips twitch at my grumbling stomach.

Eight chairs are already occupied. I hold my breath as I discreetly check out their outfits, but without exception, they are dressed casually like myself. Mitch almost sticks out in his pressed chinos and Lacoste polo shirt. It's a relief. I hate drawing attention to myself in any way, and being overdressed or underdressed could have spoiled the whole night.

Mitch pulls out a chair for me and ensures I sit comfortably before waving at the rest of the group. "Hi, I'm Mitch and this is my wife, Aeree."

Hellos and names are thrown at us at record speed. Desperately, I try to memorize at least a few, but fail miserably. My brain has always been a sieve when it comes to names—the only one I manage to catch is Tyson, a guy in his early thirties with thick brown curls who sits across from us.

A woman materializes out of nowhere. "Good evening. I'm Bobby, your guide for the next few days. On behalf of

Adventure Extreme, a special welcome to all of you who won this trip as part of their annual raffle." A smile spreads on her lips when most of the members at the table clap and hoot. "Please help yourself to the buffet now and enjoy your meal."

She speaks in a mild-mannered, almost-intimidated way, her eyes a soft brown that reminds me of a fawn. I'm sure men find her attractive—she has "protect me" written all over her fragile frame. I would kill for her waist.

When I line up at the buffet, Tyson's wife is ahead of me, her long brown hair loose in a wild mane that she tosses back a lot. Every time she does, she giggles. Mitch and I exchange a glance. When he rolls his eyes at her next snicker, I almost burst out laughing.

The food looks divine. There are barbecue ribs with sauce dripping off the tender meat, grilled chicken breast stuffed with melted cheese, and a seafood gumbo. The spicy aroma leaves a tingle in my mouth. Corn on the cob, veggie skewers, and a huge bowl of baked potatoes next to crusty French baguettes are lined up afterward, followed by an array of different sauces and condiments.

My appetite turns into my enemy—having to forgo all these delicacies is painful. With a small sigh, I turn toward the salad bar. Various antipasti, mostly marinated in olive oil, and chicken and tuna pieces are on offer, together with prefixed salads heavy on mayonnaise and at least six types of cheeses. I stick with the basics, loading my plate with a standard mix of lettuce, carrots, tomatoes, and cucumbers. To spoil myself, I choose low-fat ranch dressing and even add a few croutons for good measure.

"Is this all you're gonna have?" Mitch asks.

"Yes. My stomach feels a little tight all of a sudden." It would be impossible to purge myself in the confines of the cabin, and the public bathrooms are too risky. I could get caught by one of the other guests, who would probably gossip about it. This is not New York, where everyone does it in the restaurant bathrooms, or home, where I can hide away in the guest-room toilet next to the garage.

The others have their plates loaded and dig in while I pick at my salad. A conversation is soon in full swing. The smile is frozen on my lips while I endure their chitchat with one ear. Conversations with strangers usually bore me since I can't relate to them or their lives, and my mind easily strays to Eltas and the other guys. I wonder in which part of the world they are at the moment. For all I know, they could be hiding out in the jungle or dining at a luxurious restaurant while surveilling a leading terrorist. My dad had loved his job, the constant travels his favorite part. He had said it was the only way for him to see the world, even if the circumstances were less than ideal.

"So, what do you do for a living, Mitch?" Tyson beams at us from across the table, reminding me that I should at least make an effort to get to know these people. Starting tomorrow, all activities will be together, and it will be less painful if I have figured out a few of their quirks.

"I'm a lawyer," Mitch says before stuffing a large piece of chicken breast into his mouth.

"Oh, me too," pipes the voice of a woman from the end of the table. She's a little on the heavy side, her face painted with too much makeup. "What's your specialty?"

Mitch chews vigorously before forcing down the rest of his food with a big gulp of water. "Criminal law. What's yours, Citadel?"

"Personal injury." The woman twitches in her chair. Her brown eyes sparkle with excitement as she gazes around the table. "I just opened up my own firm. It's tough going, but better than working for someone else. We are just so thrilled we won this trip, or we probably wouldn't be here."

Mitch smirks. He despises that type of law, calling people like her ambulance chasers.

"Is there money in criminal law?" Tyson waves his fork in the air as he asks the question, almost poking his wife's eye out.

"There is when you have the right clients." Mitch's smile is smug. "My firm is one of the largest on the East Coast. You might have heard of them—Buren, Buren, and Larson."

Silence falls over the table. For the past two months, Mitch's firm has been in the news daily for defending Dario Rossi, a modern Al Capone. The case was dismissed only a few days ago when the prosecutor couldn't produce his star witness.

A guy with an easy smile finally saves the day. "Well, it's interesting for sure. I think I'd prefer that over reviewing contracts all day." His fingers are entangled with those of the man next to him, his thumb stroking the back of his hand.

"Oh, I wouldn't practice anything else, Norton." Mitch winks at me. He will keep repeating first names until he is either blue in the face or satisfied that my brain has absorbed them. Contrary to me, he never forgets a name—or a face for that matter.

"I'm a dermatologist," Norton offers without prompting. "And George here is going to stay home to raise our son. The adoption is almost final. This is our last getaway before parenthood."

"Oh, congratulations," Citadel says. "I think it's so progressive when gay couples adopt. Are you two married?"

I frown. The way she pronounced the word "progressive" practically screamed disapproval.

"Not yet." Norton squeezes George's hand. "We are hoping for a Christmas wedding."

"Well, speaking of children, *we're* pregnant." Tyson wraps his arm around his wife's shoulders. "We just found out last week and we're beyond excited."

I almost roll my eyes at him. What does he mean "we're pregnant"? Sure, being supportive is important, but he shouldn't forget that his participation was limited to three minutes filled with fun. His wife is the one who will be suffering from swollen feet and back pain; she'll probably have stretch marks across her belly for the rest of her life when it's all over. Judging from his wimpy frame, I doubt he could survive labor without permanent psychological damage.

My eyes meet the gaze of a woman who sits next to Citadel. Her lips are twitching. Without words, we understand each other. It's almost like looking into a mirror, a deep sadness hidden deep within her. Her hand is clutched tightly by the man sitting across from her, who gives her a fond smile. She mimics the gesture like a robot—those two have a rotten relationship.

After the plates are cleared and everyone else stuffed themselves, Bobby reappears at our table.

"For the rest of the evening, we have charades on the program."

I can barely stifle a groan—she has to be fricking kidding me.

"Smile, honey," Mitch mumbles in my ear. "It's a great icebreaker and we'll spend a lot of time with these people over the next few days."

My foot kicks him under the table. "Don't tell me you knew about this. I hate those types of group activities." Even though I get his shin, he keeps a straight face.

"It'll be good for you to be a little bit more social." His lips brush over my temple when he helps me to my feet. "You'll see—it won't be as bad as you think."

I shoot him a sinister look but don't argue. Secretly, I promise myself that he'll pay for this tonight.

Surprisingly, he is right and the game turns out to be a lot of fun. It's the girls plus Norton against the rest of the guys. Citadel actually reveals herself as an ace player. Her facial display of farm animals has me in stitches until Tyson's wife correctly guesses the movie *Babe*. When we win in the end, it's the cherry on top.

"I don't think I've laughed that much in years," I admit to Mitch on our way back to the cabin.

"Me either." When he smiles at me, little crinkles cut around his eyes. He looks incredibly happy.

In that moment, my heart is almost complete. It's like one of those cliché moments other couples call romantic—just me and Mitch without a worry in the world. The stars above sparkle like scattered diamonds on a dark velvet blanket. A scent of honeysuckle hangs in the air, and somewhere by the lake, the crickets give some cheesy background music their best shot.

But there is still a part of me that can't let go. It's the piece of my soul that has been aching since the baby talk, knowing that children of my own are no longer in the cards. It's the little bit of uneasiness that never leaves my side, even if the man who has sworn to love and protect me until the day he dies walks right next to me with his arm around my shoulders.

Those invisible scars, the leftovers of that fateful night, have never fully healed, constantly throbbing and oozing a little. They prevent me from moving on. On the contrary, every day, a little part of me surrenders and dies while the memories are still as vivid as the moment they happened.

A doctor at the hospital told me I was lucky to be alive. He had no clue what he was talking about. The way I see it, being alive is nothing more than a curse.

# Chapter 5

The alarm clock wakes me up way too early. I kick at the blanket, grumbling a vague curse, before flipping on my stomach. My face digs deeper into the pillow. Something tickles my ear. I slap at it and the tickle stops, just to start back up when I grunt in satisfaction.

"Good morning, honey."

I force myself to open my eyelids far enough to get a blurry look at my husband. "Go away."

He chuckles. "I would, but then you'd miss the bungee jump and I wouldn't hear the end of it."

This gets my attention. I raise my head. "What time is it?"

"Eight. I let you sleep as long as I could."

I squint at him. Not only does he wear that cocky smile that is always there when he makes fun of me, but he is also fully dressed, his hair meticulously styled like he is on his way to the office.

"What time did *you* get up?"

"Five." His tone is nonchalant, like it's the most common thing to get up that early during a weekend getaway. "I already went jogging and checked my emails."

"Fantastic." He probably worked a solid two hours on one of his cases and was more productive than I had been all week. I eye the sunshine behind the drawn curtains and decide to abandon my comfortable bed. A bungee jump is worth getting up for at an ungodly hour.

I hop into the shower, well aware that Mitch's eyes are on my butt the entire time. I'm still in my birthday suit from the night before and squirm under the attention. At least my strict diet pays off in moments like this. The warm water, pelting down on me, takes away the rest of my tiredness. By the time I stick the toothbrush into my mouth, I'm ready for my adventure weekend.

I brush, rinse, and floss, admiring my pearly white teeth in the mirror afterward. They are the only part of me I find remotely pretty. Attacking my hair next, I secure my fringe with a few clips before applying sunscreen with an SPF of fifty. That will not only prevent my skin from burning up, but also keep a dreadful tan away. Asian beauty standards are one thing I refuse to abandon. I might have been born and raised in America, but my father always taught me to be proud of my heritage.

I decide on some light chinos and my New Balance sneakers before slipping into my usual tank top. My dad's old dog tags complete the outfit. When he was kicked out of the military, I was supposed to turn them in, but played dumb and pretended I couldn't find them. Major Riley, his superior, didn't press the issue, telling me behind closed doors that he would kill the fuckers himself if someone ever touched his daughter.

Mitch is on the computer when I walk into the living room, chatting with someone on Skype. When he notices my frown, he abruptly ends the conversation by slamming the laptop shut.

"Like I said, no work." He wiggles his eyebrows. "This weekend is all about you and me."

I pour myself a glass of orange juice from the minibar. "I know that work is important to you, but for once, I just want you all to myself. I hope that's okay."

"Of course it is." He walks over to the counter with the widest grin and wraps his arms around me. "I have been neglecting you by working too much. That will change as soon as I make partner. The easy days are just around the corner."

I doubt it but keep my opinion to myself. Jonathan Buren, his old boss, pushed ninety hours a week until he was appointed to the bench. Three marriages bit the dust in the process. Since Mitch was the only one who was there for me after I got out of prison, I intend to stick it out with him no matter what, even if his constant travel and work will be a challenge. Sometimes, it's really lonely, but then moments like this make up for it tenfold. I consider myself lucky having found a man like him. He is my Prince Charming, and I've always believed that one has to fight for their happy ending. No one is perfect. It's up to me to make my dreams come true. Mitch is worth the fight.

Sipping my orange juice, I let him sway me to music only audible in his head, a light humming keeping me mesmerized. His hot breath tickles me behind my ear. All of a sudden, he spins me around, his lips only inches from mine.

"I love you, Aeree. Never forget that."

"I love you, too."

His embrace tightens while he pecks my forehead. "We should go or we'll be late. Can't have the bus leave without us."

I wouldn't even have minded that much as I long to spend more alone time with him. A bungee jump is awesome, yet getting him all to myself without him thinking about work is almost impossible. For a moment, I seriously consider just staying at the camp, but he heads for the door. I follow, slightly miffed.

The others are already gathered around a large Jeep. Bobby is standing on the passenger seat, barking orders at a few waiters who load packed lunches and water bottles into the trunk. Another guy leans back in the driver's seat, chewing gum and watching the commotion with a sullen expression.

"Okay, listen up." Bobby claps her hands until our group falls quiet. "We'll start out with a hike up into the mountains until we get to the Steel Gulch Bridge. That'll take about two hours and also includes a wall climb. At the bridge, we'll do the bungee jump. I have eight participants, so I'll split you in two groups. Your partner can take pictures or videos from across the ravine while you jump and then we'll switch places."

A few mumbles and nods accompany her words. I'm pumped up, my brief sullen spell forgotten. Hiking and wall climbing are some of my favorite activities, and the jump will be the ultimate thrill. This promises to be an epic day.

The trip in the Jeep takes about half an hour. The girl with the sad eyes sits next to me, her face hidden behind huge sunglasses. A bruise on her cheek is still visible. Her husband clutches her wrist as if he is trying to restrain her with handcuffs. They don't mutter a single word, but only stare straight ahead like frozen statues.

She tears herself loose when the Jeep comes to a stop, jumping out without waiting for him. A few angry words are hissed under his breath when he joins her, which she shrugs off.

"Boy, I really hate when men hit women," Norton mumbles to George.

I couldn't agree more. My father always taught me that only cowards beat their partners to control them and compensate for low self-esteem. He called it the "small-dick syndrome." Special-ops guys are crude that way, probably a side effect of spending most of their time around other men without the influence of the opposite sex. His unit is still off-limits to women—slush operations are considered too dangerous for us. It's a concept I have yet to grasp.

Armed with our backpacks now holding water, snacks, and a survival pack, we start to clomp up the forest path winding through the woods. A roof made of treetops shields us from the blazing sun, which is already high in the sky.

It's a peaceful morning. I catch a glimpse of a beautiful bird of prey circling above in the cloudless sky. Insects buzz around me, attracted to the sweet smell of sweat already pearling on my back. The sun cuts like blades through gaps in the trees, burning hot on my skin when the rays catch me. So much for the cool mountain climate. The humidity is through the roof and I can practically taste the thunderstorm on my lips.

The pregnant girl, Julie, is puffing next to me, her face red as a beet. Her husband isn't doing any better, even without carrying the extra weight around. They both look like they are about to collapse. Why in God's name would they sign up for a tour like this? Citadel, on the other hand, is pushing ahead without breaking a sweat despite her advanced age. She is by far the oldest of the group. Her husband trots behind her, like a child behind his mom. If she had introduced him as her son, no one would have questioned it.

At a creek, we take a break. I sip from my water bottle, watching how Julie takes off her shoes to stick her feet into the cold stream. Three painful-looking blisters decorate one of her toes and both of her heels. She must have made the rookie mistake of wearing new hiking boots.

Tyson gently massages her feet before they force them back into the shoes. At least he seems to care about her. The husband of Sad Eyes is the complete opposite; he glares at her the entire time while making little snotty remarks.

"I told you to wear more sunscreen. It's your own fault if you burn, so stop whining."

She remains quiet, playing with her cuticles.

"And you should have worn different socks. I hope you get blisters. Serves you right."

Mitch explodes. "Would you just shut up, Kendall?" He tosses the guy an evil glare. "Truthfully, I don't want to hear your nagging and I'm sure the others agree. We're here to have a nice time with our partners, so don't spoil it for the rest of us."

Silence follows his outburst. Kendall's face is burning up, though I can't tell if it's anger or embarrassment. Being at least a foot shorter than my husband and knowing that he won't stand a chance in a physical altercation, it's probably a little bit of both.

We continue our path. Bobby chats like the incident at the creek never happened, pointing out various flora unique to the Green Mountains. I listen with one ear, soaking up my surroundings. My fingers entangle with Mitch's and he squeezes my hand. "I love you," his eyes say and my insides tingle. He is such an awesome husband.

The wall is a joke, no taller than the training climb at my gym. Support handles have been hammered into the rock to make it even easier. A child could master it without any issues. I hide my disappointment by snuggling against Mitch while Bobby climbs up effortlessly as a cat would scramble up a tree.

A support rope is tossed down and we are ready to go. Citadel is first, mastering the wall within minutes. Norton and George follow. George pretends he is about to fall when he is almost at the top, and an excited Norton shrieks in horror. It makes for a good laugh. The tension that hung over the group since the creek resolves when even Kendall smiles.

"Let's take a selfie before we climb up." Mitch peels his phone out of his jeans pocket, holding it up as I lean in for a quick photo in front of the wall.

"I hope you're not going to check your emails."

He smiles, stuffing the phone into his back pocket. "I couldn't, even if I wanted to. No reception."

"I guess I should insist on a weekend retreat somewhere in the mountains when you're rich and famous."

"Wealth and fame come with a price, my dear, but don't worry. I'll try to cut back a little on my work on the weekends." He pulls me into his arms and gazes down on me with a smug smile. I lower my gaze. When he looks at me like this, I always feel he is making fun of me.

One by one, we make it up the wall. Julie is last and takes longer than the rest of us combined. Midway, she panics, refusing to move on until Bobby gets back down to show her exactly which handles to choose. By the time she pulls herself onto the plateau, her shirt is drenched in sweat, the vein on her forehead swollen like it's about to pop. She nevertheless grins from ear to ear as she wipes a few sweaty strands of hair out of her eyes.

The path meanders along the edge of a ravine. The views are breathtaking and I fall behind, my mind captured by three pillar-like tops of a nearby mountain range. From a distance, they appear as if they are holding up the sky. Loving history, I wonder what these rocks have seen. Did they provide shelter to soldiers waiting to ambush a troop of enemies who were riding along the ravine? Did lovers ever kiss under the stars? If these mountains and trees could talk, a whole world of wonder would be at my fingertips.

"Aeree, hurry up!"

Mitch's call tears me out of my imaginary world. He waves at me to rejoin the group, which has halted about two hundred yards away. I sprint uphill along the path. It would prove a mistake. By the time I reach the others, I'm panting, sweat pouring down my face. Mitch comes to my rescue once again. With a smile, I accept the offered water bottle, downing half before pouring the rest over my head. The relief is instantaneous.

"Okay, this is where the others will wait while the first group completes their jump. We found it the perfect spot for pictures, and the trees provide enough shade that you don't have to shoot against the sun. Now who wants to go first?" Bobby's gaze scans over the group.

"Aeree here."

I nudge Mitch in the side when every head turns to me. A mushroom, growing wildly out of a tree stump, attracts my fake interest. When I'm no longer the center of attention, I sigh with relief.

"Sure, I'll go," Sad Eyes offers next.

"Count me in." George winks at Norton, who is a little pale around the nose.

"What about you, honey?" Citadel asks her husband, whose name still escapes me. So far, he has not uttered a single word and only sat in a corner during the charades game.

He nods, his hands forming signs in a hurry. It's the first time I realize he is mute.

"Yes, I'll catch the next one." Her lips form the words quickly, but he understands her without effort. They are a well-attuned team.

"You sure that you don't want to jump?" Bobby asks Tyson.

Tyson nods. "Positive. We are both afraid of heights, and Julie couldn't even jump since she is pregnant. In hindsight, we should have booked something less strenuous as a last-minute getaway."

I'm baffled by his statement. Why would they even waste money on something they apparently dread?

We hike another half mile until we get to the bridge, which glimmers peacefully in the midday sun. It's made of solid steel and spans the ravine. At the bottom, a small stream fights its way through the rocky terrain. The whitewater probably turns into a powerful rapid in the spring, fed by the melting snow that transforms the mountains into a white wonderland during the winter season.

In the middle of the bridge, a three-by-three-foot ledge stretches out over the ravine. The bungee equipment is mounted to the bridge's pillar itself. It looks safe, yet my heart is pounding in my throat.

*It's gonna be fine. Hundreds of people have jumped before and survived, so you can do this.*

My legs still turn into lead when Bobby gives me an encouraging smile. "You wanna go first, Aeree?"

*Not really,* I want to scream but my head develops a mind of its own, bopping up and down with vigor.

I step close to the rail and peek down. The stream looks far, far away, more like a small string of wool. I clench my jaw as I slip on the harness. It feels snug on my hips and my shoulders. Bobbie cuffs my feet before attaching the bungee cord. It's only about two and a half inches thick—a joke, considering that my life depends on it. Talk about hanging by a thread.

Bobby pulls a few times on the harness before I wobble to the ledge with my feet tight together. My mouth dries up when I edge forward, feeling like a pirate walking the plank. With horror, I stare down. Shit, it's at least four hundred feet. There is no way I'm going to jump.

I gaze over at the little group by the trees. Mitch will have the camera up. If I chicken out, the others will make fun and I would never want him to see me as weak.

I close my eyes and take a deep breath. *You can do this, Aeree.*

My knees bend and my arms stretch out when I let myself drop forward. For a few seconds, time stops. I feel like one of those cartoon characters that hang in the air, wondering what the hell went wrong before zooming down. Then I just fall. My stomach tries to squeeze into my chest, somersaulting a few times, while my lungs burst from a scream explosion. My fall is rapid. Like a bird of prey, I nosedive into the ravine. It's the most amazing feeling I've ever experienced and utterly exhilarating.

The ground is approaching fast and I hold my breath. The expected jerk is replaced by a gentle pull on my legs before I catapult upward. When I fall again, a wide smile spreads on my lips. I kick myself for almost peeing my pants earlier—this is the best experience yet. I wouldn't want to miss it for the world.

The ride ends way to soon. For a moment, I dangle over the ground, stretching out my fingertips to touch the glistening water's surface. It's silly. I'm still at least a hundred feet above the stream. The sun stings my eyes, which have teared up from the wind. With a sigh, I hook the harness to the carabiner like Bobby explained to get myself back into an upright position before snapping the lifting wire into place for my ride up. A couple of minutes later, I rejoin my fellow jumpers on the bridge.

"How was it?" Sad Eyes asks.

"Wow," is my only response. My head is still spinning, the whole experience totally surreal. This one will be hard to top.

When I look up, Citadel's husband is just about to jump. I lean over the rail of the bridge, watching him fall. He bounces up and down before hanging freely. A sudden bang disturbs the still air, followed by a gush of cool wind, giving me goosebumps. I stare across the ravine, squinting to see if I can make out the source of the sound. Since there's no hunting in the summer, it's probably just some kids setting off early Fourth of July fireworks or practicing with their dad's rifle. I look at the cliff where Mitch is waiting. To my surprise, everyone is gone.

"Something is wrong," Bobby mumbles more to herself than to us.

My forehead wrinkles. "Why?"

"He didn't connect the lifting wire. It will be difficult to pull him up."

Together with Bobby and the others, I gaze over the bridge's rails to determine what's wrong. Citadel's husband hangs lifelessly at the end of the cord. At first, I want to call out to him, but then I remember that mute people are also often deaf. He might not be able to hear me.

With great effort, Bobby starts to retract the cord, and after a moment, Sad Eyes, George, and I pitch in. Together, we are able to heave the body back up onto the platform.

George wipes the sweat off his forehead. "Are you all right, man?"

Sad Eyes's scream, bouncing off the canyon walls, is the only reply.

I turn to see what all the fuss is about. The guy's face is pale as a ghost, blood dripping from a wound in the center of his forehead. Glassy eyes stare into the sky. He is dead.

# Chapter 6

It takes only a second for my survival instincts to kick in. I crouch, my gaze traveling back to the cliff in the hopes of finding the one person I need at the moment. Only a flock of rusty blackbirds is in the place where Mitch was less than five minutes ago. Where the hell is he?

After Sad Eyes's scream dies down, eerie silence follows. A warm breeze blows through the ravine, rattling the winch of the bungee equipment. I jump when a low squeak breaks through the calm. Here on the bridge, we're sitting ducks. We have to get to the safety of the forest.

I turn to alert my group when I notice a red light dance on George's forehead. As the daughter of a trained sniper, I know the beam too well. It had been the guiding light during many deer-hunting expeditions when I was a child—the tool my father used to teach me the difference between a precise shot and a sloppy kill. It's the light of a laser range finder.

The warning shout leaves my mouth just as another crack echoes in the canyon. Blood trickles down George's forehead. Like a freshly cut tree, he falls forward. Vibrations shake the bridge when his body slams facedown onto the metal sheets, which is followed by a new hysterical scream from Sad Eyes.

I just wish she would shut up. My head snaps left, then right. Which way to turn? In the end, I go for the woods adjacent to the plateau. It's my best chance to find my husband.

I start to run, my banging footsteps mixing with my breath and the pounding of my heart. The ground below me trembles as I push forward to close the gap to safety. When the red light dances in front of my feet, I instinctively dash to the side, zigzagging around the beam like I would an obstacle course. The magnified pops of the discharging rifle hurt my eardrums.

A metallic *ping* freezes my blood when the sniper finds his mark close to my foot. Luckily, the ricochet bullet misses any of my body parts.

The light keeps dancing along my path—the bastard is toying with me. There is no way a sniper makes two precise shots the way he did and keeps missing me. With gritted teeth, I dive forward when I reach the tree line. Something hot grazes the side of my neck before a burning pain spreads along my collarbone. Even before I run my fingers over the sting with the sticky blood, I know I've been hit.

Panting, I peek around the bush, which provides excellent cover. Sad Eyes falls down on her knees next to me. She is as white as a sheet, her whole body shaking. A few tears have smudged her mascara.

"What's happening?" she whispers.

I frown—isn't it obvious? "A sniper is shooting at us."

She gasps, clutching her hand over her mouth as if she is just realizing that this is not a bad dream. In her defense, if my neck wasn't on fire and blood wasn't dripping into the collar of my shirt, I could probably make myself believe that this is a very vivid and nasty nightmare.

"You're bleeding," she yelps.

"It's just a scratch." The pain pounds rhythmically and the wound can't be deep. "Nothing more than a graze."

Her face twists. "How can you be so calm about this?"

I ignore her stupid question. The alternative is to panic, which would turn our situation from dire to lethal. My eyes dart around, my mind scrambling to come up with a viable plan to survive.

"Where's Bobby?" I ask.

"I don't know." More tears roll down her cheeks. "What are we gonna do?"

"First, let's try to find the others." I nod in the general direction of the plateau. "This way."

I stay low as I sprint along, careful to stay fully hidden behind shrubbery and trees. Sad Eyes is right on my heels, wheezing. So far, she's keeping up, but could easily turn into dead weight. We would both be screwed.

Reaching a gap in coverage, I halt in my tracks. She bumps into me. For a moment, my body is exposed when I fall forward. Little grains of sand tear my eyes as a cloud of dirt hovers in the spot where my skull was just a second ago. Whoever this sniper is, he is not only really good, but has apparently chosen me as his next target.

I scan my surroundings to assess the situation. The tree line closest to the plateau is at an unattainable six-yard distance. Sprinting across is out of the question. Our only option is to walk around the swath to get to the main forest path. Hopefully, Mitch and the others have figured out by now what's going on and are on their way to the Jeep to call for help.

"We need to stay covered," I tell Sad Eyes. "Let's fall deeper into the forest."

She trots behind me like a lost puppy when I start to walk alongside the swath. The forest life has reawakened. A woodpecker chisels a fallen log nearby; a slight buzzing of bees, searching for pollen between patches of wildflowers, perturbs the still air. I catch a glimpse of the sky through the forest roof—the sun has almost reached its peak. I map out the points of a compass in my mind, not that it does me any good. On our hike up this morning, I didn't pay attention and have no clue in which direction to head to get to the Jeep.

The trees and brush get thicker the farther we move away from the ravine. My only guidance is the sun, but if I'm truthful with myself, I don't know any longer which way to turn. We could be walking in circles. When I had my dad, a compass, and a full backpack of supplies, finding my way through the woods was a piece of cake. Now, without any gear, we are screwed in the long run. Not that I would ever admit that to Sad Eyes. Clenching my jaw, I keep plodding along, pretending to have an actual clue where I'm going. The worry about Mitch is pushed to the back of my mind, my only driving force my natural instinct to survive.

Before long, my neck starts to burn as my mind is no longer fueled by adrenaline. My fingers inspect the wound. With a hiss, I pull away. Blood coats my hand. The graze must be much deeper than I originally thought. This will require stitches or I will get an infection.

As we continue to plow through the woods, the pain pounds evenly in unison with my heartbeat. I find myself licking my lips to keep my mind off my parched throat. Every swallow is pure agony. The humidity presses down on me like a steamroller; a few times, I almost fall when I trip over my own feet. My clothing has long surrendered to my sweat, sticking to my skin like a wet sheet. Forcing myself to keep a steady pace, I trudge along. When bushes rustle in front of me, my heart jumps. There isn't even the slightest breeze.

"I'm thirsty and my feet hurt." Julie's words are whiny. "It makes no sense to keep wandering around."

Sad Eyes's squeal confirms my surprise. "We're here." She starts to trample through the thick underbrush toward Julie's voice, causing more ruckus than a herd of elephants. I scurry behind her, my heart skipping three beats at the thought of Mitch and me reunited.

My hope fades when we only find Julie and Tyson, who look like someone has put them through the wringer. Their hair is disheveled, and Julie's face is puffy and crimson red from the heat. He is not in much better shape with a cut underneath his eye.

Julie clutches her hand over her mouth. "Oh my god, Aeree, what happened to you? There's blood all over your shirt."

"I got shot." I scan the area around her. "Where're the others?"

She ignores my question. "Shot? When? How?" Her eyes are as wide as Frisbees.

"There was a sniper shooting at us. Didn't you notice?"

Julie and Tyson stare at me like I just escaped the looney bin.

"You're kidding, right?" Tyson's lips tilt upward with hesitation. "You have to be. Why would a sniper shoot at us?"

I shrug, giving him a snotty I-wouldn't-kid-about-stuff-like-this look. "Where were you during the jumps?"

"Julie got really sick, so Citadel suggested I get her into the shade. All of a sudden, there was a scream and the others scrambled to look at what was going on. Everyone disappeared on us. When we looked for them, we got lost."

A prickling feeling spreads along my scalp. Something in his story doesn't add up, but at least it explains where everyone went. I wipe the sweat off my forehead. "Can I have some of your water? My husband has my backpack."

"Sorry, we drank it all." Tyson clutches his backpack closer to his chest.

I'm taken aback by his odd behavior. "Have you checked if there's anything useful in your survival pack? Maybe there's a flare or something we could use to alert the others."

He hesitates before his grip on his backpack tightens. "There's nothing." His eye twitches before he drops his gaze. "We already checked."

Even though I'm sure he is hiding something, I'm too weak and exhausted to start an argument. The heat and pain are making me dizzy, a pounding headache slowly snaking across my forehead. I massage the bridge of my nose to fight the pain. I need to find a source of water or I'll collapse soon.

"Well, let's keep moving," I say.

"I can't walk anymore." Julie groans. "We should have met up with the driver at the first meeting point by now. I'm sure he called the rangers when we didn't show up and they are already looking for us. We should stay put until they find us."

"There's no way they'll find us in these thick bushes," I point out.

"Then you go." Tyson folds his arms in front of his chest. "Like my wife said, she's exhausted. She's pregnant and shouldn't overstrain herself."

She really shouldn't be on the trip—being out of shape the way she is—but that's beside the point. Tyson's frown is such that he is no longer open to reason.

"Well, I'm going. There's no way the rangers will discover us here and I need to find water." My eyes pierce Sad Eyes. "Coming?"

She shakes her head. "I think I'll stay with them. I'm exhausted. Maybe later when it has cooled off."

Lucky for all of them, I already have my back turned when I flip them a bird. They can go to hell as far as I am concerned. Mumbling to myself about their prick attitudes, I keep stomping through the bushes, ignoring the angry thorns that tear at my shirt and arms. The pain in my neck has reached new proportions that shut out everything other than the swooshing of blood in my ears.

"You can do this," I repeat over and over through gritted teeth. Yet the loneliness is crushing. It's tough to keep pushing with me as my only cheerleader, especially with my injury. I'm at the brink of exhaustion. My only guide is the sun, which is moving toward the west. At least it will guarantee that I'm not walking around in circles.

When I get to a clearing, I double over to catch my breath. My attention zooms in on a small hunter's cabin that lies abandoned on the opposite side of the opening. The windows sparkle like gold in the blazing sun. I prick my ears to pick up the sounds of the forest. My father taught me that wildlife is my only friend in the woods, alerting me of danger before the human mind can even register anything unusual.

Birds are chirping nearby and the grass covering the clearing buzzes with insects. The sweet but sickening smell of decaying blossoms hangs in the air. I wipe the moisture off my forehead with my lower arm, the salt of my sweat burning the scratches left by the thorns. Everything appears peaceful, only my damn premonition is preventing me from crossing the clearing. The pit of my stomach has been loaded with bricks that radiate a poisonous tingle along my spine all the way to my fingertips and toes.

Two figures step out of the forest on the other side of the clearing and turn immediately toward the cabin. I squint, recognizing Norton and Kendall. Their voices drift across the opening, but I can't make out their words. They are slightly bent over from their gear, totally oblivious to their surroundings.

The chirping stops before a flock of birds takes off toward the sky. Deadly silence spreads over the clearing. My warning cry is stuck in my throat when the light of the laser range finder hops on the back of Kendall's cap, right over the emblem of the National Baseball League. It's one of those moments where events unfold in slow motion, but the bystander is paralyzed on the sidelines. I can't even breathe.

A big black spot spreads on the back of Kendall's cap before the crack of the bullet follows. I finally shake off my daze.

"Get down," I shout at Norton.

As Kendall face-plants onto the cabin's porch, he stays frozen in place like a hypnotized rabbit, waiting for the kill. Only when blood dribbles down the wooden steps does he finally move.

"Norton, get down." My second yell finally has him drop low to the ground.

The next bullet, intended for Norton's head, tears through Kendall's backpack. A water explosion follows. When the droplets splatter everywhere, Norton sprints up the steps of the cabin.

His clumsiness might have saved his life when he trips over the wooden threshold of the cabin. The bullet finds its mark in the door right where his head was just moments ago. His feet kick to find traction, but his shoes slip on the moldy wood of the deck. "Help," resonates from the bottom of his throat, causing a shudder to run through my body. It's a cry of mercy for his life.

He continues to struggle and finally gets on his feet, disappearing inside the cabin with one leap. A bullet rips through the door frame just as he slams the door closed. Hopefully, he has sense enough to stay low and away from the windows.

I let ten minutes pass before I dare to make my next move. Picking up a medium-sized branch, I toss it into the clearing, just to watch how it is torn to pieces by the next bullet. The sniper is still out there and now fully aware that I'm hiding in the safety of the trees. There's nothing I can do except wait for darkness or continue to wander around. The latter idea is disposed of quickly—the pain and dehydration render me immobile.

My eyes stay glued on the intact water bottle in the other side compartment of Kendall's backpack while the minutes wind down like molasses. I can't remember ever being thirstier.

Each new breath ripples through my body with pure agony. My lips are dry and cracked, the metallic taste of my blood mixing with the little bit of saliva I have left.

When my eyelids become too heavy, only the pain, drumming in my neck, reminds me that I'm still alive. All I can do is pray for nightfall—and that the sniper is not equipped with a night-vision scope.

# Chapter 7

I doze in and out, strength draining from my body with every breath. I miss Mitch. My helplessness drives tears to my eyes at the same time the humidity presses down on me like an indestructible wall. Even the slight breezes, flaring up from time to time, are more like hot air from a hair dryer than a relief. Every piece of clothing sticks to my skin, the sweat droplets that dribble from my hairline a constant burn in my wound.

The last time it was this hot, my dad had a barbecue with his friends at the house. I fretted almost the entire time in the shade on a lounge chair, my mind lulled from the meds the doctor had put me on after my attack. My injuries were slowly healing, though I battled nightmares as soon as I closed my eyes. The entire week, I had woken up screaming, crying myself back to sleep just to face more terrifying dreams.

"How're you holding up, kiddo?"

I squinted at Eltas, who was gazing at me from above. "I'm fine."

"That's not what I heard." He squatted down next to the chair, his hands holding on to the armrest to keep his balance. "Your dad said you've been having nightmares."

I turned to hide the rising tears. "It'll pass."

"You should go to therapy."

My head snapped around. "Look who's talking. I don't remember you going to therapy when you came home all messed up last summer."

"That was different."

"Oh yeah, and why was it different?" Spit spewed from my mouth as I wound myself up. "Because you're a guy who deals with matters differently? That's a bunch of crap, Eltas, and you know it."

"I'm a trained soldier. We learn how to deal with pain and torture." For a second, his eyes were in another world. "Besides, having electricity run through your body is totally different than being raped. It's maybe the worst thing a man can do to a woman."

His words made me cringe. My father had avoided the therapy topic, probably knowing how I would react. We had tried after my mom's suicide, but when I had thrown one tantrum after another whenever I was forced to go, he had given up. "All I need is a little bit of time."

He didn't let it slide. "Look, Aeree, we're all worried sick about you. I know what trauma can do to a person. I've seen it a dozen times in the service. If you don't tackle it the right way, it can destroy you."

"Okay, I'll think about it." Hopefully, this would shut him up. There was no way I would pour my heart out to some know-it-all shrink. They were all patronizing assholes.

"You're a damn liar and we both know it." He shook his head. "Sometimes, I don't know what to do with you, girl. You've always been so stubborn."

"I guess I got that from my dad." I gave him my sweetest smile.

"I suppose." He returned the smile, his sincerer than my own. "Well, if you ever need to talk, I'm here for you."

"Sure thing." I rested my head against the pillow. Having any type of conversation was still incredibly tiring for me. It seemed that words were like little earthquakes, tearing at the stitches holding my insides together. They had removed every nonvital organ below my waistline, and pain erupted whenever I coughed, choked, or spoke too much.

He squeezed my hand, but before he could push himself up, I clutched his fingers. "Eltas, what are you gonna do to those guys?"

His gaze dropped. "When something like this happens to a family member, the whole team takes care of it. Those are the rules."

"Is that why you're here today? To start making plans?"

He nodded. "Don't tell your dad I mentioned it. He still thinks of you as his little girl and doesn't want you to know."

I sucked in a deep breath. "I want to come."

"Impossible. There's always a chance that something could go wrong. It's way too dangerous."

"Come on, Eltas. Talk to my dad. I need this—for closure. That'll be so much better than wasting money on therapy."

He shook his head again. "Why did you have to be a girl? You would've made a hell of an operator."

"Is that a yes?"

"I'll talk to him." His exhale turned into a sigh. "But if he says no, it's gonna be no. It's his gig."


Crazy as they were, his words cheered me up that day. Now, almost five years later, I have a different perspective. If I hadn't persuaded my dad to bring me along, he wouldn't be in prison today. It was reckless and didn't help to kill my nightmares.

Sudden nausea overwhelms me. I just manage to roll onto my knees to avoid getting vomit all over my clothes. My stomach cramps as I hurl into a bush, every heave cutting into my wound like a knife.

When I'm done, I crawl over to the other side and hide under the branches of another bush. The brushwood covers me like a protective embrace. I curl into a ball. The air glimmers as I stare up into the sky through the few gaps in the green roof, the pain in my neck and head overpowering my other senses. Dizziness overcomes me and I turn my head to eye the clearing. One step, and it will be over. The sniper is a professional who shoots precisely enough to not make me suffer. I would be dead before my head even hit the ground.

The memories of my mother's suicide snap me back to reality. My heart soars before the ache is replaced by utter resentment. I despised her for taking her own life, and stepping out of my hiding place is lunacy. I'm better than that; I'm a fighter. My dad threw his life away so I could have mine, and I won't repay him by being a coward who gives up so easily. It wouldn't be fair to him, and it wouldn't be fair to Mitch.

With gritted teeth, my gaze returns to the sun, which is glaring down at the clearing. It couldn't be much later than three or four. By nightfall, I will be so parched that I could be unconscious. Finding water is my number-one priority. But where do I start? Every stream has probably dried up from the drought over the past weeks.

The fighting spirit melts away as fast as it had bubbled up. Who am I kidding? My body is too weak to walk around aimlessly in the hope of finding some water. I will probably get lost. Our campsite is hours away on foot, and I didn't see any sign of civilization on our drive up. That only gives me one certain water source—the second water bottle in Kendall's backpack.

I crawl back to the tree line and peek through the bushes before picking up another stick. My hand is shaking when I toss it into the clearing with a last-ditch effort, fully anticipating it will be blown to pieces. The afternoon air remains still. I chew the inside of my cheek, pondering my next move. Has the sniper moved on or smartened up and realized the branch is a decoy?

After another minute, I decide to take a chance. I stay hidden in between the trees as I walk along the edge of the clearing to get as close to the small hunting cabin as possible. Before I take off, I hesitate. It's maybe twenty yards, not more. Twenty steps—a stone's throw on every other day.

I toss another stick into the clearing. It bounces off Kendall's still frame and wobbles around before coming to a standstill. Pricking my ears, I ignore my racing heart, which beats hard against my rib cage. The birds are chirping and a butterfly comes to rest on the stick. I finally dare to take a step out in the open.

I hold my breath, waiting for the impact. Nothing. My instincts take over and push my body into survival mode by swallowing up the growing apprehension that threatens to paralyze me. With a few long strides, I'm next to Kendall, my hand reaching for the water bottle in the side compartment. The beam only changes the liquid to red for a second before the bottle bursts with the crack of the shot. I squeal, wrapping my arms around my head as little droplets pelt down on me. This is it—I will die. A few tears spring loose while I wait for the next bullet to penetrate my body.

There is no second shot. I glance around in utter confusion before a squeaking pulls me out of my daze. Through the cracked door of the cabin, Norton peeks at me.

"Aeree?"

His terrified eyes are all that is needed to get me to react. I push up like a gazelle trying to evade a starving lioness. I stay low as I sprint up the few steps to the cabin, my shoulder colliding with the door as I dive to safety.

"Ouch." Norton scrambles to get on his feet just when I slam the door shut and immediately crouch low to the floor.

"Stay down."

My warning is unnecessary. All stays quiet. After a few seconds, I let out the breath I was holding.

"Keep away from the windows," I hiss at Norton. The sooner he realizes I'm in charge, the better for the both of us.

He blinks at me. "What the hell is going on?"

"I don't know. Someone is shooting at us."

"I think Kendall is dead," he says, like it's some big revelation.

"Yes, and for now, we are trapped in this cabin." I gaze around to find his backpack. "Do you have any water left?"

"Yes, there are a couple of bottles. I put them in the fridge."

I almost roll my eyes. Since there's likely no electricity when the cabin is unoccupied during the off-hunting season, it's totally pointless. On my hands and knees, I crawl to the kitchen and tear the small refrigerator open. My hands enclose the water, my fingers fumbling with the lid while I bring the bottle to my mouth. As the water runs down my throat, a sigh leaves my lips. I gulp down a few mouthfuls before I choke.

"Take only small sips or you'll get sick," Norton says.

I glare at him before I remember that he is a doctor. With a small grumble, I comply. My strength returns with every sip while he watches me, the silence only interrupted by my swallows.

"You're hurt. Let me take a look at that." He rises before I can mutter another warning, but plops down after my face twists in panic. "You really think it's that dangerous?"

"Yes. That guy can shoot an apple off your head from two hundred yards away."

"Then why didn't he shoot you when you came out of the forest?"

I shrug, which painfully reminds me of the slash on my neck. "Dunno. He missed on purpose, that much is certain, but I can't tell you why. It's almost like it's a game for him."

He stares at me with wide eyes as if realizing for the first time the danger we are in. "How do you know all this stuff?"

"My father was in the military. Sniper assignments were one of his specialties."

"Oh."

"Try to stay low when you move around." I smile at him with encouragement. Under normal circumstances, I would have added, "Better yet, try to stay put," but from the terrified expression on his face, he's about ready to pee his pants.

"Have you seen George?"

His eyes have this softness in them that reminds me of a helpless puppy and I can't hold his gaze. How do I tell him that his partner is dead? There won't be an adoption or the happy family evenings that he excitedly envisioned during our charades game. One bullet took all of that away from him. "No, I haven't seen him." Sudden worry hits me like a jackhammer. "Have you seen Mitch?"

He shakes his head. "We heard a scream and all hell broke loose. Everyone ran into different directions. I was lucky to find Kendall after a while."

Staleness laces my mouth, when I imagine that Mitch could also be dead, before tears well up. I wouldn't have the strength to live without him. Over the last few years, he has been my only anchor, the only one helping me to keep it together. He takes care of everything.

I down the rest of my water in one go to flush away the worry about my husband. My focus has to stay on the here and now, or Norton and I will soon join the trail of dead bodies.

"Do you have any weapons?" I ask.

"My hunting knife. It's in my backpack."

I glance at the bag by the chair. "I'm gonna get it. Stay put."

I crawl over, staying close to the wall when I duck under the window. All stays quiet. I reach the backpack and toss it over to Norton before returning to the kitchen. The little bit of strength I had regained has left me. Like a deflated balloon, I sink flat on my stomach, my cheek resting on the cool tile of the floor.

"You must have lost a lot of blood." Norton slides over on his butt, dragging the backpack along. "Let me take a look at that."

I'm too weak to protest when his fingers examine the gash on my neck.

He rummages around in the backpack, pulling out a small bottle. Some of the contents are poured on a cotton pad. The unmistakable scent of alcohol flares my nostrils. My stomach is about to turn again, when he mumbles, "Hold still. This might sting a little."

I hiss when the cotton pad connects to my skin.

He dabs my wound, ignoring my yelps, while I fight with my tears. My neck is on fire and the pain slowly crawls into my head and down my shoulder.

"That's the best I can do without stitches," he says after he finally stops his torture.

Half my body is immobilized. "Do you have something for the pain?"

He pulls out a pack of ibuprofen, letting two of the pills drop into my hand. Secretly, I'm glad that the bullet hit George and not him. Having a doctor on my team has its advantages.

He crawls over to the fridge to get more water. I play with the pills in my hand, letting them roll back and forth to keep my mind occupied. Maybe we should stay at the cabin until the rangers find us. Julie was right; by now, they must be searching for us since we missed our pickup. Yet it could take days before they find us, and we will run out of water. Having no food could also become an issue, so venturing outside at nightfall to find help might be the better option.

I freeze when there is scraping right outside the window. The porch squeaks, muffled footsteps follow. The scraping moves to the door. I glance at Norton, who stares back with terrified eyes. The crotch of his pants is drenched, a small puddle spreading between his legs. His nerves must be totally shot.

The pills are dropped on the ground as my fingers enclose the grip of the hunting knife. I have never been good at throwing knives and miss most of the time, but the weapon will be good enough to ram the blade between someone's ribs if they come too close. Of course, if he has a rifle or a gun, all will be lost. With the breath caught in my throat, I watch how the crack of the door widens, inch by inch, until the door finally swings back with a creak.

# Chapter 8

Time seems to be crawling as the creaking of the door rips through my frayed nerves like a rusty, dull saw. I jump when the handle hits the wall. My tongue runs over the perspiration above my lip, the breath still firmly stuck in my throat.

When Bobby's face appears, it's almost a letdown. I exhale, yet my heart is still racing at least double its speed.

"Aeree, thank goodness you're alive. Who's here with you?"

"Just Norton." Another long exhale slows down my pounding heartbeat. When I relax the grip around the knife, my hand is shaking.

She fully enters the cabin. A man follows. When I notice the gun strapped to his hip, my nerve ends tingle. I try to argue away a surge of uneasiness by telling myself he must be a forest ranger, though something is off about him. He doesn't wear the standard uniform, and his stained jeans and combat boots look out of place.

His eyes scan the cabin before giving Norton and me a quick once-over. "Harley, get in here. I need you to sweep this cabin."

I gasp when a second man appears in the doorway. This guy is definitely not a forest ranger. His hair is long and greasy, a three-day stubble covering the lower part of his face. A cigarette hangs lazily from one side of his lips. He is big, a few good inches over six feet, yet what dominates his features is the three-tear tattoo on his cheek. His hard eyes further suggest he has been to prison. That a rifle hangs off his shoulder is enough to tighten my grip around the knife again.

He smirks at me before turning toward the small bedroom in the back. Pressing silence hangs over the cabin as he shuffles around before reappearing.

"It's clean." His voice is as rough as his looks. The cigarette is shifted from one corner of his mouth to the other as he gazes around. The smirk is back when he reaches me. The lust in his eyes makes me gag.

"What's going on?" I ask Bobby when no one offers an explanation. "Did you call the forest service or the cops?"

The man with the gun breaks into a brief smile. "Don't worry, honey. They're on their way."

I can't shake the feeling that he is lying through his teeth. The uneasiness is back and prickles in my scalp.

He regards me calmly, his jaw working the gum in his mouth, before he and Bobby exchange a glance.

"Have you seen Julie and Tyson?" she casually asks while beaming at me.

I'm taken aback by her question. Why is she interested in them? Her behavior combined with the two guys is more than odd, even a bit creepy. "I saw them a few hours ago but don't know where they went." A claw digs into my chest when I realize that her question could imply that everyone else is dead. "Have you seen my husband?"

"No, sorry."

I squint at her. "And why exactly are you only interested in Julie and Tyson?"

She ignores my question, her focus shifting to the man with the gun. "What do you wanna do?"

He rakes his fingers through his thinning hair with a sigh. "The area is too large to just wander around without a plan, plus there is at least one shooter who will eliminate everyone who has come in contact with them. With the amount of money involved, he won't back down until he finds them and that damn data stick, and we could end up in the crossfire. Besides, more teams will join the hunt as soon as word spreads that the data stick is up for grabs. Better to get more of our men out here before we comb the forest."

The three-tear guy, Harley, clicks his tongue. "That'll take forever."

"What did Julie and Tyson do?" They must be on the run. At least that explains their odd behavior.

"Man, this chick is getting on my nerves," the guy with the gun snarls. "She's asking way too many questions."

Pressing silence falls over the cabin as the three newcomers glare at me. My body tenses at the same time my fingers clutch the knife, my mind already preparing to throw the weapon at anyone who gets too close to me.

"Tie her up and gag her," the guy with the gun finally says. His chin points at Norton. "The fag, too. They'll just get in our way otherwise."

Harley draws his lip back, exposing a set of yellow teeth.

Like a hunting wildcat, I focus on his movement. Every muscle in my body flexes. I will not go down without a fight, but then the rational part of my brain kicks in. These guys have guns and don't look like they will hesitate to use them. I will end up dead or without a weapon. The knife could be put to much better use if I hide it.

A surge of adrenaline is released in my bloodstream to fight the panic when Harley moves closer. His eyes are fixed on my face, but his friend is no longer paying attention to me when Bobby bickers that it's his fault for not picking Julie and Tyson up last night. Their yelling and my racing heart drown out the click as the blade folds back in place. I hold my breath, sliding the knife into my back pocket. Every muscle is so strained that my whole body aches.

Harley reaches me just as I bring my balled hands back around. His gaze comes to rest on my breasts. With a smirk, he squats down next to me.

"Hold still, honey. I don't want to hurt you." When he leans into me, the smell of cold cigarette smoke and hangover liquor makes my stomach queasy. It's like déjà vu. "Put your hands on your back."

I have no choice but to oblige. Our closeness is jarring. The vicious glint in his eyes says it all—if he gets me on his own, he will turn into an animal. Grinding my teeth together is the only way to rein in my temper.

"Good girl." He grins at me as he pulls out a cable tie.

When he reaches around me, his hand brushes over my breast. I manage to suppress a whimper, but when his crotch grinds against me, I snap.

The memories from the night of my rape consume every bit of my rationality. I'm back in that trailer out in the woods, the heavy body of the gang leader crushed on top of me. His friend, who was taping the whole ordeal with his phone, chuckled with every yelp.

"Don't break her, bro. I want a piece of that ass, too."

A grunt was the gang leader's only response. With every thrust, a new piece of my soul was sliced away. By the time they switched places, there was no more fight left in me. Today will be different. Harley will not rob me of the little bit of strength I have fought so hard to regain over these past years.

My elbow develops a mind of its own when it crashes into his face. If he hadn't instinctively snapped his head back, I would have hit the center of his temple and caused some serious damage, but I only get his nose. He shouts out when blood splatters everywhere.

With a growl, I lunge at him, totally ignoring his friend and the gun. I would rather die than have another man violate me. I get in a couple of good punches until his slap across my face takes me off my feet. Shaking my head to get rid of the dancing black spots, I'm just about to jump him again when the cocking of a hammer paralyzes my muscles.

"Don't move, sweetheart." A low huff follows the demand. "What the fuck just happened, Harley? Can't you keep your goddamn hands to yourself for once?"

Harley glares at me with his hand clutched across the lower part of his face. "That bitch just broke my nose."

"Good for her." With a louder huff, the other guy pulls me to my feet, the barrel of the gun now pressing against my kidneys. He shoves me forward. "Face to the wall and hands on your back." When I don't oblige right away, he shoves me again. "Move it, bitch."

I press my forehead against the wall. Every fiber of my body is consumed by rage, but my survival instinct prevents me from fighting back. My dad always joked that even the toughest operator isn't bulletproof. All I can do is bite hard on my shivering lip as I fight with the tears that threaten to spill. Though these tears are fueled by pure hatred, I wouldn't give them the satisfaction to laugh at me or belittle me as weak. I have had enough ridicule to last me a lifetime.

The plastic of the cable tie cuts into my skin, but the pain is overpowered by a new rush of adrenaline when I'm pulled around to come face to face with Harley. I'm tempted to spit on him, but before I can make up my mind, a gag is forced into my mouth.

"Don't worry, honey. When this is over, I'll come find you and we'll finish what we started." He smirks. "I have a thing for Asian chicks. They're just so much more flexible and squeal louder when you give it to them hard."

I glare at him—I hope he'll come and find me. I would love to add another set of balls to my collection.

"Harley, for fuck's sake, would you stop?" His friend shoots him a dark look.

Harley's gaze lingers on my breasts for just a moment longer before his full attention shifts to Norton. "Now, faggot, don't give me a hard time, too, or I swear I'll toss you in the ditch next to your dead boyfriend."

"George is dead?" Norton's words are no louder than a whisper while his eyes plead for me to confirm that Harley is lying.

I can't hold his gaze. With my back against the wall, I crumble to the floor and bury my face against my bent knees. At least I could have broken the news to him gently. This must utterly destroy him. For me, a life without Mitch is unthinkable.

Norton's quiet sobs mix with Harley puffs as the latter gets to work. It doesn't take long before Norton is tied up. The gag cuts off his wails.

"Let's go." The guy with the gun waves at Harley, an impatient wrinkle cutting across his forehead.

When the door slams shut behind them, I finally turn to Norton. His face is streaked with tears that continue to stream down his face. He looks absolutely devastated and the pain in his eyes slices sharply into my defenses. A familiar hitch forms at the bottom of my throat before my own tears begin to fall. Every part of my body is throbbing, but the ache that is spreading in my heart takes over my existence. I miss Mitch—and all I want is for him to be safe.

# Chapter 9

Though the tears drain me of more energy, my determination to fight prevails in the end. My fingertips graze the top of my back pocket to work out the knife. It's much harder than I anticipated. The cable ties cut sharply into my skin as the gag turns my breath into short staccatos. By the time sweat trickles down my back, I realize that I won't be able to do this on my own.

I gaze at Norton, who has stopped crying and regards me with a frown. He is probably trying to figure out why I'm performing acrobatic moves. On my knees, I scoot over to him. His frown deepens when I start to grunt undecipherable sounds at the same time my fingertips point to my back pocket. He might be an excellent dermatologist, but in survival skills, he is a total dud.

A chuckle from the door paralyzes my muscles. "What are you doing, honey?"

My head snaps around and the tears are back. Mitch's smile fades as he soaks in the sight in front of him. With a few quick steps, he closes the gap between us. His fingers fumble in my back pocket when I give him a silent signal. The blade of the knife springs to life, setting me free. My lungs fill with oxygen as soon as the gag comes off.

I fling my arms around his neck before he even has a chance to cut Norton's restraints. The tears are absorbed by his shirt as he holds me in a tight embrace. There is so much relief that he is okay that it drowns out the dire situation. He is here, he will protect me, and we are together. That's all that matters.

"Kendall is dead, shot in the head like the others."

Citadel's voice finally causes my head to leave the comfort of Mitch's shoulder.

"I'm really sorry for your loss."

She doesn't acknowledge my condolences, her face void of emotions. My teary reunion with my husband probably bothers her. Norton has also started to cry again, his eyes full of pain when Mitch cuts his restraints. His hands shake as he removes the gag.

"Who did this to you?" Mitch asks with a frown.

I fill him and Citadel in on Bobby and the two thugs, telling them all about Julie and Tyson and that the sniper is likely after everyone who has been in contact with them to get his hands on some valuable data stick. The only things I omit are the specifics about Harley's threat. It will just enrage and distract Mitch. Everyone needs to focus if we want to get out of this situation alive.

Mitch inspects the injury on my neck. "This will get infected if we don't get you to a doctor soon. Are you in a lot of pain?"

Just as he says it, a heated throbbing pushes to the front of my brain. "Yeah." I search the floor for the painkillers, but they have disappeared in the shuffle.

"I have some aspirin." Citadel rummages around in her backpack and produces a small container of pills. "Here we go."

Before I can grab them, Mitch springs into the role of concerned husband. "You sit down. I'll get you some water. When have you eaten last?"

"Nothing since last night." Obediently, I plop down on the ground, eyeing the windows in the living room. The kitchen area is fully secluded from the outside, so we should be safe. Though Mitch and Citadel entered the cabin without being shot at, suggesting the sniper probably moved on with Bobby and her companions, he could always return at some point to finish the job.

Mitch pulls out a bottle of water from his backpack, followed by an apple and a candy bar. "Here. Two tablets now and another two in an hour after you have something in your stomach."

I grin, tempted to salute. He can be quite pushy when he is in one of his moods.

The apple is devoured in silence after I down the water in one go. Citadel speaks with Norton in a hushed voice, her hand squeezing his arm a few times when his face twists to a grimace. I'm sure they are talking about their dead partners. Though I feel guilty, I'm utterly thankful that it's not my husband.

Mitch rejoins us after searching the cabin. "I found some matches, but nothing else that could be of use. The water is turned off, so we can't refill our supplies and there's no food anywhere."

Citadel rubs her eyes. "So what do you want to do?"

It's apparent that she is only concerned about Mitch's opinion, totally ignoring Norton and me. It's something I do not appreciate, and I'm just about to voice my objection when Mitch's response cuts me off.

"Well, it's now"—he checks his watch— "almost four, which means the heat is even worse than before. The sensible approach is to wait here, especially if we consider that there's a sniper out there on the loose. But we also have limited supplies and need to find at least a water source. I suggest we stay put for another couple of hours, then search the area before it gets dark."

"Yeah, that's a good idea." Citadel slowly nods her head. "Hopefully, the sniper is busy tracking down Julie and Tyson."

"Those thugs said that the sniper will eliminate everyone who has come in contact with them," I pipe in, almost kicking myself for sounding shy. No need to be intimidated by her just because she is older with years of education under her belt. She might know the law, but in survival techniques, I'm miles ahead of her.

My interference with their conversation is ignored.

"Ultimately, we need to try to contact the forest rangers." Mitch sighs. "Too bad the phones have no signal in the mountains."

"I tell you what." Citadel rises to her feet and walks over to the window. "Why don't you and your wife look for water and food, and Norton and I try to find higher ground to get a signal? We can meet back here at nightfall."

"We should stay away from the windows," I say.

My warning is once again ignored. I'm still determined to let her know that I don't think we should split up when Mitch squeezes my hand.

"Let me handle this, honey." Absentmindedly, his lips peck the tip of my nose and he smiles before he joins Citadel by the window.

The two engage in a hushed conversation. The resentment of being excluded irks me more than I want to admit. I scoot over to Norton, who is leaning against the wall with a lethargic expression. I'm not even sure he registers what's going on.

"How are you holding up?"

His face twists in agony. "You knew George was dead when I asked you, didn't you?"

"I didn't want to upset you."

"Yeah, I guess it was better that this bigot told me."

The bitter sarcasm is like acid dripping onto my skin. I can't even imagine how hard this must be for him. Losing his partner is already bad enough, but learning it from someone who gloated about it is an even lower blow.

"I'm sorry, Norton." Unsure what else to say, I stand up and walk toward the window.

Mitch smiles at me. "Why don't you lay down in the bedroom for a while? You look tired."

Though I don't like to be told what to do, he has a point. Ever since he found me, the exhaustion and pain have been getting the better of me. Resting for a while will recharge my batteries and prepare me for our hike later on.

"Okay."

At the door to the bedroom, I turn around and gaze at Mitch one more time. He is still in deep conversation with Citadel. A longing for his embrace washes over me, but I don't want to appear weak. Having him back under the same roof with me is the best I can do for now.

~~~~

My slumber is way too short when Mitch wakes me with a sweet kiss. "Time to get up, babe. It's a bit cooler and I want to cover a few miles before darkness."

"Where are the others?" I stretch to get my sore limbs to relax, yet a stabbing pain in my neck forces me to still. The wound is pounding and burns—the first signs of an infection.

"They already left half an hour ago. Hopefully, Citadel will get a signal and can alert the rangers."

Every part of my body aches when I sit up. It feels like I had a head-on collision with a bulldozer and the bulldozer crushed me. I suppress a groan as I heave myself out of bed. My hand reaches for the headboard to keep my balance when black spots dance in front of my eyes.

"Are you okay, honey?" Mitch's question sets off a small earthquake in my head.

"Yeah." Massaging my temples, I remember the painkillers. "Where are the aspirin?"

"In the other room." His arm slides around my waist as he leads me back to the living room. His eyes mirror his concerned frown when I lower myself onto the chair.

"Are you sure you're up for a hike?"

"Positive." Two aspirin disappear in my mouth and I choke them down with some water. It will take at least fifteen minutes for them to offer me any relief, but I'm determined to tough it out.

"I'm ready." My smile is feeble at best, but the wrinkles on his forehead smooth a bit.

"Okay, then let's climb out the back window. The trees are right there and the cabin provides better coverage." With one strap of the backpack slung over his shoulder, he heads for the bedroom.

I follow him, glad I don't have to step over Kendall's dead body. After Mitch jumps off the windowsill, he helps me through the small window. He was right. The temperature is significantly lower than earlier in the day and the humidity is not weighing down as hard.

When we enter the forest, the shade cools my skin even more. A slight breeze adds to my comfort.

"Where to?"

Mitch's chin points toward the right. "Citadel and I came from the left, so let's check out the other side of the forest."

I trot behind him through the thick underwood. The ground is dry and hard under my shoes. Branches grab at my bare arms, but I grit my teeth when thorns scratch my skin. Once I stumble and would have fallen into a bush of poison ivy if Mitch hadn't caught me.

"Watch it there, honey. Are you sure this isn't too much for you?"

I shoot him a dark look and push ahead through the bushes. Around the next bend, a narrow forest path snakes through the woods.

I grin. "Mitch, I think I found something."

His arms wrap around me from behind as his chin comes to rest on my shoulder. "If we turn left, it'll take us back to the cabin, so let's go the other way."

The path winds downhill through the forest and our hike becomes much easier. Birds' chirps mix with a low buzzing of insects. Our steps are the only disturbance of the natural surroundings. Those are usually the times I cherish the most in the woods. With Mitch holding my hand, I can almost forget the dreadful situation. Yet, my eyes are in constant movement, watching the signs of nature. If the sniper is after us, the wildlife will alert us in one way or another.

"Listen." Mitch halts abruptly. "Do you hear that?"

I prick my ears. Thundering sounds of swishing water float our way. We head in that direction and don't have to wait long until a clearing cuts off the tree line. The beautiful display of nature is breathtaking. Sheets of water, falling from cliffs above, feed a small natural basin that is maybe the size of a large swimming pool. The water glistens turquoise green in the early evening light; a few scattered clouds on the otherwise perfect blue sky reflect off the sparkling surface.

"Wait." I hold him back when he tries to step out in the open. My gaze travels along the tops of the surrounding cliffs. Most of them are bare—the sniper couldn't hide up there. I zoom in on the pond and crane my neck to peek around the tumbling water. The waterfall cuts the basin off in the back. This will be the safest area to get water.

I point at the space behind the falls. "We'll be fully hidden back there."

Mitch, who has been scouting out the area himself, nods. "That's the best spot."

We stay close to the tree line as we quickly make our way along the basin. It actually extends into a small cave that is cool from the waterfall's mist. If our situation wasn't so dire, I wouldn't mind going for a swim. It's a beautiful spot to relax.

I kneel down next to the edge of the mossy green water. Dipping my hand in, I let the water run through the gaps in between my cupped fingers. "How deep do you think this is?"

"No clue. Could be a few feet or endless. You never know with these types of mountain lakes." He hands me one of the water bottles and I fill it up.

Before he screws the top back on, he drops one of the filtration tablets inside. Six bottles are filled this way, which will give us enough water for at least a day, even if we have to share it.

When we are done, I roll up my sleeves and dip both hands into the cool lake. Splattering water on my face gives me some relief. The pounding burn in my wound has lessened, but those aspirin will wear off in a few hours. This type of over-the-counter medication is not suitable for gunshot wounds. The few times my dad got shot, the doctor prescribed something with morphine, and he had to watch that he didn't get addicted.

Mitch's head points upward. "Let's climb to the top. Maybe we'll find a way back to civilization or the phone might work."

"Don't you think that's too dangerous? What if the sniper sees us?"

"Naw, it's safe. The waterfall will give us plenty of coverage. Once we get up there, we just have to be careful."

The idea is growing on me. The rocks next to the falls are steep, but there are enough ledges to make this a manageable climb. Uninjured, it would even be easy, but given my condition, it's hard once I start my ascent. I puff, suppressing tears the higher I get. My arms and legs are like jelly when I finally reach the top.

The sun stings my eyes and I shield them with my hand to get a better look at my surroundings. The forest stretches on all sides of the cliffs—not a sign of civilization anywhere. We perch behind a small wall of rocks that are curved in a way that keeps us almost completely hidden from view.

Mitch fumbles with the phone. "I'm getting a really weak signal." He dials 911 but lowers the phone just moments later with a huff. "It's gone again." His chin juts at a small plateau across from us. "If we could only make it over there. It's higher up and I'm sure we can get a signal."

"No, it's way too exposed. We would be sitting ducks."

His eyes run over the mountaintops. "If there was a sniper, we would see him from here. There's no one there."

Before I can voice another objection, he bounds forward toward the falls. Reluctantly, I follow him, not willing to chicken out if he considers it safe. We halt briefly at the edge of the falls. Slippery rocks part the water into little streams before the rapids combine again to a solid wall of water.

"I'll go first," Mitch says.

"Just be careful."

"Don't worry. You just have to make sure to keep your balance."

He straps the backpack closer to his shoulders.

I chew the inside of my cheek as I watch him make his way across. Most of the stones are wide—it almost looks like a man-made path operating as a bridge. It shouldn't be too difficult.

He halts in the middle and gazes down. "This view is amazing."

I groan—now is not the time to admire the beauty of nature. I'm about to scold him when my breath gets stuck in my throat. My warning shout is nothing but a gurgle as I stare at the back of Mitch's head—and the dancing light of the laser range finder.

# Chapter 10

The loud crack of the discharging rifle splits the silent air. Mitch falls. I'm paralyzed as the rapids engulf his body, and a terrible pain washes over me, as if someone slammed a knife between my ribs and turned it slowly. I want to give in to the mounting sorrow that threatens to destroy every fiber of my existence, but the twirling dirt next to my foot works like a wake-up call.

My head turns, and I squint at the cliffs behind me to find the shooter in the same moment my body propels itself toward the rock bridge across the falls. The sun is blinding and I can only make out the silhouette of Mitch's killer. In the position he is in, I won't be able to cross the falls, and the rocks, which served as coverage earlier, are too far away. Jumping is my only option. It's almost certain suicide, but the slim chance of survival fuels my muscles like a remote control. A low growl overpowers the pounding pain in my soul when I push off the ledge.

Just as with the bungee jump earlier, the free fall tickles my stomach, but this time, I don't have a cord around my ankles that will protect me from the impact. I have dived off enough ten-meter platforms before to know that the water surface below will be as hard as cement if I don't hit it right. My dad's words of caution take over—arms across my chest to protect my lungs and heart, legs straight, toes pointed downward. I fall alongside the water, but the only sound in my eardrums is my racing heartbeat.

I hold my breath as the water swallows me up. If the pond is not deep enough, my spine will snap like a twig. I sink, but when the expected impact doesn't materialize, my legs start kicking. My arms reach for the light. I take in a big mouthful of air when my head pops back up above water before I force my body under the surface again. From above, I will be an easy target. I have to get to the basin behind the falls. My muscles flex as I swim toward the rushing sound of water hitting rocks. When the sheets of the falling rapids almost crush me, I finally allow myself to drift to shore.

My fingers dig into the uneven rock, holding on for dear life, until my rapid breath slows. I gaze around, my vision obscured by the waterfall's mist. Tears rise without warning. When a sob rips through me, I almost slide back underwater. With my last-ditch effort, I pull myself out of the pond and crawl through the space in the rocks behind the waterfall. My body is drained of all energy when I come to rest on the smooth stones.

I don't know how long I lie there flat on my stomach while the rocks soak up my tears. My heart is weeping and I curse myself for my good reflexes. Without Mitch, fighting for my life is pointless, and it would have been so much better if the sniper had gotten me as well.

When my teeth begin to chatter, I finally sit up. The fear of finding my husband's broken body turns my stomach inside out, but luckily, there is no sign of him when my gaze scans the pond's edge. A ping of hope radiates in my soul—maybe he survived after all. He could have realized that the sniper was aiming at him and just dropped into the falls the way I did. The thought is soothing and keeps me breathing. My father had always said that the hope of seeing a loved one again is like fuel. It's something I hold onto now to keep me from going completely insane.

Cowering into a ball, I give in to the turmoil of emotions that rattle through every part of my existence. Tears mix with loud wails and bitter laughter as I ponder why all these terrible things keep happening to me. Whatever I did to the guy in charge of karma, I must have seriously pissed him off.

~~~~

Just as it happens so often in the mountains, nightfall is accompanied by a sudden chill. I must have fallen asleep at some point while wallowing in self-pity, and I wake up stiff and frozen to the bone. My back and limbs hurt from the hard ground and the pounding wound in my neck has turned into a constant burn.

With a groan, I pull myself up, stretching my cramped muscles in the hopes of loosening them up a little. Though hiding behind the waterfall would be a safe option, it's also impractical since no one will find me. I wouldn't even hear anyone calling me over the loud rushing of the water. Since the drinking water supplies went down with Mitch and the backpack, I will have to stick with unfiltered water, which could make me sick. Add my injury, and my hiding place only adds to my dire situation. Best to go back to the cabin to see if Citadel and Norton have returned. Hopefully, they were able to contact the forest rangers.

A biting breeze in the night air turns my body into a shivering frenzy as I peek through the gap in the rocks. The moon reflects off the water's surface and illuminates the clearing in a silver light. Tall trees marking the beginning of the forest toss dark shadows like long fingers onto the grass. It's almost like they are trying to grab me to drag me into the woods. I shudder—the whole atmosphere is creepy.

I finally decide to step out of hiding and head toward the forest path. I stay as close to the tree line as possible, leaning into the shadows to be invisible from above. At the mouth of the trail, I hesitate. It's pitch black inside the forest and I can only pray I won't get lost, but there is really not a viable alternative. I will have to take my chances.

The path is steep and I'm out of breath by the time I reach the first bend. My legs wobble like jelly when a sudden dizzy spell overcomes me. Now I regret not eating the candy bar Mitch offered, convinced the apple was more than enough to refuel. The thought of my husband's worried face makes me cry again. How could I go on without him?

Refusing to let my self-pity win, I clench my jaw and push on. Counting my steps to keep my mind from wandering, I stumble along the steep incline until I reach the end of the path. The hunting cabin lies still in the moonlight. Not a sign of life other than the occasional hoot of an owl.

Dragging my feet along, I climb up the porch. My stomach heaves when a whiff of death floats my way. Kendall's body has attracted an array of insects. As I hold my breath in disgust, I quickly step around him to get to the door. The door knob collides with the wall when I push it open too hard. A loud shriek, followed by breaking glass, greets me the moment I step over the threshold. In the moonlight illuminating the cabin, Sad Eyes stares at me as if she has just seen a ghost.

"Aeree, oh my god." Her arms fling around me, a few tears running down her face. "I thought I was the only one left."

I go rigid in her embrace, not eager to enlighten her that I'm not really the hugging type. It might upset her. My nerves are stretched to the limit and I will snap if I have to deal with any more drama.

"What happened to Julie and Tyson?"

"They dumped me the first chance they got. While I peed, they disappeared on me. Luckily, I was carrying Julie's backpack and there was some water in there after all." She finally let go of me. "I walked around in circles until I found this cabin. I'm so glad you're here."

"I'm sorry about Kendall," I mumble when I remember that she must have seen her dead husband when she first arrived.

"Oh, I'm not." She wipes her eyes dry on her sleeve. "In case you didn't notice, he was a real abusive jerk. I was planning on leaving him and only went on this trip after the lucky bastard won it in that sweepstakes so that my friends can get my things out of the house." She shrugs. "Whoever shot him saved me a lot of headaches."

I give her a thin smile, not really sure what to say. Though I know that abusive relationships are more common than people think, I have never understood how women can stay with someone who beats them.

"Have you heard anything about your husband?" she asks.

I ignore her question. Speaking aloud that Mitch is dead will make it final and I'm not ready for that. My eyes fall on Julie's backpack on the kitchen floor. "Did you find anything else in the backpack?"

"No, not really, but I also didn't check thoroughly. I find it kind of rude to dig around in people's personal stuff."

I roll my eyes. In a time of crisis, there's no time for civility. Without hesitation, I turn Julie's backpack upside down and pour the contents on the floor. After a close inspection, I find nothing useful except a flashlight. The box of tampons surprises me—she either just found out she is pregnant after taking off on the trip or was lying through her teeth. There are also prescription painkillers for chronic migraines that couldn't be safe for pregnant women.

The last item looks like a case to store glasses, but when I open it, I grin. A small phone is tucked securely inside, but it's not just an ordinary cell phone. The Globastar symbol on the side alludes that it's connected to a satellite provider.

I hold my breath when I turn it on, blinking a few times in disbelief when it actually springs to life. Bingo. The air escapes my lips with a small "yesss" after a couple of bars indicate reception. With trembling fingers, I dial 911. My heart sinks when I get a fast-busy signal. Something must be wrong with the phone after all.

Not ready to give up, I dial the only number I know by heart other than my husband's. Not expecting to get a ringtone, I squeal when the familiar sound fills my ear.

"Talk to me." The voice on the other end is that of a stranger, and for a second, I almost hang up, certain I must have misdialed the number.

"Hi. I'm trying to reach Sergeant Major Eltas Williams," I say tentatively.

"Sorry, but the Sergeant Major is not available at the moment. Can I take a message?"

More elation is sucked out of me. "It's really important that I talk to him. This is Aeree Cahill, a personal friend of his, and this is an emergency."

"Oh, hey, Aeree, it's River Cunningham."

The name sounds vaguely familiar.

"We met yesterday," he adds when I remain silent.

"Oh yeah, right." I could have kicked myself. He is the new recruit Eltas introduced me to.

"I'm sorry, but Eltas went to Washington and won't be back until tomorrow. Is there anything I can help you with?"

He is in Eltas's unit. I should trust him. "I'm in the Green Mountains and a sniper is after me." Sudden tears mess with my voice. "I think my husband is dead."

Absolute silence follows my words and I'm already afraid I lost the connection.

"Where in the Green Mountains?" His voice is colder; he probably thinks I'm pranking him.

"In this small hunting cabin in the woods. I have no clue about the exact location, but there was a bridge we hiked to called Steel Gulch that shouldn't be too far. I tried to call 911 but couldn't get a connection. Half our group is dead and there are thugs who are after some data stick and a sniper." I realize I'm rambling and I'm likely confusing the crap out of him. "You need to alert the forest rangers."

"Hold the line. I'm gonna try to have a technician trace your exact location." He mumbles with someone in the background.

I tap my foot before realizing that Sad Eyes is staring at me. I can't tell if she is amazed that I found a phone or distressed about my revelation that my husband might be dead. Either way, her intense gaze rattles me and I wish she would stop.

"The GPS tracker in the phone is turned off or has been removed."

River's voice brings me back to the conversation. "So what should I do?"

"I'll call the forest rangers and leave right now. Major Riley has authorized a chopper and I should be there within the hour. Try to turn the GPS on and stay put. I'll call you when I'm airborne."

My head bobs up and down in sheer relief until I realize that he can't see me. "Thanks, River." My voice is thick when tears rise again.

"Hang in there, all right? We'll figure things out once I get there."

"Okay." I cut the line when my knees go weak. This time I don't mind when Sad Eyes pulls me into her arms.

"I'm so sorry, Aeree."

I can't fight the tears any longer when my soul shatters under her words. The truth sinks in—Mitch will never hold me like this again. I have lost the last thing important to me.

In the darkest times of my life, one feeling has always prevailed, and that is my utter need for revenge. It's not a character trait I'm proud of, but it's the one thing that has always allowed me to push forward. Today is no exception. As I weep against Sad Eyes's shoulder, the urge to survive is overpowering. This sniper better look out because I will find him—and when I do, I will put a bullet into the back of his head, just like he did to my husband.

# Chapter 11

The squeaking of the door causes my head to leave Sad Eyes's shoulder. A flicker of hope pulses in my chest as I hold my breath, willing Mitch to cross the threshold. When I realize that it was just the wind that blew the door open, my body deflates like a popped balloon. I'm terrified of the future and have no clue how to go on without Mitch.

I yelp when the phone starts to buzz on the floor beside me. Shaking my head at my skittishness, I push the green button. The background noise almost overpowers River's words.

"I'm in the air. Did you get the GPS to work?"

I haven't even checked. "No, not yet, but I'll keep trying. How far are you out?"

"A little over an hour. If I can't track your location, you have to think of a different way to let me know your whereabouts. Do you have a flare or something?"

Mitch had searched the cabin and only found matches. "No, nothing. I could build a fire in the clearing, but it would have to be small or I'll set the whole forest on fire." With the heat and dryness, even a spark could cause a disaster.

"Don't worry, I'll figure something out." He sounds confident, which takes a little bit of the edge off, though I'm not convinced he will find me with just the name of the bridge to go by.

"Did you call the forest service? They might know where the cabin is."

"No." There is slight hesitation. "Major Riley is taking care of that."

I frown, puzzled as to why Riley would involve himself in a personal rescue operation. As a matter of fact, it's odd he even authorized a chopper. He is not one to waste taxpayers' money on something not directly related to the military.

"Is there something I should know about?"

"No, all good." His assurance is too chipper. "We're just concerned about you."

I don't know him well enough to dig further, and I'm endlessly relieved that he is coming at all. Who cares about his motives? Once I'm back in New York, I intend to ask Eltas. If there's something going on in the background, he will be the only one who will spill the beans.

"Okay, I'll call you again just before we land," he says, and I grunt in agreement before cutting the line.

"Is your friend going to help us?" Sad Eyes asks as she rises. She strolls to the window and gazes outside. "God, it's so dark. Spooky, really."

"I have to try to get the GPS to work or he'll have trouble finding us." I scroll through the settings until I find what I'm looking for. I try to switch the GPS tracker to on, but the phone asks me for a code. "Shit."

I realize that Sad Eyes is staring at me, probably trying to figure out what I'm doing.

"The tracking function is passcode protected." I drop the phone in my lap and rest my back against the wall. My head is buzzing with a nasty pain radiating along the inside of my skull. With care, my fingers graze the bandage on my neck. The throbbing from the bullet wound is a constant, dull pounding, the pain spreading in every direction.

A sudden weakness resonates in my limbs that adds to my misery. I want to exchange my body for a new one, together with my soul. This endless feeling of inadequacy is getting to me. My whole existence is once again torn to little shreds and I have no idea how to fix it.

Tears rise, but I swallow them down. It is what it is and I have to push forward. That's what my dad told me before they took him away in handcuffs. The sun is always lurking behind the horizon—I just have to know how to find it.

With a groan, I heave myself up. "We should gather some firewood. When my friend gets here, we have to point him to the right spot, plus it might alert the forest rangers."

"Isn't that too dangerous out here in the woods?"

"You have a better idea?"

"I passed a lake with a huge field that isn't far from here. We might be better off starting a fire in an area where we can control it."

She has a point. "How far is it?"

"Maybe a mile."

That's doable. I flick on Julie's flashlight, the beam grazing her migraine prescription. Just one might help ease the tormenting pain in my neck. I twist the top open and reach for one when prickling in my scalp stops me. I don't really know for sure what they are. They could be mislabeled and make me sick, or they could make me drowsy. Better not risk it.

Absentmindedly, I stuff the small bottle in the side pocket of my pants. If the pain gets worse, I can always rethink my decision. The phone disappears in the other pocket.

I hand Sad Eyes the flashlight and the small book of matches. "Ready to go?"

She nods, glancing at Julie's stuff strewn across the floor. "Shouldn't we at least put it back into the bag?"

I click my tongue. Who cares about the mess? "Just leave it. We don't have time." I scan the room once more to ensure we are not leaving anything useful behind. My heart plummets when my gaze briefly halts on the back window. I wish I could turn back time and convince Mitch to stay at the cabin.

It's almost pitch black when we step outside, only a few stars twinkle in between the clouds. The temperature has dropped a few more degrees and a light breeze plays with my hair. Thunder rolls in the distance. A storm is the last thing we need. It would be outright dangerous to be at the lake with thunder and lightning raging. Hopefully, the storm will move in a different direction away from us.

I almost gag when another whiff of death drifts my way. The beam of the flashlight briefly shines on Kendall's still body and Sad Eyes chokes. She is green in the face. I hurry her along, so she won't throw up.

We walk across the clearing and enter the forest on the other side, almost in the exact spot where I had been hiding earlier.

"Do you know how to get back to the lake?"

She nods. "I used Julie's Swiss Army Knife to mark the trees to avoid running in circles again." She points at a tree trunk ahead. "There's the first one."

I don't remember seeing a knife among Julie's things. "Do you still have the knife?"

"Yeah, do you need it?"

It would make me a hell of a lot more secure since Norton's knife went with Mitch down the waterfall, but I don't feel comfortable just taking it from her. "That's fine, as long as you have it."

I follow her as she fights her way through the underbrush. Since we have to inspect almost every tree, we make little progress. No words are exchanged, only our heavy breaths break through the silence as we make our way up a hill. By the time the woods open up, sweat has formed on the nape of my neck. A sudden cool breeze not only makes me shudder but soothes my heated skin.

We are standing on a small plateau, the glasslike surface of the lake glistening below us. The clouds have moved away, allowing the moon once again to bathe the mountains in a silver light. The area around the lake is huge, probably even big enough for the helicopter to land. Now we just have to find a way down.

"How did you get up here?"

"I climbed. It wasn't really that difficult."

I frown, taking a step forward to gaze down. There are plenty of cliffs jutting out, which could support our climb, but without a rope, it's still a risk, especially in the dark. We will also be out in the open, so if the sniper is still around and equipped with a night-vision scope, he could pick us off like targets in one of those carnival shooting booths.

"There's no other way down," she says when she notices my hesitation. "The cliffs are almost like steps. Don't worry, it'll be fine."

I continue to stare down, still not convinced this is a good idea. My arms and legs feel like rubber and the throbbing in my neck has magnified. Maybe it would be better if we build just a small fire here on the plateau and hide afterward in the bushes until the chopper arrives.

Before I can tell her about my new plan, she has already started her descent. All stays quiet. The cliffs offer very good support, and I decide to follow after one more look around. My body presses against the rocks as my feet fumble for support. It's tiring, and a few times I almost lose my footing. Luckily, the cool wind keeps me alert.

A thump confirms that Sad Eyes has reached the bottom. The beam of the flashlight hits the rocks next to me.

"Just a few more yards," she shouts, her magnified voice bouncing off the mountain walls like a booming boomerang. I could strangle her. If the sniper is in close proximity, he sure will know where to find us now.

I grit my teeth, my foot fumbling for the next ledge. In my mind, I can already feel firm ground. Like it is so often when one almost reaches a finish line, I become overeager. My hand lets go of the cliff before I have shifted my weight completely, my foot slipping off the newly found support.

"Fuck." I dangle in the air. Only my fingers, which claw into a small crack in the rocks, prevent my body from falling.

"Aeree, be careful." Sad Eyes's yell is jarring and makes matters worse.

I suck in a deep breath, trying to calm my trembling body. *Don't panic.* My tongue runs over my lip when I flex my arm to pull myself up. The sharp edges of the cliff cut into my hand before something warm and tickly runs slowly down my arm. Sudden panic takes over and the tips of my hiking boots scrape against the rough rocks as my legs scramble to find support.

"More to the left," Sad Eyes shouts.

Sweat forms on my forehead when my right foot moves to the left. I groan. My fingertips threaten to tear off from the burning pain in my arm. My muscles slacken. More and more strength drains out of me as my foot continues to scrape against the rock.

Just as my foot finds the ledge again, my fingers fail me. I can't hold on. Almost in slow motion, I start to fall, preparing myself for the impact the way I did when I jumped into the waterfall. My arms fold across my chest and I squeeze my eyes shut, my mind ready for the imminent pain.

The wind is knocked out of me when I hit the hard ground. My mouth opens and closes as I gasp for air, flashes of agony radiating from the center of my small back to my fingertips. Unable to move, I stare into the sky, wondering if I cracked my spine. When my knees are able to bend, a sigh of relief takes some of the pressure off my chest.

"Oh my god, are you okay?" Sad Eyes's face appears right above me.

Still dizzy, I grunt yeah, which comes out as incomprehensible sound.

Her hand slides under my back and she helps me to sit up. Forcing myself to breathe deeply in and out, every lungful is torture. My thumb runs over the cut on my hand to inspect the damage. It's pretty deep. Today is definitely not my day.

"Can you stand up?"

I nod, and with her help, I manage to pull myself to my feet. My body throbs as if I just had a head-on collision with a wall, though my legs follow my brain's direction. I limp toward the lake and lower myself on a fallen tree stump at the edge of the tree line.

"We need to collect firewood." I point at a small patch where the grass is burned off and surrounded by small rocks. "Look, there's a fire pit." It's a little exposed, but since the sniper didn't shoot us coming down the cliffs, it's the safest place to start a fire without risking burning down the whole forest.

Sad Eyes stops me when I try to get up. "I'll do it. You rest."

I'm too sore and weak to protest, so I watch how she gathers branches and twigs, assembling them in a small stack that is built like a pyramid. The pain is slowly easing and I can almost breathe freely again. That's when the buzzing phone causes me to jump, triggering a new wave of pain to shoot through my body.

"We are just passing over the bridge," River shouts over the rotating swoosh of the helicopter blades. "Have you figured out a signal yet?"

"We found a safer place to light a fire."

"Okay, I'm sure we'll find it. See you in a few minutes."

I end the call and nod at Sad Eyes, who starts to fumble with the matches. The third one strikes, a few twigs setting the rest of the dry wood on fire. It's not a huge light source, but it's definitely something a low-flying helicopter will be able to spot.

Sad Eyes disappears between the trees to gather more wood. I bury my face in my hands. The ordeal of the past hours is weighing down on me, the pulsing pain in my body and soul draining me of the last bit of energy. Now might be a good time to take one of Julie's painkillers.

I'm just about to get up to dig the small bottle out of my pants when a prickling sensation creeps up my scalp. I slowly turn and meet Harley's gaze. In the moonlight, his lustful eyes glow like those of a bloodthirsty wolf. My mouth opens to scream, but only hot air escapes.

He is on top of me before I can take my next breath. My back collides once again with the ground when he pushes me off the stump. I whimper. My legs kick furiously, but his heavy body immobilizes the rest of my movements.

"I told you I would be back for you," he hisses. The foul stench of his nasty breath is overwhelming. His erection presses against my crotch. I want to hurl, but the bile is stuck in my throat.

His hands slide under my shirt and into my bra. Tears well in my eyes when his calloused fingers run over my skin. I want to scream, but only gurgling sounds leave my lips before he seals my mouth with his. When his tongue demands entry, my jaw locks in a way that he couldn't pry it open with a crowbar. Finally, my brain takes back control of my body, and I wiggle underneath him to free myself while my fists beat on his back.

"You son of a bitch." Sad Eyes's trembling words echo through the night. Something dark swings through the air and hits Harley on the side of his head. For a second, he rears up like an angry bear before his arm blocks the second blow of the swinging branch.

"Fucking slut." He is up on his feet. Sad Eyes tries to punch him, but he catches her fist midair with a laugh. "Do you seriously think you can fight me?" He laughs again. "Don't worry, you're next."

I try to get up to help her, but all my strength has left me. An incredible pain throbs through my body every time I twitch or try to move. The only thing that doesn't hurt are the tears that roll down my cheeks as I curse my helplessness.

He picks her up by the throat, like a small child, and tosses her though the air. When she hits the ground, she cries out. Her body misses the fire by mere inches. Harley closes the gap between them with three long strides. His leg swings back before his foot catapults forward, hitting her square on the side of her head. She stills without a further sound.

I manage to roll onto my stomach and push up to get onto my hands and knees. My eyes dart around, trying to find a hiding place. Before I can even make up my mind in which direction to crawl, Harley's foot crushes down on me. My elbows buckle. When my chin smashes hard into the ground, my teeth slam together, the pain penetrating the depths of my jaw.

"Maybe I should take you like the little bitch you are." Harley's words are a growl.

My nerve ends curl at the sound of his dropping pants. I try to crawl away again, but his body flattens me before I can even bring my shoulders up. His knife slices through the fabric of my pants and panties, the tip scraping the sensitive skin of my lower back. When he folds back the corners of my pants, all I can do is squeeze my eyes shut to keep control of my burning tears.

# Chapter 12

Harley's heated breath grazes my cheek when he bends forward. His fingers entangle with my silky hair before his lips suck the sensitive skin under my earlobe. I struggle and kick, but he is too heavy to be thrown off. The helplessness that is so familiar is like a sharp scorching knife that slices into my heart and burns my soul at the same time. All I can do is whimper when his hard cock presses against my naked behind.

"Your skin is so soft," he mumbles before his tongue disappears in my ear.

The disgust cramps every muscle in my stomach. Once again, I try to break free, but his burly body holds me firmly in place. My tears are soaked up by the soft grass as my fists pound the ground like they are beating on drums.

His laugh drowns out my sobs. "Yeah, baby, you finally get it. You can't fight big daddy, so don't even try."

A loud swooshing cuts off his cruel chuckle before a sudden brightness breaks through the darkness. I squeal. For a second, I fear he has snapped my neck and this is the end, but then the sound of rotating blades breaks through my desperate mind.

"This is the US Army. You're in direct line of fire. Step away from the female with your hands behind your head."

Harley lets out a curse. His body shifts on top of me as he mumbles something under his breath. He rises at the same time the *frapping* of unwinding nylon rope drifts our way. I turn my head, squinting to make out several dark figures dropping from the helicopter hovering over the clearing.

My gaze returns to Harley, who is standing only a few feet away in the middle of the bright searchlights. His fingers are locked behind his head, his face contorted in an ugly grimace.

He squints at the approaching soldiers, who carefully surround him with their guns drawn. With his pants down and his dick still sticking horizontally in the air, he looks pathetic. If my teeth weren't chattering so violently, I would probably laugh.

A young soldier kneels beside me. "Are you okay, ma'am?"

I nod and roll on my back when I notice him staring at my butt.

"What's your name?" Two of his fingers press the side of my throat just above my bandage.

I grit my teeth to battle the sharp pain that shoots up my neck. "Aeree. Aeree Cahill."

His fingers pry my left eye open before the beam of a small flashlight turns the world into a sparkling star. The exercise is repeated on my other eye.

"Can you stand?" he asks.

"I think so." I clutch his arm as I slowly heave myself up. My knees are wobbly and my head is fuzzy, but otherwise, I'm still in one piece. When my pants start to slide down, my fingers clutch the waistband. My cheeks tingle when I realize my behind is still exposed. The helplessness once again gets the better of me as tears prick the corners of my eyes.

River approaches us with a few quick strides. "I got this." Carefully, he drapes a blanket around my shoulders just as my knees buckle. Before I stumble, his arm slides around me. "Shh, it's gonna be fine."

When he pulls me closer, my hands push automatically against his chest to keep my distance. His touch is jarring; after all, I hardly know him.

"Sorry." He takes a step back, tossing me a crooked smile. "I didn't mean to intrude."

I can't hold his gaze when I remind myself that he was only trying to comfort me. I probably offended him with my bitch act. "No, I'm sorry. It's not your fault. I just don't like it when strangers touch me."

With a shrill snicker, I try to lighten the sudden awkwardness that is even more unsettling than his touch. It's not working. His eyes are directed to the ground as he shuffles his feet. It's obvious he would run for the hills if he had that option.

Luckily, the young soldier returns. "The other female is unconscious. She might have a concussion and needs medical care."

"Okay, let's move out."

"What about the guy? Are you going to arrest him?" the soldier asks.

River's shoulders slump. "We have no jurisdiction. Aeree has to press charges before he can be arrested, unless"—his lips split into a wide grin—"unless he's a witness." With hopeful eyes, he turns to me. "Do you know him?"

"He's one of the thugs who is after two members of our group. They stole some type of data stick."

River smiles in triumph. "That's good enough. Wrap him up. Once we get to the city, we'll call in the locals and Aeree can file a report for attempted rape and assault. That should get him off the streets for a while."

Climbing into the helicopter proves difficult with one hand holding up my pants and the other clutching the blanket. River reaches forward for support, but his hand shoots back when his fingertips graze my skin.

"Sorry," he mumbles.

My eyes try to send him a silent apology, but he makes no further attempts to help me. I'm finally taken out of the awkward situation when another soldier comes up behind me. Without any fuss, he lifts me up by my waist. I mumble a thanks before falling on one of the wooden benches that line both sides of the helicopter.

"Where to?" one of the pilots calls from the front.

"Mount Sinai Hospital. Call ahead and tell them we have an unconscious female that we can't assess."

"Roger that, Sarge." He gets on the radio just as the chopper lifts off the ground, tilting to the side as it gains altitude.

My hand clutches the side bar to avoid being tossed off the bench. My stomach tightens. When I was little, my father had taken me on a couple of helicopter rides and I had always gotten sick. Hopefully, I won't barf all over the floor.

"Aren't we going back to base?" I ask him to get my mind off the bile that is twirling around in my throat.

"No. We are supporting an FBI operation and you've been identified as a witness, so we're taking you to the city. The feds will take over from there."

I frown. "What FBI operation?"

"Sorry, can't tell you." His smile is crooked. "It's classified."

Figures, but that explains why Major Riley authorized the chopper. My dad's unit has often liaised in joint government operations over the years—it's one of their specialties. If the feds are involved, it's likely either terrorism or arms smuggling.

I lean back, pressing my sore cheek against the cool metal of the helicopter wall. The bench vibrates under my exposed behind and every bump seems magnified. The rhythmic humming of the engine and the muffled sounds of the rotating blades lull my senses. I'm exhausted, but the adrenaline pulsing through my body keeps me from dozing off.

I can barely control the tears when my gaze falls on Harley, who sits across from me on the other side of the bench. His hands are casually folded in his lap and more bile rises in my throat. Imagining them on my skin sends a shudder through my body. My ear feels sticky and the sweet smell of his sweat seems to be stuck in my nose. I finally force myself to look away when a smirk spreads on his lips. His eyes still burn into me, which makes any form of distraction an impossible task.

When my mind finally drifts to Mitch, images of a dim future take over. What am I supposed to do? My husband has always been in charge of all the finances, and I'm not even sure how much money is in the bank. What if I can't do it? I have never lived alone, and Mitch has been my guiding light, the one who had taken care of everything. Since my release from prison, I have been totally dependent on him.

I suppress the rising tears, determined not to act like some sobbing star in a Hollywood soap. Somehow, things will work out. I have to first make it through today and clear my head before making any rushed decisions.

"Are you okay?" River's words break through my foggy mind. "You look like you're about to puke."

How charming. I shoot him a sullen look, but graciously accept the little paper bag he holds up, just in case.

"You should try to get some rest."

I nod, closing my eyes obediently just to shut him up. The adrenaline is causing havoc; I always get this incredible itch in my legs when I want to walk around but have to sit still. Back in school, it had been torture.

Flexing my muscles, I roll my feet back and forth as more and more unrest spreads through my body like wildfire. I want to jump up and scream before punching Harley in the face. Unfortunately, with my criminal record, they would probably give me another year in jail for assault, even if they found mitigating circumstances since he almost raped me.

Over the next hour, I try to keep my mind occupied by balling my hands into fists and opening them again before resorting to counting sheep in my mind. Yet the raging pain in my body works as a constant reminder of this new nightmare. I wish River would talk to me, but he is avoiding my gaze at all cost, probably afraid I will snap at him again.

We finally set down on one of Manhattan's rooftops, where a whole battalion of people awaits us. Half of them are nurses and doctors who lunge for Sad Eyes when the soldiers lift her out of the chopper on a stretcher, the other half feds with badges around their necks and the FBI logo printed on their bulletproof vests. My heart almost jumps out of my chest in panic at the mere sight of them. Since my arrest, I hate all law-enforcement personnel.

I reach for River's hand. I'm in need of a friendly face. "Will you stay with me?"

His mouth twists. "I can't. My orders are to go back and help comb the area with the others." His smile is contrite, like he would prefer to stay, but that doesn't help the sudden surge of abandonment I feel. Only the reminder that he doesn't owe me anything keeps the tears at bay. After all, we aren't even friends.

"I understand." Luckily, the engine of the helicopter roars in that moment to hide the tremble in my voice.

He climbs back into the chopper with that typical stance of an operator who values his job above everything. That's how my father used to leave the house. It was the one thing my mom could never accept.

"Excuse me, are you Mrs. Cahill?"

My focus shifts from the ascending helicopter to the woman in front of me. Her dark brown hair is pulled back into a neat ponytail, and she wears a starched blouse under the bulletproof vest over navy-blue dress pants. The hint of subtle makeup highlighting her brown eyes and full lips hides her age, but if I had to take a guess, I would probably put her in her mid-thirties. All in all, she portrays the typical senior field agent with the Bureau.

"Yes, that's me." I smile at her, trying to hide my animosity.

"I'm Special Agent Francesca Dinkle with the Joint Terrorism Task Force." She examines the bandage on my neck before assessing the damage to other parts of my body. "Please be advised that you have been identified as a key witness in a federal investigation. You're not allowed to leave the hospital without my clearance."

"Am I under arrest?"

"No." Her smile is cool. "Like I said, at the moment, you're just a witness, but I'll let you know if that changes."

With a small nod, she turns me over to the nurse who has arrived with a wheelchair before strolling off under my stare. My mouth forms automatic responses to the nurse's questions as I'm slowly pushed toward the door that leads inside the hospital, though my eyes stay on Dinkle.

My eyebrows knit together when she shakes Harley's hand, her offered smile considerably more genuine than the one she gave me. She tosses her head back, laughing, after he mumbles something to her with a crooked smile—that's when I realize they know each other.

I pull the blanket closer, uncertain whether the goosebumps on my arms are the result of the soft wind on the rooftop or my growing uneasiness. Somehow, I doubt that this ordeal is over—as a matter of fact, it feels like a new one is just about to begin.

# Chapter 13

My eyelids twitch from exhaustion, and I would pay big money to be able to lie down, despite my fear that nightmares will follow as soon as I close my eyes. It's stuffy and hot in the small room at the FBI headquarters, the lack of oxygen making me drowsy. By now, it must be early morning, but I can't be sure. No clocks or other time devices are in the windowless room, and neither Dinkle nor her colleague, whose name escapes me, wear a watch. It feels like I have been confined in here for hours, the conversation turning in circles.

Another set of photographs is placed in front of me. "What about these guys? Have you ever seen any of them?"

With a sigh, I stare at the pictures. None of them looks even remotely familiar. "No, I haven't."

After the fifth set of photographs, I gave up asking who these people are. All I ever get is a mild smile, followed by a lame apology that they can't give me insights in an ongoing federal investigation. The only good thing is that the exercise has totally fried my brain, allowing my numb mind to lock away most of the painful thoughts about Mitch. There were only a few times I was on the brink of tears, which I fought fiercely. Public drama that always accompanies an open display of emotions is a total horror for me.

I massage the bridge of my nose to fight the slight pressure in my head. The painkillers they stuffed into me at the hospital before releasing me into the care of the FBI are slowly wearing off.

"Is this gonna take much longer? I'm really exhausted and don't see the point of continuing this. Like I told you, I only met Julie and Tyson yesterday and hardly know them." Shifting in my seat, I try to get my sore body into a more comfortable position. The chair is hard and closer to a torture instrument than a seating device.

"Almost done, I promise." Dinkle offers me one of her fake smiles. It's the third time she claims this.

"Could I at least have some more water?"

"Sure." She nods at her colleague, who gets up with a sour face before disappearing from the room. Dinkle shuffles around in her files while we wait.

My fingers drum on the table, my gaze scanning the room for the hundredth time, just to have something to do. The bright neon light reflects off the white-washed walls and is almost blinding. The dark linoleum floors are polished to perfection, not a speck of dirt anywhere. The cleaning crew at the federal building must be much more diligent than those of local precincts. A light scent of lemon even lingered in the room when I first arrived, now replaced by the smell so typical of too many bodies cramped in a small, confined space.

The guy returns with the water, before planting his wide behind back into the chair. For an FBI agent, he is rather out of shape and couldn't possibly be a field agent. Too many donuts have settled in his soft midsection, making his waist appear humongous. To top it all off, he is sweating like a pig with his hair sticking up in every possible direction. Dinkle, on the other hand, looks like she just stepped out of a fashion magazine despite the late hour. Only a thin layer of perspiration above her lip suggests that she might be uncomfortable.

"So let's take this from the top."

I almost groan.

"When you were on the bridge and the shooting started, you didn't see your husband or anybody else in his group?"

"That's right." I twist the top off the water bottle, taking a few mouthfuls to drown out the sudden stab of pain as my mind briefly strays to Mitch. A small smile is forced on my lips when I'm done to indicate she can fire off her next question.

"And Julie Flynn and Tyson Roberts were among that group?"

I nod. "Neither of them wanted to jump. They said they were afraid of heights, plus Julie was pregnant and they thought it might be too dangerous."

"And you don't know when they split from the other group?"

I shake my head.

Dinkle exhales through tight lips. "I'm sorry, but as I told you before, you need to verbally respond for the recording."

"Sorry." The red light blinks on the small device that has been capturing my every word. "No, I have no idea. I also don't know where they went. I didn't see them until I encountered them in the woods."

"And were they acting suspicious at that point?"

"At the time, I would've described it more as odd, but I guess you can call it suspicious."

"But they didn't tell you about the satellite phone?"

"No, of course not. Otherwise, I would've insisted on calling the police and the forest service."

"Despite your feelings about law enforcement in general?" Dinkle cups her hands behind her head, glaring at me in challenge.

I frown. "What's that supposed to mean?"

"Well"—the fake smile doesn't match the coldness in her eyes—"I know about your conviction, Aeree. Didn't you blame the police for your rape?"

"I blame Paul Turner, who happens to be NYPD, but no, not the police force in general."

It's a lie. After I filed an official complaint against Paul, his bosses looked into the allegations about his gambling problem that led to him setting me up. The investigators came up with nothing. They told me that the gang must have made the story up, probably to expose Paul, who was working against them undercover. Then they even dared to imply that I had botched the operation by giving Paul's identity away. The bitter feeling of being screwed over by everyone has always left a nasty aftertaste in my mouth.

"What about your husband? Did he like the police?"

Mitch had hated cops with a passion since they always tried to screw over his clients. "Truthfully, I have no idea."

She leans forward. "That's an interesting statement. Have you been truthful to us, Aeree?" Her eyes are focused on my face, as if she's trying to hypnotize me. "Somehow, I get the feeling you have been lying."

"Should I ask for a lawyer?"

Her head tilts backward when she laughs in fake amusement. "Why would you need a lawyer?" She leans forward again. "Unless you have something to hide. Tell me, Aeree, is there something you aren't telling us? If you come clean now, I can help you, but if we later find out that you're somehow connected to this case, I'll personally make sure that you won't see the outside of a prison until you're past your retirement age."

Her threat doesn't sit well with me. "I really don't know what gives you that idea." Deep down, a little voice nags me to get a lawyer—that's what Mitch would have done—but I fear this will make me look guilty. Innocent people don't ask for lawyers.

"Okay, let's see." She leans in even closer. "I find it odd that a sniper who seems to be a hell of a shot keeps missing you."

"I was running."

"And Walt Jamison was bouncing on a bungee cord and was still shot in the middle of his forehead. See what I'm saying."

"Yeah, but that's different. It's easier to shoot someone in a predictable line of sight than someone who follows an unpredictable path."

She laughs. "You know an awful lot about this."

"My father was a sniper. That's how I know."

"Yes, and that's also really convenient." She rolls her eyes like I just gave her a bunch of bull before she gazes at her colleague, who has been following our exchange on the edge of his seat.

"Look, Aeree, we are not accusing you of any wrongdoing here," he says in a soothing tone. "I mean, you got shot and your husband died. That must've been a horrific ordeal."

"It was." Despite my best efforts to keep the tears locked away at the mention of Mitch's death, my voice slightly trembles. The lump in the bottom of my throat multiplies. For a few moments, the pain steals my breath until I regain a grip on myself. Losing my composure in front of Dinkle and her partner would take the meaning of embarrassment to a whole new level.

"Agent Dinkle is just doing her job, you know that, right?" The guy beams at me.

I catch on that it's their "good cop-bad cop" routine.

"Sure. All good." My arms fold in front of my chest. "Is there anything else we haven't covered?"

"Yes, just one last thing." Dinkle's voice has dropped three octaves and sends a chill down my spine. The gloves are off. "Now that your husband is dead, how much money are you bound to inherit?"

I gasp. "What are you implying?"

"Nothing." Her face feigns innocence. "Just answer the question."

Even with my limited legal training, the accusation that I killed Mitch for my inheritance screams clearly in my face. The pain reaches a new level and I almost wail. She has no idea how much it hurts to lose Mitch, and the mere suggestion that I could have had a hand in his death is so preposterous that I want to scratch her eyes out.

Instead of lunging at her, I suck in a deep breath and exhale slowly. Assaulting a federal agent in front of a witness will guarantee me a new prison stay. "I'd really like to talk to a lawyer." I try to keep myself from flinching as my fingers rub along my wrist. I can already hear the sound of the snapping handcuffs.

"Oh, that won't be necessary." She rises. "I'm done for tonight. You're free to go."

With hesitation, I get on my feet. "What about the charge against that guy, Harley? You know—for attempted rape."

"We called NYPD and they sent a detective who is waiting for you next door." She ushers me toward the exit, all of a sudden eager to get rid of me. "You can file a complaint with him if you like."

"Sure." A sudden chill in the hallway sends goosebumps all over my bare arms. I gaze up at the air conditioner that hums evenly, pushing out more clouds of cool air. It's like a refrigerator.

Turning toward the large glass window of the room next door, I halt in my tracks. My jaw drops. Of all the detectives who work for the New York Police Department, they sent Paul. My hand comes to rest on the doorknob, but I can't get myself to push the door open. Every nerve end in my body recoils at the mere sight of him.

"Is something wrong?" Dinkle asks behind me. The amusement swinging in the words does not escape me.

"That's Paul Turner."

"Oh, seriously?" This time she can barely stifle a laugh. "Isn't that the NYPD detective you assaulted?"

I squint at her, not finding this in the slightest amusing. This is not a coincidence, but a clear setup. For whatever reason, they are trying to prevent me from filing charges against Harley, though I can't think of one for the life of me.

"Can I file the complaint with someone else? It's clearly a conflict of interest." I leave out that his voice alone might push me over the edge after everything that happened today.

"I'm afraid not. As you know, it's the Fourth of July weekend and all the authorities are working with a skeleton crew. I'm sure there was no other detective available or they wouldn't have sent him."

I push myself to open the door. Since the night I separated him from some of his manly body parts, I haven't seen him. He hasn't changed much. That smug, patronizing smile I used to find sexy is still dominant in his features. His body is in top shape; I don't detect an ounce of fat where it doesn't belong. Add a nice tan that highlights the dimples in his cheeks and he looks the part of the playboy he is.

When our eyes lock, a wall of coldness that easily matches the temperatures in the hallway freezes every limb of my body. Forcing my legs to move forward is an effort. An invisible force is trying to shift my steps into reverse, and by the time I reach the table, cold sweat has formed on my back.

"Aeree, how are things?" He slowly inspects me from top to bottom. I can only imagine what I look like in the surgical scrubs they gave me at the hospital after peeling me out of my ruined clothes.

My cheeks sting when his gaze lingers on my breasts for a significantly longer time than it should. I want nothing more than to slap him across the face. Everything in his body language screams disrespect, from his slouched stance that has lost all professionalism to the sudden mocking in his eyes.

I lower myself to the chair across from him when his chin signals me to sit down. My back is straight as a stick, my feet firmly planted on the ground. If he makes one wrong move, I will bolt.

"Hello, Paul." I try to give my voice an extra chill but fail miserably. Holding his gaze is painful. Since he has always been much stronger than me, I didn't play fair when I knocked him out the night I assaulted him. Even if my rational mind insists that he can't hurt me in a federal building, I have plenty of reasons to fear him.

"The FBI indicated that you wish to file charges for attempted sexual assault?" His snarling voice sends more goosebumps along my arms.

My mouth dries up, and I can't get a sound to roll over my lips. Twice, I have to clear my throat before my voice is halfway back under my command. "Yes, that's right." My fingers twist together to control my trembling hands.

"The alleged perpetrator is a man by the name of Harley Salyers?" His demeanor is now all business. Leaning forward in his chair, he gazes at me expectantly.

"I don't know his last name, but his first name is Harley, so I assume that's him."

For a second, Paul's glare drills into me. "When I questioned him, he claimed it was consensual."

"And you believed him?" My laugh is shrill. "He had a knife and was forcing himself on me. There were witnesses who saw me struggle."

"That doesn't mean anything. Since that fifty-shades thing, a lot of girls are into BDSM. They like it rough."

"Not me." With folded arms, I stare at him. The apprehension I felt just moments ago is slowly replaced by anger. "You know I'm not like that."

"Do I?" He chuckles. "Truthfully, the Aeree I remember was always a little bit on the slutty side, spreading her legs for pretty much anyone. Just because you've gotten married doesn't mean you've changed."

"That's a fucking lie." This time, I can't keep the tremble from my voice. My face is heated as anger seethes. This is ridiculous. Why am I even talking to him? "I want another detective to investigate this."

"Well, that's unfortunately not how it works. Besides, I'm only here as a courtesy to the Montgomery Sheriff's Department since the case falls under their jurisdiction. Feel free to contact them and plead your case, but my report will clearly state that you made all this stuff up. There was no attempted rape."

Tears of hate pool in my eyes. "Ask the girl who Harley knocked down. She'll know."

"She's still in the ICU with a severe concussion. The doctors aren't even sure she'll make it." His face turns serious. "For all I know, you attacked her; after all, you have a vicious streak. Probably blamed her for your husband's death the way you blamed me for the gang assault, even though I was innocent. Something is wrong with your head, Aeree."

I'm on my feet. "You're a fucking liar." My cheeks are burning up, my face probably as red as a beet. A single tear springs free and rolls down my cheek. The smirk that spreads on his lips is belittling—oh, how much I hate him! I should have killed him when I had the chance.

Dinkle's head pops around the door. "Is everything okay in here, Detective?"

"Yeah, I got this. Aeree was just freaking out a little. She can be a bit of a loose cannon, if you know what I mean."

"Yes, I noticed." Her smile is as belittling as his. When she steps inside, she leaves the door wide open for everyone else to hear, probably hoping I'll make an ugly scene.

With a huff, I glare at her. "Did you find my backpack? I want to go home." If I have to stay in the same room with them for just a minute longer, my nerves will shatter. Raging tears will be next, which I want to avoid at all cost. I have shown enough weakness for one night.

"I'm sorry, but all the items found as part of our investigation have been logged into evidence." She doesn't look at all sorry, as a matter of fact, gleeful would be more accurate. "You get your things back once the case is closed."

That could be months. "My wallet is in there—and my keys and my phone. What am I supposed to do? I can't even get home without money."

A wicked smile twitches on her lips. "Now, that's not really my problem, is it?"

# Chapter 14

Under Paul's and Dinkle's mocking eyes, I flee from the room to save the little bit of dignity I have left. Their loud laughter, following me down the corridor, hurts to the core. My nerves finally snap in half, which manifests itself in the worst possible way—tears. I lunge into the bathroom and slam the stall door shut, sliding to the ground just as sobs shake every part of my body. I hate that my emotions are no longer under my control.

When the bathroom door opens, I bite into my shirt to muffle the crying sounds. My body is still shaking, but the tears are silent. Someone pees in the stall next to me before shuffling around with the toilet paper like they have no worry in the world. Mitch always wondered how much of his taxpayer money was spent on cigarette-and-bathroom breaks. He would have a field day with this. Thinking about him opens more floodgates, yet all I can do is breathe through my mouth to stifle the sniffles.

Water is briefly turned on before the bathroom door closes again. I prick my ears—not a sound. It's now or never. After heaving myself off the floor, I open the stall door a tiny crack and peek around the room. Empty. My gaze falls on the mirror, and I cringe when I notice my puffy red eyes. Damn traitors. I will make a fool of myself if I bump into anyone on my way out.

With a few strides, I'm at the sink. The cold water splashing against my heated skin feels divine. More tension seeps from my body when I press a cold, wet paper towel on my cheeks just below the eyes. Two more deep breaths and I'm presentable.

I hesitate before I step into the hallway, wishing I at least had my sunglasses. Never in my life will I rely on a backpack or a purse again. At the moment, the only thing left to my name is Julie's migraine prescription. In the hospital, they didn't even realize it isn't mine when they went through the pockets of my ruined chinos. Since anyone with a criminal record is always on the target list of law enforcement, I didn't want to give the FBI a chance to allege I stole the medicine and pin a new crime on me, so I kept my mouth shut. Now the small bottle shifts awkwardly in the front pocket of the scrub pants, making every step a reminder of all the horrors of my trip. My heart weeps, but this time, I manage to keep the tears locked away.

Just before I make it to the elevator, I feel eyes upon me and turn my head. My forehead wrinkles as I meet Norton's stare, who quickly diverts his gaze the moment he catches me looking at him. The room he is in has a conference-style setup with large glass windows in the front and back, which show off an incredible view of the early morning city.

He is not alone, but with a bunch of people who are huddled around a colorful map that almost entirely covers one of the two windowless walls of the room. I recognize the projected area as the Green Mountains. Citadel leads the conversation, pointing at certain marked spots on the map. She is so engrossed in her conversation that she doesn't even notice me.

Even though I should probably be happy that she and Norton survived, I'm taken aback by the polite faces of the agents. Everyone is treated civilly except for me. Just because I have a criminal record, I clearly must have done something wrong. What else could it be? Both Citadel and Norton also lost their partners, but from the looks of things, neither of them is being accused of having a hand in their demise for some inheritance. It's so unfair.

I stomp down the hallway, hitting against the elevator call button repeatedly when the doors don't open. I sigh, tapping my foot, before pressing the button again. Finally, a little *ding* announces the arrival of the elevator. When the doors slide open, I gaze right into the eyes of an older guy in a wheelchair. He rolls back a little to make more room for me when I step in. After a mumbled hello, I press the already lit button for the ground level a few times for good measure.

"In a hurry?"

I choose to ignore his question, only offering him a small smile. If I engage in any type of conversation, small talk would undoubtedly follow. That's what people do on an elevator. Unfortunately, a new *ding* signals a new stop on the next level. A tall guy with long hair that he has pulled up into a warrior bun like a samurai squeezes in.

"Oh, hey, Bill," he greets the guy in the wheelchair. "I was just on my way to see you."

"What can I do you for, Joseph?" Bill's lips are pressed together and I can't shake the feeling that they don't like each other.

Joseph briefly glances at me before continuing. "I was wondering if I could borrow your boy for a few days."

"My boy?" Bill's curt smile is cold. "That's an interesting way of putting it."

Joseph laughs. "Come on, man. You know what I mean. He would've never gotten the job here if it wasn't for you."

Bill's arms fold in front of his chest. "If you feel that way, what do you want with him?"

"Undercover gig." Joseph's smile is sheepish as Bill continues to glare at him, probably his idea of an apology after he so obviously put his foot into his mouth. "I have this case that's about to blow up, even the fricking Pentagon is breathing down my neck. Your boy"—he stops himself when Bill's eyebrows rise—"I mean, Brown would be perfect for the job."

Bill's attention shifts to me before returning to Joseph. "We should discuss this in my office. I was just getting a coffee next door, so"—he checks his watch—"is half an hour all right?"

With a small jolt, the elevator comes to a halt just as Joseph grunts his agreement. Under Bill's piercing gaze, I dart from the confined space as soon as the sliding doors permit, feeling like an intruder. Even though I don't know why, Joseph made me incredibly uncomfortable.

Out on the street, I can breathe again. The morning air has a slight tinge of coolness—it can't be that late. Judging from the blue sky above, the sidewalks will be melting within the next few hours. Coupled with the tiredness that sits heavily in my bones, I should get home as soon as possible. Only question— how do I do this without money, a phone, or even house keys?

A grin spreads on my lips when I remember the hideaway key under the silly garden goblin that Mitch got me from Switzerland. That will get me into the house. Our emergency cash is kept in a small metal box next to the sugar, and I just saw Mitch stick a hundred dollars in there the other day. This will be plenty to pay for a cab.

My arm rises when I step to the curb, and less than a minute later, I sink back into the soft leather seats of the cab after giving the driver my address. The traffic is light and the car pulls into my driveway only thirty minutes later. The whole affair costs me sixty-five dollars.

"Could you please wait here for a minute? I just need to get the cash out of the house."

His response is a dark glare. As I bounce toward the house, sharp daggers pierce my back. A car door slams shut when I walk around to the back. He probably wants to make sure I don't just disappear on him. The garden goblin is partly hidden by the rhododendron bush. Its pink petals have turned brown over the past few weeks and a slight tinge of overly blossomed flowers tickles my nostrils when I bend down to pick up the goblin. A bee hums nearby, which I shoo away.

My smile fades when I find the little compartment on the bottom empty. I scan the area on the ground—where the hell is the damn key?

A honking of a horn distracts me from my search. The cabby is getting impatient. I walk around the house, rattling the back door to make sure it's indeed locked. No chance to break in, unless I want to kick down the door. It's tempting, but in the weak state I'm in, not a realistic option.

I jump up a little to get a good glance inside the house when I pass the living room window, a quick shot of pain through my sore body my only reward. Mitch always ensured that everything was locked when we went out of town, and there's not the slightest crack I could use to pry the window open. As I make my way back around the house, the honking echoes through the morning air at shorter and shorter intervals.

A woman's shout finally puts the cabby in his place. "Hey, buddy, would you pipe it down?"

I glance around for the owner of the voice as I approach the taxi, realizing it's the new next-door neighbor. She stands in her yard with arms akimbo, glaring at the cabby with narrow eyes. The noise certainly pissed her off. Probably woke her kids.

A small wave accompanies my apologetic grin before I mouth a *sorry* her way. She still gawks with interest. Nosy neighbors are the last thing I need at the moment. The situation is already embarrassing enough. I turn to the cabby, who is glaring at me. Anger streams from his nose with every puff.

"I'm sorry, but I can't find the hideaway key to get into the house and I have no money on me. Do you maybe have a business card and I'll send you a check?"

"Sorry, lady, but I'll have to call the cops. Payment is due at time of drop-off."

I would roll my eyes at him if the situation wasn't so dire. The cops will run a warrant check, and my conviction will pop up. If anyone else questions me today, I'm going to lose it. Why can't he just cut me a break? With a long huff, I let the bubbling anger escape to prevent myself from punching him in his smug face.

"Is there anything I can help you with?" a voice asks all of a sudden.

My body turns to face the neighbor who has snuck up on us. I'm just about to decline when the cabby decides to enlighten her about my situation.

"She owes me sixty-five dollars for my fare from Manhattan and claims she has no money." He snorts like this is the biggest lie he has ever heard. "I was just about to call the cops."

"Oh, I don't think that's necessary." She smiles sweetly at him. "Do you take credit cards?"

"I prefer cash." The taxi driver jumps back when the big guy I saw last week starts to stroll toward us. Though he is not very tall, his bulging muscles remind me of those of a boxer who is about to step into a ring rather than a regular guy prying into his neighbor's business.

His face is grim when he halts next to us. "Kids are asleep again. What's the problem?"

"Pay the man, Marcel," the neighbor lady says. "It's too hot for this type of problem."

He grumbles "Why do I have to pay?" under his breath, but obediently pulls out a stack of rolled up twenties from his front pocket. "How much?"

The cabby swallows hard, taking another step back. "Sixty-five, man. I'll give you a receipt if you need one."

"No, that's fine." Money exchanges hands and the annoying cabby is on his way.

After he turns the corner, I smile sheepishly at the neighbors. "I'm really sorry for all the inconvenience. I don't have my key and the hideaway one we keep in the yard is gone. Could I maybe call a locksmith from your house?" I have no clue how to pay for the locksmith but will figure something out. Maybe I could use the emergency cash and pay back the neighbors after the holidays when the banks open back up.

"Don't worry, I got this. Just let me get my tools," Marcel mutters.

I shuffle my feet while we wait, not really sure what to say to the neighbor lady. Her eyes are in constant movement, like she's expecting someone to jump out of the hedges and attack her. Finally, her gaze comes to rest on my face.

"Sorry, I totally forgot to introduce myself. I'm Kelsey Walker." Her smile is natural. "I believe you already met my husband, Finn, the other day."

"Yes. I'm Aeree. Aeree Cahill." My fingers twitch while I debate whether to offer her a handshake, but I disregard the idea when her own fingers twist together into a knot. Just as with her husband, the situation turns a little awkward.

Finally, my chin points toward my house when the silence becomes unbearable. "I have cash in the house and can pay your friend back."

She laughs. "Don't worry about it. After all, we know where you live."

It's an unsettling thought. The big dude looks like he's persistent when it comes to collecting his debts. Owing him money for long periods of time is certainly not my first choice.

After he returns, it only takes a couple of minutes before the front door swings open. With a small bow, he invites me into my own home. Since most of the blinds are drawn, it's nice and cool, but I still hesitate on the threshold when I notice Mitch's dress shoes by the door. A big lump in my throat, already tainting my spit with salt, is bravely swallowed down.

"The money is in the kitchen," I mumble to hide the shake in my voice. "Why don't you come in?"

Entering the house feels surreal. In a daze, I stumble down the hallway, still battling my tears. There's no way I will lose it a second time in public today. Kelsey and Marcel will think I'm a lunatic if I start to bawl in front of them.

*Just get the money and they'll leave* is the one thought that drives me forward.

I tear the kitchen cabinet open and go straight for the little box with the emergency cash. When the top pops open, all color leaves my face. It's empty. What is it today with me and Murphy's Law? It seems that the world has conspired against me.

"I'm sorry, but my husband must have taken it." My face burns up when I gaze at Marcel.

His eyes narrow slightly until Kelsey nudges him in the ribs. "That's fine." He forces a smile on his lips. "Just pay me back whenever."

"I'm really sorry." My gaze drops when I lose the battle with the tears. This is all too much.

Spinning around, my fingers clutch the edge of the kitchen counter. I don't want them to see me cry. My shaking shoulders still betray me.

Marcel clears his throat. "Well, I'll head back. Give me a shout if you need anything else."

I nod, frantically wiping my face with the back of my hand. Chewing the inside of my cheek, I try to get the tears under control.

Kelsey's hand rubs over my back. "Is there anything I can do?"

I shake my head, unable to speak through my tears.

"Do you want me to stay?"

My head shakes again before I can even think. Though her soft voice is soothing, I could never open up to her. She is nothing more than a total stranger.

Her hand rubs my back in a circular motion, which soaks up some of my tension. "I'll leave then. Like Marcel said, we're right next door if you need anything."

This time I nod. "Thanks." The word is barely audible through my stuffy nose.

My knees buckle as soon as the front door closes. Rocking back and forth on the floor with my arms hugging my knees, sobs shake my body. The longing for Mitch slices so deeply into my soul that my breath fails me. I doubt that things will ever be okay again. For the second time in my life, having survived is nothing more than a curse. There's nothing left worth living for.

# Chapter 15

The next hours drift by in heartbreaking slowness. I can't stop crying, and neither the bitter reminder that I'm acting like a big baby nor my indulgence in ice cream help. After getting sick from eating too many sweets on an empty stomach, I get rid of the extra calories without having to induce vomiting. Afterward, exhaustion takes over and I fall asleep on the cold bathroom floor.

Every single one of my muscles aches when I wake up again, just to repeat the cycle of crying and getting sick. My stomach is now empty and I only choke up dry air, but the strain on my body is brutal. My injuries are throbbing, my throat so raw that I can barely swallow. I'm sure if the neighbors could see me now, they would think me a pathetic human being.

Eltas's tip about cold showers springs to mind when I can't calm my emotions. The freezing water numbs my mind and awakens some kind of natural survival instinct in my soul. Afterward, I feel a little better. I stare at the dark circles under my eyes in the mirror, which are in sharp contrast to the reddish whites and highlight my dull irises. Saying I look like a total mess is an understatement.

The cold shower also stirs my appetite. I gobble down a helping of scrambled eggs and toast, followed by a numbing portion of painkillers they gave me at the hospital, before focusing back on my surroundings. My dramatic episode has lasted a little over twenty-four hours, which puts me right into the early afternoon of this year's Independence Day. I peek through the gaps in the curtains to learn what's going on outside my house. The street is filled with parked cars—the neighbors must be having some kind of Fourth of July get-together at their house.

The thought that I still owe this Marcel guy money, allowing him to stop by my house at any time, doesn't sit well with me. Chewing on my lip, I ponder how I can repay him before the banks open tomorrow. An idea strikes. Mitch kept a few presigned checks in the bottom drawer of his desk in case an unexpected contractor stopped by to fix something around the house. I could use one of those to pay Marcel back.

All the drawers of Mitch's desk are locked as usual, but I locate the key in the little container with the paper clips. Since he has left me in the dark about everything pertaining to our life, claiming it would just be a burden for me, the urge to snoop through his paperwork is tempting. In the end, I only go for the checkbook. I'll figure out the rest later. Four checks are left—three of them presigned.

Filling in the amount is easy, but I get stuck on the name. Originally, I was planning on sticking the check in an envelope and leave it in the neighbors' mailbox to avoid facing them, but I realize I don't know his last name. Of course, I could just go with Marcel and let him fill in the rest, but that's kind of rude. Five minutes won't kill me to drop the check off in person.

The next hour is spent preparing myself for the visit. Tea compresses are placed on my eyelids to get rid of the puffiness, the rest of my distress covered up with plenty of makeup. I slide into a pair of sweats and an old shirt to demonstrate that I'm not out for an invitation to their party—just some woman enjoying a relaxed day at home, only venturing outside to pay a debt. Hopefully, they'll get the message.

Getting ready distracts me from Mitch, something I'm grateful for. His scent still lingers in the house and it's painful to walk around in a place where we were once so happy. Every room holds a different memory—be it the little jade Buddha statue we bought on our honeymoon or his dress shirts, stacked up next to the washing machine and waiting to be starched and pressed. I hate ironing with a passion and always begged him to take his work shirts to the cleaners. Now, there is no more need for me to do any ironing. He will never walk through our front door again.

Biting back the tears, I unhook the latch to the back door and slip outside into the yard. A solid wall of humidity greets me—there's so much moisture in the air that every breath stings. A whiff of grilled meat drifts from the neighbor's yard. They must be having a barbecue, just like the majority of the American population today.

My stomach growls despite my late breakfast when my nostrils are teased with more of the amazing scent. I'm famished and my body demands fuel. Maybe I can make me a small salad with the leftovers in the fridge after I come back. There might even be instant ramen noodles in the cabinet. It would be a small treat I could live with—something I probably deserve after my loss.

With slumped shoulders, I saunter along the garden path until I reach my front gate. The coast is clear, no prying eyes that can stop me before I make it next door. I hurry into the street and reach their house with a few long strides. Navigating around the cars and a motorcycle in the driveway, I arrive at their front door.

For a second, I hesitate, ensuring that the check is in the pocket of my sweats. With my chin raised as high as I can muster, I ring the doorbell.

"I got this," a voice that is definitely not Kelsey's shouts from behind the door. Great, now I have to meet even more new people.

When the door opens, I gaze right into the face of the typical American poster-mom. Her dark blond hair is pulled back into a ponytail, her crystal-blue eyes giving me a curious once-over. She is older than me, at least in her early thirties. Probably Kelsey's sister or another relative.

"Hi, I'm Aeree." My finger points at my house. "I'm the next-door neighbor. Is Marcel here?"

A small girl with cornrows zooms like a little ghost through the hallway, hiding behind the woman's legs. When she peeks at me, I instinctively smile. She is very cute.

"Who are you?" she asks. Her voice is unusually hoarse for a girl. Lively brown eyes that remind me of Marcel inspect me from top to bottom.

I shift my body under her dissecting gaze. "I'm Aeree."

Her eyes stay on me, accompanied by a slight frown, before she smiles. "You're pretty."

"Why, thank you."

I shift my weight again, unsure what to say.

"I'm Ramona," she enlightens me. "I'm four." Her hand raises to show her age with her fingers. "I also have a brother. He's two." Two fingers are folded in. Her face is laced with pride; she must have just recently learned how to count.

The woman laughs. "That's enough now, sweetie. Go and find Finn. He's looking for help with the twins."

The girl disappears into the depths of the house just as fast as she had appeared.

The woman's eyes follow her fondly; she must be the mother. When her attention returns to me, she opens the door fully. "Come on in. My husband just got back from work and is in the kitchen with Kelsey."

So this is Marcel's wife and he's got a couple of kids. Not what I expected at all.

A piercing scream from the yard rattles the house.

The woman grimaces. "Now that would be my son. He must have toppled down again. If you'll excuse me."

She rushes off, leaving me standing in the doorway. With hesitant steps, I walk down the hallway toward the back of the house. For a second, I glance into the living room. It's a total mess with water toys and towels scattered everywhere. Music, laughter, and voices drift through the crack in the terrace door. All the action is outside.

I'm almost at the kitchen door when Kelsey's voice causes me to freeze.

"And you're a hundred percent positive it's the next-door neighbor?"

I don't need to wait for Marcel's response to know they are talking about me, but his words nevertheless confirm my suspicion.

"Yes, I'm sure. Aeree Cahill is an unusual name, so it must be her. Begay said she has not only a criminal record for assaulting an NY Blue but is likely somehow involved in her husband's death. They think she killed him for his money. The only reason they haven't arrested her is because they can't find the body. You need to stay away from her, or there could be trouble down the line for your career."

There is a moment of silence. The shock that the FBI is investigating me for Mitch's murder paralyzes my muscles—I had hoped that Dinkle was just fishing and the whole thing would blow over. Horror scenarios flash in front of my eyes. I can't go back to jail—it would kill me.

"I don't know, Marcel," Kelsey finally says. "She was devastated and I could practically feel her pain. Her behavior was inconsistent with that of a wife who hired a sniper to kill her husband and a bunch of other people in some fake rampage. No one pretends that well, especially not to a bunch of strangers."

"And the criminal record?"

"You of all people should know that we all make mistakes but are capable of changing. I mean, just look at you and Finn. You both violated the law, but that doesn't make you criminals."

"I suppose." Marcel grumbles something inaudible under his breath that sounds like "second chances."

Now would be a good time to either alert them of my presence or disappear again, but my muscles don't give in to my command. I want to know badly if they can answer a few of my questions, but they likely won't tell me anything if they become aware that I've been eavesdropping.

"Besides, how can you trust anything coming out of Joseph Begay's mouth?" Kelsey asks. "I distinctly recall him boasting that he would rather have his head chopped off than ever allow you onto his team, and he called me an FBI wannabe. Frankly, I don't like him and I can't believe you even agreed to work an undercover gig for him."

Marcel grunts. "Bill asked me to. What was I supposed to do?"

"You could have said no, Marcel, especially after their informant called you the N-word. From what you've told me, this Harley character seems mighty shady and I'm not sure you can trust him at all, even if he has been Dinkle's snitch for years. Telling them that Aeree is our neighbor would have been the perfect excuse."

I can barely stifle a gasp. So that's why Dinkle wasn't eager to prosecute Harley. He must be feeding her information about the other thug who was after Julie and Tyson.

"Well, Aeree isn't *my* neighbor, and I don't really know her." Marcel's voice is stubborn. "Bill has never asked me for anything, so I was not 'bout to blow him off."

"You live three blocks away and always hang around my house. It's just a matter of time before this becomes a conflict of interest. At least tell Bill so it won't come as a total surprise to him."

A shriek behind me startles me so badly that my heart almost breaks through my chest.

"You're not allowed to listen in when adults talk."

When I turn around, Ramona's small frame is obscured by the dim light of the hallway. With her hands on her hips, she regards me with disapproval.

My cheeks sting as my lips twist to a grimace. In that moment, I wish the carpet would peel back to swallow me alive.

The clearing of a throat causes me to spin around again. Marcel's expression is unreadable when his lips curl to a fake smile. "Can I help you with something?"

More heat flushes my cheeks. "I'm here to give you your money." Though this was my original intent, the statement now sounds like a lame excuse.

Kelsey appears in the doorway next to him. "Aeree. What a nice surprise. Come on in."

The look Marcel shoots her way is murderous. "I'm going to check on the others." His dark eyes cut into me. "Just leave the money with Kelsey."

I nod, unable to breathe when he pushes past me. The anger on his face scares the crap out of me. My snooping around was never meant to drive a wedge between them.

Kelsey's arm extends invitingly into the kitchen. "Would you like something to drink? We have beer—and soda."

"No, thank you. I just want to drop off the check for Marcel."

She steps aside when my foot tentatively approaches the threshold. The kitchen is just as messy as the rest of the house; cutting boards with chopped vegetables and small cakes and puddings are spread everywhere. They could probably feed an army with all the food. When I still had my catering business, I loved preparing food for large parties, and fixing all the side dishes for a barbecue had been my favorite type of gig. My guacamole dip was legendary among my clients.

I find a small empty space on the counter and pull out the check. "What's Marcel's last name?" Now I wish I had waited until tomorrow to give him his money.

"It's Brown." Her voice is calm. If she is mad about my eavesdropping, she hides it well.

My hand is trembling as I fill in the missing information on the check. "Here we go," I say when I'm done, holding the check in front of her.

She takes it and folds it up to stick it into her jeans pocket without looking at it.

"Well, I should go." My smile is forced. I want to escape from the house so badly that I would've run if that hadn't been so rude.

"How much did you overhear, Aeree?" The words are just as calm as the previous ones. Her gaze is searching.

I twitch, my cheeks burning. For a second, I detect a hint of disappointment in her eyes, which pushes me over the edge. I storm toward the door, but halt on the threshold.

"I swear I didn't kill my husband." A hitch tickles my throat as I swallow down the building lump. I don't dare to look at her, afraid I will lose it again.

"I never said you did."

Well aware that her statement also doesn't imply that she believes me, I take another step forward. Before my command to run translates to my legs, I pause again. "And I had my reasons for assaulting that police detective."

That's all I'm willing to give her despite my heart demanding I confide in someone. There is this aura around her that's calming—like she understands what I'm going through—but that's probably only an illusion, triggered by my loneliness. After all, how could she ever relate to being beaten and raped or losing the one person who has always had my back?

# Chapter 16

I slam the door of my convertible when I get out of the car in the private parking lot of the New York National Bank in downtown Manhattan on Tuesday morning. After some more pondering, I finally broke down and searched Mitch's desk drawers for a recent bank statement to ensure I got the right branch and an account number. Not having a dime in my pocket has been driving me nuts. In hindsight, I should have gotten my own bank account, but Mitch had always insisted that the extra bank fees were a waste of money. The paychecks from the little income I had could be easily cashed at the grocery store when I did my shopping, and for everything else, I had my credit card linked to his account.

I smooth down the jacket of my business suit to look as presentable as possible. My father has always instilled in me that one should convey a professional appearance when dealing with banks and courts—those people usually have a say over your life. If a banker is not impressed, a loan is easily denied, just as any judge can throw the book at you if they hate your guts.

The inside of the bank is impressive, all wood and heavy carpets. Coupled with the dim light and the muffled voices, the atmosphere practically screams that I should tiptoe around the place. The only plus is the light coolness, which is a relief after battling the sweltering heat outside. My eyes scan the desks and stop at the tellers—without exception, the employees seem a little snobby.

My steps are hesitant as I line up in front of the teller desk. There is a form to fill in, and I quickly add the required information as the line edges forward. When I get to the amount, the pen hovers briefly over the paper before I go for a thousand dollars. Parking alone will cost a fortune and I'd better get enough cash to live comfortably until they can send me a new credit card.

Finally, it's my turn. "Hi." I place the small withdrawal slip in front of the teller when she greets me with a cool smile. "I'd like to make a cash withdrawal from my account, please."

"No problem." She starts typing on her keyboard, her eyes fixed on the monitor. "Could I see some ID, please?"

I produce my passport, which was luckily in Mitch's desk in the same drawer as the bank statement. Otherwise, I might have forgotten all about it.

A small frown wrinkles her forehead before she grabs the passport and studies it. With a sigh, she returns it to me. "I'm sorry, Mrs. Cahill, but the account is solely in your husband's name. You need a signed check from him if you want to make a cash withdrawal."

"Oh." I curse myself for leaving the presigned checks at home. "Well, I have a credit card linked to this account, so I didn't think it would be a problem."

"Sorry, but I don't see any card on this account issued in your name. The credit card must be linked to a separate line of credit. Unfortunately, we could only give you access to your husband's checking account if you were a cosigner." The smile is professional but unyielding. There's no way she will make an exception. "Can't you use your credit card?"

I can already picture her terrified face if I admit that the police are holding my wallet in an ongoing murder investigation. "I lost it. Can I at least apply for a new one?"

She clicks around on her monitor before shaking her head. "I'm sorry, but your husband will have to do this for you since the line of credit was given solely to him and it's at his discretion to authorize a second card."

"My husband was killed over the weekend." As I mutter the words, the air is squeezed from my lungs. My bottom lip is quivering, but otherwise, I manage to keep my composure.

A small gasp escapes the teller's mouth. "I'm so sorry, Mrs. Cahill. Let me call Mr. Thornton. He's our branch manager and might be able to help."

Fifteen minutes later, I'm sitting across from a heavyset man in his late fifties with a receding, graying hairline. His office is large and airy and offers a limited view of the lower floors of some Wall Street building. A coffee is placed in front of me, together with a cookie, before his assistant disappears behind the glass door. I sip a little bit of the hot drink, but forgo the sugary treat, even though I skipped breakfast and my stomach is rumbling.

"I am so sorry for your loss," Thornton says when the door closes. His voice is nasally and he huffs at the end of the sentence. Despite the blasting air conditioner, a thin layer of sweat has formed on his upper lip.

"Thank you." I dab the corners of my eyes with a tissue. While I was waiting, I figured that a little bit of public grief might work in my benefit.

He clears his throat, apparently distressed by the open display of emotions. "I've spoken to our regional office and also to your husband's account manager, but I'm afraid we cannot make an exception under the circumstances." His lips twist. "You see, Mrs. Cahill, your husband was a member of a very prestigious law firm in New York. The bank fears if we circumvent any rules, we might get sued. I'm very sorry. I really wanted to help you, but my hands are tied."

This time, the wetness in my eyes is not only for show. "What am I supposed to do for money? I don't even have enough to pay for the parking." I can already picture myself standing at a street corner for the next hour asking pedestrians for change, just to get back home.

"We can stamp your parking ticket and make arrangements for the rest." His smile is crooked. "I would suggest you contact your husband's firm as soon as possible. Lawyers usually have a will, and if the firm opens a probate case in his death and confirms that you are the beneficiary under the will, we might be able to make certain funds available to you."

I didn't even think of that. "That's a good idea. Thank you." My fingers crumple the tissue in my hand as I rise. "I might stop by later as well. My husband left a couple of presigned checks that I want to use to transfer some of the funds into an account in my own name."

His smile fades. "I'm afraid we can't accept those since we have notice of his death. The use of presigned checks under those circumstances is illegal."

Figures I just screwed myself over by trying to play the sympathy card. Murphy's Law strikes again. I'm already at the door when I remember Marcel's check.

"I used one of the checks over the weekend to repay my neighbor for a taxi fare." This time, my smile is crooked. "It's only for sixty-five dollars and I didn't know I wasn't supposed to use them."

"That's okay. I'll make sure it won't be returned. Again, I'm really sorry that I couldn't be of more help, considering you have to pay for the funeral and all."

Since he gives me this look of pity, I don't want to admit that this won't be an issue, at least not for the moment, considering they haven't found Mitch's body yet. After that, I might find myself in jail for his murder since the FBI is apparently convinced I killed him for his money. Ridiculous, since we weren't even that rich, but law enforcement can be like starving dogs, going after a bone, when they try to pin a crime on someone. All in all, my future prospects are less than rosy.

His assistant stamps my parking ticket and instructs the carpark attendant to release my car without further payment. As I pull out of the lot, I decide at the last minute to stop by Mitch's office. The law firm of Buren, Buren, and Larson is only five blocks away, with their own personal parking spaces in the neighboring building. After I inform the security guard that I'm Mitch's wife, the barrier opens without a second glance from him.

I have only been to the office a couple of times to pick up Mitch for a quick lunch, but everything is still the same. The lettering on the door lists the partners, with my husband's name nowhere in sight, and the stuffy atmosphere is suffocating as soon as I pass the threshold. I hate these types of places—they rub it in my face that I didn't grow up around a lot of wealth. A young receptionist, manning the desk across from the elevator, looks me up and down, her nose wrinkling a little when I halt in front of her.

"Hi, I'm Aeree Cahill." I squint at her when she doesn't seem to recognize the name. "Mitchell Cahill's wife."

"Oh yes. I'm sorry, but he isn't in." Irritation swings in her voice as she checks something on her computer screen. "It looks like he is off for the rest of the week."

My eyebrows scrunch together. As far as I know, he was supposed to be back at work on Thursday for a big trial. He had even mentioned that he was going to use the firm's condo in the city so he wouldn't be distracted, so it must have been a big deal. He only stays there when the cases involve big clients.

"I'm actually looking for his boss." As I mutter the words, I realize that I don't know anything about my husband's professional life. After Johnathan Buren had been appointed as a federal judge, supervisors must have changed, but Mitch never even mentioned the new guy's name or pointed out anyone specific during the few company events he took me to.

"Mr. Millard is in with a client at the moment, but I'll let him know that you're here if you want to wait. It could be a while, though." The receptionist's smile is noncommittal. Showing up without a prior appointment must be one of the deadly sins.

Since I need to open Mitch's probate as soon as possible to get some money, I should wait, even if it takes all day. Besides, except for going back home and sulking, I really have nothing better to do.

With a small huff, I lower myself into one of the visitor chairs. A book would be a fun distraction, but of course, I didn't bring one since the appointment at the bank was not supposed to take longer than a few minutes. My fingers drum on the armrest of my chair. After some restless humming, I start to flip through a magazine on the table. Princess Kate of England is expecting another child—must be baby number three or four. She has the perfect life, especially given that her husband is still alive and she has plenty of money.

I yawn into the back of my hand when another visitor takes a seat across from me. A woman appears after only a few minutes, requesting that he follow her. There's still no sign of this Millard character. With a huff, I go for the next magazine, this time a legal periodical that almost puts me to sleep. I keep checking my watch. It has been a fricking hour.

When I get to the end of the magazine, I toss it on the table and start to pace the room. A few times, my eyes graze the row of business cards on the receptionist's desk. I pick up one of Mitch's. *D. Mitchell Cahill.* Mitch had hated his first name, David—he found it too ordinary and told me he had started to abbreviate it right after he graduated law school. Apparently, it's common practice among lawyers, even though I've always found it a little bit silly.

A sigh deflates my shoulders as my gaze wanders toward the window. The offices that are eye level with mine on the other side of the street have their blinds drawn; I can't even spy on people, so another fun distraction is blown to pieces. The angry sun rays reflect off the smooth surface as if the heat is trying to take a bite out of the glass. The humid temperatures must be unbearable with lunchtime approaching. My throat is already parched at the thought of breathing in the wet air once I leave here. Walking through a tropical rainforest couldn't be any worse.

"Hello, Aeree?"

I spin around, facing an older guy with an impeccable business suit. I vaguely remember him from a Christmas party a few years ago. His strawberry blond hair—at least what is left of it—has grayed a little more around the ears, his gaunt face unable to hide the heavy bags under his eyes. He is either sick or seriously sleep deprived.

"Not sure if you remember me. I'm Toby Millard. Why don't you follow me to my office?"

The bowels of the law offices of Buren, Buren, and Larson are like a maze. We turn corner after corner until he finally ushers me into a spacious office. A heavy wooden desk, which looks like it's made of shiny mahogany, with a gigantic black leather swivel chair occupies one-half of the room; a smaller round table with chairs around it is placed in the other half. A long sideboard with antique books neatly shelved takes up the rest of the space. His law diploma and several licenses, proudly displayed on the wall next to his desk, are the only personalization of the room. There isn't even one photograph of his family.

"Please have a seat," he says, pointing at one of the chairs by the round table. "Can I get you something? Coffee—or water perhaps?"

"No, thank you." I plop into the chair before remembering my manners. "And thank you for seeing me without an appointment."

"That's not a problem. The FBI was just here, so it took a little longer." His grayish-blue eyes are filled with a mix of curiosity and caution as he takes the seat across from me. "They told me that Mitch is presumed dead at this point."

I drop my gaze, unable to grasp how he can talk so nonchalantly about the death of one of his direct reports. "He fell into a waterfall after being shot by a sniper. I doubt he survived." The familiar tickle in my throat is back, but it's suppressed by a quick double breath. Bawling in his office will be too much of an embarrassment.

"Well, the investigation is still ongoing. Divers are searching the pond, so I'm sure they'll find something." A curt smile spreads on his lips. "If something is there, that is."

His body language has turned accusatory. My head is buzzing. What did the FBI tell him? Judging from the strained expression on his face, he has already convicted me.

"I had nothing to do with Mitch's death," I say when the sudden silence in the room becomes unbearable. I mean, that's what he is thinking anyway.

"I'm a criminal defense attorney, so skepticism is in my nature. Don't take it personally." His smile is even thinner this time. "I'm usually not a fan of the FBI but given the state of your marriage"—the smile turns into a painful grimace—"I mean, I couldn't lie."

It takes all my effort for my jaw not to drop. What the hell is he talking about? "I'm not sure if I follow, Mr. Millard." If anything was working, it was our marriage. "What did Mitch tell you about us?"

"I don't think I should discuss this with you." His hands cup behind his head as he leans back in his seat. "To be honest, I'm surprised you even came. Why are you here, Aeree?"

Something inside me snaps. After he kept me waiting all this time, I don't need to take his crap. "Sorry, Mr. Millard, but I would really like to get to the bottom of this. Mitch and I were very happy, and I think I deserve to know how you even got this ridiculous idea that there was something wrong with our marriage."

His beady eyes drill into me without hiding his animosity. When he finally speaks, I expect a sharp reply, but his voice is flat and calm. "Not sure who you are trying to fool, but Mitch was aware that you were cheating on him. He told me this had been going on for close to a year."

I gasp. "That's preposterous."

"Mitch said he had iron-clad proof, and there is no reason for me to doubt his word. In our firm, marriages break apart every day. With his workload, I can't even blame you. Being a housewife with nothing but time on your hands, it's only natural that you were looking for a little playtoy to keep your bed warm while he was working his ass off to give you all of those material possessions you crave."

The blatant sarcasm of the last sentence draws heat to my cheeks. After confessing that I'm nothing but a lying-and-cheating wife, asking about my husband's will sound like a confirmation that he was right all along. For a moment, I seriously consider just walking out the door, but then I remind myself that he is the only one who can provide the answers I need.

"Well, I came because the bank manager recommended that I get a copy of his will to open his probate." I can't hold his piercing gaze. "Do you have it?"

His tongue clicks and I shrink in my seat, feeling utterly judged as a gold-digging widow, even if that's far from the truth.

"No, I don't. This firm doesn't handle anything outside criminal matters. I suspect Mitch's will is with an old law school friend of his who handled all of his personal affairs."

"Do you have a name?"

He rubs his chin. "Colton Kittinger, if I recall correctly. His office is somewhere in Midtown."

By the time I have found the exit, I will have forgotten the name with my sieve of a brain. "Can you write it down?"

He tosses me a rather vile look before getting on his feet and strolling over to his desk. The pen he uses is made of gold with black inlays and looks very expensive. Letters are carefully crafted on a small notepad with his left hand before he tears out the page.

"This is as far as my involvement will go." He holds on to the paper when I try to snatch it. "If you get arrested, don't call here. As Mitch's employers, there's not only a conflict of interest, but none of us wishes to represent you."

I nod, barely able to control my shaking hand. What a horrible experience. His statement about our marriage irks me tremendously, though I can't figure out why Mitch would have lied to him like that. It doesn't make any sense.

"Thanks," I still mutter when he finally releases the paper, determined to keep face. My father taught me that you never show an opponent that he tripped you up. With my chin held high, I walk out of his office. Hopefully, I will never have to see him again.

# Chapter 17

The mailman is just stuffing a bunch of envelopes into the mailbox when I pull up to the curb in front of my house. Most of them look like bills. For a second, I hesitate, my head falling back against the seat of the car with a growl. How on earth am I going to pay for them? Since the house is in Mitch's name, the mortgage will hopefully be covered through direct debit, but there are the utilities and insurance I know he still paid by check. I'm not even sure Mitch's medical plan at work still covers me.

After the mailman moves on to the next house, I pull the car into the garage and slide out. On my way to the mailbox, I realize how disheveled I must look after driving with the top down to preserve gas by forgoing the air-conditioning. The business suit I'm wearing is way too thick for the pressing heat, and sweat has soaked through the fabric of both my shirt and jacket. When I meet Kelsey's gaze as she sweeps the driveway next door, my fingers automatically smooth down my hair.

I dart into the house to avoid getting sucked into a conversation after grabbing the mail. Kicking the door closed, I once again lock myself into the serenity of my own four walls before I laugh bitterly at the irony. Not only does the depressing atmosphere of the empty house weigh heavily on me, I'm not even sure it actually belongs to me. After what I heard in my husband's office today, who knows who the beneficiary of his will is?

In hindsight, my husband was almost a complete stranger to me. Outside our marriage, I have no idea who he talked to or hung out with—come to think of it, he didn't introduce me to even one friend he had before we got married. He always said he didn't have time for friends and all his relatives were dead.

Though there were times I found this odd, I never questioned it. The relief that he was there for me after I got out of prison had always subdued my need to meddle into affairs he considered his responsibility. After all, I had lost everything and he was the only one I had left. It was easiest for me to just lean back and have him take care of me. This not only made me totally dependent on him but left me now totally helpless.

Deciding to take my frustrations out on the next innocent thing that can't fight back, I kick with all my might against the shoe rack, sending Mitch's dress shoes flying. A stabbing pain in my toes releases the remaining anger like a puffing valve. Tears rise instead. I'm so thoroughly fucked. At least I don't have to worry about gaining weight since I won't have money to buy food. The dry goods in the pantry and the few pizzas in the freezer are the last groceries I have.

I flip through the mail. Just as expected, most of the envelopes contain various bills. Just before I get to the bottom of the pile, my heart skips a couple of beats. There's also my final paycheck from Shop Around The Clock. With trembling fingers, I tear open the envelope. Since I was fired after two shifts, it's not much money, but it's better than nothing. It will get me at least until the end of next week.

Already making a mental shopping list, my body freezes when something *thuds* in Mitch's study. My skin crawls with a sudden itching sensation that radiates from a lump in my stomach. I scan the wardrobe for a suitable weapon, finally settling on the large umbrella. At least I could try to poke someone's eye out or give him a good whack.

My back is against the wall as my feet slowly edge forward. Holding my breath, I attempt to be as quiet as a mouse when I get to the door of the study. My ears prick, but they are unable to detect a sound. When I push the door wide open, I curse myself that I didn't go into the kitchen first to get a knife.

"Oh, hey, Aeree, you're home."

Despite the familiarity of the voice, I shriek. My heart is pounding so hard against my chest, it makes me dizzy. The smile fades from his lips, confusion spreading on his face.

"Hell, Eltas, you scared the crap out of me." The umbrella drops to my side when my tense body deflates. I waver, holding onto the door frame for balance. What on earth has gotten into him, scaring me like that?

"Sorry, you weren't home, so I let myself in. The heat was killing me." His smile reflects total innocence. "I didn't think you'd mind."

"How did you get in?" It's a stupid question—as a special-forces operator, he sure knows how to pick a lock.

The smile is replaced with confusion. "The hideaway key in the yard." He continues to gaze at me like I'm the one who lost her mind. "Remember, you told me where it is in case of an emergency."

It takes all my effort to not raise my eyebrows at his blatant lie. The garden goblin was a recent addition and I'm sure I never told him that it also functions as the hiding place for the backdoor key. Besides, the key was gone, so there's no way he could have used it unless he was the culprit who stole it to begin with.

Just when I'm about to confront him, I stop myself. Lying to me is out of character for him, so he must be hiding something. If I start an argument about the key, he will take this as a reason to retreat, which will only leave me with more questions. Better grill him inconspicuously before tossing my cards on the table.

My hand slaps my forehead. "Totally forgot. You know how bad my memory is when it comes to stuff like that."

He smiles mildly.

"So what are you doing here? And what are you doing in the study?" After breaking into my house, I don't trust him, even if he is one of my father's oldest friends. When his brows arch, I try to downplay my paranoia. "With your appetite, I would've thought you'd raid my refrigerator."

His small smile doesn't reach his eyes the way it usually does. "I heard about Mitch and wanted to check on you. How are you holding up, kiddo?"

"Okay, I guess." My arms tingle and I want nothing more than to fold them in front of my chest, but he would immediately pick up on the hostile body language. "What exactly did you hear?"

"That he was dead. Can you tell me what happened?" He leans forward in his chair, his dark eyes cutting into me. His facial expression is the same as my father used to have when he tried to catch me in a lie. Typical operator-interrogation look.

"A sniper shot him. I don't know why, but he wasn't the only one of our group. I think that it might have something to do with this couple who disappeared. They were involved in something illegal. That's at least what the thug who almost raped me said."

His eyes go wide in shock; this last piece of information must be news to him. "You were almost raped?" Catapulting upward, he is on his feet and closes the gap between us with a couple of strides.

I let a few tears fill my eyes as I nod. He couldn't have talked to River. There's no way his subordinate would have failed to mention the incident with Harley.

His hands enclose mine. "I'm so sorry this happened." His tone is soothing. In that moment, he is just like the old Eltas, who has always been there for me when my father was still on a mission. The falling tears are real this time when he pulls my face against his shoulder.

"I don't know what's happening, Eltas." Despair shakes my voice. "The cops think I killed Mitch. It's been hell."

"Shh, it's gonna be okay." He strokes my back when the tears continue to soak into his shirt. "Things will work out, I promise."

"How?" My face leaves the safety of his shoulder, my head tilting backward to gaze up at him. "Mitch is gone. Everything was in his name, so I'm broke and have no clue what to do about money. The cops are itching to slap the handcuffs on me after Mitch's boss told them I cheated on him and I'm only out for his money. There's no one left in my corner, so please explain to me how things will work out. What if they arrest me?" Fear grabs at me when I imagine being locked up again like a caged animal. "I can't do this, Eltas, not this time. I didn't do anything wrong."

His arms drop before he spins around. "I'm always here for you. You know that, right?"

"Then why did you lie to me earlier? I know there was no key in the yard. What's going on? Why are you really here?"

A small chuckle shakes his frame—the kind brought on by desperation when you know you got entangled in your own bullshit without a way to wiggle yourself free. "Okay, the truth it is. I guess you deserve that." He turns around, his face now laced with that military diligence. "I was searching your house."

"Oh." This time, my arms fold in front of my chest as I glare at him. "And what exactly were you looking for?"

"When you had contact with Julie Flynn and Tyson Roberts, did they give you anything?"

My eyebrows knot together—how does he even know about them? "No. What could they have possibly given to me?"

"Something small, like a lighter."

"No, nothing. There was another girl who had their backpack. I found the phone in there that I used to call for help.

Maybe you should ask her if they gave her anything. She was with them for several hours."

"Do you know where she is?"

His question takes me aback, but it's more confirmation that he couldn't have spoken to River. "She got hurt. As far as I know, she is in a coma at Mount Sinai Hospital."

"And where's the backpack now?"

"We left it at the cabin."

He seems satisfied with the answer, pulling out his wallet before placing a few twenty-dollar bills on Mitch's desk. "That's all I have on me at the moment, but I'll get you some more."

"Thanks." Though the gesture is undoubtedly meant to make me feel better, it leaves a stale taste in my mouth. The prickle under my scalp is back, and somehow, I can't shake the feeling he has been using me, though I have no idea why.

"I have to go. Call me if you need anything." He looks tired all of a sudden. "Take care now."

"You stay safe out there."

After the front door closes behind him, I watch through the window as he strolls down the driveway. A motorcycle speeds up and he swings himself on the back. I don't recognize the driver. He must be another new member of the team.

As they take off, the prickle in my scalp multiplies. Come to think of it, he never gave me a reason why he would search my house instead of just waiting for me to ask his questions. It's all very odd. River or the FBI could have answered most of them, but then again, maybe they sent him to ensure I didn't withhold any information since they know we are friends.

Eltas and his puzzling visit are forgotten the second my stomach grumbles. I decide I deserve a treat after the past few stressful days, and the thought of the marinated chicken breasts that Mitch kept in the freezer for late-night dinners makes my mouth water. I could even barbecue them. There is still enough mozzarella and tomato left in the fridge for a small salad, which will make the sinful meal at least halfway healthy. Food has always been a picker-upper for me—something that has continuously clashed with my need to stay thin—but for once, I will enjoy a nice meal without visiting the bathroom afterward. My wobbly knees might not keep me upright much longer otherwise. Losing those extra calories again is a task for another day.

As I drag myself over to the shed to get the barbecue grill, the sun beats down on me without mercy. Next door, children's squealing disturbs the heavy summer air before a man's laughter joins in. The squealing is cut short by splattering water. They probably have one of those toddler wading pools that keeps everyone refreshed. Sudden envy steals my breath. I wish I could trade places with Kelsey for just one day. Even if I had to sacrifice my left arm, having a family and friends would be worth it.

The inside of the shed is much cooler, though the musty smell of overripe seeds and mulch almost makes my stomach turn. After the blinding sun, my eyes need a second to adjust to the dim light flooding in from the outside through the dirt-caked window. As ill luck would have it, the grill is buried all the way in the back behind the mower and the bricks that Mitch was going to use to expand the deck.

When I step forward, I stumble over the rake. I kick it, sending it into the mower. The sudden movement almost makes me stumble again and the wound on my neck throbs afterward. Today is not the day to let out my anger on innocent garden tools or shoe racks.

As I venture further into the shed, a spiderweb gets caught in my hair. Fantastic. My hand swooshes through the air to get the thin strands away from my face. Dust tickles my nostrils and I sneeze, my fingers suppressing a full-blown sneeze attack by pinching my nose while I breathe through my mouth. When the tickle stops, I sigh. This is pretty hard work for a simple dinner. Maybe I should have just used the grill pan on the stove.

When I finally reach the barbecue grill, my hands are covered in dust, and the remains of a huge spiderweb stick to my clothing. The damn business suit needs to go to the dry cleaner after this adventure. Cursing under my breath, I pull at the handle of the grill, but it's stuck. The only way to get it out is to give it a good push from the farthest corner of the shed.

Reluctantly, I step toward the darkness, the dim light halting just short of my feet. I ignore the crawling under my skin, attributing the itchy feeling to the filth and spiderweb strands on my clothes and skin. The coolness of the shadow awaits me. That's when a hand covers my mouth and stifles my gurgling scream.

# Chapter 18

I surprise my attacker when I stab him with my high heel, scraping open half of his shin. With a hiss, the hand drops. My elbow rams into his ribs before I spin around, my hand already reaching for the large hedge trimmers that are stacked in a shelf on the wall. I'm just about to go for his eye when I realize it's Marcel.

His jaw is hanging open. "Damn, girl, where did you learn how to fight like this?"

"The hell." A deep breath slows down my racing heart, which jumps around in my chest from the sudden surge of adrenaline released into my bloodstream. Though I'm not ready to kill him since he is something like the next-door neighbor, I don't know if I should give him the benefit of the doubt. He still scares the shit out of me and has no business hanging around my property. Especially since I paid him. "What are you doing here, Marcel?" My arms cross over my chest. "That's trespassing."

"Yo, I never expected you to come back here. Most chicks stay away from the dark corners of a shed."

I roll my eyes at his stereotypical remark. "That doesn't answer my question."

"I was watching that Eltas dude." He bites his lip, his stupid grin apologetic. "Did he talk to you?"

"Yes, he did. Aren't you working for the FBI?"

His eyebrows rise like he isn't getting my point.

"I mean, he's military. Shouldn't you guys work together? Why are you spying on him?"

He rubs over the stubble on his chin. Since I saw him last, his whole appearance has changed. His clothes have several stains and a hint of cheap liquor and nicotine surrounds him like a pesky cloud. His shoes look as if they were just pulled from a garbage bin. If I didn't know him and just accidentally ran into him on the street, I would suspect he is a bum.

"He's not exactly military. What did he want?"

"What do you mean, he is not exactly military? He took over my father's old unit."

"I can't really talk about it. You know, classified stuff."

I'm close to rolling my eyes again. Whatever happened to sharing is caring? "If this is so secret, why should I tell you what Eltas wanted?"

"Because if you don't, I'll have to call it in and one of my colleagues will have to pick you up for a formal interview." His smile is contrite. "I'm sure you'd rather not spend any more time at the FBI building."

That's the last place I want to be right now. "He asked if this couple who was on the trip with me in the Green Mountains gave me anything, which they didn't." I search his face for a reaction, but his features are totally even.

"Cool. That's all I needed to know. I'll go now." He favors his uninjured leg, his face twisting every time he puts weight on the one I scraped open. Heels are better weapons than I thought.

With one jolt, his hand frees the barbecue pit from its wedged-in position before he limps out.

"Thanks," I call after him, snickering at his grunt when he bumps his knee on the pile of bricks that are stacked in his way. Today is not his day either.

At the door, he turns around. "I'd prefer if you didn't tell my family I came around. My kids are not supposed to see me looking like this." There's a hint of sadness in his voice. This undercover job must be bothering him. Must be hard on his wife and kids, too, and I wonder how many assignments he takes on that keep him away from home.

I nod. "No problem."

My gaze stays on the door after it falls closed behind him. This is getting odder by the minute. Something is up with Eltas, though I have not the slightest clue what it could be. Maybe my father knows something. They were always really close, and if Eltas has confided in anyone outside of his unit, it will be my dad. I will ask him the next time I see him.

All of a sudden, an utter feeling of loneliness swamps me. Marcel's wife might miss him for a few days, but then he will come home and be there for her. I, on the other hand, have reached the end of the line. Mitch is gone forever, but even if he wasn't, would he still want to be in a relationship with me? After everything I learned today, I doubt it. With my dad in prison and Eltas acting all weird, I can't even get my sadness or worries off my chest. There is no one with an open ear or an ounce of compassion.

Hot tears tickle the corners of my eyes. I kick the grill so I have a reason to let them fall. My appetite is ruined. My stomach is in knots, the fear that I won't be able to manage life on my own pressing on my skull. Why do these awful things keep happening to me? First my mother, then the rape, which also tore my father away, now Mitch. What did I ever do for karma to keep dishing out these blows that keep knocking me off my feet? The unfairness of it all drives more tears into my eyes.

Trying to calm my uproar of emotions, I exhale for a long time before sucking in a deep breath. This only gets me dizzy. With a growl, I push against the grill, toppling it over. Tears drip off my chin, leaving splatters on the dusty floor. I want to stop crying—be brave like my father always taught me—but the tears keep flowing like water over a broken dam. My heart and soul weep and there's nothing to stop the pain. For the first time, I can relate to my mother wanting to end it all.

A cool breeze, caressing my face like soft fingers, finally snaps me out of my desperate mood. I fumble with the grill until my throbbing body beats me down completely. On cue, my neck stings again. It's time for a new dose of painkillers. I should also change the bandage. After that, I can take a nap. The day has been exhausting. If I hide away in my room, nothing else bad can happen to me.

I abandon the shed—in hindsight, barbecuing in the heat was a silly idea—dragging my feet over the lawn toward the house. When a sudden voice from the garden path startles me, my whole body jumps and I almost topple over on my high heels.

"Oh, hey, Aeree, here you are."

Squinting against the sun in the direction of the familiar voice, I make out Kelsey's features. Are these people stalking me?

"Hi." I'm tempted to snap at her to find out what she wants, but that would be incredibly rude.

"Marcel called and asked me to check on you"—she lifts a plate as she steps into the shadow of the trees that have always prevented the back porch from turning into a melting pot—"and I brought you something to eat."

"That's very kind of you, but I'm not really hungry."

"It's only leftovers from last night, but Marcel is an ace at the grill," she says without considering my obvious opposition to her gift. "I hope you're not a vegetarian."

"I'm not, but—"

"You're bleeding." Her gaze is fixed on the small cut on my hand that has reopened during my battle with the barbeque grill.

"Oh, it's nothing."

"Donna could take a look at that when she comes over. She's a nurse and due to pick up Ramona any minute."

Of course she is. This is all very convenient so she can keep intruding in my life. Marcel probably asked her to keep an eye on me in case I was lying about Eltas.

I decide to end their game right here and now. "Why exactly did Marcel want you to come and check on me?" Despite my best efforts, my words are laced with a hint of hostility.

"He was concerned, said you looked really upset." Her gaze is open. If she has an ulterior motive, she hides it well. "I know that this might not be the New Yorker way, but where I'm from, neighbors help each other out. I'm sorry if I overstepped a boundary." She spins around, but not before I detect a splinter of hurt in her eyes. So I did offend her.

As she starts to march down the garden path, I can't help feeling like a total jerk. My paranoia is getting to me. Not everyone in this world is out to frame me and I should take advantage of a nice gesture when I can. It's exactly one of those examples why Mitch always wanted me to have good relations with our neighbors. He would've been upset about me brushing Kelsey off like that.

"Kelsey, wait." I force a smile on my lips. "I'm sorry if I came across as rude. The last few days have been really overwhelming and this heat is driving me nuts."

On cue, both of our heads tilt back. Almost with mockery, a steely blue perfection of a sky stares down on us. There are not even a few of those puffy summer clouds that make for pretty pictures. The air has come to a complete standstill—it must be pushing at least a hundred degrees. My blouse clings to my back like a second skin, and there's no doubt that there are huge sweat stains under my armpits. The business suit is probably ruined.

"I know the feeling." A tentative smile spreads on Kelsey's lips. "Sometimes, seeing any light in the darkness can be difficult, but trust me, it's there."

My brows furrow. I never took her for the philosophical type. I stretch out my uninjured hand—I made my peace, now it's time to get rid of her. "Thanks for stopping by. I'd love to try the food."

After a slight hesitation, she surrenders the plate, probably expecting me to invite her into the house. I don't do her the favor.

"Here is my phone number." She holds up a piece of paper she pulls from her pants pocket. "You can call me anytime if you need anything."

I grab the paper and tuck it in under the plate in the hope she will go. "Bye then. I promise I'll call if I need any help."

She finally gets the message and retreats after a mumbled bye. I wait until she turns the corner before I push the back door open with a sigh. Of all the neighbors on Staten Island, why do I get the clingy kind?

I peel out of my suit jacket, letting it carelessly slip to the ground, before taking a peek under the aluminum foil tightly wrapped around the plate. My stomach grumbles as the scent of barbecue sauce teases my taste buds. Coleslaw is piled next to glazed ribs; a few chicken wings that look spicy are squeezed into the remaining space. I have to say, the food looks delicious. Something I would have made during my catering days. After a quick shower, I will stick it into the microwave.

With newfound energy, I dart up the steps, turning on the shower before I tear off my clothes in front of the mirror in my bedroom. Every single piece is soaked down to my skin, even my panties and bra. After peeking under the bandage on my neck and confirming that the stitches are clean, I head back into the bathroom.

Thick steam greets me. When I step under the shower, I'm barely able to breathe. The warm water feels heavy on my skin. I turn the dial to almost cold to get some relief, foaming up with shower gel to get the sticky feeling off my skin. Splashing the cool water on my face is divine, the pressure in my scalp easing slowly. I splutter when water enters my mouth and decide I've had enough.

While I change the dressing on my neck, I allow myself to dry off naturally. Only my hair is secured in a turban before I return to the bathroom mirror to inspect the state of my body. The bruises are in full bloom, the scratches and cuts covered with scabs. Absentmindedly, I choke down a couple of the painkillers before slipping into a loose-fitting summer dress. The plain cotton material is perfect to battle the heat.

I forgo shoes, my feet still sore from wearing my stilettos all morning. The kitchen tiles are cool on my bare skin and my toes curl in delight. As I move the meat onto a separate platter to stick into the microwave, I hum along to a song on the radio. Three minutes should do the trick. Grabbing a fork, I'm just about to shovel a generous amount of coleslaw into my mouth to test Marcel's cooking when the metal handle of the fork shoots a burning pain up my arm. I forgot to cover the cut on my hand with a new bandage.

I drop the fork onto the plate and run back into my bedroom. The scent of the warm food follows me, spurring on my appetite. My mouth waters. There should be Band-Aids in the cabinet in the bathroom and this shouldn't take more than a minute.

The back of my feet dig into the hardwood floor of the bathroom's threshold when I notice the man kneeling on the floor, his hands feverishly rummaging through my first-aid drawer. Under normal circumstances, I would be terrified and on the lookout for a weapon, but since he rescued me from that pig Harley, he's got a few bonus points in my book. A gasp escapes me when he looks up. His whole face is bruised. Dry blood cakes on a split lip and under his nose. Judging from the crooked shape, the latter is broken.

"Hey, Aeree." River's smile is timid. "I hope I didn't startle you."

I snort—what's one more surprise after everything that happened today? In a way, my life has become a grotesque farce. Exactly a week ago, my husband had surprised me with a weekend getaway on our anniversary—now I'm a widow without money, slowly finding out that nothing around me is what it once seemed.

"Eltas already beat you to it." My arms fold over my chest. "And I swear, you better give me some answers or a few bruises are the least of your worries." The last part is meant to break the ice, and it works.

His smile is as crooked as his nose. "What do you wanna know?"

"I guess we'll start with everything—and then take it from there."

# Chapter 19

Five minutes later, an array of bandages and ointments are spread out on the small vanity table in the bedroom and we are ready to rock. River is sitting on the edge of the bed, his feet planted firmly on the ground as if he is about to bolt.

"This is gonna hurt, right?" He reminds me of a little boy.

"Don't tell me you're one of those guys who acts all tough in public, but then goes crying to their mommy when they have a boo-boo. You're special ops, so suck it up."

"Yeah, I guess." His grimace isn't very convincing.

Smirking, I pour a little bit of alcohol onto a pad. My fingers pinch his chin as I slowly turn his head from left to right, determining where to start patching up his damaged face. In the end, I go for the cut under his left eye. "So why are you here?"

He flinches when the pad connects to his skin. "Not really sure where to start."

With a hiss, he pulls away when I apply slight pressure. He is such a sissy. My hand cups the back of his head to stop his erratic movements. "Why don't you start at the beginning." I dab the swollen skin, ignoring more hisses.

"Okay, but you have to promise to keep it to yourself. If Riley found out, I could get into a lot of trouble."

My finger crosses briefly over my chest. "Scout's honor."

"And I'm only telling you because I'm worried. Eltas is not the man he used to be—you can't trust him. I just don't want you to get sucked into this mess more than you already have since I really liked your dad when I met him at the prison. You are good people and I'd hate if you got hurt."

"Stop stalling, Cunningham, and get on with it." I dab the area around his eye with a cotton ball, forcing him to squeeze his eyes shut, so he won't detect my apprehension. I hate that he brought up my dad. My father is already worried enough about me. If he knew of my dire situation, he would go mental.

"So my cousin is part of one of Riley's teams and I had wanted to join special ops ever since I signed up for the military a few years ago. Problem is that I failed the entry test when I got a case of bad nerves." He grimaces again, this time a little more goofily. "Blew up a convoy by accident during one of the simulations. In real life, that would have never happened, but I was so goddamn nervous, I was sick."

"And they gave you another chance?" It's surprising. My dad always said that those who fail the entry test will at some point lose their cool on a real mission. The risk is just too high.

"Well, it was an unofficial second chance after my cousin pled my case to Major Riley. Riley wanted me to infiltrate this private mercenary group who has been contracting for different jobs, some of them illegal. I was just settling in when this stuff in the Green Mountains happened. This thing is huge. I can't tell you anything specific since the stolen data stick involves classified military secrets, but the Pentagon is involved. If we don't get the data stick back by the end of this week, shit will hit the fan. Apparently, they need it for this big summit that's being hosted in Atlanta this coming weekend."

He hisses again after I attack another cut, this time louder than before. His face is twisted in pain. Deciding to be merciful, I apply some ointment with gentle fingers and cover the cut with a small bandage.

"And what does this have to do with Eltas?" I ask before turning his head to the other side.

"He runs the private mercenary group."

My hand freezes midair. "Eltas left the military?" So this is what Marcel was talking about.

"Yes, about three months after your dad's arrest. At first, he just did the usual stuff those private firms do—you know, like training and security services, mostly for larger corporations who work in hot spots around the world. Then he met this guy, Weston Cox, who has terrorist connections, and things went downhill from there. The military suspects he has been selling classified information in the Middle East, but there was never any proof. That's where I came in."

With utter care, I dab the blood around his nose. In the movies, they always straighten the bone in front of a mirror, but I have no clue if I'm really supposed to do that. The few times my father broke his nose, the hospital patched him up and he came home with a funny bandage. I decide to let it go for now. If I straightened his nose, his scream would likely alert the whole neighborhood. Besides, an expert could probably fix it later on, even if the nose heals a little crooked. "So did Riley plant you in the group to get the proof?"

"Yes. All was good, but then Cox called Eltas while we were having breakfast and told him that two of their suppliers, who were meant to make them a fortune, went on the run. Of course, I never thought they would end up in your travel group, but apparently they did."

Figures. There is probably a one-in-a-billion chance that something like that could happen, but with my bad karma, it happens to me. Why couldn't I be so lucky when playing the lottery?

"So how did you get those bruises on your face?"

"Eltas. When you called and told me about thugs and a data stick in the Green Mountains, I was just giving my weekly debrief to Major Riley. He immediately made the connection and put me on a chopper in the hopes of recovering the stick. Eltas had given me his phone, allegedly for me to stay in touch with Cox, but he was really on to me and tracked my moves with the phone. Once I got back to the Green Mountains, he hunted me down and started to beat the truth out of me. Luckily, I got away, or he would have probably killed me."

"You were very lucky. Eltas is not someone to underestimate. I still can't believe he turned on his country."

"Something happened on one of his assignments that made him quit, but Major Riley never told me the specifics."

It's still hard to imagine Eltas turning traitor. He had been military through and through. My father had trusted him explicitly—still does. Eltas was the only one who knew our whereabouts after we went on the run.

I apply a small bandage to a cut on River's chin. His knuckles are next. Judging from the blood and swelling, he must have landed some good punches in order to get away. Under more hisses, I rub the back of his hand with the alcohol-drenched cotton ball, but he doesn't try to pull away this time. A bandage soon covers the lacerations.

"I still don't get why you came to me? Am I in some type of trouble with the military, too?" My eyes search his face for a reaction, but the shaking of his head is genuine.

"We're working with the FBI on this, and one of their guys called us when he spotted Eltas entering your house. Unfortunately, I got here too late and we lost him again. I was gonna check in with Riley to get new orders, but if he saw me after he specifically told me to get medical attention and let someone else handle Eltas, he would have pulled me for good."

I smirk. "Well, I hope my bandages look authentic enough for you to claim you've seen a doctor."

"Riley is desperate since there's so much pressure from the Pentagon to recover the stick. I'm sure it will be fine. This is my only chance to prove myself to him, so it's really important for me." His hands enclose my fingers. "But enough about me. How are you holding up?"

"Not good." I battle fresh tears. "The FBI thinks I had something to do with my husband's death, and Mitch"—I swallow hard when I realize he doesn't even know who that is— "I mean, my husband, he lied to his coworker about our marriage and I don't know why. I'm totally broke and don't even know how to make it through the month." I turn my head when a small wail escapes my lips.

"I'm sorry, it's just been so overwhelming." With the back of my hand, I wipe away the few tears that managed to spring free. He must think I'm one of those women who cry all the time.

His hand squeezes my arm. "I'm sure things will work out for you. I promise, when this is over, I'm gonna try to help you with the FBI. Now I should go." When he stands, his hand reaches for the nightstand for balance. His eyes close for a second. Exhaustion must be catching up with him.

"When did you last eat and drink something?"

"Dunno, but it's been awhile."

I smile. "The neighbor brought over some food. Why don't you have some before you go? Can't have you starve out there."

"Yeah, maybe I should." His tight muscles flex underneath his shirt when he cups his hands behind his head to stretch.

I tear my gaze away, feeling bad for even noticing.

Our trip to the kitchen is spent in awkward silence. He pulls himself onto a barstool, eyeing the plate with a slight frown. "Is that all you got?"

"I'll make some more." With a puckered eyebrow, I study the few things left in the fridge before settling on the eggs. Together with the leftover potatoes, this should fill him up.

When my head pops back above the counter, he is just stuffing the last fork of coleslaw into his mouth. The ribs have been reduced to a few bones, his attention turning to the chicken wings. How can anyone eat that fast? With a sigh, I open the freezer and take out the marinated chicken breasts that I was going to grill in the first place. Might as well turn this into a feast.

He gnaws on the chicken bones, his eyes staying on me as I slice the potatoes. The grill is heating up next to me. Just looking at the frozen meat makes me salivate. If I don't put some food into my stomach soon, I will be sick.

"What about the sniper? Do you have any idea who he is?" I drop a piece of butter into the heated skillet as I ask questions, twirling it around to spread it evenly before cracking the first egg. When I look up, River chews on his chicken with distant eyes as if he is in another world. "River?"

"Sorry." He blinks a few times, but he takes another bite and chews before answering. "We're still trying to figure out how the sniper fits into the picture. Riley thinks they might be the terrorists to whom that couple wanted to sell the data stick after double-crossing Eltas's group. Apparently, they were offering more money. However, we can't be sure. For all we know, it could even be one of Eltas's men, eliminating witnesses."

"But if that's the case, why are the feds accusing me of killing my husband for his money?"

He shrugs. "I have no idea where that's coming from. There's probably local stuff we don't know about. Besides, you know how the feds are. They love to throw their weight around in operations like this to justify their existence."

I sure wouldn't put it past Dinkle and her team to be overzealous.

"Watch the eggs!"

My head snaps around just in time to prevent a food disaster. I toss the eggs in the air, flipping them over in the skillet.

"You look like a chef."

I laugh—that might have been true when I had my catering business, but that seemed like a long time ago. Since my constant battle with calories, I have tried to stay out of the kitchen as much as possible to avoid the constant nibbling while I cook. I'm bad that way. Mitch usually worked late and ate at the office or traveled days at a time, allowing me to get away with minimal kitchen duties. On most nights, I only fixed a small salad or had a yogurt.

I quickly heat the potatoes in the microwave before spreading the eggs over them. After I'm done, I place the plate in front of him with a wide smile. "Eat up, soldier."

"Don't you want anything?"

"Oh, I'll fix some chicken." I realize I never even placed the chicken breasts under the grill. It will take forever—especially since the meat is still frozen as solid as a rock. Come to think of it, it has been in the freezer for at least six months. Who knows if it's still good?

"We can share this," he offers generously, pushing the plate in my direction.

The scent of the eggs makes me dizzy. The yellow in the center is still a little soft, just the way I like it. My dad and Eltas would devour fried eggs and potatoes by the truckload when they came home from one of their missions in the middle of the night, and I would join them—the memory alone makes my stomach rumble.

"Okay, let me get another plate."

"Well, just get a fork." He flashes me a pearly white smile. "Less to clean up afterward."

I swallow down that we have a dishwasher, remembering how much I had loved to steal food off my father's plate. It seems tastier when you devour a dish that is not your own. Even in restaurants, I have always liked to trade dishes with my partner, at least when Paul and I were still a couple. It was something that drove Mitch nuts. He was a firm believer that once you made a choice, you stuck with it.

We chew in silence, though the atmosphere is far from awkward. It's almost like having dinner with an old friend who knows me well enough for words not to matter. He makes funny faces a few times that get me to laugh. When I scrape up the last bit of egg yolk with the final potato, I'm sad that the meal is over. My soul feels content for a change and I don't even have the desire to dispose of the food in the toilet.

"I should get going." His eyes are on me as he rinses off the plate. "Are you okay with money at the moment? I don't have much but could probably spare a twenty."

I don't know him well enough to impose. My father would have never borrowed money unless it was from a good friend. Besides, I still have the cash Eltas gave me and will use my paycheck the next time I'm at the grocery store. "I'm good. Don't worry. Just have to get in touch with my husband's lawyer tomorrow to open up the probate. Hopefully, I'll get some more money out of that." It sounds so simple when I phrase it like this, though the reality is probably far from it.

"Didn't your husband keep a copy of his will at the house? Most people do."

I grab a towel just as he hands me the plate. "I didn't find anything when I went through his files in his study."

"What about the laptop in the attic? Maybe he kept a soft copy on there."

The plate almost slips from the towel. "What computer? We don't even have an attic."

His forehead wrinkles. "Well, there sure was one when I was looking for you in the house earlier and it seemed it has been used quite a bit."

My mouth dries up—another one of Mitch's secrets. "Can you show me?"

"It's your house, so I don't see why not." A chuckle shakes his frame when I toss him an evil glare. "Come on, I'll lead the way."

# Chapter 20

Despite its spaciousness, the attic is stifling. Wooden ceiling beams radiate like red-hot oven rods—that's how a chicken must feel under a grill, at least if it was still alive. The navy-blue carpet is thick and tickles my bare feet. It was undoubtedly put in to muffle any footsteps in case Mitch was up here and I came home unexpectedly. Come to think of it, I heard a squeaking floorboard a few times, which I took for the old house working.

"And you had no clue that this room was up here?" River asks from behind the desk. He is fiddling with a paperclip while the laptop boots up.

"Nope." My eyes travel over the filing cabinets before settling on the small window that is almost completely hidden on the outside by the thick branches of the huge oak tree in our yard. A heavy blind is attached to it, the kind that blocks out any light when it is drawn. Of course it works both ways, making the window invisible to the eye, even if I had wandered into the yard at night.

"I suppose the tapestry door isn't the easiest to detect," he says. "I only noticed because the wallpaper peeled off in one corner."

My response is a grumble. I kick myself for never noticing the hidden door. In my defense, it's in our storage room. Other than running the vacuum cleaner over the free floor space once in a blue moon, I've never stepped inside. Our luggage and Mitch's old college stuff is stored there, so the room was strictly his terrain.

My gaze returns to the filing cabinet and curiosity has me open the top drawer. A bunch of manila file folders are neatly stored inside. The other two drawers hold the same. They look just like Mitch's case files he used to bring home. My finger traces the edges. None of the names is familiar. Finally, I pull one out. Roland Farmer is written on a yellow sticker in Mitch's neat handwriting.

I open the file. The first three pages are a police report, alleging that Farmer had raped his niece. A heavy lump settles in my stomach. There had been more than one argument about Mitch defending rapists and child molesters. Usually, our fights ended with him throwing my conviction into my face. He never understood how hard it was for me to accept that the man I loved was protecting the very reason for my misery by getting rapists off without any repercussions.

Case discovery is next and I read over the evidence. It seems like an open-and-shut case. DNA samples clearly pointed to him and the girl was only fifteen, making it statutory rape no matter how one would twist and turn it. The last page in the file is like a slap in the face—it's a refusal of the grand jury to indict. What could have possibly gone wrong?

My forehead wrinkles when I scan over the names of the attorneys of record in the notification. Mitch is not mentioned. As a matter of fact, Buren, Buren, and Larson aren't even the lawyers who defended Farmer. It's some law firm in Queens I've never heard of. Why would he have another lawyer's file in his home office? Since Farmer won, there couldn't have been an appeal.

I pull out more of the files and the pattern repeats itself. All the cases ended up with a dismissal of some sort despite compelling evidence suggesting guilt. A few of the defendants had been represented by Mitch's firm, but most of them had different lawyers. The nature of the crimes are all rape or major assaults with a few odd exceptions. As far as I can tell, there's no common pattern or anything that connects the defendants.

Flipping through the files in the second drawer, I quickly figure out that those are more dismissals, only the crimes are more serious. All of them involve a death, be it at the hands of a drunk driver or a jealous spouse.

"Did you find anything?"

My head snaps up. I was so engrossed in my task that I had forgotten River was even in the room.

"These are all dismissal cases. Is the laptop booted up?"

"Yes, but it's fingerprint protected."

"Any way to get around it?"

"There probably is, but I'm not an IT expert. You need a professional hacker to break through the security system." He squats down next to me. "Are any of the names familiar?"

"Nope." Given that I'm terrible with names, I doubt I would recognize any of them, even if I had met the defendant before.

"What's in the envelope over there?" River points to a folder pocket. The corner of a slim envelope sticks out, only noticeable due to its bright red color.

My mouth dries up as I scan over the words on the outside of the envelope. *Green Mountain Project*. With trembling fingers, I tear open the flap. There is a printed list of at least a hundred names. "Sweepstakes Participants" is printed at the top. Further down, a name is highlighted. "Norton Garrett." I flip through the pages—the highlighted names are some of the other members of our group. What the hell is going on?

When I turn the envelope around, a bunch of photographs fall out. Again, they're members of our group. This is so odd. The pictures were taken in various settings but appear to be recent.

I go for Citadel's husband first. The photo is snapped inside a coffee shop. His hands are raised like he is forming letters, but the person he is communicating with has been cut out. I flip the picture around. *Walt Jamison–Vehicular Manslaughter* is written on the back.

Curiosity gets the better of me, and without hesitation, I turn over the second photograph that shows Kendall just leaving a pub. The words *Murder in the Second Degree* make me catch my breath. What was Mitch doing with these pictures? Sad Eyes's picture is right next to Kendall's and appears to have been taken on the same night. Her real name is Nina Humphrey and *Accessory to Murder* is written underneath it. I would bet my life that her and her husband's accusations are somehow related.

By the time I go for George's photo, taken at the entrance of the Central Park Zoo, an inner unrest is controlling every muscle in my body. *Murder in the Second Degree.* I shake my head—this is unbelievable. He had been the kindest guy during our charades game. How could my perception of him have been so off?

"It seems like your trip was some kind of a setup." River flips the photograph of Norton over. Another *Murder in the Second Degree.*

Our eyes lock. There is only one picture left—of me, as I'm getting into my car at the grocery store. I reach for the picture, but River beats me to it, flipping the photo around. I stare at the words. Blood swooshes in my ears, the whole moment totally surreal.

*Aeree Cahill—Murder in the First Degree.*

The memories unleash like a nightmare as I'm transported back in time, back to that hideout in the woods where my tormentors liked to hang out. It had been the perfect night for an ambush, moonless, with a slight drizzle that made it almost impossible to see without the night-vision goggles Eltas had organized. Orson, the youngest of the unit, had scoped out the gang over the past month and confirmed that all four of them had gathered for their weekly poker game. No girls allowed, which was a rare exception.

"Okay, Aeree, you stay attached to Eltas's hip." My father tossed me a dark look. It had been a battle to convince him to take me along, only my begging and tears had swayed him in the end.

"Got it, Dad." I briefly glanced at Eltas, who was staring ahead with a clenched jaw. We had reached an understanding, but judging from the twitching muscle in his cheek, he was having second thoughts.

I ducked close behind him when we ran though the darkness like ghosts. My racing heart, pounding heavily against my ribcage, was the only sound. I don't even remember breathing. My father's raised hand halted our group just outside the backdoor of the cabin. He peeked through a gap in the curtains before giving us an okay with his fingers. It was the signal to attack.

Orson kicked the door in and disappeared in the house first, followed by my dad and another one of his men. Eltas held me back. Time was ticking down in slow motion. The low pops of the firing weapons were almost painful, a big claw restricting my chest. Were we doing the right thing? Flashes of my rape danced in front of my eyes, and I remembered the pain and fear, the built-up rage of the past few months, crushing down on me at once.

My father reappeared in the doorway. "Make it quick."

The darkness swallowed him and the others up before I looked at Eltas. His eyes were searching. One word and he would take care of the leader for me.

I swallowed hard and pushed right past him. My knees were like jelly when I stepped over the threshold. I gasped at the gruesome scene. The three younger gang members were hanging in their chairs in various positions. One had fallen forward onto the table, his face resting in a pool of blood. Nausea crawled up my throat when I found another one's glassy stare. Only a small trickle of blood oozed from the middle of his forehead where the bullet had found its mark.

Finally, I tore my eyes off the three dead men when the scraping of feet startled me. The ringleader was still alive, slowly pulling his body toward the front door of the cabin. His knee caps were busted, two more bullets in his shoulders restricting his movement. A tight gag prevented him from making any verbal sound. He was helpless, just the way I was when he took me in the trailer that night.

The deadly fear in his eyes gave me momentum. That's how I must have looked when he had torn my insides to shreds. He had shown no mercy, so why should I? I clutched my hand over my mouth when the pain cut straight into my soul. He made me lose everything. I hadn't even known I was pregnant until the doctor had told me in the hospital that the fetus aborted because of the assault. Having kids had always been my dream—something that was gone forever. All because of him. He took this part of my life away.

Eltas took the safety off his weapon and handed it to me. My hand was shaking when my fingers wrapped around the grip. Tears blurred my vision before a small sob escaped. A plea for mercy jumped out of the ringleader's eyes. My whole body was frozen. I didn't know what to do.

"You sure that's what you want?" Eltas asked over the pressing silence.

In response, I pulled the trigger. Just like before, the bullet was no louder than a low plop. The recoil was almost nonexistent—Eltas had purposely chosen this particular gun and practiced with me until firing the Kel-Tec had become second nature. I knew I found my mark when the ringleader fell flat on his face. Eltas pressed two fingers to the side of his throat, but I didn't have to wait for his confirmation grunt to know that I killed a man.

"Let's go." He tugged at my sleeve when I didn't move.

The nausea was sudden and violent, my vomit only missing Eltas by inches. He let out a curse before grabbing my arm.

"We need to go."

My legs were no longer under my command. With a click of his tongue, he scooped me up. When the cold air hit me, I could breathe again, but my whole body was shaking.

We met up with the others by the tree line surrounding the clearing. Orson was behind the mounted rifle, aiming at the canister with the highly flammable gas that would turn the cabin into a fireball. It would be apparent to the police that this was a professional hit, and the fewer tracks we left behind, the better.

The tears started to roll when the flames licked toward the sky. I had hoped that getting revenge would make me whole again, cleanse my soul of the tormenting memories, but I instinctively knew that killing the ringleader would only add to my nightmares. I had stooped to his level and was no better than him. Whoever said that getting even would make things right was stupid. I was still just as broken as before, only now, this incredible guilt spread in my veins. It was almost as awful a feeling as being raped.

I still don't know why I didn't stop my revenge spree that night and assaulted Paul just a few days later. Maybe it was the pressure to keep my dad from killing him, too. I didn't want another dead body on my hands. In a sense, I had also blamed Paul for everything, even for the murder. He had sold me out, which triggered this whole ordeal, and had ultimately turned me into a killer.

Then the day after I assaulted Paul, my dad and I went on the run when shit hit the fan, and I had bigger fish to fry. Looking over my shoulder in constant fear of what I might find was nerve-racking. Even today, my heart pounds in my throat every time I answer the door if I don't expect a visitor. When the cops caught up with us after two weeks, my dad decided that we should both surrender, fearing I could get hurt if we tried to get away.

When I met Mitch, the guilt was slowly replaced when he saw me for who I was in my heart. Now I know this belief turned out to be nothing but a lie. Maybe this is my punishment for taking a human life.

"Aeree, are you all right?"

River's soft words tear me out of my memories. I blink at him, and it takes me a few seconds to realize that his arms are circled around me. His shirt is damp from my tears. I straighten, wiping my wet cheeks with the back of my hand.

"I'm fine."

"You wanna talk about it?"

I shake my head, sniffling to lock the tears away.

"Why do you think your husband had all those photographs and files?"

I shrug with a crooked smile. My voice is not under my command. I will continue bawling if he doesn't shut up.

"What do you wanna do?"

Strangling him is an appealing thought to stop his damn questions.

"Aeree?"

I let out a puff. "I don't know, River."

He pulls me back against his shoulder when the floodgates open again. I feel stupid crying like a small child—it's something my father would never approve of—but I just can't help it. River strokes my back until the sobs settle down. I barely notice when his phone buzzes and he pulls it out of his jeans to read the message.

"I'm really sorry to have to do this, but Major Riley wants me to report to the FBI building immediately."

I nod, my smile meager. He has the same dedication to his job as my dad. When he heaves himself up with a sigh, an idea pops in my head. Sitting around at home is poisonous for me at the moment, so I might as well be proactive in finding out what Mitch's game was. Since I have no clue how to contact either Norton or Citadel, my only lead is Sad Eyes, who is hopefully still at the hospital. She could at least tell me why her and her husband's picture were in that envelope. It would be a start. Everything else will hopefully fall into place after that.

"Could you maybe give me a ride into Manhattan?" I ask. That way, I won't blow half my money on parking and can take the subway home.

"Sure. Where do you need to go?"

"Mount Sinai Hospital." I stare at my bare feet. "Just let me grab my shoes."

"I'll be waiting."

His eyes linger on my top just a little too long for my comfort before his attention returns to the phone. It takes me a second to realize that the summer dress has too much cleavage. Better change my clothes as well. With everything that has been happening, the last thing I need is someone hitting on me.

# Chapter 21

Even before my assault, hospitals had always given me the creeps. It's a place I connect with pain and suffering—my broken wrist when I fell off the swing set, stitches after a barbed-wire fence tore open my scalp the day I decided to drive down the hill behind our house in a go-cart at breakneck speed, and my tonsillectomy when I was eleven. I can't count the tears I shed on my dad's shoulder in the emergency room—the only place where even he didn't mind the open display of emotions.

When I step through the sliding door of Mount Sinai Hospital just around the time of the afternoon shift change, the familiar smell of disinfectant gives me an instant headache. The wound on my neck throbs for good measure, probably trying to remind me that this is a bad idea. Sad Eyes will be guarded by the FBI, if they haven't taken her statement, and having to explain to Dinkle why I'm seeking her out will be a challenge. They might even arrest me right on the spot for trying to tamper with a witness. That is, if I find her room.

I try to produce a concerned look as I approach the information desk, deciding at the last second that I'd better pretend to be a relative. That way, they will have to give me her room number.

"Hi, I'm looking for my cousin, Nina Humphrey. She was admitted to the ICU on Saturday night."

The nurse pecks away on her keyboard with a pleasant enough expression until the smile fades from her face. A wrinkle spreads across her forehead. "I'm sorry, but there's a block on her file. You have to go to the main administration office on the second floor. They might be able to help you."

My smile is thin. Best-case scenario, they will want to see some form of ID, but they will, in all likelihood, call over to the

FBI to check if they can release the information. Not really a good option either way if I want to keep my visit a secret.

Chewing my lip, I ponder what I should do next. Mount Sinai has over a thousand beds, so just aimlessly wandering around in the hopes of finding her doesn't work either. I jump when a small child starts to fuss next to me. My nerves are shot. If I want to come up with any coherent idea, I will need to calm down. A nice cup of tea is just the ticket for that.

I follow the signs for the cafeteria, which is packed with an early dinner crowd. With a sigh, I get in line. Slowly, I edge my way forward toward the beverage counter. My mind keeps drifting to my picture in Mitch's filing cabinet. No one in my father's team was innocent, but he alone took the fall. How Mitch found out about my involvement is even more puzzling. There were never any allegations against me.

"Aeree, is that you?"

I spin around, almost dropping my tray in the process. I halfway expect to find a cop behind me, but it's just Norton. My heart is nevertheless bouncing around in my chest and I have to take a couple of deep breaths to calm my trembling knees.

"Norton. What are you doing here?"

"I work here."

I give him a good once-over. He's wearing the standard white doctor's coat, a name tag with "Dr. N. Garrett" announcing to the world that he is a legit employee of the hospital.

"Sorry, I didn't know that dermatologists work in hospitals. I thought you had a private practice."

"I went to school here and never left. May I ask what you're doing here?"

A tingle warms my cheeks. He's caught me like a little girl who has a candy bar before dinner. "I'm here to visit Nina

Humphrey." When his face remains even, I quickly add, "Not sure if you heard, but she saved my life, so I want to thank her."

"Oh, I didn't know. The FBI asked me a bunch of questions about you."

"Like what?"

"If you had a fight with Mitch or whether your relationship seemed strained. That sort of thing."

I drop my voice when I realize that the guy behind Norton is staring at us. "And what did you tell them?"

"The truth. That you were perfectly happy and seemed to have had a great marriage." He turns around to glance at the guy who is straining to listen in on our conversation. "Let's finish this at a table. I'm on my break, so I have a few minutes."

His hand comes to rest on my lower back as he guides me to a lane specifically reserved for hospital staff. Five minutes later, I have my tea and join him at a small table by the window. Even though the glass is thick, the heat still radiates against it. I catch a glimpse of the sky. A few heavy clouds have moved in. Add the pressing humidity, and a thunderstorm is imminent.

"So how are you holding up?" I ask Norton.

"It's been tough. I miss George." Wetness glistens in his eyes. "I was going crazy at home, so I decided that work might be a good distraction. So far so good." His smile is weak. "What about you?"

"Not good. Mitch has always been my rock in the sea, so it has been a struggle." The words are painful and stab into my soul. Where did our marriage go wrong? We had been so happy.

I sip my tea, pondering how to bring up the picture of him and George I found in the envelope. After all, I can't just blurt out that Mitch claimed the two committed murder in the second degree.

"Not sure why the FBI was so focused on your marriage, but I overheard Citadel telling them that your husband mentioned to her that he was seeking a divorce." He grimaces when I almost choke on my tea. "Thought you ought to know."

The photographs are temporarily forgotten. "He did what?" The revelation is like a slap in my face. Mitch hardly knew Citadel and was not the kind of person who discussed personal matters with anyone he didn't consider a friend. Why on earth would he confide in her?

"Well, that was her statement anyways." His pager buzzes in his pocket, and he pulls it out to check it. "I'm sorry, but I have to run." He quickly takes a huge bite of his sandwich, chewing vigorously. The words "it was nice to see you again" are barely audible with his mouth stuffed to the brim.

"Wait, there's something I need to discuss with you." I kick myself for missing the opportunity to shed some light on the photographs.

With one big swallow, he forces down the food. "Maybe later. I really have to go." Another huge bite disappears in his mouth before he takes off.

I curse under my breath as he vanishes in the masses. I don't even know which floor he works on, though finding him will be significantly easier than tracking down Sad Eyes. This brings me back to my problem at hand. I could call the hospital and request her room, and if she picks up, I could ask for her room number. Of course, there's always a chance she doesn't want to see me and she'll tell Dinkle about the call. There must be a safer way.

The memory of when my dad was in the hospital floods my mind. He had been shot and almost died, but the army made a big fuss about his whereabouts since the mission was super secretive. It took my mom three days to get us security clearance. When she finally did, they had moved him out of the ICU. I feared they would make us jump through more hoops before we could see him, but the nurse was surprisingly cooperative and gave us his new room number without a hassle. Maybe this will work here, too. I could approach an ICU nurse and innocently inquire about Sad Eyes.

With newfound determination, I finish my tea and head toward the elevator. A directory is posted on the wall right above the call button and I easily find the entry I'm looking for. The ICU is on the sixth floor in the east wing of the hospital. The ride up takes forever—we seem to stop on every floor. With every *ding* and sliding of the doors, my heart pounds a little harder. Deep down I know I'm not supposed to be here. What if Sad Eyes squeals on me or refuses to see me? God only knows what they've been telling her about me. But then again, she saved my life. Visiting her to thank her is only logical.

My palms are clammy and a few sweat pearls roll down my back when I finally walk along the corridor toward the nurses' desk. In comparison to the other floors, this one is rather quiet, my steps echoing off the walls. The disinfectant smell is now so overpowering that my insides curl. When sudden dizziness overcomes me, my intuition screams for me to walk away. As usual, I choose to ignore the nagging feeling. This is something I *have* to do.

I beam at the nurse behind the desk, who returns a professional smile. "Hi, I'm here to see my cousin, Nina Humphrey. My aunt said she is in room eight, I believe." My eyelashes flutter innocently as the lie flows effortlessly from my lips. I could be totally off with the room number, but it's a risk I'm willing to take.

She checks something on her clipboard. "They moved her. She's now on the third floor, room thirty-four ten."

I high five myself in my mind, amazed that the plan actually worked. After a mumbled thank you, I'm on my way. My steps are much lighter. With any luck, Dinkle already took her statement and had just not bothered to remove the block from her file. Otherwise, getting past the FBI agents that she undoubtedly planted in front of Sad Eyes's door will be the next challenge.

The third floor is crowded with visitors, most of them dressed in nice business attire, who probably came straight after work to check on their loved ones. With my two-hundred-dollar designer jeans and flowery blouse, I scrape by. I stroll along the corridors, my eyes scanning the numbers on the door. When I reach 3406, I turn toward the patient sign next to the door, studying it like it's the most interesting thing. Out of the corner of my eye, I assess the situation. No cops or anyone who appears to work for the FBI. It's now or never.

My feet weigh a ton as I drag them across the floor. Every part of me screams to run. There's no rational explanation, just this prickling sensation under my scalp, like if ants had built a nest in my brain. It gives me an eerie feeling that something bad is about to happen.

The door is ajar. I only hesitate for a second before my fingers wrap around the handle and slowly push it open. When I soak in the sight in front of me, my breath is caught in my throat. My first instinct is to scream for help, but only hot air escapes when I open my mouth. All I can do is stare at the man in front of me and the gun that is clutched in his hand.

"Come on in and close the door." He flashes me a pleasant smile. "You've saved me a trip to Staten Island."

# Chapter 22

It takes me a moment to place the man. If it wasn't for the gun, he would look just like a regular doctor in his white overcoat. Then it clicks—he's the guy who was with Harley and Bobby at the cabin. With his hair gelled back and that wide smile, he no longer resembles a thug.

When I don't flinch, he points the gun at the center of my chest. That finally gets me to push the door closed with my foot. Instinctively, I take a few steps back as his smile turns vicious.

"Look, no one needs to get hurt. I just want to ask you girls a few questions."

Sad Eyes's face is an exact reflection of the sudden tingling fear that spreads along my spine. I swallow down the big lump of apprehension, clearing my throat a few times to get my voice under control.

"Why are you pointing a gun at me then?"

"That's just for you to understand that your cooperation is imperative." He glances at Sad Eyes, shifting his body in a way that he could fire at her if she doesn't play along. "Now, you two were the only ones who had contact with Julie Flynn after that sniper showed up. Who took her backpack?"

"I did." Sad Eyes's words are muffled as she retreats farther under the blanket.

"And where is it now?"

"Dunno. We left it at the cabin. I'm pretty sure the FBI got it."

"Did you take anything out of it?"

"No."

The man zooms in on me. "What about you? Did you take anything out?"

"Just the phone." My arms fold in front of my chest as I fight the urge to rock back and forth on my heels like I often do when I'm nervous; I'm determined to hide my inner unrest. My father always told me that panic in a situation like this is deadly. You wait, watch, and then you strike. "It would help if you told us what you're looking for."

He ignores my curiosity and pulls a silencer from his coat pocket. "Why do I get the feeling that you're lying to me?" A small smile sneaks on his lips as he slowly screws the metal tube onto the barrel of the gun.

The spit in my mouth dries up as I edge backward until my back collides with the door. Again, I want to scream, but only a wheeze drifts from my throat. Sad Eyes has crawled to the farthest side of the bed, her eyes as wide as saucers.

When the door is pushed open with force, I'm thrown forward, stumbling over my own feet when I try to regain my balance. I focus on the gun that is approaching fast. Clawing my fingers into the jacket of the man, I fall, bringing him with me.

The low *pop* of the discharging bullet cracks like thunder in my ears. The expected searing pain doesn't materialize and I realize that I didn't get hit. My knees are still wobbly as I scramble back to my feet. I'm just about to kick the man in his stomach when a shiny metal object hits him on the side of his head. An unidentifiable but smelly liquid gushes over him before his eyes lose focus. He drops to the ground.

It takes me a second for the situation to sink in. Sad Eyes is staring down on him with this weird smile, her fingers clutched around the rim of a metal container.

"Is that a bedpan?" I ask.

She nods. "The nurse didn't get around to picking it back up." Her cheeks are slightly flushed, but I can't tell if it's anger or embarrassment.

I almost snort when I realize that our attacker is now soaked in pee. My head snaps around when someone clears his throat by the door. Norton is standing on the threshold, his pale face dumbfounded. I scan his body for a sign of injury, but the bullet must have missed him.

"What's happening?" His voice is shrill. "Why are they after us?"

I quirk an eyebrow. "They?"

"Yes." He glances over his shoulder before fully stepping into the room, the door closing behind him. "When I got back from break, the dude who tied us up at the cabin was waiting by the nurses' station on my floor. There was this other creepy guy with him and I got scared. At first, I was going to call the cops, but then I thought I'd better talk to Nina to see if she knows what's going on."

"Well, I don't know, and I'm sure not gonna hang around to find out." Sad Eyes is fidgeting with the Band-Aid that holds her IV in place. "That FBI bitch who interrogated me insinuated that I had something to do with Kendall's murder, so I doubt she'll believe that I knocked this guy out in self-defense. I'm out of here."

I have to agree with her as I gaze at the man on the floor. Knowing my luck, the FBI will blame me for his injuries.

"You can't just leave." Norton's fingers run through his hair. He looks like he's about to lose it.

"Why not? I feel much better." A stubborn pout curls Sad Eyes's lips. She is trying to pull the IV out of her hand when Norton stops her.

"At least let me do this. I'm a doctor." He picks up a small gauze pad from the nightstand and covers the needle before pulling it out. "Here, press this on there."

She steps around the man on the ground to get to the small closet holding her clothes. With fleeting fingers, she starts to dress, her thumb holding the gauze in place as much as possible.

Norton squats down next to the unconscious man, who stirs when he presses two fingers against his neck. "He'll wake up soon." Next, he inspects the gash on the side of his head. "You hit him right in the temple, which knocked him out. That was pretty lucky."

"Luck had nothing to do with it." She zips up her pants before starting on the buttons of her shirt. "My husband showed me how to immobilize a person with a few concise blows."

"What I meant was that you were lucky that you didn't bust an artery." Norton squints at her with a scowl. "You could have killed him."

"Well, he was just about to shoot Aeree, so what was I supposed to do?" The tone of her voice is nonchalant, almost indifferent. "Besides, he's in a hospital. What better place to sustain a head injury?"

I almost grin at her logic, but Norton is not amused. He mumbles something under his breath as he rises but doesn't argue further. Sad Eyes finishes tying her shoe laces before gazing at me expectantly. "Ready?"

"Where are we going?"

"Dunno, but I want to get some distance between us and those guys before ending up with a bullet in my head."

I nod. "Coming, Norton?"

His face is full of struggle, but he finally grumbles an okay. He probably figures that he can always run to the cops if things get too complicated. For the moment, I'm undecided what I should do, though I don't trust the FBI enough to ask for their help. Getting away from the hospital seems the best under the circumstances.

Norton peeks into the hallway. "All clear."

Strolling toward the elevator, we try to blend in with the other leaving visitors. My foot taps softly on the floor while we wait; I curse myself for leaving the gun behind. It could have come in handy, though if the cops find a firearm on me, they will bust me for felony possession.

A low *ding* announces the arrival of the elevator and I step forward. When the doors slide back, I stare straight into Harley's face. Recognition flashes in his eyes as his hand automatically reaches backward. I'm sure he has a weapon.

"Run!" I shout, turning on my heels. Pushing through a group of people, I head toward the exit sign over the entrance to the stairway. Hopefully, he won't open fire in the middle of a crowded hospital floor.

The beating sound of my shoes on the hard concrete echoes in my ears as I fly down the steps. Another person is right behind me. When I glance back at the first landing, I notice Sad Eyes on my heels. Norton is also keeping up.

"Marcel, they're taking the stairs," Harley shouts. "Try to catch them in the lobby."

Since there's no response, I suspect that Marcel took the elevator when Harley started his pursuit and they are communicating by cell or walkie-talkie. I focus on my rapid descent, my fingers sliding along the railing to keep my balance as I jump from step to step. My heart is pounding hard in my chest, the vein in my temple pulsing. The booming footsteps are as loud as a herd of trampling elephants. I count the landings, my legs pushing themselves faster and faster to get to the bottom of the stairs. At some point, the pounding of my heart beats in unison with my pumping muscles. By the time I reach the lobby, every piece of clothing sticks to my skin and my body aches in protest.

The elevator doors slide open as I sprint across the large reception area toward the exit leading to Fifth Avenue. My heart sinks when I meet Marcel's gaze. He's just about to block my way but freezes in the last second, allowing me to pass. His eyes burn into my back until I dart through the revolving doors. I jump down the steps and turn north on Fifth Avenue, only slowing down when I reach a red light at the next intersection. My heart beats so fast that I fear it will break through my chest.

I double over, trying to slow my rapid breath and wait for Sad Eyes and Norton to catch up. "Where to?"

"Let's stop a taxi."

I only grabbed a few dollars of the money Eltas gave me when I left home, afraid I would be tempted to spend it all in a desperate moment of depression. Half of that was wiped out in the hospital's cafeteria. "I don't think I have enough money."

"And all my stuff is in my locker," Norton says.

Sad Eyes curses. "I only have five bucks, which doesn't get us far. The cabbie will call the cops if we can't pay him."

Out of the corner of my eye, I notice Harley pushing through the crowds with Marcel on his tail.

"Let's take the subway."

The stop is only two blocks up. By the time we reach the platform, Marcel and Harley have stopped their pursuit. It's odd, but maybe they decided to check on their friend before regrouping. What was Marcel even doing there? I thought he was watching Eltas, but then I remember his conversation with Kelsey in the kitchen where she said that he and Harley would be working undercover together. That must be it. I wonder if Dinkle knows that her informant is chasing her witnesses.

"Should we go downtown?" I ask when the 6 train enters the station.

"Well, I don't know about you, but I'm going to the FBI. This train goes down to City Hall, and the Federal Plaza is just a few blocks away." Norton juts his chin at us with attitude, yet his face betrays him. He's scared shitless.

Sad Eyes hesitates but gets on the train after Norton. Not wanting to be left behind, I hop on just before the doors slide closed. A cold stream of the air-conditioning hits me and my teeth begin to chatter despite the adrenaline that still pulses through my veins.

"I have friends in the village who might be able to help me," Sad Eyes says as she plops down on a seat. "Like I said, I'm not going to the FBI."

Our eyes meet and I find nothing but questions. I have no answers—I'm still utterly confused about what I should do. Though I don't want to ask Dinkle for help, the idea of Harley chasing me sends goosebumps all over my body. If he catches up with me, who knows what he will do. Even Marcel won't be able to help me. It was apparent from the chase that Harley is calling the shots.

All of a sudden, I have the urge to call River. He might have an idea how I can get myself out of this new mess. "Does anyone have a phone?"

Norton grimaces. "That's in my locker, too."

"The FBI took mine." Sad Eyes stares out of the window with a dark expression on her face. "They said I would get it back once they finished with their investigation, whatever that means."

Sounds familiar. I stroke the bridge of my nose, fighting an oncoming headache. The adrenaline slowly seeps out of me, leaving heavy throbbing bones behind. Panic clenches my chest. Maybe I should take my chances with the FBI and hope they'll eventually figure out that I had nothing to do with Mitch's death.

"So why does the FBI think you were involved in your husband's murder?" I ask Sad Eyes.

She glares at me. After what seems like an eternity, she finally responds. "I think I told you that I intended to leave Kendall. We had a prenup that would have left me with nothing, so naturally, they assume I wanted to protect my money. I mean, I can't blame them. If I was a cop, I would probably think the same, especially..."

Somehow, I can't shake the feeling that this has to do with the photo I found. I'm just about to ask her when the train pulls into the Brooklyn Bridge Station.

"It's the final stop. We need to get off."

We fall behind a large group of tourists who turn toward the City Hall exit. When I get to the bottom of the stairs, I freeze. Marcel is casually leaning against the wall at the top, playing with a cigarette butt in his mouth. His eyes scan the faces of the passengers walking up the steps. Harley is nowhere in sight, but without a doubt, he has taken up post by the steps on the other side of the platform.

Sad Eyes, Norton, and I take cover behind a wall.

"What are we gonna do?"

My gaze wanders along the platform for an emergency exit, but the only way out are the two guarded staircases. We are trapped, unless...

An idea forms in my head as my eyes follow the leaving train. Mitch and I took a Transit Museum tour once when we first moved to Staten Island, and one of the highlights was an abandoned subway station not far from our current location. This will be a good hiding place until we can come up with a plan.

"This way." I point at the dark tunnel from which a heated gust of wind floats onto the platform.

"Are you crazy?" Sad Eyes gazes at me with horror. "We can't just jump onto the tracks. We'll get hit by the next train."

"There's an old subway station not that far in. We can hide there until we figure out what to do."

Norton and Sad Eyes exchange a glance. He nods. "I agree with Aeree. We need to drop off the radar for a while until those guys stop looking for us." His eyes travel to the camera attached to the ceiling that is angled at the tracks. "But what about the Transit Authority? Won't they send someone after us if we jump onto the tracks?"

"I think if we drop down all the way at the end, we're in a blind spot." At least, it looks that way and it's a risk I'm willing to take.

We scurry to the southern end of the platform. Norton jumps first, helping Sad Eyes down onto the tracks. I toss one more look at the camera, but it almost appears to face away. I get down in a sitting position before pushing myself off with both hands. When I hit solid ground, the dull ache from the impact resonates in my feet and ankles. I bend my knees, bouncing slightly to prevent the pain from spreading up my legs.

I'm the first one in the tunnel. Despite my confident steps, my legs are heavy, as if my bones were filled with cement. My whole attention is fixed on the dimly lit tracks to ensure I won't trip; I don't even notice that I'm torturing my lip until I taste blood. We need to make sure to take the turn that the 6 train is using or we'll end up at Fulton Street—that is, if the next train doesn't crush us first. The turn is not far and I keep to the right when the tunnel forks.

After we walk about half a mile, the tracks bend sharply in front of us. I know that the old abandoned City Hall Station is built right into the curve. Even today, the beauty of it takes my breath away. Fifteen tiled arches support the ceiling, which is dominated by panels of skylights. The dangling chandeliers, burning like bright beacons in the darkness, cover the platform and tracks with a mystical glow. It's almost like we have been transported into the past.

"What is this place?" Norton gazes up with an open mouth.

"It's an old station. The length of the platform didn't support the modern trains, so it was decommissioned sometime in the forties. My husband and I took a tour here once, so that's how I knew it was here."

Norton's hands work like a ladder when he heaves me up and I manage to pull myself onto the platform. Sad Eyes is next, and after some pulling and pushing, she ends up next to me, panting.

"Help me," I hiss when she doesn't move. I'm flat on my stomach, my arms reaching for Norton. "Take each of our hands and we'll pull you up."

It sounds easier than it is. We freeze for a moment when the tracks vibrate as a train passes by at the fork. It has been at least ten minutes since we left the station and the next train can't be far out.

"Those tracks are abandoned, right?" Norton stares up at me, sweat pearling above his lip. It's stuffy and the heat in the still air is stifling.

"Well, the 6 train passes through here to loop back to the Brooklyn Bridge Station, but there shouldn't be one for a few more minutes."

"Does it stop?"

"No, it doesn't stop."

"Fuck." His palms are sweaty when our hands interlock.

Sad Eyes breathes heavily beside me, her face contorted in panic.

We both pull and Norton tries to get traction on the wall with his shoes, but his soles keep slipping. He seems to weigh a ton. "Pull!" I shout. With gritted teeth, I gather all my strength, trying to lift him up. My arm threatens to tear from its socket and we don't seem to be gaining an inch.

More vibrating disturbs the tunnel. This time the sound of the rattling wheels on metal is closer to us. The screeching brakes of a slowing train overpowers the yaps of my wheezing breath. Sweat dribbles down my temples and into my eyes, my long fringe obscuring most of my vision. It takes all my effort to force my focus back on the task.

Inch by inch, we heave Norton up, but my strength is dwindling with every second. My arm burns like hell. Sad Eyes is quietly cursing next to me. When I glance at her, her face is beet red, the sweat practically seeping from every pore. She won't be able to hold on much longer.

The rattling of the metallic wheels is getting louder, shooting a boost of adrenaline into my bloodstream. With newfound strength, I keep pulling. We're making progress, but is it enough? The way the station is curved, the train driver won't notice us until it's too late.

The tracks are now vibrating heavily. Norton's eyes are filled with deadly fear as the tips of his shoes scrape against the wall. The headlights of the approaching train are already dancing on the tiled walls when he finally finds traction. His body catapults upward. With his chest almost fully on the platform, we are able to heave him up the rest of the way.

The screeching of brakes signals that the train is just about to reach the station. Usually, the train just whips through here without stopping, but if the driver sees us, he will call it in. My eyes dart around until they fall onto the stairs leading up to the mezzanine.

"Duck inside the stairwell," I shout over the noise of the approaching train.

Lunging forward, I close the gap between the edge of the platform and the dark shadow of the wall with a few long strides. Sad Eyes is right behind me. Just before the searching light of the train illuminates the spot where we were just seconds ago, Norton awakes from his daze and dives into hiding. The train rushes by.

When the noise dies down, I wipe the sweat from my forehead. "Boy, that was so close."

"Yeah." Norton is pale as a ghost, his hands shaking as he rakes his fingers through his hair. "I swear, I thought I was gonna die."

"Well, you didn't." I lower myself onto the dusty ground, my back resting against the cool wall. My shirt is drenched and I finally manage to push my long fringe out of my eyes.

Sad Eyes puffs next to me. "So, what do we do now?"

"I think if we want to get out of this mess unscathed, we need to be truthful with each other." I pull out the photographs that I had stuck into the back pocket of my jeans. "I found these pictures in my husband's study, and I think all this might be connected." I place them in front of me on the floor, watching how both Norton's and Sad Eyes's faces tense.

"On the back, there is mention of a crime." I turn my picture around. "Why don't I go first?"

# Chapter 23

Neither of them can hold my gaze when I'm finished with my story. I didn't omit much, just enough to ensure that the rest of my father's unit won't get into trouble if one of them decides to squeal. My confession leaves me naked and exposed; once again I realize that my revenge didn't offer the expected release. I stooped onto an even lower level than my rapists, which makes me in no way better than them.

"I guess I'll go next." Sad Eyes turns her own picture and that of her husband's over. The ugly words *Murder in the Second Degree* stare back at us in the dim light of the old subway station like a grotesque reminder of how life can change in the blink of an eye.

"My husband had always had a really bad temper, and when he got angry, he retaliated with violence. It was his answer to everything and it got worse when he was drunk. When he was in one of his moods, he'd smack you just for looking at him."

A shudder runs through her body, and I can only imagine how much she suffered in their relationship.

"One night, we went to this bar. It had been my birthday a few days before, but I couldn't get time off work, so we waited to go out that Friday. The place was packed when we got there—some college kids were celebrating their graduation. The mood was great though. One of the college guys was paying for rounds and the liquor was flowing even faster than usual."

Thickness sneaks into her voice and I squeeze her arm to encourage her to continue.

She sucks in a deep breath, forcing herself to push on. "I didn't even see what this guy did to Kendall, but it couldn't have been much—he probably just nudged him with his elbow on the way to the bathroom. Kendall exploded and got right in his face, yelling that he was going to beat the crap out of him. The guy's friends came to his rescue, and together with the pub's owner, Kendall was tossed out into the street. I guess being humiliated like that pushed him over the edge."

Her eyes fill with tears and she blinks a few times to prevent them from falling.

"I tried to convince him to go home, but he wouldn't listen. We waited in the truck for hours. Before we went out, he had stopped by the liquor store and gotten himself some whiskey. I'm not sure how much he drank, but it must've been close to a bottle. All I remember is this horrific smell of alcohol on his breath. I had to roll the window down, just so I wouldn't gag. I think the cold air made it worse."

Her wet eyes are fixed on the tiles behind me; she's back in that moment in time. The pained expression on her face makes me cringe.

"At some point, the group of college kids appeared and most of them got into this big minivan and took off. As fate would have it, the guy who bumped into Kendall was last, fumbling in his pockets in front of his car. Kendall jumped out of the truck and immediately took a swing at him." She sobs. "The guy was so stunned, he didn't even try to run or fight back. He just stood there with this bewildered expression on his face. In that moment, he reminded me of my little brother. It was horrible."

I let her sob for a moment, unsure if I should rub her back or console her in any other way. Norton makes the decision for me when he wraps his arm around her and pulls her against his shoulder. She cries into his shirt, drying off her face with the sleeve of her jacket when the sobs finally die down.

"Did Kendall kill him?" It's a rhetorical question—the picture wouldn't call Kendall a murderer if the kid survived.

"He just kept punching him, and at some point, the guy went down, but that wasn't good enough for my husband. He kicked him while on the ground with his heavy work boots." Sad Eyes's face twists in agony. "And I mean, over and over again, sparing not even one part of the dude's body despite his cries. Kendall only took a step back when he stopped moving. There was so much blood." More tears roll down her cheeks. "His face wasn't even recognizable anymore, it was that bad."

Her head drops against her thighs and she lets out a low growl. "Coward me didn't even try to stop him once. I was scared he'd turn on me, so I just stood idly by and watched how he beat a man to death."

"Did the police investigate?"

"Yep, they sure did. Kendall had paid for our drinks with his credit card, so the police tracked us down the next day and questioned us. Kendall claimed he didn't know what they were talking about. At that point, I kept my mouth shut. My dad's been in and out of jail his whole life, so he always taught me that any statement just helps the cops to make their case. They arrested Kendall right on the spot. I was relieved and even considered testifying against him, but then"—she lets her breath escape with a heavy sigh—"I got this visit from his brother. He told me that they would kill me if I didn't swear that Kendall was home with me after the pub. His exact words were, 'We'll crush you like a little cockroach.' I was terrified."

"So you went to the cops and lied for him?" Despite my best effort, a slight hint of judgment laces the words.

She nods. "I know it was a mistake, but I was just so goddamn scared. Kendall's family is all the same—violent and with a bad temper—even his sisters smack their husbands around. That's why I didn't want anyone to know I was leaving him. I was gonna move away and start fresh under a new name."

I pinch the bridge of my nose, frustrated by her whole ordeal. No matter what, she could've never come out of the situation unscathed. If she had not lied for Kendall, his family would have probably killed her to eliminate the only witness, but the guilt has been eating at her for setting a monster free. It's something she will have to live with for the rest of her life, just as the dead eyes of the gang leader I shot will always haunt me.

Though I don't really want to hear any more bad life stories, I turn to Norton. "What about you?"

For a second, he hesitates and puffs his cheeks out, then he exhales through tight lips. "I also killed someone, but I'm not sorry. You can judge me all you want, but I would do it again in a heartbeat. That guy deserved it."

"What happened?"

"As you know, I'm gay. In college, there was this guy who constantly harassed me, humiliating me in public with constant remarks that I was a faggot and asking me if my butt was sore. He taunted me with these sick jokes and his friends ate it up. It got so bad that I was scared to leave my dorm room, didn't even want to go to class anymore. I had a stomachache all the time and couldn't sleep, and when I left my room, I snuck around campus like a ghost, constantly afraid I'd bump into him. In hindsight, I should have transferred, but I was on a full scholarship and it wasn't that easy."

"Man, I really hate those types of homophobic bigots," Sad Eyes mutters.

"At some point, I had had enough. I was already a senior, majoring in biology, and I've always had an obsession with poisons. As luck would have it, the guy was a diabetic. One day, I snuck into his room and replaced the insulin in one of his bottles with tetrodotoxin. It's a drug that, if injected under the skin, kills a person through respiratory failure and cardiac arrest. In an autopsy, it's usually missed unless a medical examiner is specifically looking for it. It worked like a charm and three days later, my tormentor was dead."

I frown. "How did they even suspect you?" The way he described it sounded like the perfect murder. How would Mitch even know about it if the guy didn't die under suspicious circumstances?

"I never thought they would actually analyze the leftover liquid in his insulin bottle, but for whatever reason, they did. The whole thing came to light and his death was ruled a homicide. The cops investigated and they questioned me. Since I never had had as much as a parking ticket, I was in way over my head—made some stupid remarks that got them suspicious. They arrested me and I spent a couple of weeks in jail, but the grand jury ruled there wasn't enough evidence to charge me, so they had to let me go."

He got away with murder in the end. Though I ultimately disagree with his choice, I can see how constant bullying like that could push someone over the edge. One year, I attended school in this small town in Montana when my father was training for a special mission, and the kids constantly called me a "chink." Once I figured out what it meant, I was devastated and hated my dad for forcing me to go to that school. It was three long months with daily tears and lots of stomachaches.

"What about George?" Sad Eyes asks through the sudden silence. "Do you know why his picture is here?"

Norton's lips curl into a painful grimace. "I actually met George in the county lockup. He was accused of blowing up his house—with his abusive stepfather in it. In the end, the cops couldn't prove it wasn't an accident, so he was never formally charged. They released him after seventy-two hours, but when I got out, he was there, waiting for me. In that moment, I knew there would never be anyone else in my life. I guess you can call it delayed love at first sight."

My heart breaks for him. Something wonderful had sprung from their misery, something that was destroyed by the bullet of a sniper. Sad Eyes rubs his shoulders. "I'm so sorry all this shit happened to you, Norton."

I'm just about to agree when my ears pick up a metallic *clank* on the mezzanine. Muffled words drift our way.

"That was a goddamn rat," Harley says.

"Are you sure they're even down here, man?" Marcel's voice is as flat as cardboard. He sounds bored.

"Positive. I'll check out if there's an exit back there. You go down onto the platform."

I exchange glances with Norton and Sad Eyes. "We should hide." Since Marcel works for the FBI, he won't kill us, but if he is good at his job, he will find a way to keep his cover intact. I don't want to face Harley and risk him touching me in any way, even with Marcel around.

"What about the tracks?" Sad Eyes whispers.

Norton shakes his head with vigor. "No way I'm gonna jump on those tracks again. That's practically asking for death." He hops down the few steps to get onto the platform. "Hey, look at this."

Reluctantly, I follow. He stands next to a pile of rubble from a demolished bench, holding a short plank in his hand. Now would be a good time to reveal Marcel's true identity, but before I can tell Norton that he is not a threat, steps echo on the stairs.

"Aeree, duck," Sad Eyes hisses, diving behind the pile of rubble. "Make sure to get him good, Norton."

I stand frozen in place, my mouth opening for a warning shout until I realize that this could alert Harley. Like in a movie winding down in slow motion, Marcel turns the corner just as Norton's arm rises. The plank comes down hard.

Marcel's reflexes are impeccable, and both his arms shoot up, protecting his head and upper frame from the impact. "The fuck." Scolding eyes land on me. "What're you doin', girl? Didn't you tell them who I am?"

"Sorry." I grimace as he rubs his shoulder with a twisted face. "Didn't get a chance to."

Norton's glare darts from Marcel to me and back. "What's going on?"

"He's FBI."

Sad Eyes peeks around the pile of rubble. "You don't look like FBI."

"Yeah, I get that a lot." Marcel's arms drop, his eyes scanning the platform. "Okay, guys, if y'all want to get out of here, do what I tell ya. Harley and I will disappear in just a moment, but there's a whole group of men looking for you. The only safe place is at the FBI headquarters."

"How do we know you're not trying to set us up?" Sad Eyes glares at him with challenge. "How do you even know Aeree?"

"She's my neighbor. Well, technically, she's my friend's neighbor, but that doesn't really matter now." Marcel's hands run over his clean-shaven head. "Word's on the street that one of you got a data stick from Julie Flynn, and the guys Harley works for want to get it at any cost."

"Why?"

"Let's just say it's worth a lot of money, at least if you have terrorist connections, so don't get any ideas." His face is grim as he studies each of us. I shrink back under his hard eyes.

"These guys have an army of mercenaries at their disposal and they will hunt you until they get what they want. I've been actively trying to work against them, but there's not much more

I can do. The big boss is already getting suspicious, and only keeps his mouth shut since he thinks I'm friends with Harley."

"Is that Eltas?"

Marcel's nod is barely noticeable and his confirmation crushes the little bit of doubt I had after talking to River. Eltas has truly crossed over to the bad guys.

"How is Harley involved?" Sad Eyes asks.

"He's an FBI informant, has worked with them for years. I know you guys might not be the biggest fans of the FBI, but they're the only ones who can help you. We need to get you safe, then we can figure out the rest."

"Sorry, but I don't trust Dinkle." Sad Eyes's lips curl with attitude. Judging from the stubborn frown on her forehead, she is not about to budge.

"Fair enough, then go to my boss. His name is Bill McCarthy. He runs the White-Collar Crimes Unit."

"I don't know—"

"Marcel, did you find anything?" Harley calls from the top of the steps.

"I have to go." Marcel's voice has dropped to a mere hiss. "Gimme your shirt." His fingers twitch as he points at Sad Eyes.

"My shirt?"

Harley's shoes click on the steps.

Marcel is now practically waving his arm. "Yes. Quickly."

Sad Eyes shakes out of her shirt and hands it to him with a dumbfounded expression. Luckily, she still has a thin top underneath or she'd be half naked. Marcel doesn't waste any time. He's already heading up the steps before one of us can shoot off another question.

"There's no one down there. I found the bitch's shirt with the tracker. That's why the GPS still shows this as their location."

"Fuck. What are we gonna do now?"

Marcel's response is drowned out by the echoing steps that fade the farther they get away from the platform.

When the air is still again, I sigh. "Thoughts?"

"I think that's a no-brainer," Norton says. "I've always suggested to go to the FBI."

Sad Eyes nods her agreement. "I guess we could give it a try with this McCarthy dude."

For once, I decide to go along with the majority. "Okay, let's do this."

It takes us a good half hour to find our way back to the surface. Pedestrians are staring when the manhole cover is pushed aside and we emerge on the sidewalk, but New Yorkers are used to odd sightings and no one questions us. After we find our bearings, we head north on Centre Street.

Norton rushes us along, his arms waving whenever we slow down. "Federal Plaza is just four blocks up."

My heart is pounding hard in my chest—are we really doing the right thing? Marcel could have set a trap to get us back into FBI custody. What if they arrest me? Under the right amount of pressure, Norton will easily crack and tell the cops everything he just learned about Sad Eyes and me. Not only will they charge me with first degree murder of the gang leader, but this will give them extra ammunition in their theory that I killed Mitch. They will claim I tried to silence him after discovering the files in his study.

Sad Eyes's steps become equally hesitant the closer we get to the FBI building. When we reach the south end of Foley Square, she stops without warning. "You two go ahead. I'll catch up with you later." Without affording us the benefit of another glance, she disappears in the masses of rush-hour pedestrians.

Norton's gaze is pleading, clearly screaming for me not to abandon him, too. My thoughts stray to Marcel and the few occasions I met him. So far, he's struck me as the trustworthy type, even if his methods seem unconventional at times. With heavy legs, I trot behind Norton. It's one of those moments when my rational mind is not aligned with my instincts. The worst part is that I can't even figure out which is which.

We are just walking along the African Burial Ground Memorial when Norton face-plants next to me. I suck in a breath as I stare at the blood soaking his hair. With all the noises of the city, I didn't even hear a shot. The scream of a woman next to me tears me from my daze. I spin around. The light of the laser range finder is invisible to me, but the sensation still prickles right in the center of my forehead. I squeeze my eyes shut, bracing myself for the end.

# Chapter 24

My father has always insisted that the reason why kids survive in a war zone is that they instinctively know when to duck. Without a second thought, I do the same and drop to the ground. My knees take the full impact. I groan as pain soars in my thighs, yet my efforts are rewarded when dirt sprays up behind me. The sniper missed me by a good few inches.

I don't give him the chance to readjust, but sprint toward the memorial. The tall stone wall to the right provides excellent coverage. The cool granite against my back gives me comfort while random questions zoom around in my mind. How did the sniper track us down? Is he connected to Eltas and his friend Weston, or does he work against them? What could be on that data stick that is so important to pick us off one by one? The thoughts make my head buzz and I dig my fingernails into my palms to focus on the here and now.

Cops run up from everywhere as the screams around Norton's still body multiply. From the other end of the road, Dinkle and the guy with the long hair from the elevator sprint toward the memorial. His arms gesticulate wildly as he yells at someone through a walkie-talkie. If Norton hadn't been dead, the situation would have been comical.

"I want a chopper in the air now," he shouts. "Turn those buildings upside down. I want the bastard found who is picking off my witnesses." With a frustrated huff, he lowers the walkie-talkie.

Dinkle, who has been shooing away a nosy cluster of pedestrians, tosses him a dark look. "It's Norton Garrett. He never had a chance."

"So who's left?"

"Aeree Cahill and Nina Humphrey." Dinkle flashes her badge at two cops when they try to push her back with the crowd. "Oh, and Citadel Jamison, but we have a security detail on her."

"We should put an APB out for Cahill and Humphrey as persons of interest and take them into protective custody. If they get shot, the department could be sued."

Dinkle's face distorts like she just bit into some yucky food. "Let's first check in with Agent Brown and see if Williams or Cox was somehow involved. It'd be embarrassing..."

The rest of her words fade away as they stomp back the way they came. The cops and some other suits who probably work for their team have started to question the people huddled around Norton. A few are looking my way. Better disappear now before someone figures out I was with him. The way Dinkle cringed when she heard my name shows that she still believes I'm somehow involved. Besides, ever since she covered up Harley's attempted rape, she is on top of my shit list. I don't trust her as far as I can throw her. Now with Eltas involved, I wouldn't even put it past her to claim I'm working with him since we are friends.

Trying to appear casual, I fight my way against the oncoming stream of rubberneckers who are just itching to get a glimpse of the crime scene. Some people have their phones raised on extended selfie sticks. Since Norton was killed so close to the memorial, chances are someone caught it on camera. Dinkle will find out sooner or later that I was with him. Knowing her, she will probably conclude I lured him into a trap. No way I'm turning myself in to her, no matter what Marcel says.

At the next street corner, I step into a small shop that sells sandwiches and other snacks. Grabbing a bottle of water from the cooler, I ponder what I should do next. I could go home, but chances are that the FBI will come looking for me. River is probably still chasing Eltas or hanging out at the federal building, which is Dinkle territory. Besides, I don't even have his phone number. With the few dollars in my pocket, I can't check into a hotel, so all in all, I'm screwed. There is no one I can ask for help.

As I dig through my front jeans pocket to peel out a couple of dollar bills to pay for the water, my fingertips graze a folded piece of paper. It's Kelsey's number. I had stuck it in my pocket just before I left home in case I was pressed for a ride. Maybe I should finally take her up on her offer of help. Sure, she is FBI, but she works for a different division; maybe she even has the same boss as Marcel. Since I don't really have many options, I should chance it.

I hand the clerk two dollars and smile. "Hey, could I use your phone for a quick call?"

His eyebrows scrunch together in this over-my-dead-body kind of way.

"It's local and will honestly just take a minute."

"Okay, twenty bucks and the phone is yours for five minutes."

My jaw drops. "You want twenty dollars for a fricking phone call."

"Yeah, you know, my number will show on your friend's caller ID. Who guarantees me they aren't gonna call me back, trying to sell me something, or worse, harass me?" He shakes his head. "Sorry, lady, but this could be some ploy to get my number. I need to be compensated for that risk."

"Well, I don't have twenty dollars." I pull out a few crumpled bills. "Here, see."

"I guess you won't be getting my phone then." His smile is smug as his eyes move to the man standing right behind me. "Next."

My hands shake in rage as I snatch the water bottle off the counter. What an asshole.

Outside the shop, I twist off the cap of the bottle and take a few good swigs. The cold water soothes my nerves. What should I do now?

"Excuse me, but I couldn't help overhearing your conversation with that jerk."

I jump at the sudden voice behind me, my neck twisting to get a look at the owner. It's the other customer. His smile is friendly, and judging from his navy business suit with matching tie, he is gainfully employed and probably not out to harm me.

"Yeah, and?"

He holds out his phone. "Here, you can use mine."

For a second, I squint at him, wondering whether there is really that type of decency in this world, but then I decide not to look a gift horse in the mouth. I pull the paper with Kelsey's number out of my jeans and dial it quickly before he can change his mind.

She answers on the second ring, though her voice is thick as if she has been sleeping. "Hello."

"Sorry, Kelsey, it's Aeree Cahill. Is this a bad time?"

"No, no, not at all."

"I really need your help." I turn away from the guy who gave me his phone and drop my voice to avoid him eavesdropping as I fill her in about Norton and my Mitch-computer predicament. Though I try my best to keep my desperate panic under control, the more I talk, the more unrest settles in my bones. The whole situation is truly fucked up.

"So you need a place to stay?" she asks.

"Just for a couple of days, until I can figure things out." When she clears her throat, I fear she is going to remind me that she is FBI as well and bound by some bullshit restriction. "I'm not saying I don't want to cooperate with the FBI, just not now."

"I understand. People with criminal records tend to stay away from the police whenever they can. My husband is the same."

My eyebrows rise—I wonder what Finn did to get himself a criminal conviction. "And I need to figure out why my husband was lying to me." The words tremble as I fight the hitch in my throat. "It seems my life is falling apart at the seams and I don't know how to stop it. Please, Kelsey, I have no one else I can turn to. Will you help me?"

"Of course. I actually might have a solution for both your problems. When Finn and I were traveling, we met this guy who is a computer whiz. We stayed in touch with him over the years, and at the moment, he is studying for his PhD at Rutgers–New Brunswick in Jersey. If someone can break into your husband's laptop, it's him. He also lives alone and has a spare guest room, so that might work."

"Okay. But how do I get my husband's laptop?"

"I could go over to your house and get it, and then we could meet up at my friend's house. Just take a cab. That's the easiest. Oh, and make sure you don't tell him who I work for. He hates government agencies and will freak if he finds out."

"I don't have enough money for a cab. Besides, my house is locked."

"Don't worry. Sam can loan you the money when you get there and I'm sure my husband is able to pick your lock. Just tell me where the laptop is."

It all sounds so easy coming from her mouth and my resistance is dwindling. I glance at the owner of the phone. He has started to tap his foot and keeps staring at his watch. It's time to end this call.

I give Kelsey quick instructions on where to find the laptop before asking the phone guy for a pen to write down her friend's address. With a contrite smile, I hand him back his phone. "Thanks again and sorry it took so long."

"That's okay." He talks to my breasts instead of looking into my eyes. "You wanna grab a cup of coffee sometime?"

Figures he didn't just give me the phone to be a Good Samaritan. Everyone has an ulterior motive these days. "Sorry." I raise my hand, displaying my diamond wedding ring. "I'm married."

"Oh." His lips twist.

"But thanks again for the phone." Without giving him time to respond, I step to the curb and signal for a cab. He stares at my butt as I slide into the car. Pervert.

An hour later, the cabby drops me off in front of a town house on the corner of Neilson and Hiram in New Brunswick. His glare is deadly when I inform him that I have to run in to get the money. The meter clocked out at an impressive $103, and I can only pray that Kelsey's friend has a credit card to cover it. Repaying him will be a challenge for another day.

Sweat tickles the hairline at the nape of my neck when no one opens the door, even after I've rung the doorbell multiple times. I use my fists to pound on the door next. A few times, I glance at the cabby, whose face darkens with every second. I'm sure he is considering alternative options to be paid, including calling the cops.

Finally, there's shuffling behind the door.

"It's my friend Aeree," Kelsey whispers.

"Is she alone?"

"Guys, open up." My desperate plea gets the chain on the door removed. "I need money for the cab."

When the door opens a crack, two piercing green eyes gawk at me. They remind me of one of those murky ponds my father took me to in the woods when we were catching tadpoles.

"How much?"

I grimace. "Hundred and three dollars."

"Fuck. That's all the cash I have."

"Give her the money, Sam. This is an emergency."

"When do I get it back?"

"Soon, I promise."

"Finn said that the last time you guys borrowed money from me, and I still don't have it. That was two years ago."

"Sam, please."

He grumbles something inaudible under his breath.

"The driver takes credit cards," I add helpfully.

Sam's eyes narrow. "I don't own any credit cards. Did you know the government can track your moves and spending patterns with those?"

My smile is crooked. He seems a bit paranoid. No wonder Kelsey doesn't want him to know she is working for the FBI.

He disappears and a minute later, some crumpled bills are pushed through the gap. "Don't give him too much tip or he'll remember you."

I doubt the cabby will forget the Asian woman who ran up a huge fare and made him wait in the street for a considerable amount of time while talking to someone through a cracked door, but I mumble okay when I take the money. After I pay and the cab vanishes around the corner, the door finally opens, admitting me into Sam's realm. The interior of the house is plain but functional. There's not one piece of furniture or decoration that doesn't have a purpose. What sticks out are the little cameras that undoubtedly record every movement.

"They're to deter burglars," Sam says when he notices my questioning look. His gangly frame, stringy hair, and super pale skin give him a ghostlike appearance. In high school, we would have probably called him a geek. Yet his eyes make him unforgettable. They are vibrant with this dissecting stare that gives me the chills. Somehow, I feel he can see into my mind. Lying to him would never occur to me.

Sam ushers me into a room at the end of the hallway that is stuffed with state-of-the-art electronic equipment. I count five monitors and three different game consoles, headphones in various colors, and several laptops and desktop computers. One wall is entirely covered with a huge flat-screen TV on which a frozen guy, holding a gun, stares back at me with a determined expression.

"Have a seat." Sam's head points at the couch in front of the television. "I'm just running diagnostics on your husband's laptop to see what type of security we're looking at."

"How much longer will it take until we have access?"

"Soon." His forehead is wrinkled as his fingers fly over the keyboard. "There's a secondary password, but I can bypass that." He grins. "I'm in."

I peek over his shoulder as he opens random files. Most of them seem related to Mitch's work. All of a sudden, a document catches my attention. My heartbeat accelerates when my finger lands on the screen. "Open that one."

Sam shoots me a lethal look. "Would you mind *not* touching the equipment? Those screens are sensitive."

"Sorry." Like a scolded child, my finger retreats.

My cheeks burn when I meet Kelsey's smile. *Don't let him rattle you,* her eyes say, and I can't help but grin. Pulling up a chair, I stare at the document. It reads, Last Will and Testament of David Mitchell Cahill.

I read the opening paragraphs in which my husband declared that he was of sound mind when he drafted those words before I get to the part I'm looking for. A gasp escapes me and I rub my eyes to ensure that I'm not mistaken. My name is mentioned, but not in a way I've ever imagined. Of all of Mitch's fortune, I'm left with nothing more than *one* fricking dollar. The rest is going to some woman by the name of Maureen Higgins.

Kelsey has been peeking over my shoulder. "Who is she?" From the shock lacing her voice, she is as dumbfounded as I am.

"I have no idea." The truth that I'm left penniless is hard to stomach. Mitch just cut me out of his will like I meant nothing to him. What the hell went wrong in our marriage? And why did I not notice anything?

Unable to hold back the tears, I wipe over my eyes to keep them contained. Bawling in front of Kelsey and Sam over a bunch of money is pathetic, but this new betrayal tears open more wounds. Did Mitch even love me? He couldn't have since he was obviously not very concerned about how I would make do without him. How am I going to survive without a home, money, or a job? He had controlled every aspect of our lives. I don't even have to clue where to start.

"Is that even legal?" Kelsey asks. "I mean, Aeree was his wife."

"No clue." Sam has clicked out of the will, typing in Maureen's name in the internet search bar. "My aunt's a lawyer. If you want, I can call her and ask."

I silently shake my head; that would cost money I don't have. From the looks of things, I'm thoroughly screwed.

"Okay, so from the date of birth that was mentioned in the will, I was able to locate her. She lives at Sixty-Five Maple Avenue in Stamford, Connecticut. That's close to two hours from here."

Kelsey checks her watch. "If we leave now, we might still get there at a decent hour." Her eyes cut into me. "You up for this, Aeree? Otherwise, we could do it tomorrow."

No way I want to delay getting to the bottom of this. "No, let's go now."

Kelsey holds up her keys with a smile. "Okay, I'll drive."

# Chapter 25

Kelsey and I drive with the music blasting so loudly that conversation is impossible, something that's fine with me. Since we left Sam's house, I can't shake the feeling that she got more than she bargained for—after all, she's risking her job—but she appears to be one of those people who can't say no to others. For a moment, a wave of guilt washes over me for taking advantage of her before I remind myself that I'm in desperate need of a break. The drive turns into an excruciating exercise when her phone keeps ringing, which she ignores. Passing the city limits of Stamford is a relief.

She pulls up behind a minivan a few houses down from the address Sam gave us and finally turns off the music. "So you have no idea who this woman is?"

"The first time I ever saw her name was in Mitch's will, and I've no clue why or what their relationship is."

"Maybe it's something innocent. She could be a relative."

"Mitch didn't have any relatives. His father died when he was just a baby and his mother a few years later. Mitch grew up in foster care since there was no one else who could have taken him. Since he didn't cut me out completely, it must have been some lawyer trick. He knew what he was doing." I leave out that it has felt like a slap in the face—I was nothing more than the unwanted spouse who didn't deserve any of Mitch's fortunes.

"Leaving someone a dollar is a typical tool to disinherit close family members," Kelsey says. "When my mom made her will, her lawyer said she should leave a dollar to my brother to ensure he couldn't run to the courts and claim she accidentally left him out. I thought it was kind of silly since he's in prison and won't be getting out anytime soon, but the lawyer said that it was the safe thing to do."

I try to hide my shock with a crooked smile. First, Finn with his criminal record, and now this brother who is doing some serious prison time. It just shows how perceptions can be deceiving and that everyone has a few skeletons hidden in the closet.

She opens the glove compartment and retrieves her badge. "Let me do the talking, alright?"

Though I'm dying to grill this woman about her involvement with my husband, I have to admit that Maureen Higgins might be more open to talking with an FBI agent than to a stranger off the street. Besides, if she admits she was sleeping with Mitch, I might punch her in the face.

The house is a medium-sized colonial with yellow shutters and a small yard out front. An attached garage is on the right with a newer-looking SUV in the driveway. All in all, the whole property is well kept. I crane my neck to get a glimpse at the back, but a garden shed hides most of the fenced-in yard from view. Judging from the neighborhood, it's not a cheap area of Stamford to live in.

Kelsey rings the doorbell.

"Just a minute."

The voice is young and causes my heartbeat to accelerate. I dread coming face to face with this rival who is currently threatening to take everything from me. She is the living proof that our marriage was nothing more than a farce.

The woman who ends up opening the door can only be described as stunning. Her hair is a deep copper and reaches just below her shoulders with natural, bouncy waves that would go well with a shampoo commercial. Cat-like green eyes give me a good once-over before focusing on Kelsey. "Can I help you?"

"I'm Agent Walker with the FBI." Kelsey flashes her badge. "Are you Maureen Higgins?"

"I am." The woman wraps her arms around her chest, her face defensive. "What is this about?"

"Could we maybe come in?"

A frown spreads on Maureen's forehead. "Do you have a warrant?"

I stifle a gasp as Kelsey and I exchange a glance. This is something Mitch would have asked.

"No, we do not." Kelsey smiles, undoubtedly trying to defuse some of the sudden tension in the air. "We're not investigating a crime and only require a few minutes of your time."

Struggle is written on Maureen's face, but when the smile stays on Kelsey's lips, she at least doesn't slam the door in our faces.

"I'm sorry. My husband said I shouldn't let law-enforcement officials into the house without a warrant. He's a criminal defense attorney."

This time, I have to hide the gasp with a small cough.

"I totally understand." Kelsey's tone is pleasant. "Do you know a Mitchell Cahill?"

"You mean David Cahill? That's my husband. Mitchell is his middle name." She flushes slightly. "Well, technically, he's only my fiancé. We're getting married next month." Her hand strokes her abdomen. "I'm expecting, so David is eager to make it official."

The news hurts like ten burning daggers slicing into my heart. Not only did Mitch cheat on me, but he got her pregnant. She could give him the one thing I could not. No wonder he was going to leave me for her.

"When was the last time you had contact with Mr. Cahill?" Kelsey asks.

Her lips pucker. "He called me Friday afternoon from the airport before boarding a plane to London. His work often requires him to investigate cases out of the country when his clients are foreign nationals."

That was the day we left for the Green Mountains. I remember the phone call. I was getting myself a bottle of water for the trip, and Mitch excused himself when I was waiting in line at the cash register, claiming he had to call his secretary after forgetting to turn on his out-of-office reply for his emails. I swallowed the lie without the slightest suspicion. I picture his face—it had been totally innocent—without even a trace of deception. Maureen probably couldn't tell, either, that he wasn't truly going to England but had planned a romantic getaway with his wife. Maybe the trip was intended to sweeten the news that he was planning to divorce me and he just never got around to telling me before the sniper shot him.

"And when do you expect him back?"

"On Thursday." She glances at me before refocusing on Kelsey. "Now could you please tell me what this is all about?"

Kelsey's face turns official. "I'd really prefer if you sat down."

"Something happened to David, didn't it?" Maureen's already fair skin has paled a few shades and her hand clutches the door handle. With tear-glazed eyes, she stares at Kelsey. When Kelsey remains silent, she finally opens the door for us to step in. Without another word, she turns around, steering toward the back of the house with unsteady steps.

Kelsey takes this as an invitation to come inside. Like an intruder, I follow suit, soaking up the interior as I drag my feet over the polished hardwood floor. The curtains are drawn, and despite the heat, the temperature is comfortable. I catch a glimpse of the living room, which is equipped with a mix of antiques and modern furniture. It's Mitch's typical style and the house's interior is almost a replica of my own home. Even the same Picasso lithograph hangs over the fireplace. Come to think of it, it was his favorite.

I halt when I notice a photograph in the hallway. The last tiny doubt that this is all a horrible mistake is erased. My husband stares back at me with an audacious sparkle in his eyes, his arms wrapped around Maureen from the back. The big smile on his face cuts into me like a new set of daggers. I don't remember seeing him this happy when he was with me.

The hurt is replaced with anger the next second. I want to kick the wall, maybe even toss a few of those precious vases that are crammed on the hallway table onto the floor, or better yet, smash his precious photograph. All this time, he had just been playing the act of a loving husband, probably thinking about Maureen every night when I snuggled in his arms. My fingers trace my lips. None of those heated kisses meant anything.

Tears prick my eyes when a wave of betrayal crushes down on me hard. Like a fool, I spooned up all of his lovey-dovey bullshit while he probably laughed his ass off about my stupidity every time he was up in his secret attic or had dinner with Maureen during his many "business" trips. No wonder he worked so much overtime and traveled at least every other weekend. All those nights he claimed he stayed at the firm's condo in the city were probably spent with her. His deception stings almost as much as his death.

With weak knees, I stumble forward, my vision blurry from my tears. Somehow, Kelsey's eyes cut through my pain. They warn me to keep it together. I drop my gaze when I enter the kitchen, swallowing hard to get my emotions back in check. Not that it would matter. Maureen has lowered herself onto a chair by the kitchen table, her fingers wrapped around a lemonade glass so tightly that her knuckles have turned white. Her expression is vacant—she must know what's coming next.

When Kelsey clears her throat, Maureen's head snaps up, her eyes pleading for her to stop.

"Ms. Higgins, I'm very sorry to inform you that your fiancé was involved in a shooting this past Saturday. He's presumed dead at the moment, though his body has not been recovered."

I turn away when Maureen buries her face in the palms of her hands with a wailing sob. The pain threatens to choke me— she has no right to grieve for *my* husband. When her shoulders continue to shake, I can't help but indulge a little in her misery; I want to blame her for stealing everything away from me that mattered. Deep down, I know those thoughts are out of place and Mitch is the only one to blame, but it's still easier to fault her than the man who once meant the world to me.

A sudden urge to know whether she was aware about Mitch's second life overwhelms me. "Did your fiancé ever tell you about his first wife?"

The look Kelsey tosses me is deadly.

At least my question stops Maureen's tears in their tracks. She blinks a few times. "What first wife?" From the confusion on her face, she has no idea what I'm talking about.

"Her name is Aeree. He married her two years ago."

"You must be mistaken." A deep wrinkle cuts across her forehead. "David and I have been dating for over a year and a half. If he had been in a relationship when he met me, he would have told me."

That she had no clue about his double life makes me feel better. At least I wasn't the only fool.

"Well, we should go." Kelsey rises, her eyes signaling me that I better zip it or she will kill me.

With slumped shoulders, I trot behind her. Just as we get to the front door, my gaze comes to rest on a different photograph, this one small and in a stand-up frame. From the way it is angled on the table next to the vases, it's facing the kitchen. I must have missed it when we walked in.

I can't resist picking it up to take a closer look. Mitch is much younger, maybe in his late teens, his arm casually placed on the shoulders of another guy about his age.

"Who's that man in the picture with your fiancé?" As soon as the words leave my mouth, my scalp begins to prickle.

"Oh, it's one of his best friends, Colton Kittinger. They were in the same foster home together and later went to the same college. They're just like brothers."

The name sounds vaguely familiar, but I can't immediately place him. Mitch had always insisted that he was too busy for friends; plus he didn't like to hang out with the same people he worked with. That I felt left out and isolated didn't bother him, something Maureen apparently didn't have to endure. With a sigh, I set the photograph back down.

"Well, thanks for your time, Ms. Higgins, and sorry again for your loss." Kelsey nudges me in the back.

"Yes," I mumble, unable to offer her words of condolence. Even if she had no clue about me, she was still the other woman in my husband's life. I battle more tears when I realize that she knew him better than I did, and I was the one married to him while she was just the fiancée.

Back in the car, I let out a long sigh, determined not to show Kelsey how shaken up I am from our meeting with Maureen.

"I think you should turn yourself in and let the FBI handle it from here," she blurts out without warning.

The abruptness of her statement sets off a few alarm bells and my head slowly turns. What is she implying? "Are you out of your mind? I have to get to the bottom of this to clear my name. As it stands, I had even more motive to kill him. Dinkle will claim I found out about the affair and shot him out of jealousy before he could divorce me." Hell, what if she tries to pin the other murders on me?

"Your husband apparently led a double life, Aeree. You don't have the resources to uncover the truth. There's even a chance he was involved with the couple who was selling the data stick. If you don't turn yourself in, you're making it worse."

I glare at her. "How do you know about Julie and Tyson?" Unrest spreads in my body. All my instincts tell me to get out of the car and run. In hindsight, her unexpected interest in helping me doesn't add up. Who would risk their career for a neighbor they just met?

"I'm really sorry it has to come to this." A gun rests in her hand. "Please step out of the vehicle."

A surreal buzzing spreads in my ears, just as my mind starts to swim. Why is everyone betraying me these days? Catching a break is not in the cards for me.

In a daze, I slide out of the car when the gun stays pointed at me. A few car doors slam behind us. Dinkle approaches with the widest grin on her face.

"Aeree Cahill, you are under arrest for interfering with a federal investigation."

I manage to keep my tears at bay while the cold handcuffs close around my wrists. My gaze is fixed on Kelsey, who looks absolutely guilt stricken. I should have known better than to trust her. The Miranda warning is a waste of everyone's time—there's no way I will mutter a single word with or without an attorney. Screw them all.

# Chapter 26

They book me before they even try to interrogate me. I endure the fingerprinting and photos with gritted teeth, but by the time they do the search, the familiar hitch is back in my throat, warning me to hold it together. When the deputy puts on the glove for the cavity search, my soul shatters. The tears burn hot on my skin as she digs around in my insides while Dinkle stares at me with this big grin on her face. They tape it, allegedly to ensure that procedures are followed, which adds to my humiliation and pain.

Totally numb, I sit in the shower with my back against the wall, hardly noticing how the lice shampoo burns into my scalp while the tears keep rolling. By then, I don't care anymore that I might appear weak. The deputy signals when the five minutes are up and I complete my rinse under lukewarm water. Everything inside me aches as the pain that has settled in my chest radiates through my body like toxic rays. In that moment, I wish the sniper had gotten to me.

The orange jumpsuit is still too big and hangs around my small frame like a potato sack. They refuse to give me a spare towel for my wet hair and my collar is soaked by the time we leave the jail. The rubber shoes squeak on the linoleum floor as Dinkle ushers me down the long hallways of the federal building toward the interrogation rooms. The sound sends chills down my spine—it's like someone is scraping their fingernails over a chalkboard.

The interrogation room they stick me in is small and windowless, the bright neon light biting my eyes. The summer heat still makes it through the walls and the temperatures are unbearable. Sweat pearls on my forehead by the time I lower myself into the chair. They don't remove the handcuffs. Dinkle plops into the chair across from me. Her partner soon joins her and we are ready to roll. This will be a brief event since I intend to ask for a lawyer right away, at which time they will have to stop the interrogation.

"Aeree, first of all, we have to advise you that this conversation is taped."

I snort at the casual tone of her voice. If she thinks we will have a little chat like old friends after what she just put me through, she has something else coming.

"I want to talk to a lawyer."

"Look, invoking your rights is really not in your best interest here. We received confirmation that Vermont has issued a warrant for your arrest in the murder of your husband. They have requested assistance to extradite you, so you'll be held without bail at Rikers Island until the matter is resolved. If you cooperate with us, I could probably pull some strings and get you transferred to a nicer jail upstate until Vermont can get the proper paperwork signed, or better yet, if you agree to the extradition, I could put in a good word with the prosecutor. You could have a parole date instead of spending the rest of your life in prison. Of course, that only applies if you fully cooperate with us now."

I smile at her. She must think I'm stupid. As a federal employee, she doesn't have authority to make deals on behalf of a state. It's just a trick to get me to talk.

"Like I said, I want a lawyer."

"You should really think about that."

I pucker my lips like I am thinking real hard, then smile. "I did, and I still want a lawyer."

Her partner lets out a growl of frustration. "I warned you—"

Dinkle's deadly glare shuts him up. "Look, I don't know why you wanted your husband dead, but I'm sure he did something. Was it because he was banging that other woman? I mean, if that's why you did it, I'll understand. I would claw my partner's eyes out if he did this to me."

"I didn't even know about her until today."

"So you say, but personally, I think you're lying. Most women can sense when their men sleep around." A smug smile plays at the corners of her lips. The mere fact that I'm talking at all must be a victory for her. On top of that, she's obviously trying to provoke me to get a rise out of me, maybe even get a spontaneous confession. Little does she know that the detectives who interrogated me after I assaulted Paul were much tougher and more intimidating. She won't be getting anything out of me.

"Like I said, I had no clue he was seeing another woman." My smile is as smug as hers. "Now I want my lawyer."

She huffs and opens her mouth, obviously still under the belief that she can break me, when a buzzing draws our attention to the opening door. The guy with the long hair, whom I saw in the elevator and who was with her after Norton was killed, enters. His face is twisted in rage with steam practically pouring from his nose. He reminds me of an angry bull.

"Francesca, a word please."

It's the first time that her arrogant composure wavers. She shrinks under his glare as she storms out. He leaves the door cracked open and I prick my ears in the hopes of picking up parts of their conversation. It's unnecessary—the guy is a screamer and apparently not concerned about who might be listening when he cuts into her.

"You had her booked?"

"I wanted to show her what she can expect if she doesn't cooperate."

"Fuck, Francesca, did you even look at her file? She was raped. Searches are even more intrusive for someone like her. Kelsey said—"

"Now you're listening to a rookie. Come on, Joseph, I know what I'm doing."

"Is she cooperating?"

There is a moment of silence. "Not yet. She asked for a lawyer."

"Fuck. You're off the case, I'm taking this over. I'm not having you botch this whole operation. The Pentagon is screaming about why we haven't recovered that damn data stick and you're toying with our only lead. Not happening. When this is over, I'm gonna have internal affairs look into this and you better pray you did this by the book or there'll be some serious consequences."

The door is torn open just seconds later. The guy is all red in the face and a vein pulses on his forehead. He shouldn't get so upset or he might have a heart attack.

He zooms in on Dinkle's partner next, who cowers in his chair like a spooked rabbit.

"Could you ask Agent McCarthy and Agent Walker to join me, please?"

Dinkle's partner jumps up after a muttered, "Certainly, sir," before rushing from the room. My handcuffs are removed before the guy plops into the chair that was just occupied by Dinkle.

"Ms. Cahill, my name is Joseph Begay. I'm the Senior Special Agent in charge of the FBI Joint Terrorism Task Force. First of all, I want to apologize for Agent Dinkle. She was under the mistaken belief that you are under arrest, but we're only looking at you as a person of interest in a case we're working on."

I quirk an eyebrow—he can't be serious. "So I'm free to leave?"

"Not exactly." His smile is forced. "We did get a request from the State of Vermont to hold you on their behalf while they investigate your husband's death, but from our end, you're not under arrest, so you're not entitled to a lawyer."

"I still don't want to talk to you."

"And that's your right, but I have to advise you that in 2013 the Supreme Court ruled that the silence of an out-of-custody suspect can be used as evidence of guilt. I'm sure you don't want us to think you did anything wrong, do you, Ms. Cahill?"

"I didn't kill my husband and don't feel comfortable talking about him."

"I can appreciate that, and I'm quite frankly not interested in your husband's murder. I'm willing to agree that anything about him is off the table—I'm not going to ask you a single question about your marriage or personal life. All I'm interested in is your contact with Julie Flynn and Tyson Roberts, and the dealings you had with Nina Humphrey. In turn for your cooperation, I'll ensure that no federal charges are brought forward. Unfortunately, with the state charges, you're on your own." His curt smile is thin. "But then I'm sure you already knew that."

I like his straightforward approach. For the first time, I feel someone is truthful with me and not playing some type of game. The constant battle with the authorities is exhausting. I have nothing to hide about Julie and Tyson, and if I help him recover that data stick, the Vermont courts might view this in my favor. Since I'm probably going to be charged with Mitch's murder regardless, I can at least try to make it as easy on myself as possible.

"Okay, what do you want to know?"

On cue, the door opens again and the guy from the elevator wheels in, Kelsey trotting behind him. She can't even hold my gaze. There's a pain in her eyes I cannot explain—it's almost like this case is affecting her on a personal level.

Begay makes introductions, and the guy in the wheelchair insists I call him Bill when he shakes my hand. I like him immediately. Kelsey pulls a chair to the side of the table and we end up in a circle that reminds me more of a group of friends than adversaries.

"So, Aeree, why don't we start from the beginning? When was the first time you met Julie Flynn and Tyson Roberts?"

I start with the dinner and charades game at the lodge before walking them through the events of the next day. Begay is constantly scribbling down notes while Bill is leaning back in his wheelchair, soaking up my words with hooded eyes. Kelsey is playing with her cuticles, and I'm not even sure she is paying attention. I notice that she has torn her skin in a few places and crusted blood is around her nails. Despite the heat, she's wearing a long-sleeve shirt, which I find odd. Come to think of it, I've never seen her with bare arms. She must not like to expose her skin in public.

Bill's next question makes me refocus on the conversation. "So when you encountered Julie and Tyson in the woods, you never got a chance to look through their backpack?"

"No." I dig deep into my memories, replaying the scene in my head. "He flat out refused to let me touch it. I thought he was hiding something, but I was too exhausted to argue with him. I then went on without them."

"But at that point, Nina Humphrey stayed with them?"

"Yes. I caught up later with her at the cabin and she had Julie's backpack, but I never saw Julie and Tyson again after that."

Begay and Bill exchange a glance.

Survive

"Okay, after your rescue, why did you seek out Nina Humphrey at the hospital?"

"That reason involves my husband, so I'm not going to talk about it. Let's just take it as a fact that I did."

"Fair enough. At any time, did Nina ever indicate that she received or took something from Julie and Tyson?"

"Never. Honestly, we didn't even talk about the Green Mountains."

That gets Bill to raise his eyebrows. His curious gaze is burning holes into my skull, but I stick to my guns, giving him nothing about the pictures and the stories that go along with them. It's none of his business and irrelevant to his case.

"Okay, I think our best bet is to seek out Nina Humphrey. Chances are she got the data stick; otherwise, why did she refuse to go to the FBI and ask for protection? Even if she doesn't have it, she must know something," Begay says.

"I agree." Bill's attention shifts to Kelsey. "Are you okay, Agent Walker?"

She wakes from her daze. "Yes, sir. Sorry, I was distracted there for a moment."

His smile is soft. "Marcel is a big boy. He can handle himself."

"I know, sir."

"He has worked undercover for a really long time and knows how to get out of tight situations."

Her smile is crooked, her eyes full of doubt. The worry oozing from her is catching.

"Is everything okay with Marcel?" I ask.

Bill's natural smile turns fake. "We lost contact with Agent Brown, but that happens sometimes in undercover operations. There's really nothing to worry about."

The words are as fake as his smile. I can tell he is upset, but he's keeping up a strong front since that's expected of a senior FBI agent.

After a few moments of pressing silence, Begay brings the conversation back on track. "Since Nina Humphrey trusts you to a certain degree, Aeree, would you consider going in with Agent Walker to try and track her down? Once you make contact, we want you to ask her about the data stick. Pretend your friend Eltas has connections and could easily sell it for a cut."

"Sounds dangerous." I lean back in my chair, knowing this is my one chance to strike a deal. "What do I get out of it?"

Bill chuckles just as Begay's face turns furious again. He is about to snap at me when Bill's hand comes to rest on his forearm to calm him.

"What do you want, Aeree?" Bill asks.

"I want the state case to go away. I didn't kill my husband and shouldn't have to defend myself for it."

"We are the FBI. We can't get involved in state cases."

"This is a matter of national security. You can get anything you want under those circumstances." That's what my father used to say and I can only hope he is right.

Another glance between Bill and Begay. Though Begay still appears mad, his eyes hold a new glimmer of respect. He must realize that I'm not the pushover he thought I was.

"I'll call the Pentagon and get it done. You have my word," he says.

My chin juts at Bill. "I want his word."

Bill chuckles again. "You got it."

"And I want something else." I suck in a deep breath— here goes nothing. Ever since I found the picture, the night of the gang leader's murder has been popping in and out of my mind. I need to know if Eltas's theory that one of my father's men betrayed him is right. "My dad was convicted because someone from his unit might have snitched on him. I want to know who it was, if it's true."

"That's impossible." Begay shakes his head. "That type of information is sealed within the service records."

"I'm sure the Pentagon can get it."

Begay looks like he is having second thoughts about my cooperation when Bill adds insult to injury. "She's got you by the balls, Joseph. You better do what she says or explain to Major Riley why you haven't secured the data stick—or his man—after you insisted it was a piece of cake."

Begay mumbles something through gritted teeth before shooting me a dark look. "Okay, I'll get it done, but I swear you better get me some results, and fast. We've only got until Friday, so seventy-two hours, or the deal is off."

"Okay, when do I start?" My eyes dart between Begay and Bill. This is the lucky break I so deserved.

"Right away. Kelsey will take you over to the jail to process you out and can brief you on the rest of the operation. Do you have any other questions?"

"Yes. Do you have a lead on Julie and Tyson?"

"They're dead." Begay sighs. "The rangers found their bodies not far from where you were picked up last night. Gunshot wounds to the head. We are still awaiting ballistics on the bullets."

"Was it the sniper?"

"Didn't appear that way, but it was a professional hit. Military-style execution."

"What about that tour guide, Bobby? She seemed to be involved somehow."

"Dead as well. We haven't figured out yet what role she played. Anything else?"

So only Sad Eyes, Citadel, and I are still alive from our group. The odds that I'll get out of this situation unscathed are dwindling, but at least I'm not going in alone this time. Kelsey might have betrayed me, but she is still a body than can stand between me and a bullet if push comes to shove. What none of them knows is that I can hold a grudge—and I'm intending to milk the FBI for everything I can after what they did to me.

# Chapter 27

"Still no word from Marcel?"

"Nope." Kelsey stares straight ahead, holding the bag of gummy bears under my nose when I suck in a breath to ready myself for another question.

I grab one with a sigh. Over the past two days, my calorie intake has been horrendous, forcing me to take regular trips to the bathroom for purging. All Kelsey ever eats are sweets and junk food. She claims this keeps her alert. Where she puts all that food is a total mystery to me; even after the two kids, she is as thin as a stick, apart from the muscles she has developed during law-enforcement training, which are not many. For an FBI agent, she is a little bit of a wimp.

I glare at the house across the street, secretly praying that Sad Eyes will turn up soon. Police stakeouts are definitely one of the most boring activities in the world, though Kelsey's taciturnity might be a contributing factor. Not that I necessarily mind since I don't know her well enough to share my life secrets with her. Mitch and his second life have been mostly on my mind, and not talking has given me a chance to start processing it all.

That I never suspected a thing has been bothering me the most. How could I have been so blind and only seen what I wanted to see? I guess during my prison term, I was so grateful that he stuck with me, continuing his visits even after his firm had worked out a deal. Slowly, I fell in love with him. He had been funny and kind, always making me laugh when I was at my lowest point. In a way, he gave me hope. Without him, I couldn't have survived while being locked up like an animal.

After I got out, it was easy to continue following his lead. We got married quickly to avoid me having to go into a halfway house, something I was eternally grateful for, so this made his control issues and frequent travel bearable. Total financial reliance was just the next step and convenient when I couldn't keep a job. Mitch had proven his devotion while I was locked up, so it was time to show mine by supporting his dreams and career. At least that's what I thought I was doing. That I practically gave him a carte blanche to cheat on me by playing the submissive wife never occurred to me, though I still don't grasp why he didn't divorce me immediately once he met Maureen. That he might have felt sorry for me is the only thing I have come up with so far.

All in all, the whole ordeal has been a painful experience, to say the least, with times where I was on the brink of tears. Only Kelsey's presence in Finn's old pickup truck has prevented me from bawling like a big baby. Usually, the reminder that dwelling in self-pity is pointless is enough to snap me out of my sullen mood.

I fan myself with a few papers that are scattered on the dashboard. It's to no avail. I can't even remember a time when my clothes have not stuck to every part of my skin. The small portable fan that hums softly from the middle console barely keeps the temperature in the enclosed space at a level that permits human habitation. I sip from a water bottle to soothe my raw throat. Vomiting all the time, together with the dry air, has taken its toll. Every swallow is an effort. At least the bruises and cuts have stopped throbbing, leaving the graze on my neck the only painful injury still healing.

"Is there a plan B?" I ask.

"Not that I know of."

"But there are no guarantees she will even show up."

"All her stuff is in that house, including her passport. Sooner or later, she'll show up." Kelsey munches on the gummy bears.

"We don't even have twenty-four hours left."

"I'm sure she'll show. Just stay positive."

I have to admire her patience; she doesn't seem rattled at all by the wait. My leg muscles, on the other hand, have been twitching and tingling, demanding I move around. I keep fidgeting and only Kelsey's scolding look convinces me to exercise at least some self-restraint.

"Are you sure the friend who's keeping all her stuff hasn't made contact and given her everything she needs?"

"Yep. Dinkle has a tail on her whenever she leaves the house."

My face twists at the sound of the name. Having to work side by side with Agent Dinkle still takes some getting used to.

Kelsey snorts. "Yeah, she can be a real bitch."

I snicker, surprised to hear those words from her mouth. "Don't all you FBI guys stick together?"

"Supposedly, but that still doesn't mean we have to like each other. Most of those guys don't accept me since I only have a bachelor's degree in criminal justice and didn't have any work experience before hiring on. For the FBI, that's underqualified. A lot of the agents have law degrees or at least a master's and a few years of local law enforcement under their belt."

"So how did you land the job?"

"Bill pulled some strings, same as for Marcel. Of course, most of the agents know and have been giving us a hard time. It's getting better, but someone like Dinkle makes snotty remarks whenever she can. She can be vicious when she doesn't like you."

"Well, she hated me from the start."

"Yeah, but that's because you have a criminal record. Dinkle thinks that criminals are scum who don't deserve second chances. I'm just glad she doesn't know about Finn's background, or they would probably get into a huge fight during an office get-together. He can't stand people like her."

I snicker. Though I barely know her husband, he seems right up my alley.

The bag of gummy bears is shoved into my face again, and I reluctantly take a couple, glad that the pressing silence is finally broken.

"Dinkle was way out of line booking you," Kelsey says. "I hope it didn't upset you too much."

"It was fine." I can't shake the slight tremble in my voice. Tears sting when the memory of the female deputy's fingers inside me during the search push to the surface.

"You don't need to pretend. I saw your file and can imagine what a cavity search might do to you."

"How could you possibly know?" My accompanying hiss is much harsher than intended.

"I was raped, too."

The gasp is out before I can help it. I glance at her to ascertain whether she is lying to get on my good side, but the tears in her eyes suggest that she is telling the truth.

"How old were you?"

"Sixteen. I was kidnapped, and for three months, my abductors kept me locked up and did horrible things to me." The words are strained as she fights with the tears. "I'm sure you can fill in the rest."

I have no clue how to respond and stuff a few more gummy bears into my mouth to stall. She follows suit. For a while, we chew in silence. A thousand questions race through my mind, most of them none of my business.

"What happened to your kidnappers?" I finally ask.

"The first time, nothing. The one guy got off on a technicality, and they couldn't even identify his friend. As you can imagine, I was pretty messed up. Three years later, they took another stab at me and grabbed me and another girl. During our escape, Jed was killed, but the other—" A few tears trickle down her cheeks. "The other one went to prison."

I swallow another question that has been lingering on the tip of my tongue when pain twists her face. Somehow, she doesn't seem happy that her abductor was captured. It's odd, but hey—who am I to judge? There were plenty of people who didn't agree with my punishment for Paul.

"Look." Kelsey nudges me in the side as she shoots up in her seat. "Is that Nina Humphrey?"

I squint at the woman who is just getting out of a cab. She has the same height and build, but her hair color is off. The rest of her face is hidden by huge sunglasses.

"It could be her, but I'm not sure."

"Let's check it out. If it's her, it might be our only chance."

I want to remind her that Begay told us to be absolutely certain before making contact, but she is already out of the truck. After a slight hesitation, I follow. She's the FBI agent after all, and hopefully, she knows what she is doing.

"Hey, you got a cigarette?" she asks when she reaches the woman, who spins around in response.

Even with the sunglasses, I see her eyes go wide when her gaze falls on me. She glances around like a hunted animal. Before she can take off, Kelsey's fingers wrap around her wrist.

"Look, all we want is to talk. The cops have been chasing after my friend Aeree and we need to figure this out together. Let's just go inside, alright?"

"You police?" Sad Eyes's gaze darts from Kelsey to me and back.

Kelsey chuckles. "Do I look like police?"

Sad Eyes lets the glasses slip to the tip of her nose and studies her calmly over the rim. "I guess not. Let's go inside."

She seems in an awful hurry as we rush up the driveway, her face strained with tension. While we are waiting for the door to open after she rang the doorbell, she nibbles on her thumb.

"You okay?" I ask her.

"It's my brother-in-law. My friends say he has been looking for me since he spoke with the FBI because he thinks I had something to do with Kendall's murder. I'm scared he's gonna kill me if he finds me. He's one of those types who punches first and asks questions later."

The door opens and we stare straight into the face of a big dude with a beard and greasy hair. His resemblance to Kendall cannot be denied.

"Hello, girls. We were wondering when you'd show up." A baseball bat swings softly back and forth in his right hand.

Sad Eyes's shriek is not necessary for me to figure out that this must be the brother-in-law who has been looking for her. She spins around and takes off down the driveway. When the guy raises the bat, I decide to follow. Kelsey is on my heels. Why the hell doesn't she just pull her gun?

Kelsey overtakes me and shouts for Sad Eyes and me to get into the truck. I have barely slammed the passenger door shut when the guy reaches the car. The bat flies toward the windshield. Just as spiderweb cracks spread through the window, Kelsey accelerates. If the guy hadn't jumped out of the way, she would have hit him. Not that I would have minded.

"Oh my god. Oh my god." Sad Eyes is paler than a ghost. "What was he doing at Rebecca's house? I have to call her to make sure she's okay."

"Hold on." Kelsey makes a sharp right turn and Sad Eyes's body squeezes the wind out of me.

"Oh my god, are they following us?" Sad Eyes cranes her neck to peek out the back window.

"Not yet." Kelsey takes the next curve with breakneck speed.

I'm getting sick to my stomach. "Slow down or you're gonna kill us."

"If this guy catches us, we are gonna be dead." Kelsey's words are laced with panic, though I'm sure she is exaggerating. One phone call and the area would be swarming with cops. She is probably pretending to keep up her cover.

"We need to go back." Sad Eyes is on the brink of tears. "All my stuff is in that house."

"Forget your stuff." The car sways as Kelsey makes a sudden U-turn, heading up the ramp to the highway on the other side. The signs show it's the way toward Manhattan. "I guarantee you if you go back to that house, you'll be dead in the next few hours."

Sad Eyes stares at her, her mouth opening and closing like she's struggling to find the right words. When her shoulders slump, she must have realized what she is up against. "So where are we going?"

"Not sure yet, but for now, we need to get away. That guy is not someone I ever want to see again."

# Chapter 28

The next miles are spent in silence. Kelsey keeps glancing in the rearview mirror as she continues to speed down the highway. Finally, she sighs. "I think we're in the clear. No one is following us." The car slows down a little.

"So where to now?" I ask.

Sad Eyes's focus is still on the car behind us, but she finally turns around. "I guess Aeree's place is out since I assume the FBI has a team there in the hopes she shows up. They were doing the same at my apartment. Can we go to your house?"

"Aeree and I are neighbors." Kelsey puckers her lips as if she is considering alternatives. "My brother-in-law has a condo in the city. We could go there. I'm sure he won't mind. You could call your friend to make sure she's okay and figure out what to do."

"Yeah, I suppose." Sad Eyes falls back into her seat. "Where does your brother-in-law live?"

"Downtown Manhattan, between Lexington and Park."

"That's a pretty upscale area." Sad Eyes's gaze has turned curious. "What does your brother-in-law do?"

"He's a model."

She snorts. "Like in fashion?"

"Yeah. What's wrong with that?"

"Nothing." Sad Eyes snickers. "I guess I just never met a guy who was into fashion. Kendall would have had a conniption. He thought that guys who didn't work some type of hard labor were sissies."

"What did Kendall do?" I ask.

"He worked construction." She snickers again. "He never grasped that those sissies with brains actually earned a lot more than him."

My forehead furrows. How could he have afforded such an expensive trip to the Green Mountains? Then I remember that most of the other members of our group had won the weekend gateway in a sweepstakes. Mitch had been the rare exception. But considering how cheap he was and the fact that he was probably trying to save every dime for his life with Maureen, I couldn't even be sure.

Fortunately, the traffic hasn't reached rush-hour peak and we get a parking spot right across the street from the apartment building. The air-conditioning in the lobby is refreshing, blowing cool air at us nonstop while we wait for Kelsey's brother-in-law to clear us. She ignores us for the most part by jumping into a conversation with the security guard about the upcoming football training camps.

"So how are you holding up?" I ask Sad Eyes.

"I'm so scared. Sooner or later, Colin or one of Kendall's other brothers will catch up with me." She sniffles, her eyes filled with despair. "Kendall has a big family and they will all start looking for me if they think I had something to do with his death. I guess I need to find a way to cross the border into Mexico or Canada if I want to get away from them."

"You know, the feds are looking for some data stick that Julie and Tyson had. It's top secret, even the Pentagon is involved. Did they give you anything?"

"I wish. If I had anything of value to the Pentagon, I could ask for witness protection."

The hopelessness in her eyes is heart-wrenching—no doubt she's telling the truth. It's another dead end. Maybe the feds are grasping for straws, and Julie and Tyson got rid of the data stick before they even went to the Green Mountains. For all I know, the classified data could already be in the hands of a global terrorist, leaving us to lead a wild-goose chase. It puts me in a precarious position. If I don't deliver some result to the FBI by tomorrow morning, they will neither help me with my state case nor give me the information about the snitch who ratted out my father.

In that moment, the elevator doors open and a young man steps out. I do a double take to ensure my eyes don't betray me. Sad Eyes's breathy "Oh my god, it's Cameron Walker," confirms she is just as stunned as I am. Compared to the bus ads and the many billboards that feature him for famous designer labels at every street corner, he is even cuter in real life.

"Hey, Kelsey." They briefly hug. "Is everything alright?"

"Yeah, we just need to lay low for a few hours. Sorry for the invasion."

"That's no problem." With an inviting grin, he ushers us into the elevator after nodding at the doorman. "I have to warn you, though. We had a party last night and the cleaning crew stood us up this morning, so the apartment is a mess."

"I hope you've got some leftovers. I'm starving."

"Oh, there's plenty of food." He flashes me a pearly white smile that reminds me of a toothpaste commercial. "Don't you want to introduce me to your friends?"

"I'm sure they know who you are."

He chuckles.

"This here is Aeree." Her hand lands on my shoulder. "And this is Nina."

I mumble a hi under my breath, which is drowned out by Sad Eyes's loud hello. Luckily, the elevator pings and ends the awkward ride. Cameron's apartment is the penthouse, the sliding elevator doors opening straight into a huge living room with an open-plan kitchen. Floor-to-ceiling glass windows offer a stunning view onto the surrounding city.

"Wow, that's what I call style," Sad Eyes mumbles.

I have to agree. The room is tastefully decorated with minimalist black leather furniture that is accentuated by cream tiles. A huge pool table takes up the majority of the space next to the kitchen, but the grand piano on a small podium by the windows stands out. The only downer is the hint of cigarette smoke; I can't help wrinkling my nose in disgust.

"Sorry again about the mess. Food's in the kitchen."

I notice a few dozen glasses and plates with leftover finger foods scattered on the sofa table and sideboards before turning my attention to the kitchen counter. A guy is slouched on a barstool with his face buried in his huge hands. From his low groans, he is about to die.

"Yo, Harrison, we have company." Cameron slaps him on the back before he flings himself on the stool next to him.

"I told you before, don't yell." Harrison squints at us with bloodshot eyes, barely able to sit up straight.

All he gets from Cameron in response is a mild smile. "Harrison can't hold his liquor." He winks at Kelsey, who bursts out laughing.

The familiarity between them is obvious—that's how it used to be between me and Eltas. His life now is almost as foreign to me as the second life of my husband. It seems like I didn't know either one of them at all.

Kelsey and Sad Eyes attack the buffet on the counter and help themselves to a generous amount of food they start to devour.

"Don't you want to dig in?" Kelsey asks while chewing. "You haven't had a decent meal since yesterday's lunch."

If a burger and fries, with a subsequent trip to the bathroom, can be considered decent.

"I have a slight headache," I claim just as my growling stomach betrays me.

"You're probably just dehydrated." Cameron pushes a water bottle my way.

"And I'll fix you a plate," Kelsey offers. "Just sit down on the couch and relax."

Since everyone is staring at me, the couch is the best place to hide for cover. I slide out of my sneakers and lean back. The cushions are overstuffed and incredibly comfortable. For a second, I just indulge in sitting on something other than the sagging car seat during our stakeout. The soreness in my muscles is all too evident when I shift my weight.

"Here." Kelsey squats next to me and hands me a plate. "You really need to eat something."

"Yeah, I know." With a frown, I add up the calories of chicken wings, mozzarella sticks, and mushroom caps. All fried, so it's a bundle. Add the tortilla chips and dip, and this one meal constitutes what I usually consume in a week. I start to nibble on a small piece of meat. "I spoke to Nina and she said that Julie and Tyson didn't give her anything."

"Do you believe her?"

"Yeah. She could use the data stick to work something out with the feds, so there's no way she'd miss out on that opportunity."

"So we're back to square one."

I bite off half a mozzarella stick. "Seems that way. Do you think Bill and Begay will still help me with my state case?"

"There's no state case. They just told you that to ensure your cooperation."

"Seriously?"

"Yep. I'm sorry, Aeree. I hated lying to you, but my hands were tied."

"So I guess they also won't help me to figure out who squealed on my dad?"

"I doubt it. The FBI is actually not as powerful as you think. Someone like Major Riley doesn't give us the time of day. Those army guys are all snobs."

Oddly, my father used to say the same thing about the Bureau.

"So I'm screwed. I did all of this for nothing?"

"You helped Nina Humphrey. That should count for something." She squeezes my arm. "I'll let you eat in peace. Since Nina doesn't have the data stick, I'll have to make contact with Begay and let him know what's going on. Not sure about his plans after that."

"Okay." With a sullen face, I choke down most of the food to avoid getting hassled by Kelsey again for not eating. Since I will purge myself anyhow, the end result will be the same.

As I place my plate back on the counter, I smile at Cameron. "Where's your bathroom?"

He points down a narrow corridor that branches off the kitchen. "Third door on the left."

On my way to the bathroom, curiosity gets the better of me and I peek into his bedroom. A king-sized waterbed with silk sheets dominates the room; the floor is scattered with an array of clothes. A male thong sticks out like a sore thumb. Mitch wouldn't have been caught dead with them.

The second bedroom is converted into an office and adjacent to the bathroom. Though I'm tempted, I forgo a further inspection of the apartment. I'm afraid to be caught snooping around. A low curse runs over my lips when I notice that the bathroom doesn't have a key to lock the door. Hopefully, the others will respect my privacy, or I'll be in deep shit for an explanation.

I go down on my knees and bend forward over the toilet. Inhaling deeply, I push two fingers deep into my mouth. I try to keep the gagging sound to a minimum, afraid that someone will catch on. When it is over, the little bit of energy I had regained has drained out of me.

I calm my rapid breath before dabbing the forced tears from my eyes with a piece of toilet tissue. With a low groan, I heave myself back to my feet. Turning around, I gasp as I stare straight into Kelsey's face. She is leaning casually in the doorway, watching me intently.

"I must have had a bad piece of chicken." My smile is crooked. "Got sick there all of a sudden."

"I don't believe you. From what I saw, you did this on purpose." She steps into the room and closes the door behind her. "I think it's about time that you and I have a little chat."

# Chapter 29

"You know, throwing up like this is a form of self-harm."

I snort. "What could you possibly know about self-harm?"

In response, Kelsey pulls up the sleeve of her shirt. My forehead wrinkles when I count several scars that look like she was trying to slash her wrist—they are spread over her lower arm all the way up to her elbow.

"I used to cut because I was scared to deal with the trauma from my kidnapping. The rape was the worst." Her voice is thick. "Once I cut so deep, I almost died. That's when I finally got help."

"How did you get over it?"

"I realized that the cutting kept me from letting go of my memories. I tried to kill the pain with a different pain, but all it really accomplished was trapping me in a vicious cycle. Finn told me once that we have to keep pushing no matter what is thrown our way. You can't let life slip through your fingers by living in the past. Best advice I've ever gotten."

"Yeah, but I don't throw up because I'm holding on to the past. I throw up because I need to be thin."

"Do you really? Or is it because you feel dirty and damaged and think that if you don't fit a certain beauty image, someone might notice?"

Tears prick my eyes and I can't hold her gaze.

"Aeree, after my rape, I felt the same way. I thought that men would look down on me, but that's not true."

"It's not that." A few tears slowly trickle down my cheeks and onto my shirt. "I can't have children anymore. They took that from me. My looks are all I have left."

"No man who loves you will blame you for it. This wasn't your fault."

"But that's what Mitch did. Why else would he have had an affair and gotten another woman pregnant?" The words hurt so much that my chest threatens to tear apart.

"I don't think this had anything to do with it. Something is totally off with that situation, and I promise I'll help you figure it out once we find the data stick, but for now, this has to be my number-one priority." She squeezes my shoulder. "And I'll help you with your bulimia. One thing they taught us in therapy, which really helped, was finding an accountability partner who I could call when the urge to hurt myself hit me. How about we give that a try?"

"You mean it?" My tentative smile is genuine this time.

"Absolutely. I know how hard it is to go through something like this on your own. But first things first. As far as I can tell, you haven't had a good meal in days. Honestly, I'm surprised you're still functioning. Let me fix you something that's healthier than this fried stuff, and you promise you'll eat it and keep it down. No more trips to the bathroom."

I laugh awkwardly, overwhelmed by her kindness. "Okay."

With one jerk, she pulls me back to my feet.

"And please, don't tell the others."

"Of course not. That's something that's just between us."

I trot behind her into the kitchen where Sad Eyes in on the phone, whispering. A few tears roll down her cheeks before she turns away. Kelsey starts to rummage through the fridge, ignoring Cameron's question about what she is doing. The sudden tension in the air is daunting. I slide onto the barstool and smile at Harrison, who gives me a painful grimace in return. He must have an out-of-this-world hangover.

Sad Eyes finishes her call and walks over to me. "My friend Rebecca is okay. Colin and his other two brothers burned all my stuff in her backyard after we left and told her that they will beat her up if she ever helps me again. She is so scared, she almost didn't want to talk to me. All my other friends got warnings, too, so no one is eager to help me. Seems I'm totally screwed."

"You could still cross into Canada through Niagara Falls. When my husband and I went up there once for a long weekend, all we needed to show was our driver's license when we drove across Rainbow Bridge. Then you could go to the embassy in Toronto and ask for a new passport, claiming yours was stolen."

"I guess that could work. I took out all our savings and have a little bit of money, which should get me through the first few weeks until I find a job. Only question is how do I get up to Niagara Falls? What if Kendall's family watches Grand Central Station or the Port Authority Bus Terminal since they know it's my only option to leave the city?"

"Aeree could take you out of the city and you could catch the bus upstate." Kelsey places a sandwich in front of me. "I got called into work, which isn't too far from here, so I could take the subway, and you guys can take my husband's truck."

"You sure you don't mind?" Sad Eyes asks.

"No. This might be your only chance to get away." She smiles, squeezing my arm, then looks at the sandwich.

I better keep my end of the bargain and eat something or her generosity might run thin. With a small smile, I take my first bite. It's tuna melt on rye and she took it easy on the mayo. It's a meal I can live with.

"What about you, Aeree? Would it be okay if you drive me?"

I nod while chewing. Without a state case, the FBI has no more leverage over me, and the only things waiting for me at home are problems. Maybe a road trip will take my mind off Mitch and the mess he left me.

"I know the bus stops in Albany. Is that too far?"

"No, that's fine." It's about a three-hour drive. If Kelsey loans me some money, I could stay overnight in a motel, and on my way back tomorrow, visit my dad at the prison. He will be thrilled to see me, and he deserves to know of all the crap that has been happening, especially about Eltas. I wonder if he knows that his friend quit the military and is probably betraying his country. Would he have told me if he did know?

By the time I'm done eating, my batteries have started to recharge. A small boost of energy gets me through the goodbyes. In the elevator, I wash it all down with a bottle of water. When I slide into the driver's seat of Finn's truck, I'm actually looking forward to our trip.

"Thanks for not just abandoning me," Sad Eyes mumbles from the passenger seat.

"I know how it is to be on the run. My dad and I dodged the police for two weeks before we were arrested." I start the car and reverse out of the parking space. "Just try to lay low for a while, and hopefully, Kendall's family will stop looking for you."

"Yeah, hopefully."

From the pain in her eyes, she must be full of doubts. I feel sorry for her. Eventually, I will pull myself back together and go on with my life, but her struggle will never end. Even if Kendall's brothers eventually give up, the fear alone will force her to glance over her shoulder every single day.

Traffic is just picking up when we cross into the Bronx, congestion slowing us down before we even hit Woodlawn Heights. The temperature in the stuffy car becomes excruciating; even the air-conditioning is unable to offer enough relief. I feel like I'm slow roasting in an oven.

"There's a gas station with a rest area. Let's take a break until the traffic eases up," I say.

"That could be hours."

"Yeah, but sitting under a tree and waiting it out is better than having a heat stroke in a hot car. We don't even have enough water to stay hydrated."

"Okay, I guess."

I pull behind a truck into the gas station. We are not the only ones seeking refuge from the scorching sun; plenty of families and truckers have found comfort in the shaded areas by the picnic tables. The only downfall is the occasional whiff of a burning cigarette. I have never liked the smell, but ever since the night of my rape, I can't stand it. My attackers' breath was laced with it. Cigarette smoke makes me shudder every time my nose picks up the stench.

I fall back into the soft grass and stare into the sky. There isn't a single cloud. Over the past few days, I haven't kept up with the weather forecast, though from the looks of things, the heat and dry spell will continue. Here in the shade, the temperatures are just about bearable.

Wiggling around in the grass, I try to get more comfortable. Sad Eyes hardly manages to keep her eyes open. I try to relax, but my mind keeps racing at a hundred miles per hour. Now I'm glad that Kelsey made me eat the sandwich or my energy level would likely be at an all-time low. Replaying our conversation, I try to refute her assertion that I feel dirty and damaged, surrendering when I'm unable to come up with a single counterargument. Before my attack, I had never struggled with my weight; to the contrary, I had always felt good about myself. Not once did I fall victim to some societal beauty standard of the fashion industry, even when they tried to shove it down my throat with their constant advertising.

Things first changed when I went to prison. Having women who enjoyed my curves forcefully touch me was enough reason to starve myself to a point where they didn't find me attractive. Later with Mitch, it became an obsession after he called me his little China doll. Now in hindsight, his words could have easily been interpreted as racist, but they didn't bother me at the time. I was determined to keep up with his expectations, terrified he would leave me otherwise. That I lost myself in the process didn't even occur to me. In the end, it was all for nothing. Our relationship was no more than a well-orchestrated sham. Now I just need to figure out why he stayed married to me.

I sit up when the tingling sensation of being watched once again sets off my alarm bells. Gazing around, I find a set of curious eyes staring at me. The boy couldn't be older than nine or ten and is fascinated with something on my face. Instinctively, I rub my cheek with my palm, stopping when he continues to stare without even flinching. His parents should teach him some manners. It's rude to stare.

"Is something wrong?" I ask, forcing a small smile on my lips when the words come out a bit snappy.

"Why do you have a red dot on your forehead?"

I freeze. "A red dot?"

"Yeah, like a light." He edges closer. "Right there." His finger pokes toward the middle of my face. "What's that?"

The spit dries up in my mouth. Without even thinking, I lunge forward, my body burying the boy underneath me. I expect the impact of the bullet that will end my life. When it doesn't hit me right away, I manage a desperate shout. "Nina, watch the sniper!"

I might as well have screamed "fire" in a crowded theater. People around me start to panic. Screams mix with shuffling feet. I shield my head with my arms when stomping shoes get close to me, too afraid to get up and leave the boy to his own devices. He could be trampled to death with no one to blame but me.

Two strong arms finally lift me up before helping the boy to his feet.

"Daddy, I'm scared." The boy's arms wrap around the man's neck before he is carried off without even a small thanks.

Ducking low to the ground, I take cover behind the hot-dog stand. The fabric under my armpits is soaked and sweat trickles down my side. My breath is quick and ragged. With wide eyes, I scan the area for Sad Eyes, but she is nowhere in sight.

On cue, the door to the gas station bathroom opens. For a second, Sad Eyes's frame seems frozen in place. When her gaze meets mine, I have a déjà vu moment. The warning shout leaves my mouth at the same time the crack of the discharging bullet disturbs the heated summer air. I gasp, unable to take my eyes off the scene unfolding in slow motion. Blood spews from her neck in pulsing gushes that burst out of the wound. The bullet pierced a main artery.

She falls forward on her knees, her mouth opening and closing, the rattling sound in her throat stalling my breath. I jump to my feet, ready to sprint over, when a hand holds me back. It's the little boy's father.

"Let go of me."

"Get real. You can't help her."

"But I have to."

He tosses me his phone. "Get the cops and an ambulance up here. That's all you can do."

Tears run down my face as I punch in the numbers to call 911. Every empty ring is pure torture. Sad Eyes's hand reaches out for me as she tries to crawl to safety, her pleading eyes locked with mine. Her lips form silent words. I know she's calling my name. Being so powerless tears me apart on the inside but helping her is a suicide mission.

"911, what's your emergency?"

"There was a shooting at the rest stop on I-87, just before Woodlawn Heights. A woman is critically wounded."

"Ma'am, are you at the location?"

"Yes, yes, I am."

"Okay, we'll send a car and an ambulance right away. Now, what's your name?"

"Aeree Cahill."

"Okay, Aeree, you need to stay calm."

My only response is a heavy sob.

"Is the shooter still in the area?"

"Yes, I think so. It's a sniper. I think it's the same one who killed a man a few days ago at the Federal Plaza in Manhattan."

"Ma'am, do you know the victim?"

"Yes." With all my effort, I tear my gaze away when Sad Eyes's glassy stare cuts into me like a knife. "It's Nina Humphrey. I think she's dead."

# Chapter 30

My teeth chatter despite the blanket around my shoulders. Glassy eyes seem to watch me from every corner, the horrors of the last few days finally catching up with me. I can't get Sad Eyes out of my mind. Why did the sniper shoot her and not me? He had a clear line of vision with me a sitting duck on a silver platter.

The ambulance came shortly after she was hit, but even the desperate revival attempts of the paramedics failed. When the cops started to ask questions, I broke down and begged them to bring me in. I was too shaken up, scared that the shooter would return if I stayed out of police custody. Though I hate being back at the federal building, a certain safety comes along with it.

"Hey, how are you holding up?" Kelsey squats next to me, rubbing my cold hands in hers.

"I don't know." Tears rise though I hate my continued drama queen act. "Why does this keep happening? What does this sniper want from me?"

"He must believe you have something he wants."

"And how did he even find us?" A shudder runs through me when I imagine him waiting right outside the building, the barrel of the rifle aimed at the double glass doors in the hopes that I'll be foolish enough to step through them. He must've been following us. There's no other way.

"We have no idea yet, but we brought Citadel Jamison in and she agreed to protective custody for now. You two are the only ones left."

I had totally forgotten about her—Mitch hadn't kept a file with a picture of her. Not that this would make her any safer from the maniac killer sniper.

"Anything on Marcel?"

She shakes her head. "Unfortunately not. His wife is going crazy."

"I hope he's okay."

"Yep, me too."

I'm startled by the knock on the door frame. Peeking around Kelsey, my eyebrows shoot up. What is Major Riley doing here? He has hardly changed since I last saw him four years ago; only more gray has snuck into his salt-and-pepper hair. His smile is reserved, just the way it used to be when he accidentally bumped into my dad and me on the base. I've never seen any emotions in his eyes—they always remind me of a frozen glazier in the middle of winter.

"Hi, Aeree. Would it be okay if we talk for a few minutes?" His attention briefly shifts to Kelsey. "Alone."

"No problem, sir."

Kelsey clears the field and Major Riley's heel prods the door closed before he pulls up a chair. With his chin propped on the back of his hands, he gazes at me with that same noncommittal expression. Without a doubt, this is an interrogation.

"Aeree, you need to be truthful with me or I can't help you."

"I have been truthful."

"So you don't have the data stick?"

"No. Otherwise, I would've turned it over. What on earth would I do with it?"

"You could sell it to Eltas Williams. We know he stopped by your house." His eyes drill into me, my body twitching when he doesn't even blink.

"Are you implying I'm a traitor?"

This time, a small smile teases the corners of his lips, but that doesn't alleviate the coldness of his gaze in the slightest.

"You tell me, Aeree. Your husband's will left you penniless, and I know you weren't happy about your dad's conviction. No one would blame you for trying to get your fair share from a country you felt betrayed by."

This is getting better and better. First they try to pin Mitch's murder on me, and now Major Riley is claiming I'm some international spy. "Do I need a lawyer?"

"Forget the lawyer, Aeree. All I want is for you look me straight in the eyes and tell me you never had the data stick. That's good enough for me."

"I never had the data stick." This time, I don't even twitch when he glares at me.

"Okay. What can you tell me about Eltas then?"

"I walked in on him searching my house. He asked me the same question you did and I told him the same thing. I don't have the data stick. One of your men, River Cunningham, told me later that Eltas had left the military. I had no idea, so you probably know much more about what is going on with him than me."

"We spoke to your dad yesterday. He told us that you and Eltas were close. Did Eltas ever tell you what happened in Fallujah?"

"No, he never talked about his missions."

"Even when he came home that summer after he escaped captivity? Your dad said he was over at the house all the time, that you and he used to whisper for hours. What was that all about?"

I drop my gaze. Though Eltas never went into anything specific, the pain and anguish were too palpable to ignore, his scars leaving little to the imagination. After six months of torture, they had broken him.

"He was hurting and needed a friend. That was all."

"Did he ever voice any radical ideas? Anything that could have suggested he switched sides?"

"No. I always thought Eltas was loyal to his country. He was a soldier through and through, and I never imagined he would switch sides, no matter what." I frown. "And to be truthful, I'm not convinced he did. Wouldn't that have been caught during one of his psychological evaluations? I mean, guys who work special ops have plenty of those."

"Eltas was the best at his job, so tricking a doctor shouldn't have been too difficult for him. After a while, he flat out refused to see the shrink and quit instead. That's not that uncommon, and I even forked some work his way when he first started his private security firm. The alarm bells only went off when he got into bed with Weston Cox a few weeks ago."

Major Riley's intense glare is like fuel for my twitching muscles. Even though I did nothing wrong, it sure does feel that way. Should I have noticed something odd about Eltas and alerted my dad? Eltas and I had been close ever since my mom died; he had always offered me a shoulder to cry on. Was I too scared to lose the one person I truly felt connected to by ignoring the obvious signs?

"You made Eltas the leader of the unit once my father went to prison. I would have thought you'd pick someone else if you had any doubts about his loyalty."

"Let's just say we owed him, so there wasn't much of a choice." With a huff, Major Riley turns to the door when there's a knock. "Come on in."

The door slowly opens and River's broad frame appears in the gap. The goofy grin can't hide the worry in his eyes. At least he hasn't turned on me yet.

"Any new lead on Williams or Cox?" Riley asks.

"No, sir. The FBI also confirmed they lost all contact with their informant, Harley Salyers. They have reason to believe that he might have turned on their missing agent."

"Fuck," Riley mumbles through gritted teeth. "This operation is going belly-up."

He stares in the distance, and I'm not even sure the last part was meant for my ears.

"What are you going to do, sir?" River asks as he lowers himself onto the spare chair in the room.

"Well, I was wondering why Eltas didn't kill Aeree at the picnic area when he had a clear shot. The only explanation I could come up with is that he still thinks she's got the data stick. Our last hope is to lure him into a trap." He smiles one of his cold smiles. "With Aeree's help, that is."

Something snaps inside me. I'm so sick and tired of the government using me in their games that I don't even care what happens to me. Let the sniper get me. Overall, I might actually be better off dead. "And why would I want to help you? Neither you nor the FBI can guarantee my safety if Eltas really turned on his country. You said it yourself, he is the best there is. Quite frankly, guys, I'm done. Just leave me the hell alone." I'm already halfway on my feet when Major Riley's firm hand on my arm forces me back into my seat.

"You need our protection, Aeree. Eltas will never stop if he believes you have the data stick."

"It's a risk I'm gonna take." Ignoring the slipping blanket, my arms fold over my chest. "Besides, how can you be so sure that Eltas is the sniper?"

"Who else could it be? Eltas has plenty of trained snipers working for him and wants to secure that data stick at all cost. Those kills were made with military precision. No offense, Aeree, but I'm someone who usually views evidence for its face value. Everything points to Eltas and Cox, unless you are privy to some information you haven't been sharing with us."

Major Riley's explanation makes sense. Who else would have a motive? Even if I don't want to believe Eltas turned traitor, the evidence against him is overwhelming. Everyone has a price and with the money he expects from the data stick, his new buddy Weston must have found his.

Major Riley clears his throat and tears me out of my conspiracy world. "Well, Aeree, what would it take for you to help us?"

"I want my father released from prison."

"You mean an early parole date?"

"No, I mean a full pardon." I smile, knowing that I have the upper hand. My father always said that the government would work any deal if they were desperate enough, and with the clock ticking, Riley must be under tremendous pressure from the Pentagon. Being immune to blackmail might be the official stance, but when it comes down to the wire, everyone is out for a practical solution. "This data stick must be a matter of national security, or you wouldn't be involved. Then there is the embarrassment if it turns out that one of your former men is the one who turned traitor and sold those secrets to a terrorist. If you want my help so badly, you better get my dad out for good. I'm not risking my life again for a wet handshake and a smile."

"Your dad is a convicted murderer." Major Riley shakes his head. "Don't know if I'm comfortable with your stipulation."

"You yourself said that you would've killed those bastards if you had been in his shoes. Was that just a bunch of bullshit to stop me from crying in your office, or are you a man of your words?" I beam at him. "And don't think I don't know that a pardon has to be signed by the attorney general. I'm not going anywhere unless I have that document in my hands."

This time, the small smile on Major Riley's lips is genuine as he slowly rises to his feet. "I'll make the call."

~~~~

A few hours later, I have returned to the waiting game, this time at my house. Three unmarked vehicles are watching the entrance from a safe distance and an FBI team has taken up camp in Kelsey's home next door. They are blind as a bat when it comes to indoor surveillance after Major Riley refused to take the risk of tipping Eltas off in case he swept the house before talking to me. Only a small voice transmitter that is camouflaged as one of River's shirt buttons keeps them in the loop.

"We should order something to eat. I'm starving." River shoots me a famished look from the couch. I'm still amazed by the amount of food he consumes.

"Sure. What would you like?"

"How 'bout some pizza?"

I smile thinly. Of course he'd choose a calorie nightmare. "Get a salad for me. I'm not really a big fan of melted cheese."

"Okay. Let's just order online and you can pick what you want."

Five minutes later, I complete the transaction with Mitch's credit card on file with the delivery service. That might land me in trouble with the probate court, but I'm not willing to dip any further into my cash reserves, especially since I'm not convinced the government will reimburse me.

The thought that Maureen will inherit everything under Mitch's will laces my mouth with bitter bile. While I was waiting for the pardon to go through, Kelsey asked me about my plans for the future. With my dad home, there will be another mouth to feed, which will make finding a job a top priority. Kelsey suggested I start my own business. Reviving my catering business is intriguing, but also ironic for someone with an eating disorder.

"I'm gonna go upstairs and freshen up a little. If the food comes, there are napkins in the kitchen."

River grunts something from the couch. He has found a basketball channel, and like any other man, he's totally entranced by the squeaking of rubber soles on a gym floor while their owners bounce a ball from one side of the court to another, earning millions in the process. As far as I'm concerned, those sports players are all overpaid.

I trudge upstairs. It's stifling. I wish we'd installed air conditioning in this old house. For a second, I'm tempted to open the window, but that would constitute a security breach. Major Riley stressed that we should limit the entry points to the front and back doors to give his men and the FBI the opportunity to monitor anyone who tries to get into the house.

I stroll into the bathroom and glance at the bathtub with a grimace. I would kill for a shower right now, but that will take too long. With a sigh, I turn toward the sink. The cool water I splatter on my face feels divine, and I take my time washing my hands and brushing my teeth. The bandage on my neck looks grungy. I better change it—an infection is the last thing I need.

When I tear the bandage off, the wound burns like hell. Pus has formed around the stitches. I should get this checked out as soon as possible. Rummaging through my nightstand, I find the bag with the sterile bandages the hospital gave me. My eyes fall on the unfamiliar medicine bottle next to it. I dig through my brain, wondering where I got them from, and then it clicks. Those are Julie's migraine pills. The doorbell rings just as a prickling sensation spreads along my scalp. This couldn't be. I had opened the bottle at one point when I had wanted to take one of the pills and would have noticed the data stick. Of course, I had been under a lot of stress and it had been dark—I was also in a lot of pain. There's always a chance something small could have been buried underneath the pills that I could have missed.

With trembling fingers, I fidget with the top, wiping my moist hands a few times on the comforter until I finally manage to pop the bottle open. I pour the contents on the bed. A gasp escapes me when I notice the small card that's not even the size of my fingernail. It's a micro SD card. I fist-punch the air. With flying fingers, I shove the pills back into the bottle. I'm just about to pocket the microchip when the floorboard squeaks right outside my bedroom.

"River, guess what—"

The rest of my words are stuck in my throat when someone other than River appears in the doorway. The barrel of a gun points right at the center of my chest.

"Really sorry it had to come to this, Aeree."

I glance at the bed, but the microchip is fully hidden by the folds of the navy blanket. "If you shoot me, you'll never know where the data stick is. However, if you answer one question, I'll give it to you."

"Oh, what the heck." Amusement spreads in Eltas's eyes, though the aim of the gun is still firmly fixed on my heart. "What's the question?"

"I want to know why you ratted out my father."

# Chapter 31

"Why do you think I ratted out your father?" Though Eltas's voice is still light, the amusement has vanished from his eyes.

"'Cause you were the only one with a motive. You knew Major Riley would never make you commander of a special-ops unit, not without my dad's consent."

"True, but your dad was always very supportive of me." He steps into the room. "Why should he withhold his consent?"

"Because I think he was on to you after Fallujah. He could see you had changed, but he didn't have proof you switched sides. So you figured you'd kill two birds with one stone when you ratted him out. Getting rid of him didn't only make you the leader of the unit but stopped him from digging."

He laughs in the most artificial way. "You think you have it all figured out, but you're just like your dad. Making allegations without proof is a dangerous game and can get you killed."

"So tell me it's not true. Look me in the eyes and tell me I'm wrong."

A sudden coldness wraps around me like a sheet of ice. Finally, he sighs. "I can't."

"Then tell me why? What did he do to deserve your betrayal?"

His eyes cloud in memory as he glares in the distance. Only the ticking of the old-fashioned alarm clock on Mitch's nightstand disturbs the pressing silence. When his gaze refocuses, his lips are reduced to an angry line. "You have no idea how it feels when you get left behind. I was running toward the helicopter, but your dad gave the order to take off. I know he thought he was doing the right thing since he would've risked everyone's life otherwise, but that still doesn't make it any better when you're the one standing in the middle of a war zone, knowing there's no way out. Without that order, I wouldn't have been captured."

"He wouldn't have left you if there had been any other way."

His smile is sad. "I know you believe this, but your dad is not as perfect as you think. He made mistakes, got good people killed. In combat, you have to make life-and-death decisions, sometimes in a split second, and occasionally, you get it wrong. Leaving me was one of those times."

I realize that no matter what I say, he has convinced himself that my father made the wrong choice. Reasoning this point with him is useless.

"Then why did you quit just a few months after you were made commander of the team? You got what you wanted. Why are you betraying your country?"

"The ones who captured me showed me the truth. This country doesn't give a damn about anyone—we are all dispensable when we become a burden. The government didn't even try to bring me back. To the contrary, they denied I was ever part of the military and claimed I acted of my own accord. They abandoned me just like your dad, and when I came back, they acted like nothing had happened. Business as usual. I didn't even get a commendation for spilling my blood for my country."

"I'm so sorry, Eltas." I take a step forward, which causes him to raise his weapon again. There is a distance in his eyes, confirming he is long gone. I still try to reach out to him. "Selling secrets to the enemy is not the answer. You risk the lives of many innocent people if the information on the microchip falls into the wrong hands."

He snorts. "Who's saying anything about selling? These are my brothers and I support the cause. The classified secrets on the stick will give them an advantage in this war and save the lives of many."

I hide my shock by grinding my teeth together—during his captivity, they must have radicalized him through and through. The Eltas who is standing in front of me has no resemblance to the man I once knew. That I never suspected a thing is mindboggling. So many chats, so many spilled tears—and not once did he criticize his country or my dad in any way. His building anger flew totally under the radar of anyone.

"So where does this leave us?" I ask.

For a second, he diverts his gaze, but when our eyes meet again, the darkness in them gives me the chills. "Where's the data stick, Aeree? You said you had it."

"I lied. I don't know where it is."

"Wrong answer." With one fluid move, his fingers enclose my wrist and he drags me out of the room toward the steps. When we reach the landing, I try to tear myself loose, but his grip only tightens. Half pulling, half shoving, we make our way down the steps. At the threshold to the living room, my heels dig into the floor in an attempt to avoid the inevitable. Eltas jerks my arm impatiently. My shoulder almost pops out of its socket, the roaring pain forcing me to stumble into the room. I'm shoved onto the couch. Though the cushion is soft, my spine throbs from the impact.

"Stay there and don't move if you don't want me to hurt you." When I flinch, Eltas points a warning finger at my face. I still.

My eyes connect with those of the guy from the hospital, who is slouched back in the armchair with a smug smile. A big bandage covers the side of his head where Sad Eyes got him with the bedpan. I hope he's in a lot of pain.

Harley has taken up post by the window, peeking through the drawn curtains. "It's still quiet out there. Riley must not have noticed that we took out his men." He smirks at me before his lips pucker for a kiss. When I drop my gaze, he laughs until one glare from Eltas shuts him up.

"Are you ready?" Eltas asks the last man in the room, who nods.

The man is young and someone I have never seen before. He stands beside River, who is gagged and bound with cable ties to one of my dining room chairs. The man's dark curls hide part of his face, but when he finally turns to look at me, my insides recoil. His eyes are cruel with bloodlust. Not only has he killed before, but he is someone who enjoys causing people pain.

Eltas removes the gag from River's mouth. "Meet my friend Ali, kiddo. I met him a few years back in Fallujah where he showed me the true meaning of pain. He's a natural when it comes to torture."

Though Eltas is looking at River, there's no doubt he is talking to me. When he spins around with a wide smile, my hunch is confirmed. "Do you know what's the worst?" The pain in his eyes contradicts the smile playing on his lips.

When I remain silent, he gives Ali a small nod.

"It's not the electricity or the boiling water. No, it's the little things that get under your skin. And I mean that literally." He stretches out his hand and Ali hands him a little stick he had produced from a duffle on the floor. "This is made of bamboo, the tip sharpened to perfection. During interrogation, it gets pushed under your fingernails. The resulting pain is maybe the worst I've ever experienced." He squats next to me, holding out the little stick. "You don't want River to experience this, do you, Aeree?"

"Please, Eltas, you took an oath."

"So did your father. We always lived by the motto that no one is left behind. When push comes to shove, words don't mean anything."

He scratches the tip of the little stick gently over my lower arm. I flinch when the skin breaks as he pulls away, some of the blood dripping on the carpet. The pain is manageable, but this little stick is a potent weapon.

"Where's the data stick, Aeree?"

I glance at River. He gives me a brave smile.

"I have no idea."

Eltas hands the stick back to Ali, who kneels by River's side. I cup my hands over my ears when he slowly inserts the tip under River's middle fingernail. The tormented shout still hits me full force. My stomach cramps as nausea runs up my throat. By the time the shout breaks, I'm ready to barf.

"Please, Eltas, *stop*."

"You're the only one who can stop this." Eltas's thumb wipes a stray tear from my cheek. "Just tell me where the data stick is."

"I honestly don't know."

"You see, before Weston shot Julie, she told him that the stick was in her backpack. After we interrogated this FBI agent, Marcel, he confessed that you were the only one of the group who searched it. Since the FBI turned it upside down and didn't find anything, it's only logical that the stick is with you."

I can't hold his gaze. "But I don't have it."

"You've always been a desperate liar." He gives Ali another small nod just as my hands cup my ears again. The scream is even more distressing this time, lasting longer with an intensity that curls every nerve end in my body.

When the painful vibration in my ears finally stops, I stare at Harley, who's watching River's tormented frame with an ecstatic smile. Drool has formed at the corners of his mouth, the sign of a true sadist. Our eyes lock for a second and he blows me another kiss.

Eltas has followed the exchange. He chuckles. "Harley wants ten minutes alone with you. He swears he'll get you to talk. So far, I've said no, but given you're not cooperating, I might have to change my mind."

When another plagued shout from River almost splits my eardrums, I can't hold back the tears. "Stop. I'll give it to you."

"Good girl. I knew you'd come to your senses."

"It's upstairs."

"Then let's go." He pulls me to my feet and ushers me in front of him up the steps.

I only hesitate on the threshold to my bedroom for a second, taking just enough time to look at the display on my alarm clock. It has been almost thirty minutes since Eltas invaded my home with his men. Standard unit protocol requires periodic check-ins during a stake out, and even if Eltas knocked out every single one of Riley's men, someone must have noticed the radio silence by now. Help should be on the way.

I rush over to the bed, squinting when I notice that the microchip is gone. My hand runs frantically over the comforter, but there's nothing. The chip has vanished in thin air.

"It's gone." My voice trembles as I spin around. "I swear it was just here."

Eltas grimaces. "I think you're bullshitting us, Aeree." He steps aside, making way for Harley, who followed us upstairs. "You've got your ten minutes."

"Please, Eltas, no." My words are no more than a whimper. Tears stifle my breath when Harley steps inside the room, closing the door behind him. One swift turn of the lock seals my doom.

"Here we are again." Harley grins when I back up, step by step, until I can't go any farther. "No one can save you now, honey."

My hand wraps around the stand of my bedroom lamp. I will give him a run for his money.

"Tsk, silly girl." He ducks when I swing the lamp, the punch to the side of my cheek taking me off my feet.

I shake my head a few times to get rid of the swooshing in my ears. On my hands and knees, I crawl away, getting back on my feet as soon as I put a little distance between us. As I spin around, my fists rise.

His laugh is mocking. Overconfidence is a fighter's biggest downfall—something I will try to beat into his thick skull.

I watch his pupils as he approaches, his whole body bulldozing forward like he's planning to flatten me. I sidestep out of his way, my elbow ramming right into his kidneys. He growls like a big bad bear, but he can't turn his body around fast enough to avoid a kick to his kneecap. With a howl, he goes down.

Grinning as I gaze down on him, I draw my foot back to kick his most sensitive parts when he lunges forward, ramming his shoulders into my shins. The force of the impact, followed by a sudden sharp pain, is enough to toss me on my butt. Before I can get back on my feet, Harley crushes me. I cry out when pain shoots up my ribcage and into my lower back. He once again has the upper hand, if solely by mere body weight. I kick erratically, my pounding fists on his back only making him laugh.

With glee in his eyes, his hands enclose my neck, squeezing tightly. I instinctively gasp for air, which he takes as an opportunity to push his tongue into my mouth. The sour stench of his breath cramps my stomach. I bite down hard, his bellow mixing with the metallic taste of his blood.

His grip loosens, his body going limp for just a second. I take advantage of his moment of weakness, crossing my arms and grabbing his wrists. With all my strength, I push down with my elbow closest to my body to keep him from choking me further, my foot wrapping around his lower leg at the same time. It's the move Eltas, of all people, showed me after my rape. I roll over, amazed when I can actually free myself. Ignoring the stabbing pain in my side, I push myself back to my feet.

Without giving him time to recover, my foot flies forward, burying itself deep into the soft area between his legs. He clutches his crotch, mouth wide open, his face contorted. My gaze darts around, finding the lamp just a few feet away. With one leap, I close the distance and regain control of the lamp. As my arm rises for the blow, he tries to shield his head with his elbows, but his movements are sluggish. The lamp hits him right on the side of his head. Glass shatters, thick blood trickling onto the carpet. I don't need to look at his limp body to know I knocked him out.

I double over, fighting the nausea and raging pain in my ribcage. With the back of my hand, I wipe the blood from my mouth, hissing when I come in contact with a split lip. Sudden heaviness settles into my bones and I sink to the floor, resting my aching back against the bed. My lungs sting like someone set them on fire, pain flaring with every breath. I still can't prevent a snicker as I gaze at Harley's crumpled frame. I fought back and it feels damn good.

Pondering what to do next, I flinch when the moan of splintering wood rolls through the house. An array of shouts follows, their meaning drowned out by the commotion of trampling footsteps. Though I should probably stay put, I'm still high from the rush of adrenaline pumping through my veins. Tossing caution aside, I heave myself back to my feet.

With one long step, I'm at my bedroom door, my fingers fumbling with the lock to get it open. In my haste, it takes three attempts, and by the time the door swings back, a new silence has settled over the house. I scamper along the hallway before taking cover behind the balustrade. Peeking downstairs, I find Wesley lying facedown on the floor. Two dark figures with masks hold Eltas in check. He's on his knees with his hands locked behind his head. There's no sign of Ali.

"Sir, we're clear." One of the dark figures removes his mask and I recognize him as another special-ops operator who runs his own unit.

Heavy boot heels bang together as several men stand at attention when Major Riley strides into the house, his face wearing a smug expression, like he just saved the world. "Did we secure the data stick?"

Kelsey steps forward. "I did, sir." Carefully, she places the microchip in his outstretched hand. "Aeree Cahill was the one who found it and she turned it over to me."

My sigh of relief is only audible to me. If she hadn't given me credit for the discovery, the deal with my dad would be off. For a second, my mind drifts back to the first moment I saw her on the swing set. Back then, I never imagined us becoming friends, but oddly enough, she is the one person I trust at the moment. I will never be able to thank her enough.

"Is he dead?" Major Riley stares at Wesley's still body as he waits for confirmation.

"Yes, sir, and we detained Ali Shazar as he was trying to escape through the backyard."

"Then we are done here." Major Riley's chin juts at Eltas. "Wrap him up. We're taking him to Guantanamo."

# Chapter 32

The FBI insist on taking me to the hospital. After a few X-rays, it's officially confirmed that three of my ribs are broken. I end up with a tight bandage around my torso and the advice to take it easy. Since I don't intend to get in any more fights, I gladly sign myself out with the promise to return if I have excessive pain.

Armed with a new prescription for painkillers, I'm wheeled out of the emergency room. Kelsey is standing by the window with her phone pressed to her ear. She is crying. Mumbling to the nurse that I can take it from here, I dismiss her and wheel my chair over to Kelsey.

"Hey, what's the matter?" I ask after she ends the call.

"There's still no sign of Marcel. I'm going crazy. Eltas isn't talking and I'm under strict orders not to question Harley while he's in the hospital. Dinkle is such a bitch. She doesn't even care."

"I'm sorry." I reach for her hand, giving it an encouraging squeeze. "Is there any way I can help?"

She shakes her head. "How are *you* doing?"

"Surprisingly good. Though every part of me hurts, it's still a great feeling that I showed the son of a bitch that he can bleed."

"Yeah, I should have stuck around after finding the microchip in your bedroom, but I was getting ready for the raid. I underestimated the situation. I'm sorry." A blush colors her cheeks. "I'm also sorry I couldn't help River, but we were under orders not to interfere without backup. We could have botched the operation otherwise."

"River is a big boy. I'm sure he'll be fine." As a special-ops soldier, interrogations are nothing more than a work hazard.

He knew what he was getting into when he signed up for Riley's team. "How did you even get into the house?"

"Some guy from SWAT and I were actually planted in the attic before you got home. Kind of like an insurance policy, but they didn't want to tell you in case Eltas interrogated you." She laughs. "It was kind of funny because we were climbing up the huge oak tree in your yard and Ramona saw us. She thought we were burglars and shrieked, almost alerting the entire neighborhood. Luckily, Finn calmed her down before she could give the whole plan away."

I snicker as I picture Marcel's little daughter shouting at Kelsey in the tree with her bossy know-it-all attitude. That girl is something. Her parents can be proud of her.

A sudden uneasiness settles in my stomach when I realize that there's a chance Marcel is dead. Eltas said they interrogated him. After meeting Ali, this can only mean a lot of pain for Marcel if he actually broke under the pressure. If he is still alive, he must be seriously hurt.

"Harley is the only one who can tell us about Marcel. We need to talk to him."

"I know, but Begay said I'm not supposed to—"

"Screw him. He's not even your boss."

"But he's a senior team lead. I can't just ignore his direct order or I'll lose my job. Hell, as a federal employee, I can even go to jail if I question a suspect outside protocol."

"Well, I'm not a federal employee, and quite frankly, I don't give a damn what Begay says. Where's Harley?"

"Third floor."

"Then let's go."

She only hesitates for a moment before pushing me toward the elevator. I keep hitting the button while we wait, twitching in the wheelchair. The muscles in my legs tingle as if a thousand little ants are about to move in, the uneasiness growing with every breath. Marcel is a good guy. He doesn't deserve to rot away in some basement while the only one who is able to find him is being pampered by the FBI.

It takes forever before the ping of the elevator announces its arrival. Kelsey wheels me inside after the doors slide back. Her face is stoic, her movements mechanical. Only the fact that she's chewing her lip is a reflection of her shot nerves. Her fear that my plan to confront Harley might not end well is palpable, but her need to help her friend must be more important to her than her career. It's a dedication I wish my father would have shown me all those years during his military service.

Only a few people loiter around the nurse's station when we get to the third floor.

"Where's Harley's room?" I ask as she pushes me toward a vending machine.

"It's all the way at the end of the corridor. Dinkle put two agents in front of his door, so what are we gonna tell them?"

My thirst for action is knocked down a peg. I have no idea how to get by the guards. "Can't we just tell them the truth? I'm sure they're going to understand that we need to find Marcel."

She gives me this who-are-you-kidding look.

"Well . . ." I try to come up with a logical explanation why we would need to talk to Harley, but my mind is blank. Chewing the inside of my cheek, I stare at the little blue specks on the wallpaper as if they could turn into some magical wisdom to help us out of our predicament. The sudden squeaking of wheels has my head snapping around.

Bill's eyebrows are raised as he gazes at us. "What are you girls doing here?"

"Aeree wanted hot chocolate." Kelsey blushes under the obvious lie.

"And they don't have that in the cafeteria?"

My cheeks start to tingle as his eyes dart back and forth between Kelsey's face and mine. Since I don't have anything meaningful to add to the conversation, I decide to stay quiet. Kelsey must feel the same, his question hanging in the air like pesky smoke.

"I was just going to relieve our two colleagues down the hall so they can grab something to eat. Care to join me, Agent Walker?"

"Sure thing, sir." Kelsey's smile is tentative.

Bill leans forward, his lips close to my ear. "Lose the chair and wait in the bathroom until the coast is clear. We'll see you in a few minutes."

It finally dawns on me that he is on the floor for the exact same reason as us. As head of another FBI division, he has no business hanging around Begay's suspect unless he wants to question him on the sly.

When I stand up, a brief dizzy spell hits me, but after a few steps, my body readjusts. Walking is nevertheless incredibly painful and I grit my teeth as I stroll inside the bathroom. Washing my hands is the only thing to do since I'm afraid that peeing will worsen my condition. I take the opportunity to study my face in the mirror. The fight with Harley has left its mark; half my face is swollen from his blow to my cheek. My eyes have also changed. The dullness that was present since Mitch's death has vanished, a new determination in its place. I will survive this. Life can knock me down as much as it wants, but like a phoenix, I will rise again. Burning to ashes is just part of the process.

I squint at myself. Where was my head these last few years, sulking and whining, and having a man take care of me? Before my assault, that would've been unthinkable. Kelsey is right. Living in the past just wore me down, and I have to push forward no matter what. The only one who can take my future away is me.

The adrenaline kicks in again, my body driven by a new high as I walk along the corridor toward Harley's room. The throbbing pain is barely noticeable—it's like my soul has been ignited by some powerful fuel. I catch myself humming, a small smile playing on my lips. If I can only help save Marcel, this day will have turned into the best day in a very long time.

Bill's hushed words to Kelsey are cut off when his eyes fall on me. His eyebrows rise again, but he doesn't say anything. His chin simply juts to the door next to him. Just before I enter, he holds up a small stick.

"You might need this."

It's the bamboo stick that Ali used to torture River. I take it, though I'm not sure if I truly want to use it.

"You've got ten minutes."

I grin at the irony, though I'm convinced I won't need that long. Harley is a coward at heart who will break under any type of pressure.

The window shades in the room are drawn, the blue light of dusk only cutting in through a few gaps. It's so dim I have to squint to make out Harley's frame on the bed. When I step closer, I notice that his whole head is wrapped in bandages. The lamp must have caused more damage than I originally thought.

He blinks at me, his eyes unfocused before recognition flares up. The monotone beeps of the heart monitor multiply. His breath is heavy as he squirms to get away from me until the confines of his bed stop his efforts. The gleam of metal catches my eye—both his wrists are secured with handcuffs. He couldn't defend himself if he wanted to.

"Hello, Harley." I plop into the visitor's chair next to the bed.

"What do you want?" His voice is rough, his face contorted into a painful grimace.

"Marcel Brown. Where is he?"

"I already told Dinkle. I want immunity or I won't say nothin'."

Bile knots my stomach. He's gambling with Marcel's life to get himself a deal. People like him are leeches. I can only hope he'll go to prison for a long time. Society deserves to be safe from animals like him.

"I don't do deals." I pull out the stick, staring at the tip as I roll it back and forth between my fingers. Such a potent little weapon. Though Harley deserves to feel some of River's pain, his shouts will likely alert the nurses. Hopefully, the sight alone will be intimidating enough.

His tongue moistens his lips as he stares at the stick with wide eyes. "You can't use that. That's torture."

My chuckle is bitter. "Did you afford the same courtesy to Marcel before you sold him out to Weston and Eltas?"

His left eyelid twitches uncontrollably until he drops his gaze.

"Where is he, Harley?"

When he still remains quiet, I decide to go for it. With all my strength, I turn his hand with his palm facing down. He tries to curl his fingers to fists, but my hand crushes his fingers flat underneath it. The tip of the stick has barely scraped his fingertip when he cries out.

"Stop. I'll tell you."

I only glare at him. My patience is running thin.

"He's in Queens. House is abandoned, close to Hamilton Beach, right on the corner of First and Russell Street."

I can't hide the triumph in my smile. "Thanks, Harley. Get better soon. A prison cell is already waiting." As I walk out,

I don't even bother looking back when the door shuts behind me.

~~~~

It takes some serious convincing before Bill agrees that Kelsey and I can tag along on Marcel's rescue mission—and only as concerned bystanders. Apparently, some conflict of interest bullshit prevents Kelsey from actively participating in an official capacity and civilians are personas non grata during FBI operations. They even make me sign a waiver, so I can't sue them in case I get hurt.

We take Kelsey's car and pull behind a truck across from the abandoned house. The four SUVs of the SWAT team block the road. The agents are dressed in full gear, the number of guns and rifles enough to start a small war. After a short warning, the door is broken down with a battering ram. The splintering wood reminds me that I'd better get my own door fixed if I don't want burglars to have a field day in my house.

I lean forward to get a better look when smoke drifts out of the house into the driveway. Everyone is now inside. The expected shots don't materialize; the only thing floating our way is the occasional shout of "clear." The seconds wind down like minutes. When the wait becomes unbearable, I jump out of the car.

Expecting Kelsey to call me back, the "I don't give a damn" already rests on my tongue when she overtakes me. She is just about to enter the house with neither a vest nor a mask when one of the SWAT guys holds her back.

"They found him and he's alive. Ambulance is on its way."

"I want to see him." She struggles in his arms, but he doesn't budge.

"Sorry, Kelsey, but you have to wait out here."

She growls. "Let go of me, Trevor."

"Kelsey, stop. He's just doing his job." My hand comes to rest on her forearm. "You can't help Marcel right now. Those guys are a well-attuned team and you will only get in their way if you storm in there."

He tosses me a grateful smile. Without words, we understand each other. All units, be it SWAT or military, operate in the same manner. They are strongest when they can work together like a well-oiled machine.

Kelsey finally stops fighting the guy, her body deflating when she lets out a long breath. "I'm just so damn scared." Tears glisten in her eyes.

"It'll be okay. This will be a long night for you, so you should preserve your energy."

Her hand clutches her mouth when they carry Marcel out on a stretcher. His face is covered in blood and swollen beyond recognition. An oxygen mask is placed over his mouth and nose as soon as they lift him into the ambulance. Kelsey is now frozen in place, her "oh my god" the only constant, running over her lips on repeat.

My hard shake snaps her out of her daze. "Let's follow with the car. I'll call his wife on the way."

She holds me back when I'm just about to dart across the street. "Thanks, Aeree. I would've probably already gone insane if it wasn't for you."

"Don't mention it. That's what friends do for each other, right?"

That finally gets her to smile.

~~~~

The horizon is already painted a deep morning orange when a cab drops me off in front of my house. The air smells like rain after several thunderstorms raged over the city for most of the night, the rolling thunder even audible in the waiting area of the emergency room. Just after four a.m., the doctors moved Marcel's status from critical to stable, causing a sigh of relief to run through our group of visitors.

Marcel has a big family. His mother and nephew even drove down from Connecticut when they learned about his condition. His wife, Donna, cried in Kelsey's arms, leaving Ramona shell-shocked on the sidelines until I pulled her aside and told her what my mom had said all those years ago when my father had gotten hurt.

"Your daddy works for the good guys. Because of that, God gave him a special protection around his heart, so whatever happens, he'll always love you. You need to stay strong for him, because it helps him fight."

After that, she held her chin up high the way I used to, battling her tears with a brave smile. Finn distracted her by reading to her while she snuggled with her little brother and the twins before the five of them went home with the promise that Kelsey would call if anything changed with Marcel.

As I stand in my driveway, I ponder whether I should check in on him and the kids but discard the idea. Though we talked for a couple of minutes at the hospital and he seemed nice, it's not my place to keep him company when Kelsey is not at home. A jealous fit could seriously compromise our blossoming friendship.

A light breeze offers hope that the brutal heat wave might be broken. For a second, I just let the wind float over me and play with my hair. The crispness in the air is refreshing. Maybe I'll drive down to the beach later and take a nice long walk to get my head clear. The taxi drive took another bite out of my dwindling cash, and I'll probably have to apply for social benefits soon. At least my father will be home to help me figure things out—he has always had a knack for finding solutions to difficult problems.

My front door is boarded up, so my money won't have to be spent on an emergency call to an expensive carpenter over the weekend. I turn toward the yard, walking along the path to get to the backdoor. My forehead wrinkles when I pass below the living room window. The curtains are drawn, though I could have sworn they were open when I left.

Humming a song I heard on the radio during the taxi drive, I open the backdoor and step into the kitchen. The prickling sensation that spreads along my scalp has me halt in my tracks. If I didn't know better, I could swear someone else is in the house. With a click of my tongue, I dismiss the notion as paranoia.

My throat is parched, and I pour myself a glass of lemonade from the fridge. Making a mental note to finally go grocery shopping, I slip out of my sneakers. The floor feels cool under my feet despite my socks. I stretch slightly, careful to not put pressure on my ribs. Before I left the hospital, I took more painkillers, so the throbbing is manageable, but the exhaustion is slowly catching up. A nap sounds incredibly appealing.

Glancing into the living room as I pass by on my way to the stairs, my steps come to a screeching halt. The lemonade glass drops to the ground, the cold liquid splattering against my legs and soaking into my socks. I barely notice. My eyes are about to bulge from their sockets as I stare at the man sitting on the couch with a wide grin. He must be a hallucination. Words fail me as my mouth opens and closes like that of a mindless idiot.

"What's the matter?" He wiggles his brows. "Aren't you gonna say hello?"

# Chapter 33

"Paul." As the truth sinks in that he is not a figment of my imagination, I spin around to run and collide with a wall of a man. With my pitiful five feet one inch, I barely reach his chest. He smiles down on me before one shove transports me into the living room. I fall onto my knees right in front of Paul's feet, the painful impact vibrating deep within my bones. Though I had only seen a photograph of him, I'm certain the man who pushed me is Mitch's friend, Colton something.

"The fuck, Paul? What are you and your friend doing in my house?" Even as a police officer, he has no right to just waltz in here. Given recent events and my full cooperation with the FBI and the military, he couldn't possibly have a warrant.

A chuckle from the ottoman by the window draws my attention to the third person in the room. My jaw drops. Like she has no worry in the world, Agent Dinkle is seated with one leg crossed over the other, her torso gently rocking back and forth.

"What the hell is going on? Why are you here?" As my finger points at Dinkle, I hate that my hand is shaking. My gaze returns to Paul. The same vicious gleam he had when I saw him at the federal building just a few days ago has snuck into his eyes.

"We're here to finish the job. You see, Aeree, many years ago, some of us who work in law enforcement and with the courts figured out that our justice system, as it stands, doesn't really work. Cops, judges, and lawyers alike were sick of watching guilty people walk free. So we decided to do something about it."

I swallow hard as a million questions zoom through my head, but I don't dare to interrupt him. Not when I'm finally getting some answers.

"Over the years, we've built up our network, and we're all on the lookout for those injustices. Once we find an instance where a possible culprit went free, a few of us investigate further. Then we have a minitrial without all that procedural bullshit and a bunch of witnesses who just muddy the waters. One of us argues for the state, another one for the accused, and a third is the judge. Once found guilty, we decide on a punishment. All in all, it's fair and swift."

I smirk to show him that he doesn't rattle me, though I'm scared shitless. "I'm sure those who were punished don't agree with you."

"Probably not, though we try to make the punishment to fit the crime. You rape someone, we have you raped; you beat someone, we do the same. If you took a life, we take yours. An eye for an eye. It's the law of the land since the beginning of time. You surely don't want to imply that all those generations got it wrong?"

Since it's undoubtedly a rhetorical question, I remain quiet. My jaw clenches to prevent my chattering teeth giving away my fear.

"Your case was different," he continues, his eyes now in the distance. "It involved a personal element. Since you assaulted me, the group gave me some discretion on how to handle it, especially once I convinced them that you might have assisted your dad in murdering the gang that raped you."

"But you never had any evidence I was involved."

"Nope, but the others didn't care since they all sided with me. At first, I wanted to kill you, but after Dave"—he briefly smiles—"sorry, I mean Mitch, after he got to know you while he was working on your case, he figured that putting you behind bars for the rest of your life would be a much worse punishment. That's when we came up with the Green Mountain Project. It was the perfect plan. Have a sniper shoot all the guilty criminals in your group and pin it on you. You would've never gotten a parole date."

"And how could you have possibly pinned all those murders on me?" I try to put a mocking spin on the words but fail miserably because my fear is all too palpable.

"Simple. The cheating spouse who convinced her new boyfriend to go on a shooting rampage to get rid of her husband and kill a bunch of people at the same time to make it appear like some random serial killing. We were all set. Mitch had been telling people about your marriage problems and that you were cheating on him. He was supposed to stage his death by jumping into the falls after I shot in the air. Of course, he was meant to survive and eventually be discovered wandering around by the forest rangers. All that would have been left was his claim that you confessed your plan to get rid of him just before he dropped into the waterfall. Open-and-shut case. Any jury would have convicted you."

"But why did he have to marry me?" I smirk at him in challenge in a desperate attempt to show him that his plan was ludicrous. There must be something seriously wrong with his head if he and his buddies went through all this trouble just to take their own twisted version of revenge.

"A boyfriend wouldn't have been convincing. No, it had to be a spouse." He leans forward, his cold eyes sending goosebumps up my arms. "Mitch and I grew up in the same foster family"—he glances at the big dude who pushed me down—"together with Colton here. We were inseparable. Unfortunately, my grades weren't good enough for me to go to law school, so I became a cop. After you assaulted me, we got together and started to cook up this plan. Mitch put your case on his boss's radar, so he could meet you without anyone getting suspicious. David was a common enough name for you not to figure out that my good friend Dave I had been telling you about was the same man, especially since Mitch had already started going by his middle name. Once he met you, he volunteered to marry you. He thought you were cute, so it wasn't too much of a sacrifice. It's something good friends do for each other when the stakes are that high."

Flashes of distant memories spark in my mind. It was true. When Paul and I were dating, he had mentioned his old friend Dave who was away at college, so I didn't get a chance to meet him. And I never made the connection.

Even now, this whole story sounds more like an elaborate plot of some thriller TV show than something that could happen in real life. Cops, lawyers, and judges who consider themselves to be the ultimate Solomon—who would have thought of that? Even if I had known about it, any jury would have declared me insane or paranoid if I had used this as a defense once my husband pointed the finger at me.

"Too bad your plan didn't work."

"Yeah, that's unfortunate. I wanted to pull out the day you were leaving on your trip once I found out that Julie and Tyson had also signed up when I called the lodge to confirm everything was set. Mitch insisted we go ahead since he was starting to freak out about Maureen. You see, he met her a few months after you tied the knot. Love at first sight, if you believe in that, and ever since then, he's been eager to wrap this up. Idiot almost botched the whole operation when he gave everything to her under his will, since any good investigator would have questioned their relationship. Well, I guess that doesn't matter anymore. The plan went belly-up once those private military guys got involved, though they will be the perfect fall guys now."

"I'm so sorry they ruined your plans." This time, I manage sarcasm as I smirk. "Was it tough getting all these people you wanted to kill together in our group?"

"Naw, they were just greedy. We made a list of all those we suspected of murder and sent out sweepstakes emails with the trip as prizes. Those who responded the quickest got the gig, giving priority to couples where both of them were involved." He snorts. "Call it killing two birds with one stone." His smile is smug. The plan with the sweepstakes must have been his concoction.

"And Citadel Jamison?" As far as I can tell, she had never hurt a fly.

"We were going to let her live—same as the tour guide and that couple Julie and Tyson. They were innocent and there was no need for us to kill them. We didn't know at the time that Julie and Tyson were classified data thieves, or we might have even taken care of them."

My gaze briefly diverts to Dinkle, who is still sitting on the ottoman like she owns the place, before my eyes return to Paul. Why they just let him run off at the mouth is a miracle to me, but they probably don't want to ruin his moment of revenge. It's personal to him and I'm as good as dead. "And I guess Agent Dinkle kept you in the loop?"

"Yep, it's great to have someone like her on the inside. After your rescue, we were still trying to hold on to the original plan and pin all those murders on you. We knew we would catch up with Norton Garrett eventually, and we were going to let Kendall Humphrey's family take care of his wife for us, but those guys are incompetent idiots and let her get away. Luckily, we found out about your plan to help her escape to Canada after you told the FBI, and it was easy for some cops in our group to track down the truck you were using." He smiles as his finger points right at the center of my forehead. "I had a clear shot and could have taken you out, but I knew that Mitch would have wanted you to go to jail. He had wasted two years of his life with this relationship, so that's the least I could do for him."

"And now you're here to arrest me?" With a taunting smile, I gaze at Dinkle and Colton. "Why did you bring them? Were you afraid you couldn't get it done alone?" My smirk widens. I'm unable to resist despite the building fear sickening my stomach. "Looks to me you lost your balls." My lips twitch. "Oh, I forgot. You actually did."

"Bitch." The slap sets off a painful explosion in my head, but I still can't help gloating that I got to him.

"Don't lose your cool, Paul," Dinkle says. "Let's just get this over with. You already said too much."

"Well, it's not like she'll live to tell anyone." Paul's lip is still quivering with rage. "Unfortunately for you, Aeree, a few divers pulled Mitch's body out of the pond in the mountains a few hours ago, so there is no more reason for me to let you live."

"He's dead?"

"Yes. Apparently, after he fell, his backpack got entangled in some of the underwater rocks and he drowned."

"Must have been a horrible death. This will be so devastating to Maureen." My words drip with so much sarcasm this time that he flinches back.

His hand rises for another slap when Dinkle's hiss stops him. "She is just provoking you to buy some time. Shoot her, or I'll do it for you. We don't have time for this."

"No, I'll do it." Paul's eyes rest for a second on my face before a smile curls his lips. His thumb runs along my jawline until I jerk my head away. "You used to be so beautiful. What happened to you? Mitch said you puked up all your food. Is that true? Did you turn into a little freak?"

"Fuck you, Paul."

"Maybe I should fuck you one more time before killing you. I know that would be the worst death for you."

"Paul." Dinkle groans. "Stop toying with her."

"Alright, alright." He pulls his gun from the holster and stands.

The realization that I'm about to die draws cold sweat from every pore. My pee weighs heavy in my bladder. Crazily enough, I send up a prayer asking to be spared the humiliation of wetting my pants as my departing gesture from this earth instead of pleading for protection. I expect tears to flood my eyes, but I manage to keep it together. I'm determined not to beg for my life. I can only hope that one day Paul will be judged for killing me the way he's judging me now.

A whimper still escapes me when the cold barrel of the gun presses against my forehead. I close my eyes, fully prepared to die.

# Chapter 34

As I'm captured in the darkness of my mind, every breath feels like an eternity. I wait for the bang, the imminent pain, which will end my life. A surreal swooshing in my ears turns into a pounding river as raging fear threatens to tear me apart. Despite my best efforts, I can't hold back the tears. As they roll down my cheeks, they tickle my chin in mockery before dripping onto the carpet. In that moment, I wish for Paul to pull the trigger and get it over with.

"Do it," Dinkle says. Her voice barely carries over my heavy breath, which echoes painfully in my head.

What will happen to me once I'm dead? My father has never been big into religion, stressing that we are the makers of our own destiny. My mom, on the other hand, believed that our spirit—our soul—would move on, our body just a carrier until this indestructible piece of us could rise above our tangible existence, almost like a reward for managing to get through life. Until she killed herself, I had believed her. Afterward, I had my doubts. Who would reward someone for quitting? It didn't make sense.

I read my share of articles about the actual death experience from people who were revived after their heart had stopped beating. A lot of them said there was a bright light; some said their whole lives had run backward in front of their eyes. I can't remember if anyone had talked about pain. That would be a pertinent fact right now, though if I'm lucky, the bullet will destroy that part of my brain before the pain can even register.

When the *pop* finally cracks like thunder, I crumple to the floor. The feared pain fails to materialize, and I exhale, waiting for death to claim me. Something heavy dropping next to me throws me off track. When more shots are fired, my eyes fly open. A wailing cry gets me to raise my head. I blink, totally disoriented, until the unexpected images rolling in front of me like a grotesque movie scene filter through my skull.

Paul lies still next to me. His glassy stare is fixed on the lamp above him, swinging softly in the morning breeze. A small trail of blood trickles from the middle of his forehead down the side of his face before seeping into the carpet. My first thought is that Mitch would be so mad at his friend—those stains will probably never come out. Dinkle lies equally still in the door frame, her chest rising and falling with accompanying groans.

River kneels next to her, pressing a cloth against her shoulder. "Clear through-and-through gunshot wound, but we need to get an ambulance here fast since she's losing a lot of blood."

"I'm on hold with the operator," Kelsey yells back from the kitchen.

I finally focus on the other person in the room, who is perched in a corner. A gun in his hand is pointed at the floor. I blink once, twice, but the man is not an illusion.

"Dad?" The sound has almost become unfamiliar.

The biggest smile is on his face. "You alright, Pooh Bear?"

All I can do is nod. The whole situation feels totally surreal. Maybe I died and this is the afterlife.

I finally snap out of my daze when my father's arms wrap tightly around me for the first time in over four years. Like a little girl, I weep against his shoulder as the tears keep rolling, and for once he lets me be without complaining. He's home and all will finally be alright.

~~~~

It's almost noon before things settle down again. With the ambulances came the police, but after Kelsey flashed her badge, things stayed civil. The statements confirmed that my father acted in clear self-defense when he shot Paul with one of River's service pistols. River even got an approving slap on the back from one of the cops for reacting so fast when Dinkle pulled her own gun. Kelsey played her part by tackling Colton as he was trying to flee through the back door before kicking him in the balls and handcuffing him to our radiator.

When the last police car turns the corner to leave us to our own devices, I can finally breathe freely again. It's like this incredible burden has lifted, taking away my grief and misery. When I search my heart for traces of Mitch, I realize that only the bitter sting of betrayal lingers, but I will get over that eventually. After all, I'm a fighter.

Eltas's words replay in my mind, the bitterness of his hissed words about being left behind like venom stuck in my brain. While I'm still convinced my father had no choice, I also understand the utter resentment Eltas must have felt. Being abandoned by people one trusts is like a constant beating. Mitch did the same to me when he left me without a dime after carrying on an affair during our entire marriage, all while pretending to love me. Sometimes, fighting back is the only way, but while Eltas chose the wrong means, I intend to not let my need for revenge guide me this time. Maybe I should explore legal options and battle Mitch's testament with his own weapons.

"I'd better go and check on Finn and the kids." Kelsey squeezes my shoulder. "You okay here?"

"More than okay," I say as I beam at my dad. "Thanks again for everything."

She just smiles, holding her fingers up to her ear in a phone motion as she walks away.

It feels great to have a friend now who I can call anytime I need to. With a sigh, I lean back on the hammock swing, gazing at my dad and River through hooded eyes. They are slouched in lawn chairs. River has his feet up on the table, the sun playing on his skin. I wonder if he can get a sunburn.

"So, guys, care to fill in the blanks?"

"Why don't you brief my daughter, Staff Sergeant?" My father rises, bending over to peck me on the cheek. "Sorry, Pooh Bear, but I still smell like prison. Heading up to take a shower if that's okay."

I wish he would just drop that stupid nickname. So what if I was obsessed with Winnie the Pooh until I was twelve? Before he leaves, he and River exchange this glance that forces my spine to stretch in suspicion. This smells like a conspiracy to give River and me a chance for some alone time. What's up with that?

River gives me this goofy grin before his head falls back against the cushion. "Since I got hurt, Major Riley didn't think it was a good idea for me to go to Guantanamo, and he ordered me to pick up your dad and bring him here after the doctors gave me the green light. It took half the night to get him processed out of the prison, and of course, we had to stop for breakfast because we were both starving. I tell you, your dad can eat. You owe me twenty-four dollars for his share of the tab."

I roll my eyes—when I asked him to fill in the blanks, I didn't want a minute-by-minute recount. Still not wanting to interrupt him, I let it slide.

"Just before we got here, Major Riley called. He said they interrogated Eltas, and while he wasn't even denying the espionage, he claimed he had nothing to do with the sniper. Only Julie and Tyson, and that guide Bobby, were killed on his orders. Riley wanted me to talk to you and investigate further."

"I'm surprised Major Riley believed him."

"Something never added up in my book and he must have questioned that, too. Eltas was a highly trained sniper with active combat assignments and wouldn't have bothered with a laser range finder. Those things can give away your location. Even Weston had too much military training for that. A laser range finder is only used by someone who has had some training but doesn't shoot long range regularly."

"Like a cop who doesn't work SWAT."

"Exactly."

"I guess that was sloppy thinking on Paul's part."

"Not sure if that mattered to him since he originally wasn't planning on pinning those shootings on a military sniper. Anyways, we got here and ran into Kelsey, who was just getting home. As we were standing there in the street making introductions, I noticed someone had messed with the front door. A couple of us had boarded it up, but someone had cracked it open wide enough to slide in."

Tired as I was when I got out of the cab, I must have missed it.

"We figured it could be burglars and wanted to check, so your dad and I each got a gun from my car. When we walked around the house and peeked through the living room window, we saw Paul as he was just about to shoot you. Your dad was a little quicker, so I guess he saved the day."

"Wait a minute. You just drive around with an arsenal of weapons in your trunk?"

He grimaces. "Wanna be prepared for all eventualities. I guess that's what special-ops guys do."

I hide my grin since I was only pulling his leg. My dad had always had plenty of guns and other goodies at home and they had become second nature growing up. I was actually shocked when I discovered that not all parents had a secured gun closet in their bedrooms or drove around with a suitcase of guns in their cars.

"So do you have any special plans for this week?" he asks.

"No, not really." With my father at home, I'm planning on playing it by ear. "Why?"

"Because I made reservations at this fancy restaurant in Long Beach for Tuesday night."

I gaze at him with raised eyebrows. "You mean like a date?"

"Uhum."

That gets me to sit up straight. "Now hold on, soldier. Aren't we rushing things a little? I mean, I barely know you."

"Yeah, but I'm only on medical leave till Wednesday." River's eyes have turned puppy dog. "After that, a call can come in at any time. This might be our only chance."

I fall back in the swing with a groan. What logic. "So I guess you got your second chance with Riley?"

"Yep, I'm officially the newest member of his team."

The swing rocks softly back and forth, the low squeak like a cackling laugh. It's too early. "I don't know if I'm ready."

The sweetest smile plays on his lips. "Are you seriously sending a man who helped save your life back to war without a proper dinner?"

I laugh, not really sure how to counter such a sound argument. That I once swore to myself that I would never date a special-forces operator is pushed out of my heart. What the heck. It's time for me to stand on my own two feet and make those decisions without looking at the past all the time. I can die from living, but I'm already dead if I don't at least try to find a little happiness.

~~~~

My fight against bulimia is put to the test at dinner when my dad and River ambush me with a gigantic pizza order, fully paid for by Major Riley as a welcome-home gift for my dad. I try to get away with a slice until my father's deep frown forces me to dig in. Four fully loaded slices later, I'm not only stuffed to the brim, but awfully tempted to fall into my old habits. Escaping to Kelsey's house is my only weapon.

Marcel's nephew, Rashey, who I had met at the hospital, opens the door before I can even ring the doorbell. A cigarette hangs lazily from a corner of his mouth—Kelsey likely told him to get lost when he tried to smoke inside the house. During the stakeout, she confessed that she and Finn have fought for years about him quitting this horrid habit, so far to no avail. Banning him and any other smokers outside is the best she can do at the moment to at least keep her kids away from secondhand smoke.

"Kelsey home?" I ask when he steps aside to let me pass.

"Yep, in the kitchen."

Next, I bump into Finn, who is fumbling with a cigarette pack in his hand. I can only silently shake my head—he should know how bad that stuff is for him. They don't put those warnings on cigarette packs for nothing, and he has a family to consider. His smile is apologetic when I squeeze by him before he follows Rashey outside.

Kelsey looks up when I enter the kitchen. She is feeding one of the babies—I figure it's the boy, since he is wearing blue, but I can't be sure. Neither of her twins has any hair and they look almost identical. His mouth is smudged with sweet potato and he coos, his arm stretching out when I crack a smile. He is adorable.

"Sorry, I just needed some distraction." I plop into the kitchen chair. "I hope it's not a bad time."

"No, I could use some distraction myself."

"How is Marcel?"

"Better. He's still gonna have to spend a few weeks at the hospital, but then he should be like new."

"I'm glad."

"Yeah. Rashey came by to tell us that they set the execution date for his brother. Marcel will freak when he finds out, so we need to get the timing right, or it'll interfere with his recovery."

"Rashey's brother is on death row?"

"Yes. He was the golden boy in the family, the only one who didn't get into trouble as a teen. Full merit scholarship to the University of Montana. They say he killed a girl, but Marcel is convinced it was a setup. Don't really know the specifics since he hates to talk about it."

Unsure what to say, I watch as she shoves another spoonful into her son's mouth. Though I usually find silence awkward, it's different with Kelsey. Just being around her is calming.

"So what's up with you?" she finally says. "Your dad must be thrilled to be home."

"He is. And River asked me out on a date."

"Seriously?" She turns to me, the spoon with the mashed sweet potatoes hanging in the air. Her eyes sparkle with curiosity. Only her son's coos get her to refocus on the task.

"I said yes. I mean, it's just a date, right? After all, we're friends. Friends can go out to dinner together without it turning into something more serious."

She laughs. "I'm not the one you need to convince. You're a good person, Aeree, and deserve some happiness. Heck, we all do. If it was me, I'd go for it. River is kind of cute, too."

Her words warm my cheeks some more, but luckily, her focus has fully returned to the baby. The urge to puke after my meal is forgotten. Having Kelsey in my life is definitely a good thing. Now I just have to figure out if the same holds true for River.

# Chapter 35

The sky is just as blue as it was the day Mitch and I left for the Green Mountains, but a slight breeze makes the temperatures bearable. For a second, my gaze lingers on the sign mounted to the wall of the building. "Larissa Mendéz, Esquire". Mentally, I sharpen my claws. Let the games begin.

Maureen Higgins is already seated behind the large windows of the conference room with her own lawyer when I get buzzed in by the receptionist. Larissa's offices are nowhere near as pompous or luxurious as the ones of Buren, Buren, and Larson, but she is down to earth and has proven that she stands behind her clients. I'm grateful that Sam hooked me up with her, which reminds me that I still owe him $110 for the cab fare. Need to settle that soon.

"Hi, Aeree." Larissa briefly hugs me before her chin points to the conference room. "Ready?"

"I guess." Though I try to keep my chin up with a certain degree of confidence, being in the same room with Mitch's lover is still a challenge. Mostly, I feel sorry for her now as she sits there like a pile of misery with her pregnant belly straining the summer dress. She lost significantly more than I did. Her eyes are rimmed red—she must still be crying over him.

Larissa pours me a glass of water from the pitcher before claiming her seat beside me. Paperwork is shuffled around by both lawyers before we are ready to go.

"As you can see from our petition, Mr. Cahill was legally married to my client," Larissa starts. "Under New York State law, he couldn't fully disinherit her under his will. My client wishes to avail her spousal share, as she is entitled to it. That would be twenty-five thousand dollars in cash, her car, and one-third of the rest of the estate."

Maureen can't even hold my gaze when her lawyer clears his throat. His silver hair is slicked back, the collar of his polyester suit slightly stained. Larissa told me that he usually specializes in personal injury, and she has no idea why Maureen even hired him.

"I discussed all the legal options with my client," he says in a nasally voice. "At this point, my client is likely going to reject her claim to any of the inheritance, so we have no objection to your client insisting on her spousal share."

Larissa frowns. "Your client doesn't want any of the inheritance?"

"We expect significant liability lawsuits from victims of Mr. Cahill's vigilante group. My client would rather not deal with the hassle."

"I'm also not comfortable taking any of David's money." Maureen's smile is almost shy as she looks at me. "I had no idea he was married and I'm so sorry if I caused you any pain."

All of a sudden, I feel like the wicked witch. "I'm sorry, too. I guess he played both of us for a fool."

She nods, a few tears springing loose and rolling down her cheeks. Having to raise his child on her own after everything that happened will probably be tough. My heart goes out to her. I thought she would be a total bitch about the inheritance, but once again, I'm shown that perceptions can be deceiving. I should work on not judging people so harshly all the time.

"Will I have to deal with the lawsuits?" I ask.

Maureen's lawyer jumps in before Larissa gets a chance to reply. "I doubt it. You were a victim yourself. Didn't you get shot by the sniper?"

"I did." I omit that it had just been a graze that became badly infected. Only now, after three weeks, am I able to walk around without a bandage and the need for constant painkillers.

"Okay, I guess we're done here." Larissa gets on her feet, her arm extended toward the exit. "Thanks for coming in today. I'll prepare the paperwork and submit it to the probate court."

She signals me to stay in my seat as she walks Maureen and her lawyer out. Less than a minute later, she is back.

"This was the best you could hope for, Aeree."

"It doesn't feel like a victory."

"No, it doesn't. This is a rare case where there are no winners. Yet the law is blind to this. You need closure and to move on with your life, and this money will help. You would be stupid not to take it. Like he said, you earned it."

"So you think Maureen should have taken her share of the money, too?"

"I would have advised her to take it. Lawsuits or not, chances are that she could have kept something, especially with a child on the way."

"What will happen next?"

"I will file the paperwork with the probate court today. We already gave notice in the paper for any other potential claimants to come forward, so you should be able to get your money in the next two weeks. Will that work?"

I nod. My dad's old team and the other units had taken up a collection after his release from prison, which has been keeping us afloat. Together with the money I will be earning from a few upcoming catering gigs, it should be enough to bridge us over.

"Any special plans for what you will do with the money?"

"I want to start a small company."

With Finn's help, I have made a business plan and calculated that the money will be enough for a van and the necessary kitchen equipment to get a top-notch catering business started. It's something that has kept me going, and more so, diverted my mind from everything that had happened during the Fourth of July week.

"Okay, I have to run." I smile at Larissa. "I have to prepare for a barbecue this afternoon."

Thirty minutes later, I pull into my driveway. My eyes come to rest on my front door. I picture myself walking through it with Mitch, laughing as my arm links with his. If someone had told me that our happiness was nothing but a charade, I would have declared them insane. Maybe I didn't want to see the signs—his controlling, belittling, his rolling eyes when he didn't agree with me. I was so obsessed with my happy ending that I failed to realize he spent more time away from me than at home. Now the memories just leave a stale taste in my mouth.

Determined not to let my thoughts pull me down, I get out of the car. The dimness of the hallway greets me when I cross the threshold. Though everything that could possibly remind me of Mitch has been packed away, I'm still not sure whether I should keep the house. If Kelsey didn't live next door, it would be a no-brainer, but with our friendship growing stronger every day, it's something I will really need to think about. My father will probably have a say in it, too.

I set my purse on the ground and remove the thin scarf, which has been hiding the scar on my neck. "Dad, I'm home."

"We're in the living room."

I halt in the doorway when I notice Major Riley sitting on the couch, not sure if I'm interrupting a meeting. All of a sudden, two arms circle me from behind, making me squeal. A chuckle adds insult to injury when I recognize River's aftershave.

I wiggle out of his embrace, punching him hard in the shoulder. "You scared the crap out of me. Don't do that." It's the second time this week he has pulled this stunt, claiming he's practicing his combat skills. Apparently, he needs to know how to stalk an enemy without being detected. That I'm his guinea pig is not appreciated.

When my attention returns to the living room, both my dad and Major Riley have that stupid grin on their faces that screams "caution—kids at play." I can't help but blush.

"Well, I should go." Major Riley catapults upward like a stick the way only military men stand. His hands run over his uniform to straighten it before he grabs his hat off the table. "Your plane leaves at nineteen hundred hours, Staff Sergeant. Don't be late."

River gives an acknowledging salute, standing at attention as he walks out. I only get a nod goodbye with a little wink. As soon as the door closes behind him, my head turns to my dad. "What did he want?"

"He briefed me on Eltas. They turned him over to the feds after he confessed. They will indict him for espionage and treason. It's unlikely he'll get out again."

The news saddens me more than I want to admit—Eltas had been the closest thing to a friend I had for many years. I will miss him.

"And he told me about a friend who runs a private security firm and wants to hire me."

"I hope it's nothing like Eltas's old shop," I tease.

"Of course not. It's all legit." The biggest smile is on my father's face. "So it looks like I'm not going to be a burden on you after all."

I get on my toes and peck him on his cheek. "You're never a burden, Dad." We both know he would have gone insane just sitting at home, doing nothing, so I'm glad he found a job. Hopefully, it won't involve too much travel since I kind of like having him around.

They both follow me as I stroll into the kitchen. When I open the fridge, River peeks over my shoulder. "Is that a lemon meringue pie?"

"It is." When he goes for a fork, I add, "But it's for Marcel's homecoming barbecue."

The smile fades. I can't believe he is hungry again. All he and my dad ever seem to do is eat, the portions more than I ever imagined possible. They claim it's my cooking, but I think they're just greedy.

"Well, I'm bringing this over to Kelsey. Marcel should be home soon, so join us whenever you want."

"Let me carry this for you."

I swat River's hand away when he tries to grab the plate, tossing him an evil glare. "I'm perfectly capable of carrying my own pie, thank you very much." If he thinks he can get his hands on dessert before anyone else with his chivalry, he has something else coming.

A few minutes later, I arrive at Kelsey's front door, which is wide open. She has gone all out with the decorations—the whole house is stuffed with "Welcome Home" balloons and banners. Ramona zooms down the hallway, chasing playfully after her little brother, who tries to get away from her with little squeals. The happiness and excitement on their faces is catching. I'm really looking forward to the afternoon and getting to know Kelsey's friends and family better.

She is in the kitchen, trying to sort through the mountains of food piling up on every free space. Her face twists when she spots the pie. "Another dessert? Gee, Aeree, how long did it take you to make all this stuff? By the way, it looks and smells amazing."

With tingling cheeks, I scan over the food. Maybe I did go a little overboard. Donna's budget for the party had been generous, so I wanted everything to be perfect. After I dug up my old recipes from my college catering business, I pretty much tried out every dish. The temptation to constantly nosh on the creations was pure torment, but I beat the urge most of the time. This success alone has helped tremendously when the bulimia devil roared its ugly head after my meals, and I've avoided trips to the bathroom. Though I've gained a few pounds, I feel better about myself than I have in years.

Kelsey leans against the kitchen island, her hazel eyes spilling over with curiosity. "So how did date number three go?"

"Great." I grin when I remember how much fun River and I had over dinner last night, which ended in a small food fight. "And I figured out why he never orders alcohol. He's younger than me, won't be twenty-one for another couple of months."

Her jaw drops. "Seriously?"

"Yep. I ordered a bottle of wine and asked the waiter to bring a spare glass, but when he asked River for an ID, he finally fessed up." I giggle. "You should've seen his face. I swear he almost died of embarrassment. Afterward, we had a good laugh about it."

"I like that about him. He's so easygoing." She leans forward slightly, her voice dropping to a conspiratorial whisper. "And? Any action?"

My cheeks heat. Conversations about guys are something new for me. Since we moved around so much as I was growing up, I never had a true girlfriend, the constant severing of bonds not only heart-wrenching but exhausting. After my mom's death, I pretty much withdrew into a shell. Why bother if I had to leave in a few months anyhow? With Kelsey, it's different. She doesn't let me get away with vague answers, though I can't shake the feeling that she is at least as desperate for a friend as me.

"We took a walk on the beach after dinner and he held my hand, but that was it."

"You know, it's perfectly acceptable today for women to take the first step."

I snort. That won't happen. Maybe he really just sees me as a friend, and I would never live it down if I misread the signals.

Trying to get off the subject, I open the fridge, my forehead wrinkling as I try to find space for the pie. The platters with the fish appetizers are already stacked in three layers, the rest of the shelves taken up by bowls of salad and raw meats, ready to hit the grill. I finally stack the hot dogs on top of the burgers to squeeze the plate in.

"Daddy's here." Ramona's excited shriek booms through the house, alerting us that the guest of honor has arrived.

When Kelsey and I get to the front door, Finn and River are just helping Marcel to slide from Finn's truck into a wheelchair. Donna fusses with a blanket despite the heat. Marcel's face is contorted into a painful grimace as he fights off his wife's smothering attempts, but he gives in with a small huff in the end. Pulling his son onto his lap with his hand entangled with Ramona's, the group moves into Kelsey's backyard. The lightness in the air is palpable through laughter and eager chatter. A few tears of joy tickle my throat—I'm grateful that Marcel is home and surrounded by people who love him.

The party is in full swing within the hour. Lots of compliments are shot my way about the amazing food I made. I even have a booking for a fiftieth birthday party when a man passes me his business card, whispering to keep it a secret since he wants to surprise his wife. Andrew Walker, with an address for a car repair service in Maine. I wonder how he fits into the wider family constellation.

Bill arrives just after four, delivering the latest update on the investigation of Paul's vigilante group. After they had learned that quite a few officers were involved with the group, the case was turned over to a special investigative team of the NYPD, but Bill has stayed in the loop for my sake, which I appreciate.

"The snitches have started to line up to get themselves better deals. This group was huge. It's a disgrace what has been happening under everyone's noses for years." His wheelchair squeaks as he navigates me a little bit away from a group of adults and children on the makeshift dance floor who are competing to see who can yell the loudest.

"How many have been confirmed so far?"

"At least fifty. Most of them are police officers, but there are also enough judges, prosecutors, and lawyers to warrant plowing through old case files for potential victims. The ones the investigative team were able to track down who hadn't been killed had all been warned that really bad things would happen to them if they didn't keep their mouths shut about their punishments. NYPD is also reviewing cold case files and suspicious deaths that could have been camouflaged as an accident or suicide with the right resources. It will probably be a year before we get them all."

"Did they ever find out what Citadel's husband did?"

"He ran a small kid over while driving drunk, but the jury let him go because he lost his hearing in the accident. They felt he suffered enough. I guess I can see why the group might have disagreed, though self-justice is never the answer."

A lump sits heavy in my throat. Though Bill has never asked me why the group was after me, the knowledge that I must have done something terrible to be on their list has been hanging over us like a heavy cloud.

"You know, Bill, I'm not proud of some of my choices."

His hand squeezes my lower arm. "I read your file and know what happened to you. Whatever you did, it's something *you'll* have to come to terms with. It's not my place to judge you." For a second, his eyes rest on Marcel, who is teasing Ramona by coloring her lips with frosting. "Did you know I'm sitting in this chair because Marcel shot me?"

My jaw drops.

"He was young, just turned sixteen, and one insane moment of peer pressure could have destroyed his life. It took a lot of pull to keep his case in juvie and get his record expunged, but when I see him in moments like this, I'm glad I made that choice. He deserved that second chance, just like you deserve yours."

"But weren't you ever out for revenge? I mean, he shot you and you'll never walk again."

"Oh, I was angry at first, even went to the jail one day to confront him. I wanted to look him straight in the eyes and tell him what he took from me. Even life in prison seemed too easy of a punishment back then. I wanted him to suffer the way I suffered."

"And what made you change your mind?"

Bill's smile is sad. "I expected this stubborn kid who had joined a gang to be tough and who had no remorse whatsoever. Marcel was totally different. He even cried, telling me how sorry he was, and that he would trade places with me if he could. Sad part, I believed him. He ended up pouring his heart out to me. Though his mother tried her very best, the ghetto sometimes gets its claws in you. Marcel never had a chance, so I decided it was time for someone to finally cut him a break."

I drop my gaze, unsure what he expects me to say.

"Forgiving Marcel made my burden easier, helped me to move forward with my life. I still sense a lot of bitterness in you, Aeree, not for what those guys did to you, but for yourself.

Forgiveness starts with you. You need to let go of the past or it will destroy you one day. Admitting your mistakes is the first step."

Tears glisten in my eyes as I nod. Though it will be hard, I know he is right. It's finally time to leave my past behind for good.

~~~~

Just before seven, I drop River off at the gates of the base. He has changed into his uniform and allowed my dad to give him another haircut. The result is that he is almost bald.

"Stay safe, soldier." I hold up a small paper bag.

His eyes fill with delight. "Is that some of the pie?"

"Yep. I saved you a piece before it was all gone."

"The other guys might fight me for it."

"Then you better defend it with your honor."

He smiles. Though it is time for him to go, I can sense he is not ready.

"You know, I wanted to kiss you the other night." His cheeks flush slightly, the tip of his boot drawing little circles in the dirt. It's adorable.

"Then why didn't you?"

"I guess I was too chicken." His gaze is searching when he raises his head. "With everything that happened with your husband, I was scared it was too early. I mean, you yourself said you didn't know if you were ready."

"Well, maybe the next time, you should just give it a try."

Without warning, his lips find mine. His kiss is soft, and when I allow him access, his gentle tongue is almost teasing. He doesn't take the lead the way Mitch and Paul used to do—it's an equal back and forth as our bodies slowly melt into one. My knees are a bit shaky when we finally break apart.

"Since I don't know when I will be back, I thought waiting was a bad idea. I mean, you never know. You could meet some other guy tomorrow."

"Don't worry. I'll be here when you get back."

"You promise?"

I nod. That's what women do who get involved with special-ops guys. There is nothing else. Though I had never wanted to be in this position, the thought doesn't scare me any longer. Baby steps, that's all I can do. The rest will eventually fall into place.

After he disappears inside the base, I decide to drive home with the top down, for once not concerned about that dreadful tan. I'm going to live my life the way I want to without the constant worry of what others think of me. The wind cools my face as I cross back into Staten Island, and the salty air, carried in from the ocean, prickles delicately in my lungs. Even if it never goes any further with River, what is life without taking a risk once in a while? Fear is just as unproductive as all the guilt and anger that has been eating at me for far too long.

As I speed up to get home faster, an exhilarating shout springs from my lips. For the first time in over four years, it feels terrific to be alive. I'm a survivor—and no one will ever be able to tell me otherwise.

# THANK YOU FOR READING!

★ ★ ★ ★ ★

Please consider leaving a review! Reviews help indie authors like myself find new readers and get advertising. If you enjoyed this book, please tell your friends!

# Here's a FREE GIFT to you!

## WAR ORPHAN

## A TOMÁS ARAYA STORY

*Life has been a struggle for Tomás Araya. Orphaned after the execution of his parents by the new regime of Malaguay, he elbows his way up the ranks of the national army. At nineteen, his life looks bright. A fast-track career beckons in the military, his sweetheart carries his child, and his music is to lift him to the stratosphere.*

*But the higher you rise, the deeper you fall.*

*As Tomás's life explodes, he needs to act.*

*Fast.*

*One wrong turn, and it's game over.*

Get War Orphan as a free download when you sign up to my mailing list at
www.salmasonauthor.com

# Want More?

## BOOK I OF THE WAR BRIDE SAGA IS OUT NOW

## WAR BRIDE

*On the internet, you never know who's on the other side of the screen.*

*Trying to escape from her conservative parents and her boring life in backwater Indiana, eighteen-year-old Stacy Degray sets off to visit Felipe, a charming guy she met on the internet.*

*All too soon, her dream vacation turns into a nightmare when she becomes trapped in poverty-riddled Malaguay, a small South American nation known best for its child soldiers and thriving drug trade; a place where war rules and a life is worth nothing.*

*A pawn in a ruthless game of political power play, terrorism, and deceit, Stacy's life becomes a struggle for survival. Her only remaining move is to learn the rules and start playing.*

*The stakes are her life, the players are callous, and the odds are stacked against her.*

# PROLOGUE

The hot, stale air in the small room is stifling. A fuse in the ancient air conditioner has blown again. Leaning back in his chair, Felipe wipes the sweat from his forehead with the back of his hand. A sweltering draft floats through the cracks in the broken window frame. *Hijo de puta.* Why does Miguel make him use the computer in the main compound? He could be sitting by the pool at the mansion with the laptop, enjoying a cold drink, but of course that's not acceptable to his cousin. Felipe has no clue why Miguel always seems pissed off at him, but it's been that way for as long as he can remember.

Ramon lights a cigarette and takes a deep drag, letting the smoke escape through the corners of his mouth. "How is it going?"

Felipe grabs the pack of Camels off the table and sticks a cigarette between his lips. "I've got three possibilities, two Americans and one German. How 'bout you?" He strikes the match on the sole of his shoe, holding the flame under the cigarette tip. As he inhales, the nicotine lulls his mind and takes the edge off his frazzled nerves.

Ramon grins. "I just got shots of a redhead in a bikini. Come check her out."

He doesn't have to ask twice—soon, both men are huddled over the computer screen.

"Wow, she's hot." Felipe clears his throat to distract himself from the pull in his pants. "Where's she from?"

"Ireland." Ramon takes another drag. "She's coming over next month."

A small whistle escapes Felipe. "Congrats, *mano*. She your first recruit?"

"Yep." The smoke from the cigarettes hangs over the musty room, robbing it of the last bit of oxygen. Ramon coughs into his fist. "She's being matched with Tomás. He's a lucky dog."

Felipe smirks—Tomás is his best friend and they have always believed in sharing their possessions. The redhead looks promising. In times like these, he loves his job. Recruiting foreign girls to match them with high-ranking soldiers sure beats dodging the bullets that fly around in active battle.

Ramon extinguishes the cigarette and cups his hands behind his head. "When do you think I'll be matched?"

"No clue. Talk to Miguel."

Ramon's lips twist as if he just swallowed something nasty. "You know how short-tempered he is. I don't want to get on his nerves by asking him when I finally get to score."

Felipe nudges his shoulder. "I'll ask him for you."

"Thanks, *mano*." The usual easy-going grin is back on Ramon's face.

"Don't mention it."

Felipe returns to his own computer and opens the link to the forum he has been following for the past few months. He'd uploaded a few poems he had found online from various unknown authors, claiming them as his own, which resulted in a few bites, but they all led to dead ends. Most of the women were either too young or too old to meet the recruitment criteria. Maybe he should move on to another forum.

Every girl between sixteen and twenty-five is a go, though adults without a college education or steady job are preferred. Those from broken homes are best—no one will come looking for them when they don't return home, and they are easier to tame since they secretly long for a family. In recent years, the shortage of women has become a pain in everyone's ass. Girls with half a brain prefer to move away to explore opportunities in neighboring countries, and most of the others have never set foot in a school. High-ranking officers in the Malaguian army don't take kindly to the prospect of having their offspring raised by an illiterate spouse.

Felipe scrolls through the inbox, quickly scanning the messages, on the lookout for his next victim. A few sentences from a girl catch his eye—she seems really sweet. Her name is Stacy and she is from some hick town in Indiana he's never heard of. After he hits the return button, he writes a mushy reply; maybe she will take the bait and turn out to fit the profile. Hell—he hasn't had a girlfriend in over a year and could try to claim her for himself. For all the hard work he does for the cause, he deserves some fun, especially with Tomás joining the ranks of married men soon.

With hooded eyes, he continues to browse the forum, leaving a few thread comments and taking drags from a fresh cigarette from time to time. His stomach growls—lunch is approaching—and he fully intends to take the afternoon off. Maybe he should go to the shooting range. Training has never harmed anyone and he could hang with Tomás afterward.

When the door flies open, he is so startled that he almost jumps out of the chair. Sun floods the small, dim room and blinds his eyes. He blinks at the silhouette in the doorway.

"Yo, Felipe, I need you to run an errand with me."

His cousin's cold voice sends a shiver down his spine. Miguel is in one of his moods where he will beat the crap out of anyone who mouths off.

"I'll be right there." Felipe logs out of the forum and shuts down the computer. "*Hasta luego*, Ramon."

Ramon pecks away at the keyboard without paying attention—he's probably chatting with the redhead about her upcoming trip. Being a romantic at heart, he gets a few good bites from cute girls every week while Tomás has the emotional insight of a fly. The girl will be in for a surprise once she arrives in Malaguay, expecting to find a Romeo and instead is married off to Hannibal Lecter, minus the liver and fava beans.

Miguel is waiting out by the open-sided military truck. He flicks away a cigarette as soon as Felipe steps out of the building. His eyes seethe with anger and the two soldiers with him hide in the driver's cabin.

Felipe frowns. "What's the matter? You look like you're about to kill someone."

"The rebels set one of the fields on fire and destroyed half a million dollars of merchandise."

"I told you—"

Miguel's death glare cuts his cousin off. "I remember what you told me. We need more soldiers to guard the fields, so let's get some."

"Where are we gonna get them?"

"The orphanage." Miguel signals the driver that he is ready to go after Felipe pulls himself into the truck.

With a sigh, Felipe leans back, letting the airflow cool his heated face. The orphanage is run by Pearson Moore, an American idealist who tries to save Malaguian boys from becoming child soldiers. Miguel hates him with a passion and the confrontation won't be pretty. It puts Felipe in a tight spot—he was raised in the orphanage until he was fourteen. Pearson is like a father to him.

They ride in silence through the center of town, which is almost deserted. A few kids with runny noses take off as the truck approaches, and a mother calls out to her son, who has been playing with a stray dog. The boy is young, maybe ten or eleven, but that has never stopped Miguel before. When he needs soldiers, he pretty much takes anyone off the streets. The law requiring boys to be at least fourteen to enter the military doesn't apply to him.

The road begins to slope upward as soon as they leave the last house in the city behind, and the truck follows the windy trail, wrapping itself around a mountain. The orphanage is five miles out in the middle of the woods—five small buildings in total, consisting of several dorms for about twenty-five boys and a handful of girls, a school, a mess hall, and an administrative building.

Pearson is funded through donations, mostly from softhearted Americans, and even though he enjoys a certain degree of protection from the US embassy, they won't involve themselves if a few boys are taken. The political climate between Malaguay and the superpower has been strained since the overthrow of the old Malaguian regime eighteen years ago, and neither of them are keen to rock the boat.

When the truck screeches to a halt in front of the administrative building, a few boys playing soccer on the nearby pitch turn around to watch. Miguel squints at them before grabbing a machine gun off the stand. Grinning with viciousness, he strolls over to them.

"Hey. Who of you is over twelve?"

Without exception, the boys evade his gaze and act as if they swallowed their tongues.

Miguel flicks the safety of the gun. "I asked you boys a question."

One of the youngsters is stupid enough to make eye contact. "Mr. Moore said we're not supposed to talk to you."

Miguel doesn't even bother to respond. Without hesitation, he aims the gun at the kid's feet, spraying the ground in front of him with a spurt of deadly lead. The boy jumps back, white as a sheet and shaking.

"Hey, what the hell do you think you're doing?" Pearson trembles with anger as he rushes toward the little group, a rifle aimed at Miguel's head.

Miguel regards him calmly. "Unfortunately, I have to borrow some of your kids."

"Get out of here before you regret it." Pearson slides his finger inside the trigger guard.

Miguel's eyes narrow. "*Tonto del culo.* I'm the president's son, and if you shoot me, this orphanage will burn within the hour, with everyone inside. I'm sure you don't want the death of innocent children on your hands."

Tense silence follows his words. The wind howls in the canyon, echoing off the tall mountain walls. All eyes are fixed on Pearson's finger. Felipe prays he won't pull the trigger. The soldier's machine guns will turn his body into a human sieve if he so much as puts a scratch on Miguel.

After what seems like an eternity, Pearson lowers the rifle. "Please, don't take the boys. They're only children and they've already lost their families."

The triumph is all too visible on Miguel's face—Felipe is certain there'll be more visits in the near future. "I tell you what. Since you're cooperating, we'll only take five today. How does that sound?"

Pearson curses under his breath, making Miguel laugh.

He turns to the boy he intimidated earlier, who stares back at him with wide eyes. "Now, *pendejo,* how old are you?"

"Thir—Thirteen." Tears glisten in his eyes.

Miguel smirks. "Today is your lucky day, kid. You're getting out of this shithole."

He turns to the next boy, and ten minutes later, five of them are loaded on the truck. Pearson has disappeared, probably calling the president's mansion or the embassy to bitch about Miguel. His complaint will fall on deaf ears—he is too small of a fish in the pond to matter.

*"Vamonos."* Miguel hits the side of the truck and the vehicle turns around, swaying up the hilly road. Pulling out a pack of cigarettes, Miguel lights himself a smoke.

"What's your name, kid?" he asks the boy he had intimidated, offering him one of the cigarettes.

The boy takes it without even the slightest hesitation. "Charo."

"I'm Miguel."

"I know who you are, sir." Charo takes the offered lighter and flicks it open under the tip of the cigarette. Eyes closed, he takes a deep drag.

There's no coughing or spluttering—this couldn't be his first smoke. Pearson is strict and doesn't allow any drugs on the premises, so the boy must have either snuck off into the woods, like Felipe and Tomás used to do, or he hasn't been at the orphanage long.

Miguel studies him with a chuckle. "You don't need to call me sir." He blows the smoke right into the boy's face. When he doesn't even flinch, Miguel says, "Tell me, Charo, what do you want to do when you grow up?"

"I want to be rich—live in a big mansion like you."

Miguel chuckles. "And I bet you'll do anything to get there."

"I'll do whatever it takes."

"Even if you have to kill for your country?"

Charo nods slowly. "Give me a gun and I'll fight for Malaguay. Long live President Rizo."

Felipe turns away, a heavy lump settling in his stomach. As usual, his cousin left out the dying part. Only four out of every ten child soldiers live to see their eighteenth birthday, half of them disabled from a bullet wound.

As the truck makes its way back toward the city, Felipe glares up at the mountains. He loves his country, but sometimes he wonders how it would have felt to grow up without war and violence—in a place where a life mattered.

His sullen mood only lasts a moment, his mind drifting back to Stacy. "Listen, Miguel, there's this girl I met online I'd like to recruit, possibly for myself."

"Seen a picture yet?"

Felipe smiles as he remembers Stacy's cute email. "No, but there's this innocence in her writing I really like."

Amusement flickers in Miguel's eyes. "Go for it, Felipe. You've got my approval."

A smirk spreads on Felipe's lips. All of a sudden, he can't wait to get back to the recruitment center. Maybe Stacy had already answered his message—if she has, and looks halfway decent after she sends him a picture, he will do everything in his power to get her to Malaguay.

# Special Thanks

One person can write a book, but it takes many more to publish it. Thanks to all of you who have accompanied and supported me in my writer's journey so far—I couldn't have done it without you.

A special thanks goes out to my kids for being my towers of strength. You keep me motivated and full of dreams. Keep it up, guys.

My next special thanks goes out to my editor, Nicole Ayers. A writer is nothing without his or her editor and Survive was a tricky one (How did you ever make it through the first draft????). Thanks for turning this diamond in the rough into a sparkling gem and not enforcing deadlines. This book wouldn't have seen the outside of my computer without you.

Next on the list is my awesome cover designer Lucy from render/compose. Thanks for the amazing cover and doing a fab job in branding the series.

Beta readers are an important part of the creative process and I'm grateful to have found Mary Nikolettou who has helped me iron out plenty of wrinkles. Thanks, and I'm already looking forward to our next adventure.

Also a very special thanks to Zarif Tanzim, who helped me flush out some teething issues. Your advice and guidance were spot on.

Another thanks to Crystal Watanabe and the team at Pikko's House for ridding the manuscript of the last pesky mistakes we all overlooked.

Of course, I can't forget my launch team, who helped me to get Survive off the ground. Thanks for all your feedback and support: Aleksa Stranjina, Alexis Dawn, Alissa Liu, Althea Blair-Mills, Amber Zettle, Ana Simons, Angelina Johnson, Annie Church, Artemis Hayes, Avanti Karkhanis, Bhakti, Bilqees Amla, Breyden Caldwell, Carter Best, Catherine H, Crystal Athena, Dhrumi, Domonic Kruger, Dora Kelly, Elle Davis, Farah, Janiyah E., Jessie Hazel, Jillian, KadeeBug, Karen Sampson-Venzon, Kelly, Lee Andrews, Louise Pallent, Maria (lil) Rojas, M Greenhill, Marilyn Jansen Van Rensburg, Mark Davis, Mary Nikolettou, Oona Chestnut, Paige Robson, Ravendra, Rumaisa Jahangir, Sakshi, Samantha Kline, Sarah Royal, Shakira, Shantia Elliott, Sheila Sanaipei, Shernah, TaCaia Thompson, Tahera Ahmed, Titta, Torri Valderrama, Trinity Brown, Wamuyu, Zarif Tanzim

www.ingramcontent.com/pod-product-compliance
Lightning Source LLC
Chambersburg PA
CBHW070644180626
46817CB00006B/2239